# GRAVITATIONAL ATTRACTION

## ANGEL MARTINEZ

Dreamspinner Press

Published by
DREAMSPINNER PRESS

5032 Capital Circle SW, Suite 2, PMB# 279, Tallahassee, FL 32305-7886 USA
http://www.dreamspinnerpress.com/

Gravitational Attraction
© 2014 Angel Martinez.

Cover Art
© 2014 Anne Cain
annecain.art@gmail.com
Cover content is for illustrative purposes only and any person depicted on the cover is a model.

ISBN: 978-1-62798-900-8
Digital ISBN: 978-1-62798-901-5
Second Edition July 2014

First Edition published by Silver Publishing, February 2012.

Printed in the United States of America
∞
This paper meets the requirements of
ANSI/NISO Z39.48-1992 (Permanence of Paper).

To Ian, without whom there would have been no GEM drive, no *Hermes*, and no lively, odd discussions about the possible yet-to-be discovered relationships between magnetism and gravity.

# GLOSSARY

T'tson'ae, the language of the Drak'tar, is uniquely suited to mouths filled with large, sharp teeth.

*Consonants:*

Labial consonants (*p*, *m*, and *b*) don't enter the language, though the Drak'tar can learn to pronounce them when speaking human languages. Most other consonants translate as the English speaker would expect, though the *ch* is a throaty *h* as in "chutzpah".

Apostrophes denote clicks, both with the tongue against the roof of the mouth and with the tongue behind the upper front teeth. While human languages use clicks as consonants, the Drak'tar utilize them more as syllabic separation.

*Vowels and diphthongs:*

*a*, *e*, *i*, *o*, *u* are pronounced as they would be in Spanish (*a* as in "father", *e* as in "hey", *i* as in "Igor", *o* as in "oak", and *u* as in "fluke")

ai: a long *i* sound, as in "eye"

au: as in *ow* or "how"

ou: a short *u* sound, as in "huh"

ae: a short *e* sound, as in "tent"

ei: a long *a* sound, as in "tale"

Most noun plurals are created with the addition of a palatal click and *ae*. Nouns ending in vowels are pluralized using the palatal click and *en*.

*Words:*

atenis: Heart, both anatomical and used as an endearment for one's lifemate.

aten'ae: Plural of *atenis*.

At'kros: Proper noun. A wide expanse of prairie-like lands designated in ancient times as neutral territory. Negotiations between rival groups could take place in relative safety here due to the scarcity of above-ground predators and the inability of underground predators to burrow through the thick granite shelf under the plains.

chautae: A battle companion, one you have fought beside.

chu'tsou: A Corzin battle tactic meaning "from beneath" that uses the surrounding terrain to mask approach.

dalk: The leader of a *katrak*, both in battle and as head of family.

dalk'ae: Plural of *dalk*.

Drak'tar is singular, but also refers to the race as a whole. Drak'tar'sae is plural, as in several Drak'tar.

durhai: A cat-sized predatory animal native to T'tson, normally solitary but forming devastating swarms during times of drought or famine.

drustel: Private rooms in Corzin family housing, normally only assigned to registered *aten'ae* groups and pairings.

hach lis: An exclamatory of presentation. The closest English equivalent would be "behold."

hai'kash: A full Corzin mobilization involving every Corzin within communications reach, even those below the age of majority.

hatra'os: Youngling—the Drak'tar stage between first shed and adulthood.

hech'zai: A Corzin platoon, usually twenty to thirty fighters from the same peer/age group, led by one of their own, their *tach*.

hei': Prefix denoting the singular first person possessive, "mine."

heido: An aerial life form of T'tson that Isaac describes as "flying pancakes." Their skins secrete a substance fatal to humans.

heltas: Drak'tar life stage marked by the first shed in childhood. Also refers to material specifically engineered as a neural damper, normally used by Drak'tar children during these early skin sheds.

hidach: "Calm wind," an idiom to reassure that all will be well.

huchtik: Offworlders, anyone not of T'tson—the *ch* is often drawn out at the back of the throat—pronounced this way, it implies insult.

irskai: T'tson'ae bipedal burrowing predator, saurian-avian in appearance, prized for its durable hide.

ka': Prefix denoting the plural first person possessive, "our." Used as a simple possessive at times, it can also contain connotations of affection or loyalty.

kaast'tlk: Blood feud, vendetta.

katrak: The name the Drak'tar gave to Corzin familial/social groups. A Corzin lives, trains, sleeps, fights beside, and dies beside the members of his *katrak*.

katrak'ae: Plural of *katrak*.

ke'dra: The matriarch of a group—some groups as large as cities, some smaller family groups.

ke'dra'en: Plural of *ke'dra*.

kes: Second person familiar imperative of the verb *kesk*, to drink

ket'haras: "The outward voice"—a newly minted Drak'tar word for interplanetary ambassador.

ket'sa: "Outward turning"—what the Corzin call their out-system mercenary forays.

ko: T'tson'ae herbivore, larger than a brachiosaurus.

ko'sai: Underground T'tson'ae predators that can grow to prodigious size and can live over a hundred years. Their primary hunting technique involves feeling vibrations from the ground above and surging up through the soil to snatch unsuspecting prey from below.

krisk: A T'tson'ae expletive. There is no human equivalent but indicates someone whose honor is so bankrupt, he would steal food during famine.

lau'ec: The traditional Corzin knife, meaning "the extra claw."

lechta: T'tson'ae herd animal, known for its timidity.

ledit: Another of T'tson's burrowing predators, particularly vicious as it has several mouths.

lochau: Roughly translates as "cousin," someone of your familial group who is not your brother, father, sister, mother, or lover.

rai: Fiber plant native to T'tson with wide multicolored stalks.

sart: Drak'tar hospital bed with high sides and built-in medical capabilities.

sechkran: A spicy T'tson'ae sweet, often used in food preparation for celebrations.

selfau: Specialized agricultural domes that regulate water delivery and gas exchange.

Sil'ke'dra: "She who rules," the mother to all. Turk's *ke'dra* also happens to be the *Sil'ke'dra*.

sol'atenis: The complete heart—Drak'tar'sae take several life mates, some females will have as many as a dozen before they feel complete. The Corzin are less ambitious and normally take a single life mate or sometimes two or three.

sulden: The chosen partner of one's child.

sulden'ae: Plural of *sulden*.

tach: The peer leader of a *hech'zai*, the equivalent of a field sergeant and ship captain rolled into one.

te'ha'dach: A formal greeting, only used in large groups.

tessil: A bioengineered medical device that attaches directly to the patient's skin to aid in hydration and respiration.

ter'as'lok: An ancient system of Drak'tar tunnels deep underground, the last line of defense.

terek: Third-person singular, present tense of the verb *tersk*, one of several "to be" infinitives.

T'tson: Their planet, one literal translation could be "where we place our feet."

Not a T'tson'ae word but perhaps useful: ESTO (Eridani Sector Treaty Organization)

# CHAPTER 1: THE *MARDUK* INCIDENT

"HAIL THEM again, Mr. Ozawa." Captain Drummond's voice held a sharp edge, betraying the tension beneath the stone-faced calm.

Isaac's fingers flew over his console as he repeated his hail on all the customary frequencies. "This is the C-courier *Hermes* to any personnel aboard the *Marduk*. Distress beacon intercepted. Please advise the nature of your emergency. This is the *Hermes* hailing the Judiciary Transport *Marduk*. Please respond."

"Anything? Static? Ticks?"

"Nothing, ma'am. Just the autobeacon replaying the request for assist."

"Mr. Wilde, readings would be appreciated any time now." The Captain turned to her left where Rand Wilde matched Isaac's frenetic movements at his boards.

"In range now, ma'am. Scanning. Just a sec," Rand murmured. His forehead creased. "I'm not sure this is right...."

"You're not here to edit, Mr. Wilde. Raw data will do. Life signs. Ship systems."

Rand cleared his throat. "That's just it, ma'am. No life signs. None. She's drifting. Radiation leakage aft. Probable engine damage. Life support still shows online."

"You think they ditched, Captain?" Isaac powered his chair around, one hand still hovering over the boards in case he picked up something on channels.

Captain Drummond stared at the vidscreen where the hulk of the *Marduk* occupied two-thirds of the view. Her silver eyebrows pulled together as she drummed her fingers on her chair arm. "Why leave the lights on when you've left the house?" She turned again. "Lifepods, Ms. Casalvez?"

Sylvia shook her head. "None sending anyway, ma'am. Too early to tell if any launched."

"What the hell happened here?"

The Captain echoed Isaac's thoughts. Judiciary ships ran heavily armed. Not too many things out there could take her down. To Isaac, the engine damage appeared minimal. She could have still been underway, limped into port at Kerron Station, at least. Not to mention that the crew would have to be in dire straits to leave the ship without proper shutdown procedures and a recovery buoy sending coordinates. Isaac shivered, superstitious thoughts creeping in where he needed objective, rational ones.

"Ma'am." A sudden thought hit him. "It's a transport."

"The point, Mr. Ozawa?"

"There'll be a holding deck amidships. Heavy shielding. Our scans wouldn't get through."

"True." Captain Drummond drew in a long breath. "Survivors could be holed up."

The bridge officers watched her, expectation drifting like heavy incense.

"Isaac."

The use of his first name made him cringe. Something unpleasant would come next. "Captain?"

"Feel up to remote work?"

Isaac hesitated. The captain had asked rather than ordered and relied on him to say no if he had to. He lifted a hand to press the tiny nub behind his left ear that activated his implant. A couple of quick diagnostics only produced a minor twitch in his left eye.

"Should be able to do a run," he said, hoping his voice sounded more confident outside his head. The implant picked the worst times to act up, but when it did, he would be in a world of hurt. "EV-bot?"

"If you're up to it, Isaac." Still the soft voice from the captain. The sympathy in her eyes made him cringe.

*I'm not going to break, dammit.* Yes, the tiny interstitial bot would be less of a strain, but the visuals would be too limited. They needed to know what waited inside that floating... coffin. He couldn't shake the image.

He switched on, configured for the human-sized bot, and, through his implant, unhooked the grapples that kept it moored to the side of the *Hermes*. Visuals from the bot superimposed over his view of the bridge. An ache started behind his eyes from the split vision. In short bursts, he fired the bot's aft thrusters to orient it for the *Marduk*'s airlock iris. He'd have to cut his way in, but any ship worth its polyceramics had redundant airlock closures. The damage would be minimal.

"Trav? Can you get us closer, maybe?" Isaac murmured. "So it's not so long a retrieval flight?"

"Already working on it, Oz," Travis answered, his gravel-in-a-polishing-drum voice drifting aft from the pilot's chair. "Got your back."

*Got your back.* The familiar phrase was both a comfort and a sad reminder. Like Isaac, like Travis Humboldt, many of the officers and crew were ex-military. Most were retired, though, on their second careers. Isaac was the only one forcibly discharged.

The implant behaved during the bot's flight over and Isaac dared to hope. *Maybe it'll be all right this time.* But as he concentrated on the fine work of guiding the laser saw, the twitch behind his left eye became a tic. By the time he had cut through and secured the airlock with the temporary emergency shield recessed over the iris, the tic had evolved into pulsing, intermittent pain.

*Never mind, just get it done, quick and efficient.* Isaac activated the bot's audio and sensors as he eased it out into the ship's corridor. Only the soft hiss of the ventilation system disturbed the silence.

"Quiet as a tomb," Rand muttered on Isaac's right.

"God, Rand, shut up," Sylvia hissed.

"Visual on your two screen, Captain," Isaac spoke over them.

"Put it up on main, Mr. Ozawa. We're all in this together."

Isaac guided the bot toward the ship's central decks. No signs appeared that anyone had been on board recently until the lift doors opened onto the holding deck.

"Holy. Fucking. Hells," Travis whispered.

At first, Isaac thought the dark splashes smeared on the walls and puddled on the floor were some sort of mechanical fluid, the dark rust the right color for dried joint lubricant or maybe…. His thoughts stuttered to a halt when he spotted half a hand lying in the center of the corridor. His focus pulled the bot's camera back to a spot on the wall, plastered with pieces of intestine. Nausea gripped him. Someone on the bridge retched violently.

"Life signs, Mr. Ozawa. That's why we're here. Proceed to the holding block."

The captain's sharp command helped him focus, returned his attention to the readouts. The numbers and symbols flashing across his internal display didn't keep him from seeing the gore strewn about the corridors, though, as if some gruesome human abattoir had suffered a catastrophic explosion. The bot's mechanical foot landed on something with a sickening crunch of bone and another bridge officer lost it.

The pain behind Isaac's left eye spread across his forehead, pounding against his skull. He had to hold it together, though. *What if some poor sod's alive in this hell?* Gritting his teeth, he pushed the bot on through the doors into holding, where a hand still clutched the comm console, attached to half a forearm.

*The autobeacon. Here's the man who set the autobeacon before something ripped him to shreds.* The rest of the comm officer was missing or unrecognizable amid the ruin of blood and shreds of flesh. Isaac stared, fixated by the wedding ring still gleaming from the dismembered hand. He swallowed hard, trying to banish thoughts of this man's family.

Distracted, it took him a moment to realize what the numbers flashing on his right screen signified.

"Life signs! Captain, we've got a survivor!"

"Human?"

"Ninety-eight point six. Heartbeat's slow, but has the right cardiac signature. Ma'am, if it's not human, it's close enough for me."

"Pull back, Mr. Ozawa." The captain rose from her chair, barking orders. "I need a retrieval team! Mr. Humboldt, your choice. Full exosuits and a medipod. No risks, no heroics! Anything feels off, you haul ass back here!"

Isaac concentrated on getting the EV-bot to haul ass as well. Travis would need some time to get the team assembled and run the exosuits through flight checks. He couldn't say why, but he had a terrible need to be part of the retrieval team. Someone was alive in there, and somehow, even though he had only been on the ship remotely, he felt a connection and a responsibility to get him or her out, preferably whole.

The shakes had him in their teeth by the time he stowed the bot again, though. The minor headache had exploded into a full-bore migraine. Nausea and pain competed in equal measure and he couldn't decide if he should reach for the vacuum bag under his console or lie down on the decking for a minute.

"Isaac?" Captain Drummond's voice may as well have been light-years away.

He turned to answer her and realized his choices had been taken from him as his vision tunneled inward in black fuzz.

*Someone was calling him. He searched for the voice through endless corridors... running... always running....*

"Oz? You all right there, boy?" Travis's deep voice rumbled against his ear.

He blinked his eyes open and looked up into the pilot's face. A strong arm supported his back and he realized he was lying on the decking, held against Travis's chest.

"Thanks, Trav, I didn't know you cared," Isaac croaked out with what he hoped was a convincing smile.

Travis snorted. "Yeah, you wish. Just trying to keep you from taking a header." He helped Isaac sit up. "Where're your meds, Oz?"

"I have them. I'm not an idiot." Isaac's hands shook too much to open the calf pocket, though.

Travis pushed his fingers aside and removed the packet for him. "Yeah, that's why I asked, bud. To make you feel stupid. Shit, you're so damn prickly sometimes."

Isaac flushed, but he meant it this time when he muttered, "Thanks."

With a little more help to undo his cuff, Isaac managed to rip open the packet with his teeth and slap the med patch onto the inside of his wrist. Relief would come quickly. He just had to keep swallowing against the rising nausea for a few more seconds.

"Trav?" He breathed in little sips, eyes on his deck boots as a point of focus.

"Answer's no, you lunatic," Travis said before he could ask the question. "You need to rest."

He shot Travis an irritated look. "I'll be in flight shape in a couple minutes." Travis's jaw clenched, his face set in stubborn lines, so Isaac changed tactics. "Respectfully requesting that Lt. Humboldt consider including me in his retrieval team. I have the ship schematics in my head. Mission would go faster with me on point."

Travis rose, barking orders into his wrist comm, and for a moment Isaac thought his request would be ignored. Then the pilot glared down at him. "Dammit, Oz. If you pass out and I have to drag you back by your harness—"

"You can beat the hell out of me then. But I won't."

"Damn freak," Travis grumbled. "You got five minutes to get your ass down to the launch bay, hear me?"

"Yessir."

With the chair as an anchor, Isaac climbed back to his feet, testing his balance. He shook still, but the worst of the effects had receded. "Damn implants should be outlawed."

"Less than 2 percent go bad, Mr. Ozawa." The captain eyed him dubiously.

"Yes, ma'am, so I've been told. Always helps me feel special."

"Sarcasm isn't the most appropriate use of energy right now."

Isaac chewed on his lower lip, trying to get the prickles of anger under control. He'd lived with this for five years now. Sometimes the bitterness still bubbled up. Stress reaction, probably. "Yes, ma'am. Sorry."

"Accepted. Best get moving, or Humboldt's leaving you behind."

Taking care to keep his steps steady, Isaac left the bridge with the eyes of the remaining bridge staff boring into his back. He knew what they thought, but he wasn't trying to prove anything. *Not this time.* The need to get over to the *Marduk*, to make certain for himself that the survivor would make it, was almost frantic. He couldn't have explained it in any rational way if the captain had decided to call him on it.

In the launch bay, Travis gave him a quick look up and down but refrained from further comment. "Oz, you're in number five. Lester ran the checks on it. You're good to go."

Lester Morris, from engineering, gave him a nod from across the bay. A good hundred-twenty kilos of solid muscle, Lester would be there for his strength as well as his mechanical expertise. Rand, already climbing into his suit, fumbling with the harness straps, would coax the *Marduk*'s systems into a data dump. Sylvia, the best shot on board, was along just in case, and Dr. Varga was there as well, since the survivor might not be in the best condition.

Isaac waved across the bay in thanks and pulled himself up into the suit's compartment. He strapped in with quick, efficient movements and hit the control pad to close the panels around him. The visor came down last, encasing him in weapons-grade polys and a self-contained respiratory system. Audio and display check complete, Travis hit the lock on the bay doors, which rolled back to show the *Marduk* turning slowly against the star-dappled black void.

Empty silence enveloped them as the suits left the bay. Isaac's own breaths had always sounded like a windstorm to him in the utter absence of other sounds. New recruits often passed out from lack of oxygen as they fought against breathing too loudly, panic and claustrophobia often weeding out the ones unsuited to deep-space work early in training. But for Isaac, planet-born dirtsucker that he was, the wonder of moving so freely through space, inimical to life, hostile and breathtakingly beautiful, had never worn thin.

Isaac reached the *Marduk* first to punch in the code he had left on the temporary airlock hatch. The six of them kept their face shields down as they slipped inside. Atmospheric levels might be all right, but the possibility of breathing in airborne blood particulates was not a pleasant thought.

A little whimper drifted through the audio.

"Hold together, people," Travis growled. "Oz promised to get us out and back quick."

"Sorry." The whispered apology came from Rand, his suit's helmet swiveling back and forth as he picked his way through the carnage.

"Rand, stop looking!" Sylvia snapped. "Focus on the suit in front of you."

While Isaac couldn't run in the heavy exosuit, he did pick up the pace. Unlike his first foray with the remote, now he knew exactly which cross-corridors and doorways to use. Within three minutes, he had them in the lift, headed toward the holding block. The heavy blast door slid aside to show the gruesome tableau at the comm console. A catch of breath in his pickup told Isaac that Rand had probably missed this the first time through. He couldn't be sure, but their nervous scan tech had most likely been one of the bridge officers throwing up.

"Still only showing one heartbeat," Isaac said to distract them all. "This way."

He led them down a corridor marked "A-block" where they passed one empty cell after another, not empty because the occupants had been torn to pieces but entirely empty.

"What kind of Jud ship carries one prisoner?" Sylvia asked.

"Maybe they were trying to evacuate before…." Lester's deep voice trailed off.

"Don't waste time on speculating," Travis cut in. "We're close."

The last cell held an occupant, its transparent electrified door still intact and locked tight. The man lay curled in a tight ball against his air pallet, dazed eyes half-open.

"Hey," Travis shouted through the door. "Can you hear me?"

The man didn't move, though he shivered violently, hard spasms running along massive arms and a broad back. *Probably in shock.*

Isaac found himself staring. Dark shadows marred the prisoner's skin, but the strong jaw and even features spoke to a devastatingly handsome face when he was well. He could see the man was huge, even curled up so tightly, easily two meters tall, maybe more. Golden-blond stubble atop his head indicated a recent shaving, though Isaac had no idea if he wore it that way out of choice or if prisoners were routinely shorn. He wore only a sleeveless midthigh shift. Anger rose in Isaac's chest. Bad enough they locked him up, but to take away a man's pants? Such calculated humiliation seemed cruel.

"Get the damn door open," Travis said, bringing Isaac back to the task at hand.

Rand plugged into the wall jack, and all his uneasy sounds ceased as he concentrated on hacking the door code. The door whispered open on Rand's triumphant cry.

"Attaboy," Travis said. "Now go back out to the console and download the logs."

"Out there? Alone?" The audio picked up Rand's hard swallow.

"Dammit, son, they're just pieces of meat out there. Nothing'll hurt you."

"But—"

Travis sighed. "Sylvia, go with him so the ghosts don't eat him."

Distracted by Rand's fears, Isaac had missed the moment their rescuee began to move. He had pushed up on trembling arms, hard muscles corded with the effort, and turned his head to face them, teeth bared in a snarl.

"Shchfteru scum," he whispered in a cracked, ruined voice. "Damn you…."

*He's going to hurt himself. Or lunge at Travis, and then someone's going to panic and shoot him….* "Humans." Isaac held the hands of his exosuit wide. "We're not some damn chuff, we're humans."

A low growl came from the man's chest, a sound Isaac had never heard from a person before. The man was obviously too far gone and the suits looked too menacing. He reached up, undid his helmet latches, and lifted the whole assembly off his head. "See, human. We're here to help you. Get you out of here."

The man stared at him, something flickering in his eyes through the rage. During his moment's distraction, Travis and Lester grabbed him and pinned him to the decking so Dr. Varga could get him sedated.

Isaac caught a whiff of the foul air and slammed the helmet back on his head, coughing fitfully as he got the latches secured. "Oh shit… that's horrible… how was he still breathing?"

"Don't know, bud." The servos in Travis's suit whirred as he stood back up for the return walk. "But the shchfteru, if they were here—it explains a hell of a lot."

"Explains why the crew's in shreds," Lester rumbled. "Doesn't explain why the ship's whole and the boards are untouched. Or why this guy survived."

Lester was right there.

"We need to get the *Hermes* away, Trav," Isaac said softly. "The chuff don't leave things half done. They're bound to come back to finish."

# CHAPTER 2: AN UNLIKELY ISHMAEL

"FROM THE desiccation of the remains and our patient's level of malnutrition, I'd say he was alone in that hell of a charnel house for at least two weeks," Doc said as she scrubbed.

"Two... weeks?" Isaac blinked in shock. "God. Poor bastard." His gaze returned to the man on the ICU bed. Medics worked to start IVs and to shove his hands and feet into operating restraints. "Why's he being fastened down, Doc? Don't you think he's had enough confinement?"

"Isaac, sweetie, we don't know anything about him."

"We know he was military—"

"Yes, his tat says so, but we can't get a reading on it."

"Which means?"

"He was probably in some branch's Special Ops. Some top-clearance unit. I say 'was' because I think he was probably headed for a military prison. But the *Marduk*'s records don't say a word about him. He's given a number designation, but that's it. No file. We don't know what we have here. Deserter. Traitor. Spy. Terrorist. War criminal. Some poor sod that went nuts and killed his squadmates. When he looked at you in that cell, tell me honestly, did he seem sane to you?"

"Would you be, Doc? After two weeks alone, locked up and terrified?"

"No. And most people wouldn't have lived that long, either. He's strong-willed, regardless of what else he is. And that's just my point, hon. He could be very dangerous."

Isaac sighed. The poor man didn't look dangerous, not now. Strapped down spread-eagle on his back, he looked terribly vulnerable, the dark shadows under his eyes emphasized by the harsh lights of the sick bay. At least they'd wrestled him into a decent pair of pajamas and, now that they were finished working on him, covered him in radiant-heat blankets. He hadn't opened his eyes, hadn't said a word, but at least he was safe.

The *Marduk*'s logs had confirmed one thing: shchfteru had perpetrated the slaughter. The nomadic scavengers had followed their usual pattern, luring the *Marduk* with a distress call, damaging her engines, and then sending a boarding party to teleport through the airlocks. The mantis-like chuff could 'port only a few feet at a time, thank God, or the whole galaxy would have been wiped clean of other life long ago. After boarding, their normal pattern was to slaughter the crew, take some of the meat with them if they found it palatable, and then strip the ship of any materials and electronics they could carry away.

The normal pattern had ended on the *Marduk* with the slaughter. The moment the chuff had moved into A-block, the vids broke up in static. When the disturbance cleared, the chuff were gone. Not pulling out, not regrouping, but vanished. Even their ship no longer appeared on the scanners after the vid feed returned three minutes later to show the bloodied, silent ship corridors.

"Rand's ghosts must've eaten them," Sylvia had suggested to various snorts and Rand rolling his eyes. The fact remained, though: they had no explanation.

Their recovered survivor might hold the answers if he remained sane and was willing to tell the story. As the only person to have held even part of a conversation with him, the bridge crew elected Isaac to try some gentle questioning. Not that he minded. He felt drawn to the man, who was seemingly alone in the universe. If he was honest with himself, he was even more interested after the medics had stripped him to scrub him down. Despite the effects of malnutrition, his body was still hard-packed and impressive. Isaac'd had to revise his estimate of height to well over two meters when he lay stretched out. His pale skin, interrupted by scars here and there, carried two tattoos, the black military code circling his left biceps and an intricate knot-work of blue and green weaving around his navel.

"Corzin," Travis muttered as he stood by Isaac, watching the proceedings.

"Excuse me?"

"He's a Corzin warrior. The design on his stomach. Strange but ferocious as hell. Sometimes take on mercenary work. Fought with them at Demos. Crazy bunch of mothers, but nothing gets past them. What the hell one's doing with a naval tatt…." Travis shook his head. "None of this mess makes sense."

The ICU bay cleared, leaving Isaac alone with this odd cipher. He leaned back against the counter, arms crossed over his chest, and waited for some sign the man might be waking.

A TERRIBLE jolt yanked him from the dark. *Shchfteru. Agonized screams. Rage coursing through every nerve. The white… blinding white… imploding suns… the terrible silence….*

He had no wish to open his eyes again. There had been a face, a beautiful face, but he must have dreamt it in his madness. The silence remained. If he opened his eyes, he would see the cell again, the blood-drenched walls, the gray horror of his floating tomb. No. Better to keep his eyes closed and see again those dark eyes set against flawless golden skin.

Wait. Sound. The soft sound of even breaths drawn. *Not alone. Sweet spirits, I'm not alone.*

His eyes flew open to find a miracle staring at him from across the room, the same lovely face from his vision. It must have been true. His body felt warmer and no longer as if he might go mad from thirst. Rescue… perhaps. But he needed to be cautious.

"Hey." The beautiful golden-skinned man spoke, his smile reaching his raindrop-shaped eyes. "You recognize me?"

He could only stare, hesitant to believe the evidence of his senses. They had lied to him before in recent days.

"You have a name?" The voice rivaled the face in beauty, soft and warm, caressing his exhausted mind. "All right, we'll start with mine. I'm Isaac Ozawa. And I guess I could just call you the *Marduk* Rescuee or maybe Ishmael—"

"Ishmael?" The word caught in his dry throat, barely a rasp.

"Yeah, you know, the sole survivor? And I alone survived to tell the tale? Oh, never mind. But it would be nicer to have a name."

He swallowed against the rawness, trying for more of a voice. "Turk."

"That's your name? Turk?"

He nodded and watched in fascination as Isaac shook his head, dark hair fanning his cheeks.

"Of course it is. No soft sibilants or lingual sounds for you. Oh no. Nothing but hard, strong sounds. You probably have a last name that would hurt to say."

Turk drew a slow breath, trying to keep up with events. His head ached. "Always... talk so much?"

"Only when I'm nervous or pissed off."

"Which?"

"Which is it now? Oh, nervous, definitely." Isaac shifted, head cocked to one side. "Not that strange men usually make me this nervous."

"But... I do." He forced his attention away from the captivating face. Isaac was in uniform, burgundy with gold piping. He couldn't match the colors with any unit he knew. Whose hands had he fallen into? "Water?"

"Oh shit." The beautiful smile fell. "Of course you want water. Damn. Hang on."

Turk eased his head back to the bed, waiting. Something pinned his hands and feet. In his weakened condition, he had little hope of breaking a magnetic or even a physical barrier. Isaac came back into view, water bottle in hand. A sharp, electric jolt ran down Turk's spine when an elegant golden hand slipped behind his head to help him drink. He had no business thinking about those hands.

"Better?"

"Thank you." Why did he have to be so kind? It would make what he had to do so much harder. He closed his eyes on a sigh, gauging the remaining strength in his wasted body. "Back hurts. Need to...."

"Stupid restraints," Isaac muttered. "They should've at least left you one hand free so you could shift a little."

He chewed on a sensuously full lower lip, considering, as Turk watched in helpless fascination. Isaac's jaw clenched as he seemed to come to a decision. He reached over and pressed the pad to unlock Turk's left wrist.

The moment he regained movement, Turk lunged. He seized Isaac by the throat, applying enough pressure to constrict his airway.

"What unit? What battle group? Whom do you serve?"

Isaac's fingers scrabbled at his hand, his eyes wide and desperate. "Don't... please...."

"Who are you?"

"Not... military," Isaac choked out, his coloring edging up from pink to crimson.

"Liar," Turk growled. "Implant. Fighter pilot. Behind your ear."

"Ex-Altairian... Fleet...." Isaac gasped, struggling to pull away. He was strong but not large enough to break Turk's grip. "Bad... implant. Discharged... this is... commercial ship... courier...."

His eyes rolled back and his body went limp as if someone had stolen his bones. Turk let him slide to the floor, his heart racing. With his free hand, he unlocked the rest of his restraints and rolled to peer over the edge of his bed. Isaac lay crumpled on the decking, the shadows of his thick, black lashes caressing his cheeks.

*No insignia, no rank designation, a courier ship... what have I done?*

Slowly, uncertain if his body would respond, he eased his legs over the side of the bed. Once he stood, his knees crumpled. No matter, it brought him down onto the floor with Isaac. He had made a terrible mistake and hoped it wasn't an irrevocable one. The decking pitched underneath him and he half slid, half collapsed onto his side facing Isaac.

His hand moved without his prompting to smooth a stray lock of hair behind Isaac's ear.

A telltale blue ring surrounded the little implant nub. He could see it now that he was closer. That much was true, then. The implant had not bonded well with Isaac's brain stem. Pilots with partial rejections, from what he had been told, usually committed suicide. In the most elite fighters, the promise of symbiotic flight became too much a part of young soldiers' psyches. To be one of the handful chosen, to undergo the rigorous training, and then to have the dream ripped away—he understood how that could unhinge a man.

But Isaac seemed whole, friendly, and even cheerful. *Such strength... so alluring, so desirable. I have been alone too long for a stranger to affect me so.*

The stranger in question coughed and let out a soft moan.

"Isaac?" Turk kept a gentle hand on his shoulder.

"God." Isaac coughed again. "What's *wrong* with you? A little paranoid, maybe?"

Flushed with shame, Turk placed a fist against his chest. "I have erred. My heart grieves for my errors."

"Could just say you're sorry," Isaac muttered. Then he glanced over at Turk, his eyes widening. "Oh. That's what you were doing... damn." He sat up, rubbing his throat. "Sorry. Should've explained things. Of course you're a little jumpy—"

"I should not have attacked my rescuer," Turk cut him off softly.

Isaac cocked his head to the side. "Fine. You can make it up to me, then."

Suspicions skittered along Turk's nerves. "How?"

"Two things. One, you can promise me you won't attack any of my shipmates."

He considered this, wondering if there might be a trap in the request, but his brain was too tired to come up with one. "If no one offers me threat, I will not harm anyone on this ship."

Isaac nodded slowly. "That's fair, I guess. And two, you can tell me why you were in that cell."

"Protective custody."

"Oh. What for?"

"I can't say."

"You mean you won't say," Isaac said on a little snort.

"Not... at liberty to say." Turk tried to sit up so he wouldn't need to stare up at Isaac from the floor. His muscles trembled, though, and he found Isaac's arms around him before he had managed an upright position.

"Let's get you back in bed, all right? You're so damn cold and you're shaking."

The real concern in Isaac's voice allowed him to relax. Whatever intrigues he might stumble into farther on, they would not involve this guileless, sincere soul. Isaac took more of his weight than he thought possible as he helped Turk heave off the floor and back into bed. His slender body held surprising strength, hard muscles evident in the arms wrapped around Turk and the shoulder he leaned against.

"Can you at least tell me where they were taking you? Is there somewhere you're supposed to be?" Isaac rearranged the blankets over him, tucking him in as if he were a child. Somehow, the gesture touched rather than embarrassed him.

*Lie down with me....* Absurd. As if any deck officer on duty, even on a commercial vessel, would do such a thing. "Luyten Station. Eridani Sector Treaty Organization Fleet HQ. I must be... overdue."

"Yeah, probably," Isaac said on a slow exhalation of breath. "You don't have to if it's too hard. But can you tell me what happened? On the *Marduk*? When the chuff came?"

Turk fought against the sudden chill gripping his insides. "No."

"No, you won't tell me?"

"I... can't." He seized Isaac's arm, trying to keep the sick bay from spinning.

"Whoa... hey. It's all right."

A gentle hand stroked his shoulder and he forced his lungs to draw a whole breath. "I saw them. In the hall. Screams. So many screams. Saw them shred crew outside my cell. They tried to open my door. Rage... engulfed me. White. Nothing but white. Then they were gone."

He stiffened as he found himself pulled into Isaac's embrace. He was no weakling to need comfort. He was Corzin, strength incarnate, a warrior born... and found himself clinging to Isaac like a child woken from nightmare.

"It's all right. It'll be all right now," Isaac soothed as he rubbed Turk's back and held him tight. "I'm sorry I asked. You need to rest. I'm sorry."

Turk forced himself to calm, unwilling to worry his new... what? Jailer? Protector? Friend? It was too early to say. When Isaac gave his chest a final pat and told him to rest, panic nearly rose up again.

"Isaac," he croaked out when his gentle interrogator had turned to go. Dark eyes regarded him with a mixture of sympathy and curiosity. *Don't leave me alone.* "Thank you."

"Not a problem." Isaac flashed a brilliant smile. "Try to get some sleep."

The door closed behind him. Turk closed his eyes and tried to silence the voices in his mind, the whispers that Isaac hadn't been real.


CAPTAIN DRUMMOND paced the length of the briefing room. "Luyten Station. At least that tells us who he belongs to."

"Maybe," Travis said. "Protective custody could mean a lot of things."

Sylvia waved a hand in a dismissive gesture. "Not our problem. He was on his way to ESTO HQ, he admits it, so we drop him there."

"I just wish there was something in the logs to confirm it." Isaac rolled a stylus on the tabletop, disturbed on several levels. "Or to tell us why someone on military business was being transported as a prisoner."

"We only have his word it was some top-secret mission," Rand added.

"Yeah. His word." Isaac squashed the urge to glare at Rand. They had been round and round this buoy already. He knew on a gut-instinct level that Turk wouldn't lie. He might withhold information, but the man didn't seem capable of lying. Without any evidence to back that up, though, Isaac knew how it would sound to his fellow officers. Poor, lonely Isaac, dazzled by another handsome hunk of male.

Captain Drummond stopped her pacing. "It's all we have. We go out-system. We head for Luyten and we go through channels there." She turned to Travis. "Skeleton shifts, Mr. Humboldt. Crew needs some downtime. We fire up the GEM drive in three days. I want everyone sharp when we get to Luyten."

The junior officers filed out. Isaac stayed.

"You all right, Oz? Something on your mind?" Travis asked.

"Not sure yet. But I feel like we're missing something."

Captain Drummond finally slid into her chair at the head of the table. "I think we're missing most of the puzzle. But Ms. Casalvez is right on one point. It's not our concern."

"Yes, ma'am. Of course."

"Still, you're concerned." She leaned forward, hands clasped in front of her. "Turk's been through hell, son, I know that. And I can see you feel a certain empathy for him. A strong man on the verge of emotional collapse. I understand. But I'm warning you, get involved in this, in any way, it's going to bite you so hard on the ass you'll never be able to sit down again."

Isaac ducked his head. "Yes, ma'am."

"Get some rest, Isaac. You're long overdue."

He wandered to his quarters, trying to sift through thoughts that wouldn't sit still. By the time he crawled into his bunk, his brain had deteriorated into a tangled mess of unpleasant scenarios. To make matters worse, he kept returning to the way Turk's body felt pressed tight to his, chest to chest. It had been a long time since a man had lain trembling in his arms.

# CHAPTER 3: BIOLOGICALLY HUMAN

TURK TUGGED at the cuffs of his borrowed shirt. Try as he might, the sleeves just weren't long enough to fasten. He bit back a sigh of frustration. The trousers fit relatively well, especially tucked in the deck boots. Thank the spirits someone on the crew had oversized feet.

The doctor had said he could walk a bit today if he wished. Apparently, Isaac was off-duty and had been asked to accompany him. Dr. Varga had looked at him a little oddly when he asked if Isaac was real.

"Yes, he's our communications officer," Dr. Varga told him.

"Dark hair? About so tall? Soft voice?"

"Yes, that's our Isaac."

*Isaac*....

The thought of him made Turk's heart race, as if he were some adolescent off on his first assignation. *Ridiculous.* Nothing could have been more inappropriate or more absurd than to fantasize about a man he would never see again once he disembarked.

He glanced up when the sick-bay door hissed open. Isaac strolled in, greeting the medical staff one by one with soft words and his bright smile. Turk tore his gaze away, unwilling to be caught staring. The comm officer looked even more desirable in his off-duty clothes, a black T-shirt stretched tight across his sculpted chest and dark trousers that clung to him like a pleading lover.

"Hey there!" The warmth of his gaze caressed Turk's face. "You look shiploads better than yesterday."

For a moment, Turk sat mute, snared by the lovely pools of his eyes. "I... yes. Thank you."

Isaac shook his head on a chuckle. "Still not much of a talker, though. Did they give you lunch yet?"

"No." The rules of polite conversation said he should offer more than single syllables, but the words stuck behind his teeth.

"I'll walk you to the mess, then, and we'll feed you there." Isaac turned to Dr. Varga, "Is that all right, Doc?"

She shrugged. "It's a short walk, but don't rush him and stop if he needs to rest."

"Perfect. It's a date." Isaac shot him a wink, destroying Turk's remaining doubts. The man was flirting with him.

*If you knew anything, my dear rescuer, you would not. I shouldn't be here, entangling these kind people in my darkness.* Luyten. They headed for Luyten, had changed course and put aside their own business to take him where he had been ordered to go. A shiver ran up his arms. The admiral said he would be safer at Luyten. Perhaps.

"Sure you're up to this?" Isaac rested a hand on his arm, his brows drawn together.

Turk forced a tight-lipped smile. "Yes. I'm fine."

"Yeah. You're about as fine as a faulty-coordinate GEM jump, but you still need to eat." Isaac put a hand under his elbow as he stood. "Mess is just down the hall. It's mostly synth stuff, but it's not too awful."

Turk tried a few steps, gratified when his knees held. "Food is strength. Taste is secondary." There. That had been more than single syllables.

Isaac gave him an odd look. "That's one way to put it. But I guess when you've missed more than a few meals...." He let the thought trail off as he led Turk out the door.

The sick bay had been the usual stark white of so many other medical units in his experience and he expected the normal variations of gray in the corridors. Instead, a riot of color ambushed him. Turk stopped with a hand on the wall, head swiveling to try to absorb it all.

"Oh, right. The paintings." Isaac chuckled. "Captain Drummond's a firm believer in keeping the brain active. Spacers get lazy, she says, going through the same routines, the same protocols again and again. Arts, literature, games of strategy, she's always coming up with new brain exercises for us. This"—he waved a hand at the explosion of images on the walls—"is one of three freehand zones on the *Hermes*. Anyone can come on their off-hours and paint."

A fanciful winged creature in glorious reds and oranges adorned the wall above Turk's hand. Below it a cityscape spread out in blues and greens. "Without constraint? Or rules?"

"Two rules. You can't paint over someone else's work. And no sex scenes."

Interesting, though not surprising, that one of the most natural and beautiful acts would be forbidden. Offworlders were such contradictions of decadence and prudishness. "Yours?" he asked softly. "Any of them?"

Isaac dropped his gaze, a flush blooming on his cheeks. "Sure. I mean, I'm no artist, but then most of us aren't. It's not very good."

Turk raised a brow, waiting, amused by this sudden shyness.

"That one"—Isaac pointed—"down on the right."

The painting had been rendered in delicate, careful strokes. Graceful trees stood festooned in soft pink petals on branches that seemed to flow down toward the stream bathing their feet. Despite Isaac's protests about his lack of skill, Turk found it astoundingly beautiful.

"Is it home?"

"Yes." Isaac whispered the word and Turk understood the longing in it. "It was."

They made the rest of the walk in silence, a circumstance Turk regretted. He found Isaac's voice soothing, but prompting someone else into conversation wasn't his greatest strength.

The light green of the mess hall seemed subdued after the exuberant splashes of color in the corridor. Perhaps it was meant to be restful, but the bland sameness only reminded Turk of his aching weariness. He eased into the chair Isaac indicated and waited while his escort went to forage. Other crewmembers ate singly or in small, companionable groups, so Turk kept his gaze on the table. If they stared, he would not acknowledge it, would not offer threat.

Isaac returned and placed a tray in front of each of them. He sank down across from Turk, rubbing at his left temple.

"It causes you pain?" Turk gestured toward the implant.

"Sometimes. I just overdid it yesterday," Isaac said with a little shrug. "It's not usually too bad."

Turk turned his attention to his food, pushing the brown and green cubes around with his fork. "If it hurts you, why didn't they remove it?"

Silence greeted his question. He raised his head to find Isaac staring at him, tight-jawed and tense.

After a moment, those dark eyes softened. "You really don't know, do you?"

"I suppose not. What should I know?"

"If you take the implant out, you kill the recipient."

"Ah." Turk set his hands on the table. "I spoke without forethought."

Isaac cocked his head. "I guess that was another apology. It's all right."

"But you... you survived. Is this not... unusual?"

"Since I should have ended it honorably and saved everyone all the trouble and mess?" Isaac's tone had turned bitter. He shot Turk an apologetic glance. "Sorry. Yeah, I know. Most go over the event horizon and suicide. Sure, the Fleet sets up counseling and puts you under a watch when the implant goes bad, but most failed pilot candidates find a way to end it. Guess I wasn't ready. And then they didn't know what to do with me."

Turk struggled to make sense of the tale. "You could not pilot the Novasym fighters any longer. But they offered other tasks? A jump ship? A transport?"

A sharp bark of laughter escaped Isaac. "Dear God, no! I'm not considered stable enough to pilot a ground shuttle! No, they tossed me out. Honorable medical discharge, of course, but it amounts to the same thing."

"Ah." Turk shoveled protein cubes into his mouth to prevent any more uncomfortable questions. Was it always so with Offworlder military commands? To use a man, ruin him, and then treat him with scorn? He closed his eyes, drawing slow, careful breaths. A gentle hand settled over his and his breathing ceased altogether.

"Hey, I'm sorry. Did I upset you? Do you feel all right?"

He opened his eyes to meet the concern in Isaac's and he offered another small curl of his lips. "I'm fine. Tired, a bit."

"Do you ever smile?" Isaac gave his hand a little squeeze. "I mean a real smile? Flash those white teeth?"

"I...." Turk faltered. His instincts all bellowed at him that he could trust this man, but he had no clear reason why. "I was raised to look upon a show of teeth as a threat display."

"Oh. Is it threatening when I smile at you?"

"No. You have a lovely... that is, I am becoming more accustomed to human facial expressions."

Isaac's brows drew together in a puzzled frown. "But you are human."

"I am... biologically human. Yes."

"Guess you're not going to explain that, huh?"

Turk gulped down the two bottles of water Isaac had brought him to discourage further questions on the topic. It felt wrong to have another open the petals of history to him and not reciprocate, but blood oaths held his tongue, stronger than any rules of proper conduct or the pull of a passing attraction.

Thankfully, Isaac did not take offense. Instead, he steered the conversation on to name the other occupants of the mess hall. He ate sparingly and slowly, as if even synthetic food was something to be savored.

"You want more?" He gestured with his fork to Turk's empty plate.

"Thank you, no."

"You're a big man. You have to eat."

Yes, he had to regain his strength, but the few bites he had eaten already tested his limits. "The doctor said it might take some time. Prolonged deprivation...."

"Of course. I don't mean to badger you." Isaac chuckled. "You must think I'm the nosiest, pushiest person in the quadrant by now."

"You have been more than gracious," Turk said. *And your curiosity has most likely helped keep you from ending your life.* The mess hall lurched suddenly. "Isaac... I think...."

Isaac rose and hurried around the table. "We better get you back. You've gone sort of gray."

The floor tilted under him as he stood, but Turk kept his feet with Isaac's hand under his elbow. The few steps back to the corridor took all his concentration.

"Oz, you need a hand?" a deep voice called from across the mess hall.

"I think we're good, Trav, thanks."

A low hum muted the words, as if Isaac spoke from inside a bowl of water. In the corridor, Turk stopped with a hand on the wall. *I am about to shame myself and collapse at this beautiful man's feet. Sweet winds of At'kros, give me but a moment's strength.*

"All right, you're not going to make it, and I can't carry you." Isaac palmed a door pad on his right. "Come on into this one. Passenger cabins are empty this run."

Turk's vision darkened; only a vague notion of a bunk swam before him. He lurched forward with Isaac's arm around his waist.

"That's it. Perfect. Just relax."

The ship steadied when he lay on his side. The hum subsided as he drew deep breaths. The weakness stung his pride, though he knew the sting would have been less in front of anyone but Isaac.


THE CABIN had a couple's bunk, thank goodness. Turk would have been too big for a single. Isaac pulled blankets from the wall cabinet and covered him, since he shivered.

"Guess our little outing wasn't such a good idea." He patted Turk's shoulder. "You wait right here. I'll run to medical and get some help."

A huge hand shot out and seized his wrist. "Please," Turk whispered.

*Please what?* Isaac stared at the long fingers, the grip firm but careful. One of those hands would be big enough to cup his butt, lift him against the wall.... *Damn. I can't go down that route. Stupid.*

"What's wrong? You feel sick?"

Turk shook his head, blue eyes pleading and anxious.

He eased onto the edge of the bunk, his brain trying hard to override his hormones. "You don't want to be alone."

"Please. It's… I'm not certain what's real when I'm alone."

The captain had said don't get involved. Problem was, he'd been involved the moment he picked up Turk's life signs. What difference did it make anyway? What did it cost him to offer comfort to someone in need? In a few days, Turk would return to his command, resume his life, and disappear off the scopes. Until then, he was horror-shocked and hurting, his mental gyroscopes gone crazy and his personal nav on the blink.

"I won't leave." He patted Turk's hand. "Let go a sec, though. Let me call Doc." Strong fingers uncurled slowly, as if the very act of letting go caused Turk pain. Isaac kept his place on the bunk's edge, his proximity standing as his promise not to vanish, and tapped at his wrist comm. "Doc?"

"Oz? Everything all right?" Dr. Varga's voice came back small and compressed through the comm.

"Yes, ma'am. We had to make a detour. Stopped in one of the passenger cabins to let him rest."

"Is his skin clammy? Pulse racing? You need me to come over there?"

Isaac put a finger to the pulse point on Turk's wrist. The beat sped and then settled, strong and steady. "He's a little chilled, Doc, but doesn't seem distressed. He just couldn't go any farther right now."

"All right. We'll let him rest where it's quiet, then. Call me in an hour or so. Let me know if you need help getting him moved."

Isaac clicked off and waved a hand at his companion. "Move over." When Turk scooted to the far side of the bunk, he stretched out beside him.

"You don't need to—"

"I know." Isaac took his hand, lacing their fingers together. "We both could use a rest. I'm here. This is real."

Turk freed his hand, but it was only to wrap an arm over Isaac's waist and pull him close. Depleted though he was, enormous strength still resided in that arm. Isaac held his breath a moment, wondering if Turk had anything further in mind. He relaxed when Turk nestled his head against Isaac's shoulder and closed his eyes. All he seemed to want for now was companionship, a bit of human warmth. Isaac lay with him, stroking his broad back, trying to decide if he was more relieved or disappointed.

# CHAPTER 4: MEMORY AMBUSHES

"STATUS?" CAPTAIN Drummond strode out of her office and settled into her chair.

"Nav comp laid in, ma'am," Sylvia said. "On your four screen."

The captain glanced down at the calculations, but only as a formality. Sylvia had thoroughly tested the equations and then three sets of eyes—Travis's, Rand's, and Isaac's—had checked them through before they reached the captain.

In his two years with the *Hermes*, Isaac had never found an error in Sylvia's calc, and he had tried his damndest to find one. Early on, he had resented Sylvia. The nav officer slot should have been his. He had the training, the certification. But the captain had told him, without cushioning or coddling, that if he had a migraine or a neural attack in the middle of a GEM jump, they were all dead.

"My ship, my little slice of tyranny, Mr. Ozawa," she had said then. "You accept my decisions, or you get your ass back down that gangway and off my ship now."

Isaac had swallowed his pride, apologized, took the comm officer's slot, and counted himself lucky. With his "condition," no other captain had been willing to consider him for any berth. Some even balked at having him as a passenger, since he was considered so unstable, and he had given up in despair.

He had been drinking and fucking his way through every bar on Demos station when Travis, who had been one of Isaac's instructors in his last service year, found him. Some people never believed in luck. Isaac knew better. People lived and died by luck. A second's hesitation, a moment's impulse made the difference between a good outcome and disaster. He had been close to the end then, despair gnawing away his stubborn resolve. One last, hard screw with the big Marine drinking next to him, one last look at the stars, and then he was taking a walk out the airlock.

Just as he stood to let the Marine take him to his bunk, Travis appeared in the doorway. Salvation, enforced sobriety, and a chance at a berth on a sweet, fast ship all wrapped in one gruff, hard-edged packet. Luck. If he hadn't insisted on finishing his drink, if Travis hadn't recognized him despite his being walking wreckage, he would have died that night.

"Mr. Wilde?" The captain's voice brought him back to the present.

"Clear field, ma'am. No traffic, no debris."

"Mr. Ozawa?"

"Course logged and registered. Comm is clear, Captain."

"Mr. Humboldt, the helm is yours. Set shields and power up."

Clanks announced the Mondal shields swinging out from the hull and the bow shielding opening to expose the GEM drive. During in-system flight, the big drive needed to be shielded from debris, but its shield was plain polyceramic. During gravito-electromagnetic flight, though, the ship needed protection from the monstrous gravitational forces of the drive. The Mondals, constructed of neutron-free lumanium, nullified the gravitational forces on the ship itself and kept the *Hermes* from a swift and mangled end while it shot through the continually forward-expanding gravity well.

Isaac sat back, watching the polys peel back to expose the gleaming drive. He would be just a passenger in a few moments. Sylvia and Travis had all the hard work until they re-entered system and finished braking sequences. *Good thing too.* He would have struggled to keep his mind on task. His thoughts kept drifting to a huge, hard-muscled body and a pair of strong, gentle hands.

Dr. Varga had allowed Turk to stay in the passenger cabin since she proclaimed it a "less stressful environment" than sick bay. Isaac checked on him during the day and returned to him every sleep cycle when Turk would hold him tight. He never made any sexual advances, never offered a kiss beyond a soft caress of lips to Isaac's forehead, but he would crush him close sometimes during sleep, as if only that physical reminder of his presence would keep the nightmares at bay.

An odd arrangement, but Isaac couldn't stay away. He had seen Turk's ferocious side, and it was formidable. But it was only half the man. When not in combat mode, he was polite and careful; there was a gentleness in him that Isaac wished he could explore. To have those hands stroke over his body, to see if he would be as careful preparing his lover as he was with his speech, oh, it would be glorious….

Isaac shifted uncomfortably in his chair, his trousers suddenly too tight. He was going to end up with a permanent erection if he kept on drifting into lecherous thoughts. Turk needed comfort, not some hormone-crazed spacer who needed to find a piece of serious meat at the next port. *Definitely. Going trolling first thing we hit station. Work off all this pent-up energy. Something muscle-bound and throw-you-up-against-the-wall fierce, with big hands and deep blue eyes and... dammit, stop.*

"Gyros at speed, nearing 90 percent," Sylvia called out.

Isaac hit the ship's comm. "All personnel. GEM thrust in five. Secure and strap in. GEM thrust in five."

He thumbed the control on his chair arm that powered his restraints in place, every officer on the bridge following suit. The violent change in velocity could plaster an unsecured crewman against the nearest wall with broken bones the least of his worries. Turk was already secured, Isaac had made certain. The bunks had standard safety webbing that Turk had used to secure himself with practiced, efficient movements since Isaac had refused to leave until he did.

"Powered up, Captain."

"Check in, Mr. Ozawa?" Captain Drummond's gaze was firmly fixed on the forward viewport and the drive.

"All section heads report secure, ma'am."

"When you're ready, Mr. Humboldt."

"Count it down, Oz, we're staring down the pipe."

Over ship's comm, Isaac began the count at ten, warning the crew to lean back and brace themselves. "… and three… two… one."

At one, Travis punched it, the helm control gripped tightly in both hands. The familiar feeling of a huge hand slamming him back into his chair exhilarated Isaac. He yearned for the controls, of course, but he settled for the sheer mad rush of GEM flight, letting the ecstasy take him. The sensation was terrifying to some people, but he'd been trained to it early and few other things got his heart pounding like that initial hard acceleration.

*I hope Turk's all right....* Not that he worried for him physically. It was obvious from his reactions that he had deep-space training. But he was alone down there in the low-level lighting of a GEM run, alone with his memories and his nightmares. Eight hours, that's all he had to get through while Travis wrestled the *Hermes* through the vortex currents. The most dangerous part came in the deceleration sequence, when the pilot was exhausted and mistakes could be deadly in spectacular ways. Once they hit the third or fourth downshift, though, movement about the ship would be safe again.

Eight hours was all Turk had to endure. After two weeks alone, that shouldn't seem like much.

SILENCE. NOT quite as complete as the *Marduk*, but it was oppressive, with the steady hum of the huge gyroscope powering the drive. Machine hum, but no human sounds. Isaac's soothing voice no longer drifted over the comm, no footsteps sounded in the corridor. Turk shivered and shut his eyes, but behind his eyelids were scenes of blood and destruction. He opened his eyes to focus on the cabin, lit only by the dim glow of the door panel.

Admiral Uchechi sat in the chair by his bunk. "I'll do the best I can for you, son. We'll get you out from under his eye here. I think that's the best thing. Send you to HQ where there should be more checks and balances."

"Sir, you're not really here," Turk whispered. "We had this conversation weeks ago."

The admiral's dark face gleamed as if lit from below with an eerie light, his eyes cast into ominous shadow. "I know, boy. And once we get you there, we'll rip your brain from your skull and keep it in a jar!"

His voice rose to a roar, his jaws distending to show chitinous pincers instead of teeth.

Turk clamped his eyes shut and set his jaw. "You're not here. You're not the admiral. You're not chuff. I am alone." He thought hard of Isaac's scent when he lay close, the mix of male and musk, the sweet scent when Turk nuzzled behind his ear while he slept.

He forced his eyes open again. *Alone.*


ISAAC'S HEART sank when he reached the cabin. The *Hermes* was on decel and the captain had given him leave to quit his post for a few minutes. He wanted to get Turk up, maybe move him to the crew lounge where he could sit by the viewport and watch as they raced in-system. But when he found Turk in a shivering ball under his webbing, he revised his plans. Calm and coherent was more important than a view of Luyten's outer planets.

"Turk?" He unlatched the webbing and let it slide back into its wall slot. "You all—"

With frightening speed, Turk's body uncoiled and struck. The air rushed from Isaac's lungs as his back met decking with a hard thud. He gasped and struggled against the heavy body pinning him, his arms held above his head in Turk's unbreakable grip.

"Dammit." He fought his panic to keep his voice low and soothing. "Turk, it's me. It's Isaac. I'm real, remember?"

The fierce light faded from those cerulean eyes, confusion seeping in. "Isaac? Isaac...." He eased his grip but didn't move. "I... did I hurt you?"

"A little bruised, maybe, but no, I don't think so." Isaac stared up at the strong jaw, the clean lines of the face above him, far too aware of the press of Turk's weight against his groin. "Um, did you intend to *do* anything in this position? Or are you just resting?"

Turk stared down at him, his expression softening. He released one wrist, his hand drifting down Isaac's arm. "You're so lovely," he whispered. The backs of his fingers caressed Isaac's jaw.

"Turk...." Isaac couldn't draw a whole breath. Solar flares blossomed inside him, moving up from his knees to his groin. There was a word he should say, something starting with an *N*, but it escaped him as Turk leaned down to brush his lips under Isaac's ear.

Turk moved to lick along the seam of his lips and Isaac's brain went into core meltdown. He moaned and wrapped his arms around Turk's back, melting to the tender kiss. The man was so huge, so strong, could have torn him in half without breaking a sweat, but his touch was so gentle, just as Isaac had suspected it would be. His hips pressed up, seeking the friction of hard cock against cock, frustrated by the clothes between them.

*What's wrong with me?*

With a groan, he pulled back. "Turk, I'm sorry. We can't do this."

Blue eyes blinked at him. "You don't find me... desirable?"

*Oh hell, yes. I find you all kinds of desirable.* "It's not that. This just isn't right. I... don't want to hurt you. You're not some quick screw I picked up in a bar somewhere."

"A quick screw." Turk rolled onto his side, head propped up on his hand. "Is that what you normally seek?"

"I guess. Yeah. For a few years, now. Just... relief, right?"

Turk stroked a hand over his shoulder. "It sounds lonely. Do you never allow yourself joy in your assignations?"

The question hit Isaac like a blow to the gut. He sat up, rubbing both hands over his face. "It's not like I don't take any pleasure from it. But I take what I need and go. Never much conversation. Only stick around long enough to get my clothes back on. I haven't even slept in another man's arms since"—*since Ethan left me*—"since I joined up with the *Hermes*."

One of those enigmatic little smiles tugged at Turk's lips. "You have slept in my arms."

Isaac met his gaze head-on. "Yes. Yes, I have. And I like you. And I feel responsible for you. So you're not some throwaway sex toy, all right?"

Turk closed his eyes on a soft sigh and rolled onto his back. "I will not pursue what you don't wish. But even a few hours of joy would be... better than keeping a barren heart."

"And here I didn't think you had an ego," Isaac said on a chuckle. "Man knows me for a few days and thinks he can make everything better. Besides, I'm still on shift. I have to get back to my post." He nudged Turk. "Just came to check on you. Were they bad? The hallucinations, the memories, whatever it is you see?"

"Perhaps not as terrible as before." Turk shrugged where he lay. "It would take time to adjust, they said."

"Adjust to what?"

Turk rose abruptly and turned his back to pick up the blankets scattered on the floor.

"Sorry. Forget I asked. Things you're not at liberty to discuss. I got it." Isaac stood and straightened his uniform jacket. "Would you rather stay in here for the rest of the shift or would it be better for you to be around people?"

A visible shiver ran up Turk's back. "If there is a place where I might hear people coming and going, that would be better."

With Turk installed in the chair next to Dr. Varga in the crew lounge, Isaac felt comfortable returning to work. Maybe not entirely comfortable, since his balls ached. His fingers stole to his lips, Turk's kiss still lingering there. When men kissed him, he expected hunger and bruising force. That's what he looked for when he went trolling, a man who would take him with quick ferocity. He needed the heat, the pain. *Be honest, you idiot. You want them to get it over with.* Turk's tenderness had taken him off guard, opened a door he'd long thought shut.

"Right. I need tenderness from a half-crazed military operative. Now *that* sounds healthy."

"Oz, you talking to yourself again?" Travis called over as he took his chair.

"Yes."

"Just checking. Carry on."

TRUE TO his word, Turk made no further advances when Isaac crawled into his arms the next sleep cycle. It touched him that the big man would be so solicitous and considerate. Nearly everything about Turk touched a deep recess of need inside him, a need more complicated than sex.

Isaac gazed at his sleeping face where the dark shadows had faded with the help of proper food and rest. With all the secrecy surrounding him and his strange, sometimes unpredictable reactions, a sensible person might have been afraid. *But I'm not. Maybe because I don't have a lot of sense left. Or maybe it's something else.*

Sleep had been an elusive commodity for years, but in Turk's arms, he dropped off with ease. A warm body in bed had certain advantages. There had been a time when he never slept alone, when the same solid presence had always occupied the other side of the bed.

*Ethan....*

The agony had mostly faded over the years. Sharp stabs of memory still hit him, though. They had promised forever. To be fair, those promises had been made to a different man. Ethan had sent a whole man off to his first phase of Novasym assimilation and got a wreck back when Isaac came home. The visits in the hospital, awkward and uncomfortable, when Ethan wouldn't meet his eyes and could barely touch him, should have given him some warning.

Too absorbed in his own misery, Isaac had missed all the signs. The shock of coming home to an empty apartment, to the voice message from Ethan that simply said, in flat, even tones, his family had called him home and he wouldn't be back, had put Isaac's heart through the trash compactor. He didn't recall much about those first weeks alone except the frantic calls to Ethan's family estate on Titan, calls that were never answered.

*"What was it, sweetheart, you just wanted a hero?"* Isaac recalled screaming into the home comm. *"Glory to bask in? And then when I didn't live up, you toss me out with the spoiled leftovers?"*

Such a fool. He'd been such a fool. Alone, rattling around a living space too large for one ailing, deranged derelict, he'd broken everything not nailed down and some things that were until the neighbors called enforcement. They dragged him away, back to the hospital....

"Isaac?"

Someone shook him gently. He didn't want to go back to the hospital.

"Isaac, come back. It's only a dream."

He twitched and gasped when his eyes flew open. Concerned blue eyes met his. A gentle hand stroked his hair.

"You cried out in your sleep." Turk's deep voice vibrated against him.

"I fell asleep?"

"Deeply. Difficult to wake. You were very angry."

Isaac tried for a laugh. It came out forced. "How can you tell someone's angry in their sleep?"

One blond eyebrow rose. "Unclench your fists. And your jaw. Feel the shout that rattled your lungs."

He pulled in a breath and uncurled his hands from the sheets. His fingers and his teeth ached. "Oh."

"Do you want to tell it?"

"What? The dream?" Isaac shifted onto his back and didn't protest when Turk laid an arm across his stomach. "Just fell asleep remembering something I shouldn't."

"Your lover. Who left you."

Isaac scrambled to sit up. "Who've you been talking to?"

Turk gave him space, his voice soft and even. "No need. I have been ill, but I'm no half-wit. I have eyes and ears."

"That obvious, huh?" Isaac raked his fingers back through his hair. "Sorry. Didn't mean to wake you up."

His left arm twitched, fire-footed spiders of pain racing under the skin. *Dammit, not now.* The twitch became an uncontrollable tremor, his breaths coming short as nausea swept over him. He just had to hang on a few minutes. It never lasted long.

"Do I fetch help for you?" Turk slid off the bunk to his knees. "Is this implant driven?"

"Yeah. Neural attack. Sometimes when I'm upset. Sometimes just because." Isaac took careful sips of air. His meds were in his quarters. *I'm an idiot.* "It'll pass. No need for the medics."

Turk's frown let him know he didn't approve, but he moved back onto the bed, stripping off his borrowed T-shirt in the process. Isaac didn't have more than a glimpse of his massive hard-packed chest before Turk sat behind him.

"It's not really a good idea to touch me," Isaac whispered as strong arms wrapped him close. The painful tremor spread down his left side, making it difficult not to thrash. Any touch served as an irritant, but trying to shove Turk away was like trying to shove a cargo loader.

A vibration began in Turk's chest at a pitch so impossibly deep no human voice should have been capable of it. The vibration slid into Isaac's bones as Turk opened his mouth to transform the hum into a full-throated note. It shook him to the core, making his heart skitter and jump. He twitched in Turk's grip, every nerve trembling in sympathy with that chasm-deep sound.

"What... the hell?" he gasped out as he scrabbled for purchase on the bed with his feet. The vibration reached into his skull, permeated his brain. For a moment more, he struggled against Turk's iron grip, panicked by the strange feeling.

Then the pitch dropped half a note. The pain vanished. The twitches along his nerves ceased. Soft euphoria washed over Isaac as he collapsed against Turk's chest. He turned his head so his ear rested against pectoral muscle, drinking in the vibration that had suddenly turned so soothing. A little whimper caught in his chest, and while he couldn't help feeling disgusted with himself for being so weak, he burrowed into Turk's embrace.

*Damn, this feels so good.*

The note grew softer until it faded altogether, leaving only Turk holding him tight, rocking him gently.

"What...," Isaac whispered. "How did you do that?"

Turk shrugged. "It's simply a matter of matching frequency with your magnetic field. The right resonance—"

Isaac sat up to stare at him. Turk snapped his mouth shut, his eyes guarded. It seemed obvious the big guy had said more than he had intended.

"I won't tell anyone," Isaac reassured him. His palms still lay flat on Turk's chest. Part of him said this level of closeness was a bad idea, but he wasn't in any hurry to move. "Your bizarre medical technique is safe with me."

One large hand slid up to cup Isaac's face. "I know." Turk let out a slow breath. "It's better?"

"Much. But you look tired."

Turk nodded and rolled down onto his back without relinquishing his hold. With his ear pressed to Turk's heart, resting between strong thighs and draped across a massive chest, Isaac tried to muster the willpower to roll off. But it felt so right, so comfortable and comforting, that he fell asleep before he could convince his body to move.

# CHAPTER 5: A NIGHT OF JOY

"FINE, SO he's not completely crazy." Travis put down his mug. "But sleeping with him's not one of your best ideas."

Across the breakfast table, Isaac fought against rolling his eyes. Turk still dozed peacefully, so Isaac had come to the mess by himself, rumpled and tousled from lying draped across him all night. "Sleeping, Trav. Not 'sleeping with' him. There hasn't been anything besides sleep."

"Still, you're in too deep, Oz."

The contrary part of Isaac wanted to argue he hadn't gotten in deep enough, but Travis wouldn't appreciate the humor, especially before his first full dose of coffee. "He's needed some help. Some company. A little compassion is so wrong?"

"If I thought that's all that was going on in that tilted-axis head of yours, I wouldn't say word one." Travis stabbed a fork into what passed for eggs. "But he's unstable and you're...."

Isaac waited but Travis trailed off with a shrug. "Not quite as unstable," Isaac finished for him. "I'm not planning on marrying him, Trav."

"Yeah, yeah, just friends. You keep in mind, you lunatic, that he was in a prison cell when we found him and that nothing about him adds up." Travis leaned forward, lowering his voice. "He's either some deep operative, and you don't get involved with them, boy, 'cause they play so many parts they forget who they are. Or he's some commodity for the ESTO boys and girls... experiment, new kind of conditioning, intel vessel, who knows? And then it's just too dangerous."

"Couple days we're handing him over, Trav." A hard knot formed in Isaac's throat and he swallowed against the sorrow those words caused. "So it doesn't much matter if I'm just holding his hand or screwing his brains out, does it?"

Travis scowled at his coffee. "Oz, you're a grown person. I know that. Just can't help worrying."

"Don't think I don't appreciate it. But knock it off."

TURK WOKE to an empty bed and a wave of grief. Luyten Station was only two days away. He would be alone again soon enough, which made each stolen moment with Isaac precious.

Having someone sleeping in his arms again was a balm to his tightly stretched nerves. The Offworlder custom of sleeping in isolation except for mated couples or lovers had puzzled him at first. Why did they punish themselves that way? But he came to understand that most *wanted* a solitary place to sleep and he had forced himself to adjust, as he had tried to in all things. How he longed for home, for the comfort of familiar things. Perhaps it would not be so much longer.

Isaac, though, was more than a sleeping companion. Turk's heart yearned for him when he was out of sight and leaped with eager need whenever he was near. There was only one answer to how this could have happened with a stranger, and it was one Turk did not wish to face. It was one thing to lose one's *sol'atenis* in battle, another entirely to know he lived elsewhere in the galaxy, out of reach.

*But then, no one truly knows how long he has....*

Even if he had found his completion at home among his *katrak*, death could have followed that same afternoon. He had seen it happen.

"Live as if you sip your last breath. Revel in each night as if you snatch your last view of the stars," he murmured the old saying. It had seemed mere platitude when he was younger.

He slipped into borrowed clothes, determined to find Isaac. Without anyone to turn to for counsel, he had to trust that the connection he felt was real and not another symptom of his temporary—he hoped—madness. If no sense of bond had occurred to Isaac, he would know it was part of his disconnection from reality and he would leave off tormenting the man.

The search proved absurdly easy. Isaac strode down the corridor toward him when he stepped out the cabin door. Watching Isaac's lean grace and haunting beauty, Turk lost the ability to speak. Every new sighting was like a hammer blow to the heart, stealing breath and reason.

Isaac's distracted expression transformed with his smile. "Hey! You're awake. How do you feel?"

"Well. Quite well. Rested." Turk fumbled for more since Isaac was in uniform and most likely going on duty. "Are you just starting shift?"

Isaac tilted his head, regarding him curiously. "Not much to do today. Have to check the boards. Station won't be hailing us until tomorrow. You sure you're all right? You're a little flushed."

"Yes. Fine." *This is ridiculous. Battling screaming hordes of durhai didn't rattle me so.* "I would like to speak with you. When you have a moment."

"I've got a moment now. What's on your mind?"

"Ah… more than a moment."

Isaac chuckled, a rich, warm sound. "And not out in the corridor, I guess. I'll just be a few. Why don't you grab some breakfast and I'll meet you back here?"

Turk nodded and stood transfixed as he watched Isaac walk away. The snug uniform trousers accentuated that tight, rounded backside in terribly distracting ways. He had to meditate, to center himself. If he couldn't convince Isaac he was sane, reasonable, and recovered, it would be a sadly short conversation.


*I WOULD like to speak with you….*

The simple sentence raked over Isaac's nerves. Turk had been far too serious and uncomfortable for the coming conversation to be anything on the order of "thanks for everything, be seeing you."

He had work to do, dammit. While his hands shook, he managed to answer the routine system buoy queries and forward the requested channel codes to the captain's comm. The first contacts with Luyten Station would be prior to approach, between the captain and the stationmaster. Only when they had reassurances that Turk belonged there and would be welcome would they open channels and begin normal approach procedures.

Turk was probably nervous about rejoining his command. After what had happened and all the questions he likely couldn't answer,

Isaac couldn't blame him. *Probably what he wants to talk about. Maybe he remembers something.*

Work settled him. It always had. His position on the *Hermes* had done wonders in that regard. The neural attacks dwindled to a few a month rather than the daily incidents he'd experienced before. The migraines and fainting spells stayed at bay as long as he didn't ask his implant to do any actual work. Good, solid work among good, solid people, without giving up the stars, what more could he have wanted?

*Someone who loves me....*

But that route was for dreamers and for people with the luxury of indulging each other's illusions. Stripped down to the bare bones of what a person could be and still keep going, Isaac's illusions had long been ripped away. Sex was necessary. Love was for other people who didn't have to worry about their own brains betraying them.

He finished all his necessary tasks and then puttered with the boards a bit longer out of anxiety. Finally, he rose with a little sigh, preparing to leave the nearly empty bridge. He could only put off this conversation for so long.

"Rand, I'll be back in a bit to take watch."

The scan tech gave him a halfhearted wave, brooding over something, most likely Sylvia. Maybe. He hadn't been able to figure Rand out. For all he knew, the boy was mooning over Travis instead, or Captain Drummond, heaven help him.

Back at the passenger cabin, he stopped outside the door to straighten his jacket and smooth a hand over his hair. A little laugh caught in his chest. *Acting as if you're picking him up for a date....*

He palmed the door open to find Turk pacing, his blond brows drawn together in an expression of fierce concentration.

"Hi—"

Turk lunged for him, and a gasp cut off his words. The big man seized him by his biceps and plunked him down on the edge of the bunk. For a moment, Isaac thought he might be in trouble, but Turk sank to one knee and took his hand gently. From another man, it might have been supplication. From Turk, it seemed more an attempt to get on eye level. The man loomed even when he sat down.

"First, I have yet to thank you properly." Turk turned his hand up and kissed the palm. "I truly believed I was meant to die on that ship. You found me. You have been so kind. My light in the gloom."

"Um... you're welcome?"

Turk caressed Isaac's palm with his thumb, scattering his thoughts. Apparently, Turk wasn't finished, though. "I am so grateful. I wish to give you something in return. We have so little time, but I would offer myself. A night of joy. Let me try to give you that, at least."

Isaac's cock twitched at those words but part of him bristled. He jerked his hand away. "You want to fuck me out of gratitude?"

Turk either took no notice of his anger or chose to ignore it. He moved closer, his hands sliding to either side of Isaac's hips. The heat in his eyes threatened to set Isaac's jacket ablaze. "I want to meld our bodies because you make my blood boil. I want you with a hunger that rivals the need to breathe."

"Oh." Every ounce of blood in Isaac's body rushed to his groin, leaving him dizzy and reeling. "Oh God."

A hand slid up to cup his face. "I will not take what is not given freely."

"I have to be on watch in a few minutes." Isaac swallowed hard, appalled by how breathless he sounded.

"How long?" Turk leaned in close, his breath caressing Isaac's throat.

"Four... four hours." He gasped as Turk licked along his pulse line.

"Good." Turk kissed along his jaw, murmuring against his skin. "Give me your answer when you return. Yes or no."

Isaac was on the verge of collapsing back on the bed and letting Turk have him right that second, but the big man pulled back and gained his feet in one fluid motion. "Turk?"

"Joy, Isaac. Not a quick screw. Come to me when you have the time. If it is yes, I will show you how bright your soul can burn."

"And if it's no?"

"I will always remember you and be grateful for the memory."

Isaac stumbled to his feet and somehow made it out into the corridor. He leaned against the wall, panting. What the hell was he going to do now?

"THERE SHOULD be tea." Turk sighed as he looked about the spartan cabin. "And *rai* sheets and ferns."

It couldn't be helped. While it wasn't the setting he would have chosen for courting, one had to be adaptable. He had procured a carafe of coffee from the mess and two mugs, and while the sheets were stark white instead of the bright rainbow they should have been, at least they were crisp and clean.

He was barefoot and bare-chested as was proper, but he mourned the loss of his hair. He would have worn his crest loose on such an occasion, freed from its braiding, inviting his prospective lover to touch. Barbaric custom, shearing the entire head bristle short, but it had some practical advantages under human-style helmets.

Isaac did react to him, to his touch, his voice, in a way that hinted at sweet surrender. He hoped the connection was enough to penetrate through *huchtik* sensibilities.

FOR THE second time that day, Isaac hesitated outside the door. This time, though, he had good reason.

"This is such a bad idea. For so many reasons." *Yeah, what reasons?* "He's barely sane." *And you're so normal?* "He'll be gone soon." *So you can't have now with him?* "But...." *Shut up and stop being a coward.* "Nothing worse than losing an argument with yourself."

The door slid up to reveal Turk in his half-naked glory. He put his hands over his heart with a little bow and said something in a language Isaac didn't recognize that involved a lot of hard consonants and clicks.

"Pardon?" Not that he would have understood in any language. His mind was far too focused on the honey-gold jewel line disappearing into Turk's waistband.

Turk gave him a little smile. "I suppose the best translation is 'my life pauses for your answer.'"

"Answer...." His speech center had short-circuited. He had seen Turk completely naked once before, but now, regaining his strength, his confidence, he was breathtaking. Big men usually did it for him, sure. This was more. He wanted... oh God, he wanted everything.

"Yes or no." Turk held out his hand, a little frown creasing his forehead. "As we discussed."

"Yes," Isaac murmured as he took a step forward as if in a dream. "I mean, no! That is—I don't think... oh fuck...." He buried his face in his hands. "I don't know what to think."

Strong hands closed over his shoulders. "Isaac," Turk said gently. "I didn't wish to distress you. Please. I withdraw the question. I'll simply hold you tonight, the way you like."

"The way I...?" Isaac stared up at him, flabbergasted. He had slept in Turk's arms because *Turk* had needed it. At least that was how he thought it had gone. Now with those bright blue eyes gazing down at him with such concern, he had to wonder. He laid a hand flat against Turk's chest, silken skin over steel, and stepped closer. "I want you to touch me," he whispered. "I miss being touched."

The men who normally bedded him held him tight, held him down, and held him still, but they didn't brush their lips over his jaw or lick his throat.

"Where would you like to be touched?" Turk pulled him close with a hand cupping the back of his head.

"Everywhere."

Turk's lips ghosted over his ear. "This is yes?"

"Yes."

"Good," Turk whispered, making Isaac shiver as his tongue traced the outer shell and his teeth nipped his lobe.

Careful tugs pulled Isaac's T-shirt from his pants. Turk's fingers slid underneath, cool and sure against his heated skin, tracing along the muscles on either side of his spine. His touch remained soft as he continued up to circle Isaac's shoulder blades, bringing the material along for the ride.

With little nudges, Turk urged his arms up so he could pull the shirt off over his head. He stopped with the T-shirt caught on Isaac's wrists and tangled the material in his fist so Isaac's arms were trapped above his head.

*Now... now he's got me secured and he'll take what he wants....*

Part of Isaac longed for Turk to throw him down and take him hard, but part of him balked against it. Not that his internal battle mattered, since Turk seemed to have no intention of doing any such thing. Turk nipped and sucked along Isaac's arms, into the creases of his elbows, right down to the sensitive skin of his underarms.

Isaac dropped his head back on a groan. Just when he thought his knees might give way, Turk tugged the shirt off his wrists and snaked an arm around his waist to pull him in close, chest to chest. His lips came down on Isaac's, soft touches at first that caught fire as Isaac clung to him. Strong arms clasped him tight and Turk plundered his mouth in a delirious claiming, delving his tongue deep and exploring every recess.

Turk slid his grip down to cup his butt, a cheek fitting perfectly in each hand, and Isaac whimpered into the kiss, grinding against the hard body pressed to his. So good, oh so damn good. The simple feel of skin on skin, of having a lover take his time, had him more keyed up than when some men had been inside him.

"You are so beautiful," Turk whispered against his jaw. "I thought it the first time I saw you. Such a lovely vision, I thought you were a dream."

"I'm real," Isaac gasped out as Turk's hands slid beneath his waistband. "This better be real, or I'll be really pissed."

A warm chuckle vibrated against his skin, and then Turk sank to his knees. Isaac concentrated hard on breathing so he wouldn't pass out as Turk unbuttoned his pants and slid them down to his ankles. His briefs followed, leaving him feeling more vulnerable than he had in years. Most of the time, he could turn everything off, including any body shyness, strip and use his lean, lithe body to enflame his bed partners. Now, standing there with his pants on the floor and his erection jutting toward Turk, he felt awkward and unsure.

"Turk? What are you... oh." Isaac had expected him to go right for the prize. Instead, he took Isaac's hand and kissed the fingertips one by one. Then he nuzzled along the outside of Isaac's thigh, down to kiss the back of his knee. The unexpected sensuality of that spot tore a groan from him.

"Everywhere," Turk murmured. "I don't intend to miss an inch of skin." He stretched out on the floor, gently lifted one foot at a time to free Isaac from his boots, socks, briefs, and pants, and then proceeded to suck on his toes.

No one, but no one, had ever done that for him. Isaac watched in helpless fascination, his knees growing weak under the erotic assault. "Bed… please? Before I fall over?"

Turk rose, the grace and power of his body reminding Isaac of one of the big feline predators on Altair, deadly, dangerous, and oh so beautiful. He swept Isaac up in his arms and planted a soft kiss on his cheek.

"You are certain, little one? You want this?"

"Oh yeah. You back out now and I'll die of blue balls."

"Is it just relief, then?" Turk's smile fell, his expression suddenly vulnerable.

Isaac reached up a hand to stroke Turk's face, tracing the strong jaw with his thumb. "No, hon. Not just. I… want you. Not just a hard body. You."

His face still serious, Turk nodded and strode to the bunk where he placed Isaac down gently. He opened the wall cabinet next to the mattress where the standard prophylactics were stored. "Are you egg-fertile?"

"No. Never had the extra parts put in." He had talked about it with Ethan, but that had been before. "You can't knock me up."

Turk pulled out the blister pack of antimicrobial lube rather than the spermicidal variety. "It was not something we had at home. I found it a fascinating possibility when the ESTO doctors explained it to me."

"I guess for some people." Isaac swallowed against the sudden lump in his throat.

"Shh. Do not dwell in memory." Turk tilted his head up and met his lips in a tender, searching kiss. "Life is moment to moment. Grasp the moment or allow life to slip from you."

Isaac wrapped his arms around Turk's neck and pulled him down for a more serious kiss. His spicy, masculine scent filled Isaac's head, his taste wild and sweet. He slid his hands down Turk's body to undo his pants, desperately wanting Turk naked. The big man stood to shed the rest of his clothes and Isaac's heart thudded against his chest. *He's so damn gorgeous.*

Bigger by far than any man Isaac had ever been with, broad-chested and hard-muscled, Turk didn't disappoint in any regard half-clothed. Standing naked with his huge cock standing support-beam straight from his body, he was glorious.

"Turn for me," Isaac whispered. "Let me see all of you."

With a little smile, Turk indulged him, and Isaac's breath caught in his chest. Chiseled back muscles ran down to a narrow waist and a firm, beautifully rounded ass. Perfect, every part of him perfectly proportioned for his frame, every inch was a sculptor's dream.

Turk slid onto the bed, caressing Isaac's side. His forehead creased. "Would you rather give or receive? You are a bit smaller than lovers I've had before."

"You won't hurt me. Just go slow. I want that monstrous tool inside me. You don't even know how badly." He tried to turn onto his front, but Turk stopped him.

"I want to hold you. To watch you."

The tenderness in that deep voice reached into Isaac's core, heat pooling around his heart. He rolled down onto his back and spread his legs so Turk could lie between them. With gentle nudges, Turk bent his knees up, stroking the backs of his thighs. He lowered his head to kiss Isaac's hip while his hands caressed his butt. Isaac arched up with a little yelp when Turk's tongue delved into his bellybutton. He settled back with a moan, his cock leaking onto his stomach. Turk licked the pearl drops away, tearing another moan and a squirm from him.

"You taste wonderful. Salt and *sechkran*," Turk whispered against his erection, sending shivers along his spine.

"I hope that's a good thing."

A deep laugh rumbled from Turk, the first real, uninhibited laugh Isaac had heard from him. "It is the best thing. Sweet nectar to soothe the soul."

Big hands spread his cheeks and Turk teased at his puckered entrance with the pad of his thumb. A snick announced the tip snapping off the lube pack. The narrow nozzle slid easily into Isaac, and he spread his knees wider as the cool lube injected into his channel. Turk's finger replaced the nozzle, sliding into him, slicking the lube farther inside, and stretching him gently. One finger became two and Isaac bit his bottom lip hard.

"Please—" he began and broke off with a hard groan when Turk's fingers massaged his hot spot. "I don't think I'll hold out like this." It made no sense. Plenty of times he'd had a sizeable dick shoved hard into him, and he hadn't been able to come. How could he be on edge just from a couple of fingers?

Still in no hurry, Turk removed his fingers to slick some of the lube over his cock. The sight of his hand wrapped around his own erection, pumping slowly, sent sparks of need through Isaac. He writhed atop the sheets, trying to entice Turk to hurry, but the big man wasn't through with him. He bent his head to suck one of Isaac's balls into his mouth and slid three fingers into Isaac's back channel.

"Oh God... Turk." Isaac clutched the blond head in both hands, trying to urge him up.

Turk did lift his head for a moment. "Don't fight the current, little one. Let me give you this."

"But I want you inside me," Isaac whispered.

"Patience." Obviously his last word on the subject, Turk put his mouth to better use and wrapped his lips around the head of Isaac's cock. He tongued the slit, his eyes locked on Isaac's. When he plunged down, sucking hard, Isaac cried out, his hips arching off the bunk. His tip hit the back of Turk's throat with each downstroke. His hips thrust up into the wet heat.

"Stop... please... I'm coming," Isaac panted out.

Turk just growled and suckled harder, his fingers corkscrewing in and out of Isaac. Helpless in the grip of such astounding pleasure, Isaac clawed at the sheet, tossing his head from side to side. The pressure built to critical. His panting edged into sharp cries as the build to ecstasy became excruciating. White heat shot from his core, his orgasm slamming through him, racing along his nerves with every pulse. He gripped Turk's head hard, needing a point of stability as spots danced in his vision.

"Damn... just, damn." Isaac twitched hard when Turk gave one last lick at his cock. "I'll never accept another blowjob again."

Turk slid up to lie beside him, one hand caressing his stomach. "Oh?"

"Nothing will ever compare." He lifted a shaking hand to cup Turk's face. "But you didn't get anything out of it."

Turk's eyebrows crept up. "Your joy is more than something." He leaned in to nuzzle at Isaac's jaw. "And I've only begun."

"Was hoping you'd say that."

"You make my blood sing." Turk wrapped an arm around his waist and pulled Isaac on top of him. "Your smile takes the strength from my legs. Your laugh wraps heated plumes about my heart."

"God. How did you go from one-word sentences to being a poet?" Isaac's voice shook. He nuzzled at Turk's shoulder to hide the way his eyes filled. No, oh, no, he could *not* feel this. The tug of physical attraction had edged over into so much more. Turk's body had caught his attention, but it was his unique view of the universe, his good sense, his concern, his patience, and his sweet, vulnerable moments that had clamped hard around Isaac's heart.

He heaved a shuddering breath, dreading, as he hesitated, the moment when Turk would ask what was wrong. How the hell was he supposed to explain? It would sound crazy or at the very least, incredibly stupid. But Turk didn't ask. He held Isaac close and stroked his hair, murmuring softly in that unidentifiable language.

"There is no shame if you weep in my arms," Turk whispered, his deep voice trembling.

*Oh damn.* He was upsetting his new lover and he wasn't sure he could handle it if he drove Turk to tears. Isaac swiped at his eyes with the heel of his hand and levered himself up far enough to see Turk's face.

"Now why would I want to do that when I have all this?" Isaac circled one pale nipple with his thumb. He watched it pebble before he gave it a teasing pinch. Turk's breath caught on a sharp inhale, so Isaac moved to the other nipple. "I can think of better uses of your time than turning you into a crying mat, can't you?"

One corner of Turk's sensual mouth curled up. *Better.*

"And what use would you make of me?"

Isaac sat up on Turk's stomach, running his hands in slow, soothing circles over hard pecs. "Oh well, you're big and strong. You could help me rearrange my cabin. Or let's see, you're obviously very smart. Maybe you could help out in engineering...."

"I see." Turk caressed his hips, a glimmer of amusement in his eyes. "You want me to work for my passage."

"Seems only fair, right?" Isaac reached behind him to grasp Turk's cock and then rose up on his knees. His voice fell to a husky murmur. "I'm sure we can work something out."

"I have no doubt." The heat in Turk's gaze threatened to burn Isaac's skin. He stroked Isaac's backside, encouraging him to settle. Most of his former bed conquests would have tried to ram right in after getting him off. Turk showed astounding patience, petting and teasing until Isaac was ready.

When Isaac angled that thick cock toward his entrance, Turk helped matters by spreading his cheeks. With them both lubed and Isaac relaxed again after the clenching pulses of orgasm had subsided, the head slid into his channel with little resistance. He had to stop, thighs trembling, eyes shut, breathing in careful, short sips, as he adjusted to Turk's massive girth. The burn was just short of unbearable, almost too much. Almost.

He opened his eyes to find Turk's head flung back, his expression one of erotic torment.

"Turk?"

"Stay still a moment, little one," Turk whispered. "You're skin tight."

He couldn't have moved if he tried. Turk held his hips in a vise grip. The slight edge of pain, the way Turk controlled his movements so easily, brought his erection back to full throttle faster than he thought possible.

*Nothing sexier than a powerful man.* Soon Turk shifted his hold, pulling Isaac slowly down his shaft. A hiss of pleasure escaped Isaac when Turk hit his prostate. Even with all the careful preparation, the stretch remained at an eye-watering level. Turk filled him to the limit and still had more to spare.

Hands on Turk's shoulders, Isaac leaned forward to change the angle and find some leverage. Turk held his hips still and maintained an agonizingly slow pace, pumping in and out of Isaac with languid rolls of his pelvis. Far from the quick pounding he had anticipated, the tender assault was far more sensual. It had been so long since a bed partner had cared about his pleasure.

Turk released one of his hips to cup his balls. With his middle finger, he reached back and pressed against the sensitive spot behind them, stroking Isaac's prostate from both sides.

"Oh God," Isaac panted out. "Turk, please… harder. I want you to come with me."

"My climax won't be an issue," Turk said through clenched teeth.

"Got it." *When's the last time* you *had sex, bud?* "Wrap your hand around me, hon. Hold out for me just a bit."

He was close, but Turk's muscles had sprung taut. The big man obviously hung on by a thread. Long fingers engulfed Isaac's cock, pulling a hard groan from him as Turk added a slow pump up and down to Isaac's sensual feast. It didn't seem quite fair when all Isaac had done for him was let him slide inside. He leaned forward, tearing a long moan from each of them as he changed the angle yet again, and seized Turk's mouth in a bruising kiss.

Turk tried to pull back, to say something, but Isaac put a hand on his forehead to keep him still and returned to attacking him with lips and tongue. He tasted so good. Isaac's brain shut down, his body wild with lust. Turk settled back, returning the kiss with equal ferocity, tongues tangling, and teeth nipping. Cavern-deep moans vibrated against Isaac's mouth. Turk thrust his hips up harder, his body trembling between Isaac's thighs.

Red-orange sparks shot through Isaac, his climax roaring up without warning. He gyrated his hips in an attempt to drive down harder onto Turk's cock and farther into his pumping fist. He lifted his head for breath to cry out and when the first pulse of orgasm crashed over him, he was lifted from the bed as Turk arched and bellowed, joining him as his seed hit deep inside Isaac, the heated splash sending shockwaves through his own orgasm.

His vision tunneled as the heavy pulses tapered off into aftershocks. Collapsed atop Turk's broad chest, he drifted, content and replete. He realized he might have blacked out when he became aware of Turk stroking his back, calling softly to him.

"Rrmmph," he managed as eloquently as he could.

"Are you all right?" The real worry in Turk's voice pulled Isaac out of his stupor.

"I'm so many things right now." Isaac turned his head far enough to kiss Turk's shoulder. "'All right' doesn't even begin to cover it."

Turk's warm chuckle vibrated through him. Still buried inside Isaac, he made no attempt to move Isaac or roll away. He simply held him and let him fall asleep.

# CHAPTER 6: LUYTEN

ISAAC STARED morosely out the viewscreen in the crew lounge at the bright speck that was the first sight of Luyten Station. Turk pulled him back to lean against his chest and kissed the top of his head.

"I don't want you to go," he said, knowing he sounded childish.

"If things were otherwise, *atenis*, I would rather stay." Turk wrapped both arms around him, as if he could protect him from heartache.

"What if you don't show up at HQ? They probably think you're dead by now, right?"

Turk heaved a sigh. "I have made promises. A man should keep his promises, don't you agree?"

"Oh wonderful. On top of everything else, you're a man of honor too."

"I could never return home if I felt my honor bankrupt." Turk turned him and smoothed a stray bit of hair behind his ear. "Their hold on me is not for a lifetime, though."

"How long?"

"For three years, I was promised to them. They have two remaining."

*Two years.* Isaac leaned his forehead against Turk. "What does that even mean, you were promised to them? You make it sound like you're a transport or some shiny new armament."

"Someday, little one, I might be at liberty to explain."

"I don't want state secrets. I just want to make sense of all this. I mean, you're Corzin. Far as I know, ESTO doesn't have any hold on you."

"ESTO has no hold on the Corzin."

Isaac looked up into those striking blue eyes. "Those nonanswers are so annoying. But you're really good at them."

"Thank you."

"It wasn't supposed to be a compliment."

"I know." Turk put a knuckle under his chin and tilted his face up for a soft kiss. "Isaac, no one knows what tomorrow holds. But if we reach the station and they take me away, allow me no outside contact, know that they take terrible risks if they keep me beyond the promised time. Two years. Not so long. And know when it is done, I will come to find you."

*Brave words of the moment. In two years, you'll have moved on.* "All right."

"You disbelieve me. But remember, I'm a very stubborn man. Hasn't Dr. Varga said so?"

"Yeah. She did." *It's still a pipe dream. Dreams just make you miserable.*


*I HAVE been selfish and caused the pain in your eyes.* Turk could not regret the little bit of time granted to them, but the strength of Isaac's attachment had blindsided him. Those lovely dark eyes were shadowed now, remembering old pain and anticipating new. He would find a way to erase every moment of hurt in Isaac's life, not that day, most likely not the next, but someday.

He stood by the airlock with the bridge officers, listening to the clanks and thuds of life-support hookups and the gangway tube from stationside. Isaac stood beside him and offered a brave smile. The rest of the officers were on edge, almost grim.

Captain Drummond broke the silence. "Sure this is what you want?"

"It is what must be done, Captain," Turk answered, his eyes on the lock.

"Fair enough. Call of duty and all that. All of us understand that. You just keep in mind that we'll be docked here a good week, resupplying, hopefully picking up contracts. You need us, you send up a hail. Understood?"

"Yes, ma'am."

The captain had not shared the particulars of her communications with the Admiralty. She told him that she had explained the situation and that, yes, they were pleased Turk had survived, but something about the conversation had obviously disturbed her. She was a canny spacer with years of military service behind her, so Turk trusted her instincts. If things had not gone as Admiral Uchechi hoped, though, there would be no help for him. Anyone trying to interfere would be at risk.

A succession of green lights overtook the red on the airlock's panel. When the all-clear signal lit, the captain palmed the lock pad. The heavy door rolled up with a hiss, too much like a threat display for Turk. He suppressed a shiver, not wanting to worry Isaac. The captain strode through first, down the chilled, harshly lit tube of the gangway. As he followed, the rest of the officers trailing in order of seniority, he felt like he was walking into the gullet of some monstrous predator.

Stationside, a contingent of Marines in ESTO black and gray waited. He assumed they had come to take him into custody, but the squad snapped to attention when he appeared. Relief jolted his heart when Admiral Uchechi himself stalked around them, his hand held out to Captain Drummond.

"Captain! Good to meet you in the flesh!" They shook hands, both crisp and professional. "I have to thank you again for the search and retrieval. Was sure our boy here was lost for good."

"He's iron-willed, Admiral," Captain Drummond said with a soft chuckle. "I think he would have held out as long as it took."

"I have no doubt." The admiral half turned from her. "Turk!"

He snapped to attention and saluted, as they had taught him.

"Stand easy, boy." The familiar loam-dark hand gripped his arm. "Good to see you in one piece."

"Sir. Thank you." Turk gave him a nod, uncertain what he should and should not ask. Relief at seeing the admiral warred with puzzlement. "I didn't... expect you here, sir."

"You didn't report on schedule, I had to wonder. And the *Marduk* had disappeared off the scans. Had to come see for myself what happened." The admiral's gleaming smile appeared to hold genuine relief. But then, human smiles still baffled him. They seemed to mean so many things.

"Yes, sir. I'm not certain—"

"We'll talk in a bit." The admiral's clipped voice cut him off abruptly. "First, to medical. Get you checked stem to stern. Then we get you back in proper rig, boy. Looks like you need to return someone's clothes."

"Sir, I…. Might I thank the officers before we go?"

"Of course. Good man. Right thing to do."

Turk turned back to the *Hermes* crew with a leaden lump in his chest. Such a short time with them, but he felt he understood them better than he had most Offworlder groups. There was loyalty here and trust, the understanding that each could depend on the others, the closest group to a *katrak* that he had encountered since leaving home.

"Captain, thank you for all you've done." He shook Captain Drummond's hand first. "May your ship always hear you."

She gave him a puzzled look but then smiled. "Spacer's duty, Turk. But it's been our pleasure to have you aboard."

He nodded and moved down the line. "Dr. Varga, thank you for taking such painstaking care of me."

"You behave, hon." A slight quaver crept into the doctor's voice. "Don't undo all I've done."

He continued until he reached Isaac last. His arms ached to wrap him close and he wished he could give reassurances, but they would ring false. Despite Admiral Uchechi's presence, he had no clear notion of the terrain yet.

"Isaac." He took one slender golden hand between his.

"You message and let us know you're settled, all right?" Isaac blurted out when he hesitated.

Turk inclined his head. "If at all possible, I will." Isaac chewed on the corner of his bottom lip and it was all Turk could do not to pull him in to kiss that anxious look away. He lowered his voice to a whisper. "There is always a way, *atenis*. Do not doubt me."

Dark eyes gazed up at him with fierce need. "I'll do the best I can."

A SICK feeling lodged in Isaac's stomach. He was watching an epic love walk away from him once again. He had managed—just—not to fling himself against Turk's chest and beg him not to go. Such behavior would have been stupid and embarrassing. The man had no choice.

"Trav?" he asked in an absurdly small voice.

"Hmm?"

"Where do the Corzin come from?"

Travis shifted, arms crossed over his chest as they all watched the ESTO contingent surround Turk and lead him off. "Don't know, bud. Don't know if anyone does. They show up in small bands, fifteen to thirty or so. Fight where they please. Disappear again."

"Oh." Isaac blinked against the sting at the backs of his eyes. "The ones you knew, they never talked about family, about home?"

"Far as I could tell, those little war bands *were* family. Blood relations and lovers."

He lost the battle and swiped a sleeve over his eyes. "It must be awfully lonely for him."

Travis laid a hand on his shoulder. "I'd imagine so."

BACK IN uniform, with sleeves long enough for his arms, Turk felt marginally more comfortable. He sat across the conference table from the admiral, answering questions as best he could.

"You don't have any impressions of those lost minutes?" Admiral Uchechi asked quietly as they watched the *Marduk* crew's last moments play out on the holoscreen once again.

"No, sir. Nothing."

"But you have an idea concerning what happened."

"Yes, sir." Turk stared at the table. "But I don't understand how it might be so."

The admiral's blunt fingers drummed the table. "You're scared, boy. Can't blame you. We can run some trials, though. There's a room equipped for it."

"Lumanium lined?"

"Three meters thick. It'll be safe. Maybe give us some answers if you can bring yourself to try."

"For you, sir, I would be willing. Provided—"

"I know!" Admiral Uchechi flung his hands up. "Wouldn't do that to you. That's why we brought you here." He stood, signaling the end of the interview. "Time enough tomorrow. You've been through the grinder, son, and it shows. Take the day. Get some rest. Or some serious booze and sex, whichever helps you relax."

"Could I see the room, sir?"

"Not really what I'd call R and R, boy. Next you'll want to give it a run."

"If I might. I would... feel less edgy, sir."

The amusement in the admiral's eyes warred with his stern expression. "You'll drive me to drink, boy, with your polite insubordinations. Follow me, then. Let's put your mind at ease."

As much a scientist as he was a military officer, the admiral was the only human Turk trusted to solve the riddle of the *Marduk*. After the previous year's incident with the fighter's interface, and the ill-conceived procedure afterward, the ESTO Board had assigned the project, and Turk, to Admiral Uchechi. His background in biotech and experience in xenodiplomacy rendered him uniquely qualified to calm and guide a Corzin warrior who had begun to fear his own brain.

Of course, not everyone in Command had been pleased with the assignment. Several high-placed officers believed they should have been granted the project and its living prize instead. Turk had sat through the hearings, only half comprehending the long-winded speeches concerning "proper resource allocation" and "risk-ratio justification." What he did come to understand was that Command regarded him as both a dangerous unknown and a valuable research breakthrough.

Admiral Ranulf, the most vocal advocate for using him in weapons research, had been just as vocal in his displeasure over losing

Turk to Admiral Uchechi's command. His petitions to the Board never ceased, his persistence the reason Turk had been sent from Terranova in secret. The things that man had wanted....

Turk shuddered, tamping down on the memories. The admiral led him through the station corridors to a hangar bay door.

"It's an unused shuttle bay," he explained. "We built the room inside. Big enough for our purposes, with the added advantage of being an external module to the main station."

"Ah. Good." Turk nodded his satisfaction. If anything, spirits forbid, went wrong, the room would be isolated from station's life support and power core. At the admiral's wave, he strode in, inspecting the walls. "Could you close the door a moment, sir?"

"You want me to step out?"

"If you would, sir. It would ease my heart."

The door hissed shut behind the admiral, but in a moment, his voice filled the room. "Just down the hall, son. We have you on monitors. Don't overdo it today."

"Yes, sir." Turk stopped his pacing, adding belatedly, "Am I on audio, sir?"

"Affirmative. You need something, sing out."

He planted his feet in the center of the room, closed his eyes, and let the centering note rise in his chest. The sound bounced back to him from the walls, floor, and ceiling of the containment chamber, solid, unbroken, unwavering. Good. There were no cracks or flaws in the construction.

The unbroken gray of the room held no furnishings, no objects of any kind, except a wall cabinet by the door. Turk undid the buttons of his uniform jacket and slid out of the heavy material. It wasn't necessary, but the fewer restrictions on his body, the easier the singing would be. He opened the cabinet to place the folded jacket within and smiled at its contents. A few months ago, the selection of flat, matte discs would have puzzled him. Now he was comforted to see them again. The admiral knew what he needed.

He ran a finger over the palm-sized circles, graphite, copper, plastic, and silver. The admiral had tried to explain once how these objects were diamagnetic and how his manipulation of magnetic fields affected their electrons, but the words were foreign, the concepts eluded him. He did understand that some objects, these materials in particular, were easier to hold steady within the magnetic fields he created.

With the graphite disc in his palm, he closed the cabinet and turned to face the outer wall. He closed his eyes and let the centering note rise once more, feeling for the disc's field, surrounding it, adjusting the note to a fifth below its resonance. His lips parted, the second note throat-sung to join the first, a third above the note held in his chest. The graphite's resonance completed the chord. It floated above his palm, its own field in opposition to the one he created.

This much he could have accomplished before he had ever left his *katrak*, before he had come to live among the *huchtik*, the Offworlders. The next part would be the new ability, the one that had only come after the doctors had been inside his skull with their cold metal and their chemicals. He sang to the graphite, to the fields, changing the force and frequency of pitch. The carbon disc spun in suspension faster and faster until it appeared molten. He backed from it, keeping it aloft. A third note sprang from him, and then a fourth, physically impossible except that the tones, the scientists had told him, were generated from his brain and not his lungs.

The magnetic fields spun in time with the disc, invisible, but his altered sense tracked them, felt them attain frightening speeds. The notes were his shield, all he had. Without them, he might have been ripped to shreds as the gravitational force gathered. In space, the process would have been silent. In a closed, air-filled room, the forming gravity well announced itself with a shriek of displaced air. The disc distended and vanished into the suddenly expanding gravity field.

Turk released the notes. The graphite reappeared on the opposite side of the room and dropped to the floor with a clatter. He staggered forward, dizzy from his efforts, to retrieve it. The shape, as always, had elongated into a distorted, twisted ellipse.

This was why he had refused to run trials with living subjects. To kill in the heat of battle was one thing....

"Turk? Everything up to standard?"

The admiral's voice brought him back from his morbid musing. "Yes, sir. It's perfect."

"Glad you approve," the admiral said in a dry tone. "Enough today, boy. You need to rest."

ISAAC STROLLED through the shopping district at loose ends. With the ship docked, his duties were minimal. He had no heart for the usual entertainments, but lying around his cabin while the crew had station-leave seemed pitiful. Turk had messaged that all was well, the clipped tone letting Isaac know others had been listening. It should have relieved him that the big man would make the effort at contact, but his leaden melancholy persisted.

The displays of Tharsine oranges and bright Prcyon silks seemed somehow drab and bland. Even the Altairian shop, with its familiar sweets and spices from home, failed to hold his interest.

Maybe his priorities were all twisted. Maybe it was time to stop this shadow-puppet life. *So strong, so tender...* dammit, Turk had made him feel again and he wanted it to stop. It hurt.

For God's sake, he was seeing the man everywhere. Every large body caught at the edge of vision, any flash of blond hair made his heart skip and stutter. Even that big man in ESTO black and gray striding toward him down the promenade... *oh wait, that is Turk.*

A smile leapt unbidden to his lips, threatening to crack his cheeks. He managed, just, not to race across the intervening distance to throw himself into Turk's arms. At least he could spare them both that much embarrassment.

*Damn, he looks good in uniform. Mouth-wateringly good.* Isaac had never much cared for the ESTO rig, but the jacket stretched tight across Turk's massive chest. The gray-piped black trousers clung to the bunch and flex of herculean muscles as he walked and the knee-high spit-polished dress boots didn't hurt one bit.

Turk stopped in front of him, blocking his view of the shopping district, of the station, of the rest of the universe. "Isaac. Mr. Humboldt suggested you might be here."

He recalled muttering something about shopping before he left the ship. "Um, hi," he managed, trembling racing along his nerves.

Turk settled his hands on Isaac's shoulders, steady points of heat sending shards of stained-glass light through his body. "I have unsettled you. Made you uncomfortable."

"Unsettled?" His body yearned to take that single step, the one that would take him into the circle of Turk's arms. "Surprised me a little. I thought they'd keep you—" *Locked up. Under guard. At least confined to quarters.* "—busy. It's good to see you, though."

"I had some time in the schedule." Turk's hand slid up to cup Isaac's face. "Even merely a glimpse of you. I wanted at least that."

"Maybe you have time for more?" *Your quarters or mine?*

"I only have a few moments."

Isaac's heart lurched in disappointment.

Turk caressed Isaac's jaw with his thumb as he forged on, "But perhaps you're free this evening? To have dinner with me? There is a restaurant the admiral recommends."

"Are you asking me out, soldier? Because I need to tell you, I don't usually date ESTO boys."

Amusement tugged at the corners of Turk's eyes. "Could I respectfully request that you make an exception in my case?"

"You'd have to give me some reason."

With a chuckle, Turk leaned down and planted a soft, heated kiss on Isaac's lips. "Reason enough?"

Isaac's knees turned to water. "That'll do."

He gazed up into summer-sky blue with the disorienting feeling of being able to fall into those eyes forever. Pull of lust and want, certainly, but the force of attraction for this man was so much more, something he had told himself he had with Ethan, but that had been pale delusion. Here was everything he wanted, everything he needed. Here was the answer to his emptiness.

"Turk? Maybe I should...." A wave of unease, the feeling of imminent, colossal blunder nearly choked off his words. "Maybe when the *Hermes* pushes off, I should stay."

A frown creased Turk's forehead. "I'm not sure that would be wise."

*Oh God, he doesn't want me for more than a fling... I'm such a fool.* "Why?"

"I would see you safe, little one." Turk pulled him close, despite the disapproving looks from passersby. "Ex-Altairian Fleet. This might not be the most welcoming place for you."

Isaac rested his head on that hard chest, giving in to a long exhale of relief. Of course, Turk was worried for him. What other reason would there be to want Isaac to go? "It wouldn't be so bad, hon. It's not like there are open hostilities anymore. The enlisted might scuffle in the bars sometimes, but that doesn't affect me. I could find a job. Settle in while you're here."

"If...." Turk trailed off to gaze over Isaac's head, obviously processing. He came back to Isaac with a tight-lipped smile. "We'll talk more tonight, all right? Seventeen hundred at The Heliotrope?"

"Good. Perfect. I'll see you then."

Isaac watched him stride away, his confidence and easy-predator grace clearing a path for him through the crowd that he seemed to take for granted. His uneasiness and uncertainty rushed back when he turned the corner. Turk's sudden change of mood at the mention of Isaac staying set off all his social alarm bells. He couldn't help feeling he had made a terrible mistake, simply blurting out the thought like that. *Too late to take back now.*


THE TEMPTATION Isaac laid at his feet was enormous. To have his *atenis* close, perhaps even put in a request for cohabitative quarters, to wake every morning to find Isaac beside him, was a heady, thoroughly distracting thought. In two years, his time with the *huchtik* would be finished. He would take Isaac away and explain everything, take him home and register their completion formally. Then nothing would separate them short of death....

*Or certain ESTO officers.* The thought stopped him cold. Humans often puzzled him, but he understood enough to know Isaac could be threatened, even harmed, to gain Turk's compliance. If the wrong faction arrived on station, if they gained any foothold in the project and discovered Turk's attachment, Isaac would be in danger. But only if he stayed.

He would make his position clear that evening. While he dearly longed to keep Isaac by his side, he would explain that much of the situation, which would break no oaths. The *Hermes* would leave with Isaac aboard, safe amid loyal, trustworthy crewmates. With Isaac safe, it would no longer matter what the ESTO wanted from him.

The next meeting on his schedule was with the lab staff here. More new faces, more people he had to struggle to decipher. He paused in his tiny bachelor's quarters, no more than a bunk and a comm station, to write his overdue report. Every month, the agreement between his people and ESTO stipulated, he was to message home. His first messages had been regular holovids, but the ESTO communications staff, who did not report to Admiral Uchechi, informed him they weren't getting through. They advised switching to text and politely suggested he send in Standard rather than in his native T'tson'ae. They claimed it was easier for the filters to deal with.

Turk was no one's fool. Text was easier to edit than holo. He strongly suspected ESTO dissected his messages for classified information, hidden messages, possible codes, and then censored and sent them on. Still, if he did not report, his homeworld would assume the worst. The Corzin had fought no wars of their own for several centuries. He didn't wish to be a catalyst of change in that regard.

Every message began *Sil'ke'dra, a'hat'kau'tsae*, which he assured them was the proper form of address to his matriarch. A true literal translation, however, would have been *"Sil'ke'dra, these words may have been twisted upon their tails."*

Tangled thoughts of Isaac and home pulled at his attention so thoroughly, he missed the odd silence of HQ's corridors until he reached the conference room. By then the door had hissed open and his worst fears bled into reality. Admiral Ranulf occupied the center chair, his expression all too clear for Turk to read. Gloating predators had that universal expression in common.

His instincts told him to pummel this man into the decking. His purpose, however, was largely diplomatic. In that regard, pummeling superiors would be counterproductive. Instead, he stood at parade rest and gave the man a polite nod. "Admiral."

"Turk, sit, please. We hear you've been through a terrible ordeal." The clipped phrasing undercut any effort at solicitousness. Cold eyes followed him with hungry fire. "Good to see you safe."

"Thank you, sir." Turk eased into the nearest chair, taking in the room's occupants. The aides and adjutants on either side of the admiral were familiar, but he couldn't name them. The only other man he recognized was Admiral Uchechi, who paced along the back wall.

"I'm sorry, son." Admiral Uchechi's words cut terse and sharp across the room. "There's nothing I can do at this point. I will file protest with the Board, though." These words were flung at Ranulf. "Count on it."

"Do you dispute the transfer order?" Ranulf asked, too calm, too sure. "Are there points of irregularity that should come to my attention?"

"No," Uchechi snapped. "The documents are airtight. You know it. I'm sure you had your legal swamp-rats swarming all over them."

"Admiral, there's no need for unpleasantness. If you feel all is in order, I'd appreciate your cooperation in finalizing the transfer."

Admiral Uchechi stalked around the table, snatched the stylus from the aide unlucky enough to be holding the tablet, and signed his name with unabashed ferocity. "Turk, your project has now been transferred to Admiral Ranulf by order of the Board of the ESTO Coalition. You give him the same respect you gave me. But *don't* let him bully you into anything against your conscience. I'll have this ridiculous decision reversed. Hold fast."

"Admiral, I believe you no longer have jurisdiction here," Admiral Ranulf said with a little smile, one that even Turk could see was not meant as a friendly gesture.

Armed security suddenly flanked the doorway. Admiral Uchechi glowered until they gave ground, but still he departed, leaving Turk lost and fearful.

Not that he projected any of his fears. Calm, polite, that would be the only face the *huchtik* saw. *When the enemy has captured you, give them nothing,* his mentor had always said. Nothing. No hint of anxiety, no cry of pain, no understanding of what would cause anguish. Not that Admiral Ranulf was an enemy in the strictest sense, but his ambitions rendered him just as dangerous.

Ranulf leaned forward, hands clasped on the table. "Is there anything you need, Turk? Anything at all? Different food, sleeping arrangements, someone we could bring here to make your stay more comfortable?"

"No, sir. I'm quite comfortable."

"All right after your run in with the chuff? Feel like you might need some time with a counselor?"

"No, sir. I'm quite well." He cringed inwardly at the lie, but he was much improved. The little show of kindness was most likely to put him off his guard, so he calmly went on the offensive. "Sir, you are aware that I refuse to test with live subjects."

"I didn't ask that question, but yes, I'm aware." The admiral's pleasant expression never cracked. "Your answers should reflect what your superior has asked and nothing more, crewman."

"Yes, sir."

The admiral still smiled and motioned to an attendant by the wall, who brought Turk a glass and a water pitcher.

"Do you think I'm a bad man, Turk?"

The question threw him. He blinked, trying to hide his surprise. "Sir, I... don't know you well enough to say."

"But you think what I would ask of you is evil."

"I don't agree with it, sir. Evil is often a matter of perspective."

The admiral steepled his fingers. "Do you hold executions back home?"

Again, Turk struggled to recover, off balance and out of his depth. "No, sir."

"No? A warrior culture without executions of any sort? What of acts of betrayal or cowardice? How are these punished?"

"Sir... in the unlikely event that a warrior acts without honor, he takes his own life. Too many fall in battle. We see no need to murder each other in addition."

"I understand." The admiral gave a sage nod. "But you know that we do things differently. That in a larger, multilayered society, certain types of discipline, of correction, becomes necessary."

"I know that it's done, sir, yes."

"What if one of those people condemned to die were given a choice? A possibility at life—would you help them with that?"

"Sir, I... I can't answer that." What did he truly understand about *huchtik* laws? Or morality, for that matter? Whenever he thought he understood, something happened to shift things sideways again.

"Let me give you an example. A hypothetical one at this point." The admiral leaned over the table to pour a glass of water for him. "Let's say we had a spy in our custody, someone who had betrayed his officers, his people, and the government he swore to serve. Sold secrets to the enemy. Caused the deaths of his fellow soldiers because of it. Can we agree that this man acted dishonorably?"

"Yes, sir. Shamefully." He felt a trap forming in the words. Admiral Uchechi had never done this to him, this sort of verbal tracking. Fervently, he wished he could exchange admirals again.

"Good. So, under our laws, this man would be condemned," Ranulf went on. "But if he were given a choice, die in the execution chamber or volunteer for experimentation and, perhaps, live, wouldn't you want to give him that chance?"

Turk stayed stone still but inwardly, he sagged with relief. The admiral thought he posed a difficult question. It was no question at all. He hesitated, as if he needed to consider. "No, sir. I could not."

"Oh? Because the man is a traitor?"

"No, sir. Because he would die."

"He might die. If you refuse his sacrifice, he most assuredly dies."

"But not by my hand, sir. And not so horribly."

Cold eyes bored into him. For a moment, Turk thought the admiral would continue to press his point. Instead, he rose and held out his hand to shake. "We'll talk again soon, Turk. No need to report again until after morning mess. You may take your liberty until then."

"Thank you, sir," he managed in a steady voice.

Liberty. Somehow he doubted it. As he made his way through the corridors, he took a few unexpected turns. The same magnetic resonance followed him no matter what path he took. He had no need to turn to see that he was being followed.

*Isaac*... spirits help him, they would find out about Isaac when they met for dinner. No. He could not keep that appointment. He would never forgive himself if something happened to Isaac. Nor could he message him, either to break the date or to warn him. The channels would be monitored.

Some sort of message, though, he had to devise some way to let Isaac know. He returned to his quarters to think. After an hour's pacing, he went to the runner assigned to his block and asked for paper, ink, and brush. He had seen such things in the marketplace. The young man looked at him as if he had extra limbs, but brought him all he had requested.

It had been some years since he had engaged in such arts, but the skill came back. He framed the paper in careful scale-work, interspersing the scales with flowers from home. This was more than a warning, more than an explanation. The message was also a gift for Isaac, and he took painstaking care with every dip and stroke of the brush. In the center of the paper, he drew a tree, as close as he could recall to the beautiful flowering trees from Isaac's wall painting. Around the tree, he wrote a poem he hoped would pass the scrutiny of those who watched:

> *In the heart of winter*
> *Wind reaches icy fingers to snatch breath*
> *And while my table is barren*
> *There will always be a cup for you.*

He waited until the ink dried and then rolled the paper into a scroll, addressing it as a gift to the *Hermes* before he put it into the pneumatic system. It would be intercepted and analyzed, but he hoped it would still arrive in time.

# CHAPTER 7: COERCION

ISAAC CHECKED his comm unit again. Something serious must have come up to delay Turk this long, half an hour late and counting.

"Would you like something stronger while you wait?"

He startled and gazed up into slit-pupil feline eyes. All of the Heliotrope's front-room staff were body-modified humans. Isaac's waiter, with his pointed fur-tufted ears and delicate claws, was no exception. He had heard the staff were available for other appointments after shift but had never inquired into those extra services.

"No, thanks. The water's fine." Right. That would go over well if Turk showed up harried and out of sorts and found him trashed.

"Just yell if you need anything, handsome. Anything at all." The cat-waiter winked at him and sauntered off.

A few months ago, Isaac might have been flattered by the flirting and possibly intrigued. Now his thoughts only turned to how empty and unsatisfying a night with cat-boy would probably be.

"Dammit, where is he?" Isaac murmured. He tapped the *Hermes*'s link into his comm. Maybe Turk couldn't figure out how to call person to person and had called the ship.

"*Hermes* bridge," Rand's voice came back. "Oz? You all right?"

"Fine, fine. Have any messages come in for me?"

"No, nothing on my watch." Tapping drifted over the connection. "Don't see anything archived either."

"Nothing came in from Turk? Maybe not to me, but the ship, the captain, anyone?"

"Oh, from Turk. We did get a piece of rolled-up paper from him."

Isaac closed his eyes, forcing back his irritation. "And what does the rolled-up piece of paper say?"

"Don't know. Haven't unwrapped it."

"Rand! For God's sake! What does it say?"

A huff of breath came over the connection, followed by soft crinkling. "Slag it. It's handwritten, Oz. Who does that? I can't read this scribbling. Something about winter... a cup on a table. Looks like a thank you and good-bye to me."

Isaac's heart turned to frozen sludge in his chest. It still beat, but in a painful, dull thud once every few years. "I see."

"You all right, Oz?" Rand's voice sounded strained and small.

"Good. Perfect. Thanks."

He cut the connection and stared into his water glass. There it was, then. He had managed to scare Turk off, getting all clingy, needy, and let's-stay-together-and-play-house. Stupid, great wandering stars, he was so damn stupid!

"Everything all right?" Cat-waiter had returned.

Isaac rose from the table, leaving a few creds on the payscreen as a tip. "Looks like my date won't be coming."

"Oh. Pity," the cat-waiter crooned. He ran a clawed finger up Isaac's arm. "Anything I can do to help?"

"Thank you, but no." Isaac managed a wan smile and slid past him on his way out. *I need a drink. No, I need to get trashed.*

TURK PACED the station corridors, restless and anxious. In front of a kiosk, a distracted man bumped him. He bared his teeth and snarled. Wide-eyed, the man hurried away.

*This won't do. Someone will call security at this rate.*

Hate crouched in his chest, an unwelcome and unaccustomed guest. Perhaps he simply never had cause to hate before, but Ranulf had forced him apart from his heart's desire. His body ached for Isaac. His soul keened for him. Isaac must be kept safe, though. That was the only important thing.

He could only hope Isaac understood.

While he kept clear of the main shopping district so there would be no chance of happening upon Isaac coming from the restaurant, he had thought to troll through the bars. If, by chance, he spotted someone from the *Hermes*, he could take a chance and speak a few words, send a clearer message. No one could fault him for stopping to speak to one of his rescuers, and the exchange would be polite and brief.

Yes, that would do. A short, whispered warning to keep Isaac close to the ship followed by a bright, human smile and a handshake before he strode on, nothing to pique the interest of his watchers.

He would find a way to send messages over the next two years, but only when the *Hermes* was out of reach again.


"OZ, GODDAMMIT, what are you doing?"

Isaac glanced up from his drink and squinted against the haze of inebriation. He was almost certain it was Travis looming over him. "At the moment? Drinking Apocalypse Sunrises until I can't remember my own name. And then I'm going to ask the patrons of this dive if anyone wants to fuck me senseless."

Travis slid onto the chair beside him. "What's happened, bud? Thought you were having dinner with Turk."

"Yeah. Funny how things go, huh?" Isaac muffled a half-hysterical laugh in the rest of his Apocalypse. The things tasted foul, like mildew and halitosis, but they packed a wicked kick. "He ditched me. Scared another one off. My besh... my best talent."

He turned to signal for another round or three and nearly fell out of his chair. A strong hand closed around his arm.

"All right, Oz, I get it. But this is no way to handle it."

Travis heaved and got him to his feet. The floor pitched and spun. Isaac tangled both hands in Travis's jacket to stay upright. "'M sorry, Trav. I'm really trashed...."

"I know, bud. Not much you can do now"—Travis put an arm around him and steered him toward the door—"except get to your bunk and sleep it off. I'm sorry he hurt you. Didn't think he was the kind to cut and run."

Isaac nodded, a bad idea with his brain sloshing on so much alcohol. His throat closed up and he prayed he could hold it together for the walk back.

"Trav? Am I so… so… that no one wants me longer than a quick fuck?"

"Don't think this is the time to answer questions." Travis pushed another drunk away from the doorway so they could get by. "You won't remember anything I say anyway. But you're a good man, Oz. Got a good heart. You're smart and funny—"

"If you were gay, would you do me?"

Travis huffed out a breath and got Isaac walking down the corridor. "I'm your friend, Oz. Wouldn't want to botch that up. But if I was going to start up with someone like you, it wouldn't be for a night. And I wouldn't lead you on and then dump you."

Isaac sniffed and let his head thump down on Travis's shoulder. "Thanks. I…. Cap'n will be pissed at me, huh?"

"Only if we let her catch you like this."

It took a few beats to realize that Travis hadn't come out with the automatic het-guy denial. No sputtered "Of course I'm not gay, but…." How odd. Isaac concentrated on putting one foot in front of the other. In fact, he found he had to stare hard at his feet to accomplish the task. Looking down was never a good way to avoid other pedestrians.

He bumped up against something that felt like a stone wall. On second examination, it was a broad chest. An achingly familiar chest….

"You," he spat out as his gaze met Turk's.

Turk stared at him, blue eyes wide, his jaw working, but no words forming. Finally, the big man whispered, "You can't be here."

"No? Guess I missed that part. You've got some big titanium balls to come slinking around." Isaac let go of Travis, his index finger poking into Turk's hard chest to emphasize every point. "Looking for your next little fancy bit? Managed to forget all the sweet words you whispered over my naked fucking body already?"

"Isaac, please," Turk whispered and then raised his voice. "I don't understand what you mean, Mr. Ozawa. Seems to me you're quite drunk and should probably go back to your ship."

"It's *Mister* Ozawa now?" Somewhere in a sober corner of his mind, he knew he was making a sordid scene. He found it hard to care. "Was it fun to play with the broken little pilot doll? Did you plan on throwing me away the whole damn time? If you just wanted a fuck, you could've been honest and *said* so! I would've let you do me, no strings or wires!"

"Oz, you don't wanna do this." Travis tugged on his arm.

Turk's complexion had paled to gray. "Mr. Humboldt, get him out of here. Quickly. Please." He turned on his heel and strode off.

"Oh, no." Isaac tore out of Travis's grip and stumbled after Turk's retreating back. "You do *not* get to just walk away."

Adrenaline and anger cut through some of the alcohol fuzz. He wove and shoved his way through the evening crowd, managing a near run to try to catch Turk's long stride. Isaac struggled to keep him in sight. At a point where smaller establishments clustered thick as fur-moss, he abruptly vanished.

"Dammit." Isaac fumed as he cast about, peering into several narrow side corridors. He saw movement between a seedy inhaler bar and a flesh-for-hire service, so he hurried down the dimly lit passageway, intent on catching his prey.

Halfway down, he realized the corridor was a blind alley and empty as well. He wove to a stop, palm pressed to his head as the Apocalypses caught up with him again. A wave of sorrow swamped his anger. It didn't matter, really, if Turk didn't want him long term. No one ever would, so it just meant the big man was human. But he wanted to talk to him again, rest in those enormous arms one more time. Footsteps came toward him.

"Turk?" God, he sounded pitiful, bleating like a lost lamb. He steadied himself on the nearest wall.

"This the one?" an unfamiliar female voice asked.

Isaac squinted into the gloom. Not one, but four figures approached him. Even in his sloshed state, alarms shrieked in his head. *Oh hell....*

"Yes, ma'am. No mistaking him," a younger voice answered.

Black-and-gray uniforms surrounded him. *Security*, he reasoned and pulled himself straight, trying for respectable. "Evening, officers. Can I help you with something?"

"Yes, Mr. Ozawa. You can come with us, please."

"The charges? Before I go anywhere, I need to know. And to contact my ship."

"Best if you just come along, sir."

"The hell you say. I'm not budging until I see ident and hear what I'm being hauled in for."

"Admiral's orders, Mr. Ozawa." The woman's voice was soft, more menacing for its reasonable calm than the threat in the male voices. "You either cooperate and walk on your own, or we stuff you in a packing crate."

*Packing crate?* That wasn't normal security procedure for any station, not even an ESTO-owned one. His detainers acted oddly, as well, heads swiveling at stray sounds, hands on holsters. *These boys and girls aren't security.*

Despite his chemically altered state, he retained enough brainpower to realize Turk's odd behavior had an alternate explanation. Something had gone wrong at HQ, and Turk had been trying to keep him out of it.

Four of them, with God knew how many more in shouting range. If he could get out to the main thoroughfare, with witnesses and probably Travis Humboldt searching for him, he might have a chance. *I can take four. I think.*

He let his shoulders slump, pretending acquiescence. The moment they gave him space to walk, he kicked out and took the lead soldier boy out at the knees. The one behind him had to stop or trip over him. Isaac took off.

If he had been sober or if they had been unarmed, he might have made it. Alcohol soaked, though, his dash for freedom wasn't quite a straight line. A sharp buzz gave him warning. *Pulse stun.* Fire slammed into his back and leapt up in a cataract of agony to envelop him. His muscles froze and his head met the floor with a crack when he fell.

"Close in!" the woman shouted into her comm. "Five squad, fall back on me! Move!"

She obviously felt a threat was imminent. From his vantage, flat on his back on the floor, Isaac soon understood why. A deep, inhuman snarl echoed down the passageway. His four assailants only had time to look for the source before Turk charged. They fired four, five, six shots, but they didn't affect Turk. That, or the soldiers were lousy shots. He kept coming, that deep, bone-rattling growl making Isaac's ears itch.

Isaac could only watch in stunned fascination as Turk reached them, picked the nearest soldier up by the back of his jacket, and flung him against the far wall. The second soon flew in a graceful arc over Isaac's head to land in a less-than-graceful heap against the side of the inhaler bar. Turk took out their leader with a single, swift backhand to the woman's head, and the fourth he simply punched in the face.

The Corzin's reputation hadn't quite registered until that moment. Swift, fearless, unstoppable, and oh so damn sexy. Despite the stun hit, Isaac felt a rush of arousal. *You pick the stupidest times to get turned on.*

Turk dropped to one knee beside him, his eyes full of anxious concern. "Isaac... my poor Isaac." He slid his arms under Isaac's body to cradle him against his chest. "Why didn't you stay on the ship?"

*There's more coming. Dammit, Turk, you have to go!* Unable to speak or to move even to blink, Isaac hoped Turk knew.

The moment of tenderness cost them dearly. When dozens more footsteps pelted down the corridor, Turk turned too late. He rose with that strange growl starting in his chest before three stun shots hit him at once. He still reached for Isaac as he fell. Apparently, even a Corzin couldn't take three direct shots to the torso.

"Get them crated. Move it, people!" The woman was conscious, though she gave orders sitting on the floor, cradling her head.

While they folded Isaac's limbs and stuffed him in the wheeled, plastic crate, he took perverse pleasure in their conversation.

"Admiral wasn't blowing steam. That sonofabitch is fucking *scary*."

"Don't know why they let him run around loose."

"I want him secured, you boneheads! Don't put him in the damn crate until you get him cuffed!"

"The little guy, too?"

"No, just be careful with him. He's supposed to arrive undamaged."

*Little guy? I guess next to Turk, anyone looks little.* Their obvious lack of fear of him hurt his pride, but as the lid came down on the crate, he reasoned this was the least of his worries.

TURK WOKE to several unpleasant sensations. His head pounded from the multiple stun shots. His arms ached, bound cruelly behind his back at wrists and elbows. He tried to draw a deep breath and nearly choked. Tight bands of leather constricted his chest and throat, and a plug gag was stuffed in his mouth. Someone had gone to great lengths to be certain he wouldn't be able to utter any sort of note. He lay on his side on a hard surface, other twinges and deep aches telling him he had been beaten while he was out.

Far worse, though, was his view across to the gurney next to his. Isaac lay there, stripped to the waist, and strapped down on his front. His head hung off the end of the gurney. Why, Turk couldn't imagine, but it most likely wasn't good. Lab techs in white coveralls attached monitor leads to Isaac's head and back. The final lead, different from the others in its dull, metallic gleam, attached directly to the control nub of Isaac's implant.

*Electrode.* Anger surged through him, a subterranean magma flow, his muscles straining as he fought his restraints. Spirits help them all if he got loose, doubly so if they harmed Isaac.

One of the techs tapped on a console. "Sir, they're awake."

*"Thank you, Harrington."* Admiral Ranulf's disembodied voice floated through the comm. *"I'm on my way."*

A low, miserable moan let Turk know that the tech was right. Isaac was awake and most likely suffering the combined effects of hangover and stun-sickness. He lifted his head and tugged on his wrist restraints, obviously puzzled. Then he turned his head and spotted Turk.

"Oh holy fuck," Isaac spat out. "Turk, you all right?"

Unable to answer, Turk managed a strangled sound and a frantic nod, trying to convey that Isaac shouldn't worry about him.

Isaac turned his head to snarl at the techs, "You let him loose, you misbegotten bastard sons of mongrel scat-tunnel whores!"

While Turk didn't think the imaginative cursing would get them free, he appreciated the stubborn ferocity, and it seemed to make Isaac feel better.

The door opened to admit Admiral Ranulf, who listened to Isaac's ranting with a raised eyebrow and settled in a nearby chair. "Mr. Ozawa," he began when Isaac ran out of breath. "I'd appreciate it if you wouldn't verbally abuse my staff. I will have you gagged if you persist, and I'd rather not. If you begin vomiting, you might choke."

"You're joking, right?" Isaac said on a bark of laughter. "Takes a lot more alcohol than I had tonight to do that."

"It was last night, Mr. Ozawa, and it's not the leftover effects of getting drunk that concerns us."

That sounded ominous. Isaac quieted, watching the admiral with a wary light in his eyes.

"Better. Now, Turk." Ranulf turned to him. "You might wonder at this point what I want from you. Today, nothing. Today, I simply need you to watch and remember. An object lesson, if you like. Switch it on, Harrington."

The lab tech at the console tapped a control. A hum of electricity droned. *No, no, please!* Turk flung himself to the edge of his gurney, stopped by the excess of restraints. The tech tapped once more. Isaac arched in his bonds and screamed, muscles rigid, eyes wide in panicked agony.

"Again," Ranulf said, his tone calm and reasonable.

Isaac twisted, his beautiful face contorted as he continued to scream. The current ran directly to his implant, and through it, most likely to every nerve fiber in his body. The hum shut off and Isaac collapsed back to the gurney with a thud. Now Turk understood why they had him positioned with his head hanging off the end as he retched miserably into a basin one of the techs held.

*Isaac… I'm so sorry.* His thoughts careened between the desperate need to comfort Isaac and the dark yearning to snap the admiral's neck.

"Normally, I don't condone this sort of tactic," Ranulf began. "Are you all right, Mr. Ozawa?"

"Fuck… you," Isaac got out in a strangled whisper.

"Well enough, then. Turk, I offered you several opportunities to compromise, at both the Board meetings and here again on-station, but I've come to understand that you're a man of unyielding principles. While I admire that, it's not something the project has time for. Any other man, I would have recommended more direct persuasive methods. But you're Corzin. Wouldn't work with you. So, unfortunately for Mr. Ozawa, we need to use someone you care for."

"You're an idiot," Isaac broke in. "Turk doesn't give a damn about me. He hardly knows me."

Admiral Ranulf let out a soft laugh. "We have vids from the shopping district that say otherwise. Our barbarian warrior has a tender side."

"That's invasion of private citizens' rights, you bastard," Isaac shot back. "And this is a violation of more interplanetary treaties than you could crawl out from under."

*So brave... he's so brave. Hold fast,* atenis. *There will be a way out.*

"I don't think you should be worrying about that right now, Mr. Ozawa. Harrington, again."

This time Isaac's scream was hoarse and trailed off in a soft whimper when the current shut off. How many times could he withstand the shocks before there was permanent damage?

"Again."

*Stop, damn you, stop it!* The cuffs cut into Turk's wrists as he struggled, snarling, but he found no weakness in the metal. Isaac's body stiffened and convulsed, but apparently he had no strength left to scream. He slumped, his golden complexion faded, his eyes closed.

"That's enough for now." Ranulf stood and gestured to Isaac. "Cover him. We don't want Mr. Ozawa to chill. We'll leave you with him for now, Turk, to remind you what stubborn insubordination will cost. My offer is simple. Your lover will remain in custody. Do what I ask, and he'll be treated gently but the electrode will stay attached. Refuse an order, balk at a request, offer any sort of threat, and he suffers. I think we understand each other."

Turk nodded. What choice did he have? When the room cleared, he lifted up as far as his restraints allowed and slammed his shoulder into the gurney. Perhaps if he could break the metal frame, he might have jagged pieces to use. The metal top dented in, the frame creaked as he smashed against it again and again.

"We have you monitored." Ranulf's dry comment came over the comm system. "I suggest you find another outlet for your frustrations."

*Gladly. Come in here and unfetter my hands.* He collapsed on the gurney, trying to draw a full breath against the tight leather bands around his chest.

"Turk?" Isaac's shaky whisper drifted across the room.

A strangled sob caught in Turk's chest. Isaac apparently took it for acknowledgment.

"It'll be all right, hon. Who knows how long I was supposed to live with the damn implant, anyway? I don't know what that ESTO bastard wants. But don't you give it to him. Hear me? You make me proud. Stay strong."

For the first time in his life, he felt anything but strong. He wanted nothing more than to pull Isaac into his arms and weep over him. Since that wasn't an option, he managed a grunt he hoped Isaac would take as assent. More important to keep Isaac reasonably calm until he could devise an exit strategy.

With this act of barbarism, ESTO broke their part of the bargain. No need for him to hold up his end any longer.

He had just begun to wonder if he could break his thumbs and slip the cuffs that way when the alarms started to shriek.

# CHAPTER 8:
# TRAVIS HUMBOLDT'S CAVALRY

*CORE BREACH warning. This is not a drill. Please remain calm and proceed to the nearest evacuation staging area. Core breach warning....*

The absurdly calm voice spoke over screaming sirens. In the heart of HQ, a deceptive quiet reigned, but the scene on the public side of station would be utter chaos.

"Dammit," Isaac rasped out, addressing the comm system. "You can't leave us here! Somebody come cut us loose!"

Turk was certain no one could hear but him. Isaac was too weak to raise his voice above the cacophony.

He always believed using such a dangerous power source was *huchtik* madness. Here was the proof. People would scramble to save themselves and he and Isaac would be left to die.

The door hissed open. *Ah, perhaps there are orders. Ranulf doesn't want to lose his prize.* Good. Confusion and panic would be allies in his bid to escape with Isaac to the *Hermes*. He would have to move fast, though....

But the figure in the door was no white-uniformed lab tech and certainly was not Admiral Ranulf.

"Trav?" Isaac whispered.

"Let's move, people." Travis gave his orders in a hushed, clipped voice. "Sylvia, watch the door. Rand, get the code hacked on Turk's cuffs. Lester, think you can carry Oz? He doesn't look so good."

As soon as Rand had removed his gag, Turk blurted out, "Mr. Humboldt, they have the room monitored. They'll be coming."

The pilot laughed. "Yeah, well, they would be if they were viewing real time. Sorry it took us a bit to get here, boys, but Rand had to hack into HQ and we had to do some planning. Vids on this room are on a continual loop, thanks to our scan rat." He aimed a good-natured cuff at Rand.

"The core breach? Is there time to get the *Hermes* away?"

"There's no meltdown, big guy," Rand said with a grin. He let out a little exclamation of triumph when the cuffs clicked open. "Got it."

"I don't understand." Turk sat up while Rand made quick work of the rest of his restraints. He tore off the leather bands himself.

"Told you our boy had to hack into systems. First, to find out where they had you two held. Second, to get us in here. And last, this was the captain's idea, to set off a false breach alarm as a diversion," Travis explained as he helped get Isaac free and lifted into Lester's strong arms. Isaac moaned, his head lolling against Lester's chest. Thankfully, it looked as if he had blacked out.

"How did you know we had been taken?" Turk eased to his feet, testing his balance.

Travis hefted a military-grade stun rifle as he snatched a quick look into the corridor. "Wasn't far behind Oz. I saw them stuff you boys into crates. Knew I couldn't take a whole squad alone. But was pretty sure you'd end up here, since those idiots were in uniform." He waved everyone to the door. "We go fast, we go quiet. No shooting unless we have to. Turk, feel like you can run?"

"Yes, sir. If you arm me, I'll take rear guard. Make certain you make it."

Travis frowned. "I'm not leaving anyone back who might fall behind. And I'm not sure you're in shape to be carrying a weapon."

Turk let his teeth show in a ferocious grin. "Don't arm me, then, Mr. Humboldt. I'll still guard your backs. I have no need of weapons."

"Don't doubt that, bud." Travis gave him a long look up and down. "Good enough. Turk takes rear. Sylvia, you're on point. Rand, you stick by Lester, stay behind me."

"But I've got a pistol," Rand muttered, glaring at his shoes.

"You've done more than your fair share today, boy. Let us do what we're good at now."

With his raiding party sorted, Travis gave a quick sketch of the route they would take back, not as direct as possible, but through the maintenance corridors to avoid the worst chaos of the private sector.

Running footsteps pounded around a bend in the corridor. Two lab techs careened around the corner and pulled up short at the sight of them.

*Huh. They were coming to retrieve us after all.*

Not that it mattered one bit. Turk took two running steps to reach them, knocked one flat with a kick to the head, and downed the other with a hard jab to the temple.

"Wow," Rand breathed out. "He's fast."

"And he's not even at his best," Travis chuckled and handed Turk a dual-action pistol. "You keep the laser-safety on unless you've got no choice, hear me?"

He nodded, and they set off at a run.

Squads of ESTO soldiers ran past them at several cross-corridors. Equipped with flex shields and prodders, they were obviously en route to crowd control duties and, thank the spirits, had no attention to spare.

Challenge came as they prepared to open the access door leading out of HQ. Turk, Sylvia, and Travis formed a defensive semicircle around Lester, still cradling an unconscious Isaac in his arms, and Rand, who worked feverishly to get the lock open.

"Come on, baby, come on, don't be a bitch," Rand coaxed the door mechanism. A whir and a hiss announced his success. Turk wondered if the young man had ever used his considerable skills for less-honorable purposes.

At that instant, their astounding run of luck ended.

"Halt! Where the hell are you going, crewman?" A noncom leading a squad of six strode down the corridor to intercept them. "Where's your unit?"

Turk stepped in front of the others, pistol held muzzle down. "I'm to escort these civilians back to their vessel. Guests of Admiral Ranulf." While true only in an ironic sense, it was easier for him than telling an outright lie.

"I wasn't told any crewmen were on escort detail."

"Was pulled at the last minute, Sergeant. I need to get these people to safety." Turk took note of every soldier's position and their relative ease with their weapons.

The sergeant's eyes narrowed. "I've never even seen you before. Who do you report to?"

*Enough time wasted.* "No one you would know," Turk replied pleasantly and slammed the butt of his pistol into the sergeant's face.

The man was stubborn and needed a second blow to go down. By this time, weapons had come up on both sides. Turk fired at the man farthest down the hallway while he took out the man closest to him with a kick to the chest. The crunch of bone might have been satisfying under different conditions, but he was too afraid a stray shot might hit Isaac to indulge in the joy of battle.

Sylvia took two down in quick succession, her shooting sure and unhurried. Travis accounted for the last man standing. They turned their backs on the soldiers and raced off into private-sector territory. Had the station been in actual danger, Turk would have felt the need to secure them as hostages and take them to safety. As it was, he had no qualms separating the sergeant from his rifle and leaving them all moaning on the floor.

Their booted feet echoed off nearly empty passageways as they pelted toward the docks. At one cross-junction, they had to pass through a main thoroughfare, right by one of the evac points. Civilians mobbed the security manning the pod doors. Voices shouted demands and threats. Children cried. Rand stopped to watch, wide-eyed and pale. Perhaps the consequences of his tampering with the alarm system hadn't occurred to him before.

"Come, *hatra'os.*" Turk took his arm to propel him along. "We are not safe here. And Mr. Humboldt said no one may fall behind."

"Right. Travis said," Rand agreed in a dazed fashion and hurried to take his assigned place in their formation again.

Their flight took on a nightmare quality, through twisting access ways and back corridors. Finally, they stared out of a doorway, panting, at the *Hermes*'s gangway. The dockside between them and their goal seemed too exposed and impossibly wide.

"This is where it gets dicey, kids," Travis said as he peered up and down the curved dock. "They know their guests are gone by now. They'll expect us to head for the *Hermes*. I don't see any ESTO bravos. Doesn't mean they're not there."

"They lie in wait, Mr. Humboldt." Turk felt the peculiar eddies of magnetic fields that signified life. He pointed with his chin. "Behind those loaders. And more behind that engine housing panel."

"How's he know that?" Lester whispered, shifting Isaac in his arms. Isaac shivered and muttered, but stayed out.

Travis shook his head. "Don't ask. Just believe he does. Dammit."

"If I might suggest a course of action." Turk waited until he had their attention. "Mr. Humboldt, I think you may have been an Altairian Marine at some point?"

"I was. And how the hell do you know *that*?"

"The way you carry yourself. The way you handle your weapon. The fact that you understand the Corzin as well as any *huchtik* could. You are fierce fighters."

"Thanks for that. Your point?"

"You and I go out shooting. I take the right; you take the left. We provide the cover fire. Sylvia picks off any fool who shows his head while she and the young men make a dash for the gangway."

"He's insane." Rand gaped.

"Yeah. Kinda like that about him," Travis said with a short laugh. He tapped his wrist comm. "Cap? You read me? We're coming in. I need that airlock open when we get there or you may be scraping us off the door."

"*Do you have them?*" Captain Drummond's voice came back sharp and tense.

"All accounted for, ma'am. Permission to come aboard."

"*Granted. You'll have your way cleared. Dammit, Travis, be careful. We've got heat signatures reading all over dockside. I need you back here in one piece.*"

"Have I ever let you down, Renata?"

"*Never. Don't start now.*"

Clanks and thuds sounded all around them as ships' crews unhooked gangways and grapples, desperate to get clear of station.

"Leaving my channel open, Captain. We'll be with you in seconds."

Travis pinned them each in turn with his gaze. "You don't stop. You don't turn and come back, no matter what happens. Have faith Turk and I will make it. On my count."

He held up his left hand and counted down. At one, they burst from the doorway, Lester sprinting full-out with Rand, pistol drawn, on his heels. The rest of them fanned out, guns swiveling. Sylvia darted ahead when Travis gave the signal. The moment they broke cover, the hiss and crack of shots fired peppered the decking.

"Laser fire!" Travis yelled as he laid down a broad swath of cover fire in the direction of the engine panel. "Turk, dive for cover! These boys aren't playing!"

A weapon in either hand, Turk set up continual fire into the larger group of attackers behind the cargo loader. He made his way step by step toward the partial cover of a gantry boom, trusting in his shielding growl to deflect the shots in front, and Travis to take care of his back.

He risked a glance to his left. Lester had nearly gained the gangplank. A few more steps and Isaac would be safe. A sharp cry behind him caused him to whirl. Travis was down on one knee, clutching his shoulder.

"Stay down! Coming to you!" Turk bellowed and backed toward him, firing a weapon in either direction.

His intention was to get Travis and make a hasty retreat since Lester was now pelting up the gangway. Sylvia had turned, her back to the ship, to add her firepower to Turk's. Unfortunately, Turk had forgotten that one of their party was not ex-military, and not accustomed to firefights.

"Travis!" Rand shouted as he dashed back down the gangway. To his credit, he did get off three shots, albeit wild ones, before he went down in a spray of blood.

*Blood?* Turk reached Travis and saw the red stain on his shoulder as well. The ESTO idiots were using projectile weapons on dockside. Easier to debilitate your opponent, since laser hits were clean and didn't bleed out, but absurdly dangerous this close to the outer skin of the station.

"Mr. Humboldt? Can you make a run for it?" Turk asked as he kept firing.

"Yeah," the pilot grated out through clenched teeth. "But Rand...."

"I'll retrieve him. Please get to the ship."

Turk stood, sending the growl of his personal shielding out as he went to rapid fire with both hands, keeping the enemy pinned behind the metal sheeting. Sylvia followed his lead and set down a screen of fire on the opposite side. Travis lurched across the decking and when his foot hit the end of the gangway, he added his firepower to cover Turk's retreat, grimly raking their attackers despite his injury.

A headlong dive and a quick roll brought Turk to where Rand lay. A shot had creased his skull and blood pooled under his right leg, but he was breathing. Turk scooped him up in his left arm. The boy weighed less than Isaac did. Still firing with his right hand, he dashed for the *Hermes*, where more crewmembers had filed out with rifles to secure their retreat. Captain Drummond herself waited at the airlock controls as they stormed up the gangway onto the ship.

"Dammit, Humboldt! Of all the pigheaded stupidity!" she fumed, palming the lock to bring the door down and shut out the renewed gunfire.

"Sorry, Captain. Wasn't expecting *bullets*." Travis staggered over to brush the red-brown hair from Rand's eyes. "Told you to get to the ship, boy. Why couldn't you listen?"

Rand's eyes fluttered open and his smile was one even Turk understood as relief. "Trav... you made it...."

The captain barked out orders, delaying any more dressing down, and everyone hustled to obey. The injured were whisked off to sick bay, the remaining bridge staff dashed off to stations, and engineering hurried to cast off. While evacuations continued, they had a chance to slip away with all the other ships scrambling to get clear. Once station operations discovered the fraud, the all-clear would sound, and Turk was certain the *Hermes* would be in danger of pursuit.

He made his way to sick bay and stood against the wall, watching the medics work. One of them tried to coax him into a chair to have his own injuries seen to, but he waved the woman off. His hurts were small ones, not worth their time. Guilt plagued him as he watched them attach monitors to Isaac and wrap him in blankets, his beautiful face too still, too pale. If only he had thought of a better way to warn him. If only he had acted faster. If only he had never become attached to Isaac at all. That last simply wasn't possible, though. From the moment he had set eyes on Isaac, his heart had been captured and caged.

# CHAPTER 9: TAKING ISAAC HOME

ISAAC DRIFTED. Lights floated somewhere far above, perhaps he was planetside and they were stars. No, too round, too regularly spaced. A gathering of stars... was there a collective noun for stars? Maybe there should have been. A compendium of stars. A brilliancy of stars. A frisson of stars.

He smiled at the bit of verbal fancy. His warrior-poet was affecting him in all sorts of unexpected ways. *Turk... oh God, Turk.* The image of Turk, bound and beaten, leapt up, shattering the quiet calm. The big man had been trying to get him to go back to the ship. He must have known he was under surveillance.

*Instead of listening, instead of trusting him, I get stupid drunk and endanger us both.* He struggled toward the lights, toward the voices in the distance. Turk? Did he hear him?

"Turk!" Isaac felt as if he shouted, his chest heaved with effort, but the sound came out a croaking whisper.

"He's awake, Doc."

"Oz? Do you know where you are?"

*Dr. Varga? Why is she in ESTO HQ?* "I'm... not... it's hard to see. There's... is Turk here?" Someone lay on a flat surface nearby, but he couldn't make out enough to tell.

"No, sweetie. I think he went up to the bridge. He was here, though, making sure we knew what happened."

"Who's that?" Isaac tried to point. He wasn't sure it worked.

"It's Rand. He got in the way of a couple of shots, but nothing too serious. He's sleeping, poor kid."

"Shots? Why... would someone shoot at Rand?" Not that he hadn't been irritated with Rand from time to time, but to shoot him?

"He tried to play hero while they were bringing you back."

"Fool boy was trying to come help me," a deep voice spoke, oddly subdued.

Isaac's vision cleared enough to make out Travis sitting next to Rand's bed, holding his hand. Holding his...? Maybe he still wasn't seeing straight. That couldn't be right. But as he watched, Travis smoothed a stray lock of hair behind Rand's ear in an unmistakably tender gesture.

"Trav? You all right?"

"Yeah. Mostly. I've been damnably blind, though."

"Ah." Isaac turned things over for a bit, and then the hum of the in-system engines registered. "Who's flying?"

"Captain's got the helm, bud. She said I wasn't getting near the bridge with a hole in my shoulder."

"Someone needs to go back to the start for me, I think. I'm lost." Isaac tried to lever himself up. A wave of dizzy nausea slammed him back down, pain knifing through the back of his skull. "Shit... oh... just... shit. Doc, what's wrong with me?"

Dr. Varga didn't answer right away. That worried him. She perched on the side of his bed and stroked his hair. That raised the worry factor up to near-panic.

"It's your implant. Those bastards did some damage. Probably out of sheer stupidity. From what Turk said, I don't think they knew that they would. Some of the neural net's overloaded, connections frayed."

"Oh. Not something we can fix, is it?"

"No, Oz."

"I'm dying, is that it?"

"It's too early to say. We can't say for certain how much the damage will affect normal functioning. You could still recover enough for certain things. But for now, you need to lie flat and try to relax and—"

"Or I might die. Or be a bed squid. You can say it, Doc. I'm a big boy."

"Your neural patterns are unstable. We'll fight to keep you with us, Oz, but we might lose."

Isaac closed his eyes on a little nod. "Got it."

*"Dr. Varga, you need to get your patients secured."* Captain Drummond's voice came over the comm. *"We've got fighters closing. Things may get rough in a bit."*

"Travis, back in bed." Dr. Varga stood, giving orders in her calm, steady way. "I want straps secured on all patients. Yes, you too, Humboldt. Don't give me that look. Get that cabinet locked, Heath. Brace for turbulence."

*But I want Turk...* Isaac tamped down on the petulant, selfish thought. Turk was probably secured up on the bridge by now, safer than anywhere else on the ship.

TURK WATCHED the approaching fighters onscreen in frustration. On a Corzin ship, he would have been manning the guns. On an ESTO carrier, they had at least let him do targeting. This was an unfamiliar vessel type, though, and even with the captain shorthanded, she could ill afford an untried man in one of her officers' positions.

The captain sat at helm, Sylvia on her right at nav. The scan tech seat held one of the more experienced hands from engineering, while the comm officer's chair, Isaac's chair, had a very nervous youngster commandeered from comp support.

"Ma'am.... Captain, there's a message coming in from pursuit. Do you want it...?"

Difficult not to roll one's eyes. The youngster couldn't even phrase the question.

"Of course I want it," Captain Drummond snapped.

Turk watched the young man hesitating. "He wants to know which comm, Captain."

"Bridge comm," she snapped. "Dammit, Aiden, if you can't hold together, you're worse than useless up here."

"Yes, ma'am."

The message cut across the bridge midsentence, *"... ordered to stand fast and come about. You are harboring a deserter in violation of interplanetary treaty. By order of Admiral Ranulf and ESTO Fleet*

*Command, stand fast and come about. No charges will be filed against ship or captain if you cooperate fully."*

The command to halt and come about repeated, presumably on loop until the *Hermes* chose to answer.

"Captain?" Turk rose from the jump seat at the back of the bridge. "Is it your intention to give me to them? For the safety of your ship and crew, I would understand."

Captain Drummond turned to face him, gray eyes sharp and angry. "Are you a deserter? Is there any damned reason you can give me not to? How about we have some answers, Turk, and fast. I'm more than tired of all the mystery, especially now that we've stuck our necks out for you."

"You need not. The important thing was to get Isaac safe."

"Well, he's not safe, damn your eyes! He's probably dying! And I don't hand anyone over to ESTO scum if I don't know the whole story!"

Turk stared out the viewscreen, currently showing the view astern, at the approaching fighters. It was true. The *Hermes* crew had acted as if he was one of them, and he had thrust them into peril, given them only fear and pain. He need not break oath to explain certain truths.

"My people lent me to ESTO for a three-year period. It was, in Admiral Uchechi's words, to be a mission of cultural diplomacy. I would live as one of the *huchtik*, the Offworlders, as one of their soldiers, to learn about them. ESTO asked that one of their soldiers be allowed to live with the Corzin in exchange, but this was refused. It simply could not be."

His thoughts strayed to home, to his *katrak*, his brothers, his cousins... with a little shake of his head, he went on, "So long as they broke no promises, threatened nothing belonging to the Corzin, I was to be one of them, obedient and faithful. They have broken faith. I am no longer theirs."

"Then we won't hand you over, son. What they've done is tantamount to an act of war. The Imperial family on Altair has a soft spot for its pilots. They won't take a retired pilot's kidnapping lightly. They fire on us, the diplomatic mess only spreads."

"If they fire on you, they will do their best to erase the evidence, Captain. Can you outrun them?" He turned his head to meet her gaze.

"Probably not. Best hope is to buy time until Fleet can answer our distress call."

"Armaments?"

"Stern guns and a couple chasers port and starboard. Nothing to match what they're hauling." She shrugged. "If they want a fight, we'll oblige. But we won't last long. Our biggest advantage is all the civilian ships scattered out from station. Every ship out there will be picking up what's happening. Too many witnesses to sweep away if they try to take us out."

"Give me the comm, Captain. I'll answer them. It won't deter them, but there is… diplomatic necessity."

"Aiden, move it! Give the man your chair."

The young man's hands shook as he gave Turk a quick rundown of the system. Aiden helped him with the channel and then stepped back.

Turk took a slow breath, tapped the console, and began to speak in a clear, calm voice. "This is a direct message from *tach'*Corzin Turk to Admiral Ranulf of ESTO Central Command. Admiral, you have directly and willfully violated the agreement between our respective ruling bodies. Your actions force me to terminate my mission ahead of schedule—"

"You're out of line, crewman." Ranulf's voice cut across the channel, interrupting his careful speech. "The agreement with your government was that your term with us would end only if ESTO threatened Corzin interests. We have not done so. You are currently in violation of this aforesaid agreement and are ordered to return to duty. I may be able to have the desertion charges dropped, but you need to come in, Turk. I can't help you if you continue this insubordination."

"No, Admiral. You misunderstand the agreement. The exact language was that ESTO would threaten nothing belonging to the Corzin. You have not merely threatened my *sol'atenis*, you have caused him physical harm. You have grievously injured what is *mine*, sir, do you hear me?" Turk felt his voice drop to a fierce growl, unable to stop himself. "Count yourself lucky that I do not invoke *kaast'tlk*, instead of merely breaking off contact. Your spine, at least, will still remain inside your torso."

He cut off the channel, turned to see several sets of wide eyes regarding him anxiously, and realized he was still growling. With a hand over his heart in apology, he stopped the snarling and composed himself.

"Yours, huh?" Sylvia said as she turned back to her boards. "Wonder how Oz feels about *that*."

That gave him pause. He had meant to discuss everything with Isaac, but there had been no time. "I... don't know."

"Men are such idiots," Sylvia said with a snort. "They're still closing, Captain. No change in vector."

"Was a good try, son. Get yourself strapped in somewhere." Captain Drummond returned her attention forward.

"Yes, ma'am. I think I'll head toward sick bay." Not entirely a lie, since he did head that way. What he omitted was that he kept going, all the way to the stern of the ship. If Ranulf felt his prize slipping away, Turk was certain he would destroy the *Hermes* rather than allow anyone to escape and ruin both his plans and his reputation. But perhaps there was a way out still.

In speaking with Admiral Uchechi, and in the bits and pieces he recalled, he believed he had an understanding of what had happened on the *Marduk*. His brain had become capable of generating gravity fields, wells of such density and power that they achieved the same propulsion potential as starship GEM drives. During experiments, though, these had always been in lumanium-lined rooms to contain the fields.

When the shchfteru attacked, his instincts had taken over. Weaponless and helpless in his locked cell, rage overcame him and he must have created a field in the corridor outside his cell. The chuff caught in that field would have been ripped to shreds, indistinguishable from the human remains on cursory examination. The remaining chuff would have teleported away, back to their ship.

*And the ship....* Turk shuddered and stumbled as vague memories tugged at him of creating something far larger and more terrible than anything he had before. The ship could have fled. Yes, perhaps, or it could have been sucked into a heavy, short-duration gravity well.

Was it possible? Somehow, in a desperate moment, had he reached through the hull of the *Marduk* and sent the spinning EM fields into space? There was no sound in space, not to speak of, but his notes were only to center him, to focus on the resonant vibrations. The field itself, the electromagnetic energy, *that* could certainly travel outside a ship.

He stopped at the back of storage, the very stern of the ship. Here the *Hermes* had no lumanium shielding. Since she never ran in convoy or formation with other ships, she had no need. Once again, he wished for advice, for guidance from someone wiser. Would the fighters be too far off to pinpoint? Could he do this, something he had previously only done without thought?

The ship lurched and pitched, flinging Turk against a stack of crates. Alarms sounded. A call went out for fire suppression teams. The ESTO fighters had opened fire. It was time to stop agonizing and simply do. Admiral Ranulf had instigated battle and battle he would have.

Both hands on the ship's hull, Turk reached for the resonance of the fighters' signatures. Yes, he *could* feel them through the ship. He had simply never tried before. They matched speed with the *Hermes*, keeping just astern, most likely targeting her thrusters. Deep in his chest, Turk let the first note rise, reaching outward, ever outward. By the fourth note, he knew his EM field had formed outside the ship. He could feel it between the hull and the oncoming fighters.

As he had so many times before, he changed the pitch, adjusting the field in his mind. It was his mind affecting the changes, not the notes, he understood that now. The magnetic field spun faster. He gritted his teeth, concentrating on keeping it far enough away from the *Hermes*, expanding the field to the size of a man, the size of an airlock, the size of a single-man fighter. He grew lightheaded. His knees threatened to buckle, but he had to hold out. The spinning field reached the speed where it would have shrieked in atmosphere. Without that, the gravity well blossomed in front of the lead fighter before his instruments could scream warning.

Turk toppled to the floor, senseless.

"HE DID... *what?*" Isaac had insisted they place Turk in the bed with him. With his arm around Turk and the big, blond head nestled on his shoulder, there was almost room.

"We're pretty sure it was him. Gravity wells don't just appear out of thin space," Sylvia explained. She flashed a fierce grin. "Took the stabilizers and the guidance vanes right the hell off. Crumpled the fighter's nose. Just flattened the cockpit."

"The pilot?" Isaac whispered, feeling nauseous.

"Ejected. God, Oz, after what they did to you, you care about what happens to them?"

"He was just a pilot. Just doing his job."

"They picked him up before they all turned tail and ran back to station, so stop looking all stricken." Sylvia's normal scowl returned, though more worried than angry. "How're you feeling?"

"Not so bad if I stay still. Been so damn cold, though."

She snorted. "No way you could be cold now. That big lug would keep a whole regiment warm."

"Jealous?"

"Not exactly my flavor, Oz. You get some rest."

His aching brain failed to get a good grip on the facts. Somehow, his lover could create gravity wells. Somehow, he had managed to aim one at pursuing ships, and done it in such a way that it hadn't ripped a hole in the *Hermes*. Life had so many mysteries still to solve, his gorgeous lover was back in his arms, and Isaac was dying. Just the way his luck had always run.

"SO EXPLAIN, son." Captain Drummond's fingers drummed on the conference table. "Or is it one of those blood oaths you can't break? Something the Corzin try to keep secret?"

"No, ma'am." Turk shifted uncomfortably in his seat. Once he had awakened and the doctor pronounced him fit, the captain had summoned him to meet with all the mobile *Hermes* officers. "It's simply that I'm not certain I can explain."

"Do all Corzin do this?" Sylvia asked, obviously impatient.

"No. Not... what I do."

"Have you always done... whatever this is?" Humboldt—Travis said. He was supposed to call the pilot Travis. Pale and drawn, his uniform jacket draped over his wounded shoulder, he had insisted he should attend.

"No. It wasn't…."

Dr. Varga put a hand on his arm. "I don't approve of this interrogation, Captain. Turk's been through a lot in the past few days."

"We all have, Doctor." The captain rose to pace. "We need answers. Now."

"Renata… Isaac's dying."

Silence descended in a heavy shroud. Captain Drummond finally spoke in a gentler tone. "It's certain?"

"I can't repair net damage. The implant will try to save itself. Isaac's body will identify it as the enemy and go into full rejection. His temp is elevated already. His body is at war with itself." Dr. Varga stared at her hands. "I can't fix this. Let them have what time they have left together."

Turk held up a palm to stop any further argument. "I will explain what I can. And then I have a request. One more request of all of you, who have done so much."

He had their attention.

"It began when the ESTO officers showed me a ship, an Altairian Novasym fighter captured during the wars years ago. They showed me many things in my first weeks with them. I believe they wanted to see the 'barbarian's' reaction to different sorts of tech. I… spoke to the ship."

He waited for the exclamations of surprise and disbelief to die away. "Not as a pilot would. I would not be able to meld with the symbiont, to become one creature with it. But I heard things from it, its misery, its loneliness. It reacted to me. Opened its door for me. They—"

"Went bat-shit crazy," Sylvia muttered.

"It excited them, yes. I agreed to allow them to run tests on my brain functions. But they did more than test. They tampered. They went in with surgical instruments and the spirits only know what else. What you saw today is the result. Corzin are sensitive to certain types of energy. We can manipulate them to a small extent. But my brain… apparently it now acts as a living GEM drive."

"Fucking hells," Travis blurted out.

"At least it's clear now why all the infighting and political maneuvering over you," Captain Drummond said. "Boiled down to whether you were person or weapon, didn't it, son?"

"Yes, ma'am."

She shook her head. "Humboldt, tell me how we get embroiled in these things."

"We're good people who can't walk away?"

"That, or we're cursed." She flung herself back into her chair. "You had a request, Turk."

He rose and went to the holopanel to pull up a star chart. "Yes, ma'am. I believe there is one last option to save Isaac. I'm asking that we take him"—he thumbed the chart until he pulled up the correct system—"here."

"We can't do that, son. It's a quarantined zone. No access."

"Normally, that's true. I can get you in."

Her eyes narrowed. "And why would that be?"

"Because, Captain, it's my home."

They stared at him as if he had sprouted extra limbs. Travis recovered first. "The Corzin homeworld. Turk, you sure you should be telling us this?"

He dropped his gaze a moment. No, he was not certain. There might be some who would judge him harshly for it. But he had to try. "I would not take *huchtik* there normally. T'tson is a closed world, ordered so many generations ago. But ESTO has made recontact, so we are not as isolated as before. And you, this crew, this ship, you have warriors' hearts. All of you, even little Rand Wilde, though he lacks the skill. You rescued me, and I have fought beside you. *Chautae*, battle companions, as I have not seen in any other Offworlder company. I trust you."

Captain Drummond opened her mouth to say something. He hurried to cut her off. "Please, Captain. For Isaac."

"They can help him there?"

"If anyone can, yes."

She drummed her fingers a moment more and then gave one firm nod. "For Isaac."

# CHAPTER 10: THE COMPLETED HEART

"RAND?"

"Hmm?"

"Do you know what happened to the note Turk sent?"

They had been drifting in and out of companionable half awareness while the officers met with Turk. Isaac because of the waves of pain, heat, and chill, Rand because of the "stellar meds," as he referred to his analgesics.

"Note?"

"Yes. The rolled-up piece of paper?" It was hard to get irritated with Rand now, in such pain because of what he'd done for Isaac.

"Oh, that." Rand's nose crinkled as he thought. "Um. I put it in my jacket pocket, I think."

Grunts and curses brought Isaac's head around. Rand was pulling himself up to reach for the cabinet next to his bed. "I didn't mean you had to get it *now*, Rand."

"Just a sec... I have to see...." Rand pulled his jacket out and sat back against the wall, gasping and pale. He fished around the inside pocket and produced a much-folded piece of paper. "Ha! Told you I had it."

"I didn't say you didn't, bud," Isaac said in a dry tone.

"You didn't? Oh." Rand seemed puzzled by that and Isaac attributed it to the meds. "Well, here, anyway." He reached across the gap between them, bottom lip caught between his teeth, and tossed the paper on Isaac's chest.

"Thank you." Isaac unfolded the paper and smoothed it as best he could on his stomach. When he brought it up to read, he nearly choked. This was no mere note; it was a delicate work of astounding artistry. The central weeping cherry had an ethereal, alien appearance, lovely in each careful sweeping brushstroke. The poem... oh dear God, the poem....

"Fuck." Isaac's vision blurred with tears.

"Oz? You all right?" Rand inquired softly.

"No."

Rand made an uncomfortable sound. "It wasn't a good-bye, was it?"

"No. More like a warning."

"Oh. Shit… Isaac, I'm so damn sorry."

"Don't. You couldn't read it, bud. Not your fault. I should've come back to see it myself instead of storming off like an idiot."

The sick-bay door hissed open. Travis leaned in the doorway with a weary sigh. "I leave for ten minutes and Rand looks like death on a plate and Oz is bawling. What the hell's going on in here?"

"I gave Isaac his note," Rand said in a small voice. "I didn't mean to make him cry."

"Note? Oh… that note." Travis perched on the edge of Rand's bed to pat his foot. "Lie down, kiddo. You're white as an icecap and scaring the shit out of me." He waited until Rand slid back under his blankets. "Oz? He's on his way. Maybe wanna pull yourself together?"

Isaac swiped a hand over his face. "Sorry. My first love poem. Hit me a little harder than I expected." He held it out for Travis to see. "Amazing, isn't it?"

Travis's dark brows crept up. "He did that? Huh. Man of hidden talents."

The man in question came through the door, with eyes for no one but Isaac. Where Travis's entrance had been slow and pained, Turk swept in like summer rain, swift and powerful. He smiled for Isaac and bent to kiss his forehead. "I have a question for you."

"Do you?" Despite the pain and fever, Isaac's body tightened at that simple touch.

"Would you like to see my home?"

"Oh, well, now I know it's serious. Asking me to come meet the family and all."

Turk's forehead creased. "It was a serious question, *atenis*."

"I know, sorry. Why are we going there?"

"My homeworld... our science is different from yours. The physicians there may be able to assist."

"Well, of course, if it's in the name of science...." Isaac lifted a shaking hand to cup Turk's cheek. "I'd love to see your home."

Turk's hand steadied his. He turned his head to kiss Isaac's palm, sending a shockwave of dizzy need through him. "Good. Done, then." He placed Isaac's hand back on his chest and slid his arms under to lift him.

"Turk, maybe not the best idea," Travis cautioned.

"The doctor has given permission. She hopes it will be... beneficial."

Rand gaped, his fingers twitching the covers. "Beneficial. Must be nice."

It didn't escape Isaac's notice, though, that Travis's hand was still on Rand's ankle. Maybe his stay in sick bay would turn out nicer than he thought.

"Where are we going?" Isaac asked, though he couldn't have cared less as he let his head rest on Turk's shoulder.

"To our room, with the larger bed," Turk said. "Dr. Varga says she will bring your medicines to you there. She believes you will be more comfortable in my care."

"Not going to argue that."

Isaac hit the door pad for him since Turk had his hands full. Little firefly lights bounced around his heart at the way he had called it "our room." *Has a nice sound to it.* Turk laid him on the bed as if he handled angel-hair glass filaments. It was irritating to be treated so carefully, but Isaac sighed with relief at being flat on his back again. The pain never vanished, but it did fade to bearable.

"Rest, little one," Turk whispered as he perched on the bed. He placed a palm on Isaac's chest and hummed to him, soothing him to sleep.

ONLY ONE way for human life to spark, that unlikely and frantic meeting of zygotes, but so many ways for the spark to wink out. Turk lay curled next to Isaac, willing each rise and fall of his chest. Stripped to his briefs, he curled closer when shivers wracked Isaac's sleep. Breath stuttered, halted, and began again on a gasp.

Isaac's eyes flew open, his gaze fixed on the ceiling while he slowed his breaths. He turned his head and smiled. "Hey there."

Lightning storms raced from Turk's heart to his knees. What he would give to have Isaac look at him that way every morning... "How do you feel?"

"It's not so bad." Isaac's fingers brushed over Turk's arm. "Glad you peeled out of the uniform. Don't think I want to see ESTO black and gray ever again, if I can help it."

Turk caught the wandering hand and kissed his fingers. "Isaac, I should... there are some...." Fingers brushed along his bruised jaw, scattering his thoughts.

"I'm so sorry," Isaac whispered.

"For what?"

"For not giving you a chance to explain. For not believing in you."

"Isaac...." Turk took that gentle hand and pressed it to his chest. "You disrupted your life to save me. No one would have harmed you had I not involved you. You've suffered so because of me. You mustn't be sorry."

"I just feel like such an idiot."

Turk propped up on one elbow so he could kiss Isaac's forehead. "You have good reason not to trust. I should have recalled that and devised a different way to contact you. Fear for you muddied my thoughts. I acted stupidly."

A little smile tugged at Isaac's lips. "Fine. So we're both idiots."

"Inept communicators."

"I'll take that." Isaac fanned his fingers out over Turk's chest. Turk's breath hitched when a thumb brushed over his nipple. "Make love to me."

Desire warred with caution. "I'm not a savage, *atenis*. I would hurt you."

His eyes drawn with pain, Isaac continued to stroke his chest, his expression more serious than Turk had ever seen. "Turk, listen. They talked about this in training. Someone with an implant... once there's neural net damage... it doesn't get better. Only worse. I know you want to make it better, but I don't think the chances are good. There'll come a time soon when I can't feel certain parts of my body, when I can't control my limbs anymore. It'll get to a point where I don't recognize you, where I don't even know my own name. Turk...."

He pulled Isaac into his arms, trying to calm his trembling. "We won't let it get that far."

"You don't know that. You're hoping, but you don't know. This may be the last few hours I can be with you, as myself, in control of my body. Please.... Turk, this might be the last time for me."

Turk gazed into those lovely loam-dark eyes. They shone with unshed tears, with uncertainty and pain. *This will not be the last time. It must not.* He closed the distance between them and pressed his lips to Isaac's, claiming his mouth with tender ferocity. He lifted his head far enough to whisper against Isaac's mouth, "You must do something for me, then."

"What?" Isaac whispered back.

"Take me, Isaac. I want to feel you move within me."

A dry, brittle laugh forced its way from Isaac. "Much as I'd love to, hon, I don't think that's something I can do for you right now."

"You can. You simply need a bit more... imagination," Turk murmured as he began to unbutton Isaac's shirt. There was a name for the soft, loose clothing worn for sleeping, but he couldn't recall it. "I'll help you."

"I can't even do much to get you ready," Isaac said on a shaky breath.

"Ah, that's what worries you." Turk gave him a little smile and reached over to pull the lube from the cabinet. "I will help you there as well."

His lips explored Isaac's slender, golden throat while he pulled off his briefs. Isaac slid his hands over Turk's back in soft caresses, little earthquake tremors running through him that Turk hoped was excitement rather than chill. He caught Isaac's hands and kissed his fingers before placing them gently on the mattress. With a little gesture for a moment's patience, he turned and rolled down on his back with his head by Isaac's feet, giving Isaac the perfect view as he spread his legs and bent his knees up.

"Oh… babe… damn," Isaac breathed out. "I might climax just watching you."

A soft laugh escaped Turk's chest. He hadn't even done anything yet, though he was about to remedy that. With a flick of his thumb, he snapped the top off the lube, a hard tremor running through him as he slid the tip inside and Isaac let out a desperate moan. He emptied the tube inside his channel, the cool slide of it making his cock twitch, and then replaced the plastic with his forefinger. He pushed inside with a little grunt, his neck arching as he gave himself no time to adjust and added a second finger.

"God." Isaac shifted restlessly on the bed, turning on his side for a better view. His hand stole down to stroke himself, though his gaze remained glued to Turk.

Turk stretched himself only to the point where it would ease Isaac's entry. He transferred his now-slick fingers to Isaac's erection, watching as his eyelids fluttered, his lips parting in arousal. He guided one of the slender hands to his own cock, his breath catching as Isaac's fingers curled around him, his thumb pressing the sensitive nerve bundle on the underside.

"I'm going to move you now." He licked a wet line along Isaac's ribs as he turned again so they faced the same direction. "You must tell me if I hurt you or if you need me to place you on your back again."

Isaac nodded, his bottom lip caught between his teeth. Turk sucked gently on that captured lip until he saw his lover's expression relax again. He ran fingertips over Isaac's ribs, delighting in the way his skin shivered under the touch. *Like wind over water… so lovely.*

Ideally, Isaac should have stayed on his back, but Turk was anxious about putting any weight on him. He slid an arm under Isaac, supporting his head and shoulders, and with a hand on his hip, rolled them both together so Isaac lay on top. He nuzzled at Turk's chest with a little hum and then lifted his head far enough to meet his eyes.

"Hey there, handsome. This is comfy and all, but I don't know what you think I'm going to be able to do."

He ran his hands down Isaac's back to cup his cheeks, each firm globe the perfect size for his hands. "All you need to do is feel, *atenis*. Just that."

Isaac let out a contented sigh as Turk spread his thighs to let him settle between them. Their cocks nestled together, fitted like double portico columns, and he had a moment's satisfaction in how hard Isaac was despite his physical state.

"Turk?"

"Hmm?"

"What does that word mean?"

"Which word, little one?"

Isaac traced patterns on Turk's arm. "*Atenis*. You keep calling me that. I hope it means something good."

Trust Isaac to hit dead center onto one of the things he needed most to discuss. "There is no easy translation."

"Please. You don't get off that easy."

He stroked the backs of Isaac's thighs as he considered the best explanation. "I could tell you it means 'beloved' and it does. But that is only a piece of it." He bent his knees up and slid Isaac down until the velvet head of his cock nudged against his entrance.

"Distracting me?"

"No." He licked the pad of Isaac's thumb and kissed the tender center of his palm. "More illustration than distraction. The *sol'atenis* is the completion of one's heart. The one who truly belongs with you. On my homeworld this is an inseparable bond, one recognized by tradition, by law, and by every being living there."

Isaac stilled, fisting his hand. "So you're... laying claim? Trying to tell me I'm yours and no one else's?"

He shifted his hips, letting Isaac nudge at his puckered ring. "No, *atenis*. I tell you this so you know that without you, I can never be whole." His hand slid between them, guiding Isaac's erection, providing the thrust Isaac couldn't. A gasp caught in his throat when the head pushed through. It had been so long, but Isaac fit inside him as if he had been specially forged for him. "In this moment, I am whole," he whispered against the soft cloud of Isaac's hair. "My heart complete."

Isaac shivered atop him, his hips grinding in slow circles. "How do you know it's me? How would someone you hardly know... how can you be sure?"

*I know you, sweet spirits, I know your courage and the bright fire of your heart.* "The Corzin feel that connection as surely as we feel heat and cold. The resonances match, hearts singing in tandem. You are the piece my heart was missing."

"And if I say no?" Isaac's breaths came shorter, his excitement and frustration evident in his squirming. "If I tell you I don't feel whatever this is, can't feel what you do? Can't be this for you?"

"I cannot compel you to stay with me. I would not demand it." He slid his hands down Isaac's sides to grip his hips. "If you refuse me, if you leave me, I must let you go. But I will spend my life as half a man, never whole again."

Isaac grew quiet again and Turk felt wetness against his chest. "I don't want to leave you," he whispered. "But I don't want to leave you torn in half when I die."

*Ah, that's it, then.* Now he understood Isaac's hesitation. "Against all reason, beyond all probability, we found each other. I could have spent my life having never met you, frustrated and lonely, wondering why I could not find what others have."

He pulled his knees up toward his chest and moved Isaac's hips, helping him to thrust in slow, sure strokes. "But I have lain in your arms. I have kissed your lips and slept beside you. I have known my *sol'atenis*, and been complete. Whatever happens next, my Isaac, we have all that." He tilted his hips up on a moan to meet Isaac's invading cock. "We have this."

"Turk, oh God." Isaac's fingers closed over his shoulders, digging in. "You feel so damn good. So perfect."

Tiny suns exploded behind Turk's eyes each time Isaac hit against his pleasure gland. Each breathy moan torn from Isaac lifted him one stair tread closer to that golden pinnacle. Isaac helped as much as he could, the rolling of his hips adding delicious friction against Turk's aching cock trapped between them.

"Babe... fuck," Isaac gasped out. "I'm coming. I can't—" He cut off on a strangled cry, his hips jerking, and his arms rigid against Turk's chest.

"That's it, that's it," Turk whispered to him even as he reached between their bodies to fist his own erection. It only took a few swift, hard tugs to bring him that last step, streams of wet heat shooting between them, joining them further together.

Isaac's breaths came in shuddering gulps, earthquake tremors running through him. Anxious that he had asked too much, Turk quickly rolled him onto his back and let Isaac slip free, though the pain of that loss, all too soon, was sharp and brittle.

By the time Turk had him cleaned and wrestled back in his pajamas—*yes, that's the word*—Isaac's breathing had quieted to soft wheezing.

"That was... amazing."

Turk kissed his eyelids. "You are amazing."

Isaac lay silent for a moment, though his fingers curled around Turk's where they lay on the sheets. "If I...." He closed his eyes and began again. "If somehow I manage to make it through this, I want to stay with you. If that's... what I think you were saying."

"It was. I am glad to hear it." He stroked the sweat-soaked hair from Isaac's forehead. "Go to sleep. I will watch over you."

Brave words, the ones he had given Isaac. But as he gazed at Isaac's beautiful face, too pale, pain-etched, he knew he would not wish to live if his *atenis* died.

# CHAPTER 11: T'TSON

ISAAC'S CONDITION deteriorated alarmingly after GEM jump. They cushioned him as well as possible, but the stress took a terrible toll. When they began deceleration, Isaac told him in a soft, even tone that he could no longer feel his legs. By the time Turk returned from the bridge after giving the perimeter system alarms the correct passcodes, Isaac had lost the power of speech. He still smiled for Turk, returned his kisses, and held his hand, which Turk clung to as hopeful signs.

He told Isaac about T'tson, about the Drak'tar and the enclave where he had grown up. It was difficult to say how much Isaac heard or understood, though he seemed pleased when Turk spoke to him and nestled close with a contented sigh.

"We cannot take the ship in farther than the orbiting station, but Captain Drummond says we are to have the shuttle. I'm certainly capable enough to fly it down, right to Karsk Tor. I have explained the dire need to perimeter security, so we will be allowed to come in unchallenged with all possible speed. I have not spoken to the *Sil'ke'dra* yet—"

Isaac tugged on the front of his T-shirt with a frown, a question in his eyes. So he had been listening.

"She is the planet's matriarch, the head of government." When Isaac nodded, apparently satisfied, Turk went on, "I have explained in messages to her, though, and if she has not had time to hear them yet, I will explain when we arrive."

A bit of worry seemed to creep into Isaac's eyes, though Turk was unable to fathom the source. If Isaac was never able to speak again, they would both need to learn one of the hand languages. This guessing at his lover's thoughts simply would not do.

ISAAC COULDN'T help the terrible thought that his body had become a packing crate or worse, a casket, inside which he lay trapped. Turk threw strange words and concepts around—not strange to Turk, of course—and he had to rely on the sparest of gestures and expressions to try to ask the myriad questions his explanations raised.

Were the Drak'tar a governmental body? The civilian caste to the Corzin warriors? A class of nobility? He had said the *Sil'ke'dra* was Drak'tar, so any of those were likely.

Soon he might not even recall the words, so there was no use worrying at it. Soon he might not recall who the handsome man beside him was, speaking to him with such earnest urgency.

"Isaac? Have I said something wrong?" Turk reached to wipe moisture from his cheeks, which Isaac recognized belatedly as tears. "Please don't cry. We're nearly there. All will be well."

He thought he managed a smile and he squeezed Turk's hand where it lay on his chest. It was all the comfort he could give now, when he desperately wanted to fold Turk in his arms and kiss his anxious look away.

"We're ready." Dr. Varga poked her head in the door. She pulled a mag-lev stretcher in after her. "We're just going to transfer you over, Isaac. Won't be more than a second."

The transfer from bed to stretcher, with four sets of arms cradling him, wasn't as painful as he'd feared. Not being able to feel anything from the waist down had a bit to do with it, but he was grateful for small favors.

Turk kept a hand on his chest and hummed to him as they carted him through the corridors. The deep, resonant notes eased the pounding in his head and the sharp pains along his spine, though he knew the shuttle ride down into the planet's gravity well would undo any good Turk did.

In the *Hermes*'s number two shuttle, the *Sprite*, they secured the stretcher to cargo moorings, padded him with blankets, and strapped him in. Isaac fought down his apprehension. How bad would this be and how much more of himself would he lose before they landed?

He grasped desperately at Turk's hand as he made to go forward and begin preflight, trying to convey with his eyes all the things he couldn't say.

"Hold on for me—" He bent down to cup Isaac's face and pressed their lips together in a tender, searching kiss. "—for but a little longer, *atenis*. A few more hours and you will have help."

Even if he still had a voice, Isaac wasn't sure he would have been able to say much to that.

He closed his eyes when Turk left him and the shuttle bay door clanked shut. At the roar of the engines, he realized he had drifted off and the shuttle was now in motion, easing out of the hangar bay, preparing for separation. In some other lifetime, where a single choice or two would have changed outcomes, he would have been piloting the shuttle himself. Before the implant, he had been an accomplished pilot, licensed to fly dozens of small craft types. A wave of nostalgia swept over him, memories of the exhilaration and freedom of flight he had long suppressed.

Through zero-G flight, he drifted, relatively comfortable despite the rising fever and persistent aches. But the onslaught of planetary gravity destroyed any momentary sense of peace. The shuttle trembled, despite the insulators and padding, and Isaac felt the sudden pull against his body as if a giant hand meant to yank his bones from beneath his skin. The pain in his joints rose to searing agony as the shuttle shivered and groaned into the upper atmospheric layers. Just as he thought his brain would surely begin to leak from his ears, the plummeting sensation ceased and the little vessel leveled off into true flight.

He lay gasping, his sight dark around the edges. The terrible realization crept over him that he could no longer feel his hands.

The rest of the flight and the landing proceeded in a haze of pain. Turk's voice floated back to him, speaking in his native language over comm, most likely to traffic control. The thump of landing gear barely registered. He only swam up toward full awareness when Turk came back to undo the straps on his stretcher and take him up in his arms.

"Isaac," he whispered. He buried his face against Isaac's neck in obvious distress.

*Do I look that bad? I'm still in here, babe....*

Of course, Turk couldn't hear his thoughts and soon pulled himself together enough to say in an artificially steady voice, "We are here, *atenis*. You need only rest now. You've been so brave, to stay with me this long."

He strode down the ramp, Isaac swaddled in blankets in his arms, under a painfully bright blue sky, high clouds flung out like a distant scattering of pebbles. A sharp spice-scent reached him, reminiscent of cinnamon and marsh-fennel from home. As Turk reached the ground, Isaac realized they had landed on a high plateau, surrounded on all sides by astonishing plunging gorges and soaring promontories of dark green rock shot through with veins of scarlet.

*We're in the middle of nowhere. Where the hell's the city he was talking about? What in God's name is he doing?*

The scenery might all be hallucination, he reminded himself. That was a disturbing thought. All the breathtaking, quiet landscape might actually be tall city structures and bustling thoroughfares that his brain no longer chose to see. He wished he could ask Turk. *What do you see?*

If it was illusion, it was an oddly complete one. Turk's boots rang on the plateau's hard stone, echoing off the nearby cliffs. A bite of winter chill accompanied every breath. Aerial life forms circled overhead, dark circles against the sky, putting Isaac in mind of graceful, delicate pancakes. He wondered if he would soon see syrup bottle bird-creatures as well, or perhaps flying fried eggs.

*Odd, what a person thinks of under stress. Speaking of stress....*

Turk's heart galloped under his cheek. He nuzzled at the broad expanse of chest, hoping to convey that he was still cognizant and maybe calm Turk. Moving his head gave him a better view of their path and his pleasant little illusory world took on a nightmare quality.

A sheer rock face loomed before them, no natural formation in its even planes and glass-smooth surface. It looked like a doorway into the mountain, except no door could be so huge, the polished hunter-green stone rising a full fifty feet above the path. Sentinels bracketed this entrance or monument and their appearance only cinched it for Isaac. He was obviously hallucinating. As tall as Turk, though not as broad, they were bipedal life forms, but there the resemblance to Turk ceased. They had not two arms, but four apiece, and long, sinuous tails curling out below the ankle-length, quilted coats they wore. Their heads had long snouts with nostrils rather than noses, the effect halfway between reptilian and avian, and crests of shining protrusions bisected their skulls.

*Feathers? Scales? Hair?* He couldn't quite decide, even though it was his own hallucination, which it had to be since the Corzin were, for the most part, human.

The one on the right called out to Turk in that language of hard consonants and clicks, harsher still since the sentinel seemed to be snarling. Turk answered, at first in his usual calm way, but his voice descended to snarling as well as the exchange grew more heated.

Isaac recognized only a handful of words, among them *huchtik*, which he knew Turk's people used for outsiders. Apparently, his presence wasn't entirely welcome, though they obviously knew Turk, at least, as they used his name. The argument escalated to shouting, with numerous impatient two-and three-armed gestures from the sentinels, including pointing back toward the shuttle.

Movement drew his attention away from the verbal combat. Though no seam had been visible previously, a ten-foot high section of stone depressed inward. Soundlessly, it pulled into the rock face and slid sideways to create an open doorway. Through this marched another of the four-armed nightmares, though this one stood at least eight feet tall, its head crest a spectacular fall of emerald and turquoise reaching to the center of its back. This one's dress also differed wildly from the sentinels' heavy coats. Only a sheer bit of drapery wrapped its hips, floating around its calves, and the four arms clinked with delicate stone bangles in every possible shade of red.

To Isaac's surprise, Turk fell to his knees, holding his human bundle up toward this strange apparition and speaking in soft, pleading tones. His breath hitched, and he continued in a choked voice with the words, some of which Isaac recognized, "*Sil'ke'dra, hach lis. Isaac Ozawa terek, hei'sol'atenis.*"

This was the matriarch, then, whether this was her normal form or not. She flicked her fingers at the sentinels and they retreated. Her hand reached down to cup Turk's face, delicately clawed fingers long enough to reach halfway around his skull. "*Ka'Turk, hidach.*"

Turk pulled in a shuddering breath and rose slowly to his feet.

To Isaac's shock, she peeled the blanket back with one claw to address him directly in Standard, her accent strange and fluid but understandable. "Welcome, Itzak. The reasons for your visit are heavy on my heart, but I am pleased our Turk has found you."

"Isaac cannot answer you, *ke'dra*," Turk murmured.

"So. We have only small bits of time." She whirled abruptly and led the way inside.

His eyes expected dark, his brain expected a rough-hewn cavern, so it took a few moments to understand what he saw on the other side of that doorway. Below them, stretching on toward an inner horizon, rose conical spires and ziggurats, winding thoroughfares and glimpses of rooftop gardens. Vehicles in the form of colorful rectangles zipped about on the lighted avenues, like magical flying carpets from some ancient Earth tale.

*Karsk Tor.*

Even through his dimming awareness, Isaac was forced to abandon his stubborn belief in hallucination. This was T'tson's capital city, and the Drak'tar were not even remotely human.

"WHAT HAVE you done to yourself, boy?"

Turk raised his head from his hands, blinking in the soft light of the Calming Room. "Father?"

"Perhaps. Though I'm not certain you are still my Turk. Crest shaved. In those barbarous clothes." Loric settled beside him on the soft carpet, his arm around Turk's shoulders contradicting his hard words. "You are thinner. And home before you were expected."

"Things did not... go as planned." He met his father's gaze, those lake-blue eyes, which had always pierced through him. "There are things I should say."

"Always. Especially at the end of such a hard journey." His father ran a hand over Turk's head where the braided crest should have run down the center. "But your heart has other matters to attend first."

He nodded, suddenly so unbearably tired. "The healers have Isaac in treatment. I have not heard news yet."

"Have they taken care of you?"

"The attendants came. I've had some water, but could not eat."

Loric gave him a long look, frowning. "Is your honor still yours, boy?"

The question was expected, though it still stung. "Yes. Though I wish I had done many things better."

"So... so." The paternal gaze softened. The frown remained. "And if your *sol'atenis*, this *huchtik* with a warrior's heart, loses his final battle? Do you follow him into the dark?"

Turk tore his gaze away to stare at the leaf patterns on the carpet. "I do not know, Father. Much of me will surely die."

Loric squeezed his shoulder, the grip just shy of painful. "We have missed you, my stargazing child. We would miss you all the more were you to take that leap."

He could only nod mutely, unable to offer false comfort.

# CHAPTER 12: LIKE NEW SKIN

LIGHT FILTERED in slowly. Isaac reached for it tentatively, hesitant to leave the warm cocoon of darkness. When he cracked an eye, he immediately squeezed it shut again. The light stabbed at him, too bright to focus.

"Isaac?"

The voice boomed in his head, fathoms-deep and as loud as the sea.

"Isaac, can you hear me?"

"Shh," he hissed. "Stop yelling at me. God."

"You can speak again!" Turk said in an excited whisper, though even that grated on his nerves.

"Dammit, Turk, hush." Isaac clamped his hands over his ears. Footsteps in the hall, the rustle of cloth, the nearby murmur of Drak'tar voices, everything was too loud and too bright. *Something's gone very wrong.*

Vague images tugged at his memory, looming shapes of Drak'tar healers, soft voices, a room with sharp scents. A twilight state had enveloped him during what he had to assume was an operation, but he didn't think he had ever been entirely unconscious. *Brain surgery... they keep you awake during brain surgery.*

A hand touched his shoulder and his nerve endings screamed protest, as if a live, frayed cable had been dragged across his skin. He jerked back with an involuntary cry. Turk said something, but he could no longer make out words over the cacophony in his head. The hand returned to grip his arm and his awareness exploded in a white-noise fog of neural overload. Brushfires swept across his skin. Colored pinwheels flared and died in his vision. A confusion of scents choked him.

He struck out blindly, connecting with something hard, and scuttled back until he hit a wall. That contact was no better, so he lurched forward again, curling and uncurling in a desperate attempt to find a center to the chaos. Someone threw a blanket over him, the material strangely smooth, as if it were glass or ice. The noises ceased. His skin stopped shrieking. He pulled the material around him with a grateful sob.

Somewhere on the other side of his barrier cocoon, Turk was speaking, words that sounded like frantic protest. His voice grew fainter and fainter, someone obviously leading him away.

*Turk... what have you done to me?*


IT TOOK four attendants to bear Turk down to the floor, hard Drak'tar arms pinning him from all possible angles. Some small part of his brain recognized his actions as irrational, but Isaac's distress and pain screamed over any remaining reason.

"Zadral *tach*'Corzin Turk," a fluid female voice spoke above him.

His full name and rank, something he had not heard in over a year, penetrated the fog of rage. He ceased his struggles and looked up. His miniature riot had attracted the senior healer's attention.

"Do we sedate you?" she asked, crest half-raised in annoyance.

He met her gaze, willing his taut muscles to relax. "No. I... I have erred. Please. I acted out of anxiousness."

Her nostrils snapped shut and then reopened on a snort. "Better. Let him up."

He rose slowly, careful of all the limbs disentangling. "Healer, I—"

"Come." She cut him off with that terse word and a flick of her claws. Then the hard line of her jaw softened as she took his hand and led him to the Calming Room. With the lights dimmed to a warm glow, they all settled on the carpet, the healer across from Turk. One of the attendants removed his jacket and began to knead the knotted muscles in his shoulders. The healer reached out her lower arms and took his hands, her upper right hand cupping the side of his face.

"Our Turk," she murmured. "You left us with the morning sun in your eyes and return with a shadow-haunted gaze." Her voice became brisk again, "Your Itzak spoke to you. He moved by his own will." Her thumb stroked the sore spot on his jaw. "He moved well enough to land a powerful blow, though I doubt he knew what he did. These are all good things, yes?"

"Yes, Healer. But—"

She held up her free hand to quiet him again. "We wrapped him in a *heltas* blanket. He quieted immediately."

Turk stared at her in confusion. "Isaac isn't... he wasn't... humans don't go through skin sheds." He felt stupid saying the obvious.

"True. But we believe with the neural rechanneling, his body must readjust to his brain. He mimics all the behaviors of a youngling after first shed." She stroked his hair. "We have taken him to one of the newest teaching groups, so he might learn with them."

"He's not a youngling. He's a grown male." Turk fought to smooth his horrified expression. Isaac's humiliation at finding himself in a learning group with what he would think of as children caused a sympathetic twinge in his stomach.

"Yes. He is."

"But you think he could... adapt?"

"We must hope so. It is not a certainty, given the capacity of the human brain for inexplicable reactions, but we must try. His oversensitive nerves may simply be an affliction of a few hours. Impossible to say."

*Or it could always be so and I will never be able to hold him again. But he lives, by all the spirits, he lives.*

A DIM glow permeated the room, dim enough that Isaac risked a peek out of his blanket. He hadn't been able to before, in his hurried transport through too-bright, too-loud hallways. His fairy-glass blanket, wrapping him head to toe, had kept him safe, insulated from every touch, every scent and sound. Of course, he had no idea what material actually swathed him, but the fanciful thought comforted him.

None of the Drak'tar had explained where they were taking him, or if they had, he hadn't understood. While he had an undeniable gift for languages, the spare few words he knew of T'tson'ae didn't get him far.

Now he peered out into the welcome gloom wondering where *here* was. A number of lumpy shapes littered the floor, each shape on its own soft carpet. The one by the far wall moved and whimpered, and then one closer to him followed suit. He realized slowly that each shape was a blanket-wrapped bundle, just like himself, the room filled with them.

He fought down panic brought on by the strangeness of it all, the cave-like room, the mysterious living packets all around him. The unknown had a bad habit of breeding nightmares.

*I can't go down to the cellar, Mama. There are things down there. I hear them.*

*Turn on the light, sweetie.*

That simple bit of advice only applied in a metaphoric sense. He concentrated on pinning down what he did know. The bundles in the room, once counted, weren't as numerous as his bewildered eyes believed. Twenty-two, in all, including him. As his eyes adjusted to the soft glow that seemed to emanate from the rough-hewn walls, he caught movement to his right. One of the blankets wriggled far enough to reveal a Drak'tar snout.

*A very small snout.* The realization hit him that all of the bundles were considerably smaller than other Drak'tar he had seen. *Kids. It's a kids' ward.* He wondered in bemusement if the little ones were burn victims. They sounded so miserable.

Grown-up Drak'tar entered, their shorter stature and subdued crests leading him to believe they were male, though making assumptions about an alien culture was dangerous as all hells. Certainly seemed to make sense to place him with the children, though. They were closer to his size than the adults were, after all. But he had to wonder at the logic behind it.

Belatedly, he realized that if there was logic, he might not grasp it. They had taken him in without question, presumably just because Turk asked them to, and saved his life. God, he could *move* again, speak again, even think clearly, at least under his fairy glass. Maybe he shouldn't question their motives too closely. Though so far he wasn't entirely comfortable with their style of medical intervention. What if he had to stay wrapped up for the rest of his life to prevent his devolving into a shrieking maniac?

The adults moved from one bundle to the next, coaxing each one into sitting up. From an open-topped box, they handed each child a dark globe, roughly the size of an orange, with a short cylinder protruding from the top. Hands wrapped in the blankets, the children took the globes and, with their heads still hooded, put the cylinder up to their mouths and slurped.

*Ah. It's a straw. Got it.*

In whispers softer than a human could attain, the two adults obviously spoke encouragement, stroking backs and soothing frayed nerves, their hands always kept carefully on the outside of the blankets.

They approached Isaac last and knelt on either side of him to help him sit up and support him.

"Itzak," the larger one whispered as he offered a globe. "*Kes.*"

*Kes.* Drink. Imperative, singular. Or maybe interrogative.

His body obeyed him, but even the simple task of holding the drink proved too much. His hands shook, his arms leaden. A large, clawed hand closed around his to assist, keeping the blanket between Drak'tar and overwrought human skin. He held his breath, fighting whimpers as his lips touched the straw. *Too much, oh God, too much.* Every nerve flinched and screamed at the contact, but he forced himself to drink. The liquid, room temperature and supremely bland, soothed his sore, dry throat.

Calm settled over him and his headache eased. While he normally would have objected to sedatives without full consent, he was grateful for an end to his shivering anxiety. The Drak'tar males, whom he began to think of as nurses, eased him down onto his ovoid of soft carpet, stroking his back, probably telling him everything would be fine.

He couldn't understand the words, but the gentle concern in their actions conveyed their meaning. The room's glow dimmed, the only sounds the even breathing of twenty-two patients drifting off to sleep.

AFTER A period of sleep, the room's occupants stirred. Without windows or chronometers, Isaac couldn't be sure it was morning or afternoon or any other damn time. Some of the children lay still in their blanket nests, some rocked or fidgeted restlessly. He tried to sit up propped against the nearby wall but found himself still too weak and exhausted to manage on his own.

He watched, instead, as different Drak'tar adults, distinguishable from the nurses by their more colorful clothing, came to see the children, a small parade of them, one or two at a time, each new visitor kneeling by a different child. Isaac thought they might be parents or other relatives. A foolish lump rose in his throat that his own mother wouldn't be among the visitors, as if he were a neglected child on visitors' day at a boarding school.

Then Turk appeared at the doorway like the sun piercing the clouds in glorious hues. He set aside his previous anger at procedures done without his consent. When he had thought about it in a cooler moment, he had been beyond consent, and Turk had been the closest person available to stand in for next of kin.

In nothing but loose trousers of bright blue and a black knee-length vest, Turk looked more himself somehow. A hand weapon rode on his right hip, a wickedly curved blade on his left. His hair, just beginning to grow out of the military buzz cut, had been shaved on both sides to leave a golden crest down the center of his scalp, in imitation of the Drak'tar. He craned his head, peering into the gloom, but didn't enter.

His behavior puzzled Isaac until the big man took a step forward and was immediately intercepted by one of the caretakers. An urgent conversation ensued, with the nurse stroking Turk's shoulder, obviously sympathetic, but unyielding. Turk was not allowed on the ward. His face radiated misery.

Isaac managed to lever himself up on one elbow and to wave a blanket-encased hand. Turk's sharp eyes caught the gesture. He placed a hand over his heart and bowed in return, formality taking the place of the more intimate gestures tender longing would have preferred.

Turk leaned in the doorway, arms crossed over his massive chest, watching with mother-raptor intensity as the nurses sat Isaac up to feed him some bland, room-temperature paste. Even with their careful coaxing, he only choked down a few bites, taken from the end of a utensil that looked like a cross between a spatula and a miniature shovel. The sensation of something sliding over his tongue and down his throat left him shuddering and gagging. The drink, thicker than the previous one, which he suspected was meant more for nutritional than anesthetic purposes, went down easier.

The whole process left him drained and limp, and he began to drift off soon after the nurses let him lie down again. They stayed by him, talking over him in those nearly inaudible whispers, perhaps worried that he wasn't progressing like the kids. The little ones had no trouble sitting up and feeding themselves from their beautifully carved square stone bowls. Whatever afflicted them was clearly different from what ailed Isaac.

When he woke again, Turk had vanished from the doorway, the parade of parents over. *Probably a set schedule for visiting hours, just like every other med facility.* Movement in the corridor caught his eye, and he had to revise his theory, at least for certain visitors.

She took up an alarming amount of space in the wide doorway as she stripped the red bangles from all four of her arms and set them on the ledge in the hallway. It puzzled him that he didn't hear a single click or rattle as she did so, but then it occurred to him that he hadn't heard any noises from the hall since he had arrived. *Most likely a sonic barrier on the door.*

The *Sil'ke'dra* swept into the room. The nurses rose to their feet, not quite at attention, but with a sort of quivering anticipation, nostrils flared, eyes wide. She stroked their crests as she went by and both males visibly relaxed. Was one of the children hers? More than one?

Her steps took her past all the Drak'tar youngsters and straight on to Isaac by the back wall. He struggled to sit up, but she put a hand on his shoulder and pressed him back down.

"Itzak." She spoke in that same peculiar subdecibel whisper as the nurses. He wondered that he heard them all so clearly. "There are few Drak'tar who speak *huchtik* tongues. The Corzin do, but they may not enter here yet. You have questions, perhaps?"

He nodded, unsure if he could trust his own voice.

"So... yes. Turk is well. Back in the arms of his *katrak*. He worries for you, but his health holds. That first."

Isaac pulled his blanket close, as if it could substitute for Turk's arms. He indicated the children with one blanket-wrapped hand and then pointed to his own head.

She tilted her head to one side but seemed to understand him. Her speech was clear, though slow and cautious, especially around labial consonants like *m*'s and *p*'s. "The little ones had no neural reshaping. They will be *hatra'os* soon. The time between. This is their first shed. The first is... difficult. The nerves feel too close. Too much. Everything too much."

"Like me," he tried a spare whisper and found he could keep his voice as soft as hers.

"Like you." She petted his ankle over the blanket, touch apparently vital in communication. "It is like new skin for you, this change. The live little machine in your head, it wished to have its own way. The healers coaxed it into...." She hesitated, her snout wrinkled.

"Cooperation?"

"Yes. But they... rebranched? Some of your nerve paths. Grafted onto your trees."

"Grafted? What did they graft onto me, ma'am?"

"Drak'tar nerves. Better able to... adapt."

He blinked in shock. "Oh." Good God. Now not only did his brain contain an unhappy bioengineered symbiont, but alien biomatter as well? "Ma'am, I... how... are we even compatible?"

A soft trill caught in her throat, cut off on a sharp exhalation. Was she exasperated or laughing at him? "With certain preparations, yes. You are not our first human, Itzak."

*Laughing, definitely.* "No, ma'am. Guess not." His natural curiosity won out over any self-concern. "The Corzin—they live with you. Can I ask how?"

"It is not something we give to outsiders. But you are *ka*'Turk's own heart and no longer outside." She sat cross-legged, apparently settling in for the explanation. "Many generations back, a ship came to our system. We had explored our sister planets but no farther, had listened without understanding to the words coming from the void. We knew there were others, but had not met them. Rolf Corzin's ship was damaged. Beyond repair. The humans aboard were all in canisters, helping them live. Many canisters had failed."

"How many?"

"We recovered nearly eighty. So many more died." She stopped, twitching at the silken material covering her knees. "They were... new. We acted, to our shame, as if they were animals."

"You kept them as pets?"

"We used them. To learn. What is the word?"

A chill ran up Isaac's spine. "Experimented. You experimented with them."

"We did. More died. Shame mounted on shame."

"But you recognized at some point that they were thinking, feeling beings like you." This was obvious, since the progeny still survived, but he wanted to nudge her away from her rising distress.

"Yes. Rolf Corzin and sixty-eight of his crew still lived, much changed. In reaction time, in sensory functions, in other ways. Still human, but more than. Different than."

"So they stayed with you."

"They stayed. It is the covenant between *Sil'ke'dra* Karsk and Major Corzin. The Corzin are the outward face, the Drak'tar the inward face, but T'tson is home to us all."

*Do they serve you? Are there parallel societies? Or one, symbiotically intertwined?* He kept these questions to himself, though, uncertain if the concepts would carry across the way he intended.

"And me, ma'am? I'm not Corzin."

She gazed at him so long with her strange golden eyes that Isaac wondered if he would burst into flames. "You are not, Itzak. You are something else again. But the planet has called you here. Perhaps it has called you home."

# Chapter 13: Heart Resonance

The next few days Isaac spent in observing and being observed. No longer consumed by misery, the children had noticed him. They stared openly, and no one reprimanded them. They pointed and asked questions, which the nurses answered without evident censure or condescension.

Curiosity was obviously encouraged. Isaac did his best not to feel like a zoo exhibit. He often heard Turk's name mentioned in the explanations, as well, which always seemed to be some key to understanding since the questions usually stopped there.

Turk spent visiting hours propped beside the doorway, the dark circles under his eyes clearing more each day. People often stopped to speak to him during his vigils, Drak'tar and other Corzin alike, with frequent touches and embraces. While it was strange to see Turk in one of those four-armed bear hugs, it was almost stranger to see his Corzin kin.

Men and women, they all shared Turk's body type: tall, broad-shouldered, muscles sculpted to perfection. Turk was by no means the largest. They all went armed, against what Isaac couldn't imagine in what seemed a civilized, lawful society, and all of them wore their hair in braided crests, often interwoven with brightly-colored beads. In fact, much of the conversation seemed to center around Turk's hair. Each Corzin reached up to indicate his short crest with sad murmurs and head shakes. Turk always gave them that tight-lipped smile and said something reassuring. Isaac amused himself by supplying imaginary conversation.

*Oh my word, what did they do to your hair? How awful! What barbarians!*

*Don't worry. It's growing back. They're not all bad people.*

After visiting hours, the children had a new occupation for their time. A Drak'tar male, his movements slow and measured, his crest bright cerulean, came to instruct the youngsters. Isaac reasoned he was an elder by the way the nurses deferred to him, helping him down onto the carpet they spread for him, fussing over him until he shooed them off.

The first day, he spoke to the newly shed children for some time, their bright eyes shining from under blanket hoods, intent on his every word. Isaac longed for a translator. The second day, he had them all sit up straight and they practiced breathing. *Ah, meditation techniques.* This, at least, he understood. Since he was strong enough to sit up on his own, at least for a short while, he joined them. Always through the nose, even, measured, mindful breaths during which the teacher counted. He began to learn Drak'tar numbers, if only to ten, and slept far better that night.

The third day brought a return to confusion for Isaac. The teacher spoke first, gesticulating at his throat and mouth. Finally, he demonstrated the point of his lecture, a deep, resonating note rising from his chest, soon joined by a second and third tone.

*Just the way Turk does it ... but why?*

The little ones gave it a try. The technique obviously was not new to them, but maybe their own developmental stage had prevented them from trying before. The teacher made his way around the room, coaxing and encouraging. With some of his students, he seemed to be making corrections. It took Isaac awhile to realize they were corrections in pitch. Not that any of the children seemed to be singing the same notes, or even harmonizing with each other.

*A matter of matching frequency with your magnetic field. The right resonance....* Turk's words came back with startling clarity.

Was it some sort of self-administered pain management, then? A ritual rite of passage? A nonverbal form of communication?

He startled out of his reverie when the teacher crouched in front of him. "Itzak."

*Nice that everyone knows my name but no one bothers with introductions.* The slightly bitter thought rose unbidden. He mashed it down and returned the teacher's gaze attentively.

"You." The teacher waved a hand at the children. "Like them."

"I don't think I can, sir."

"You have…." He drew in an exaggerated breath, patting a palm against his bare chest. "No air?"

"I'm breathing fine. But I don't know how."

The teacher pointed to his own throat and began with a sound like a creaking door. Isaac managed a fair imitation, though he was unable to maintain it as the teacher increased his volume and added the second note.

He shook his head. "I'm sorry, sir. I don't think I have the right parts for this."

The teacher inclined his head in a sideways nod, patted his shoulder, and moved on. Strange, no one had treated him with anything but kindness, so why did he feel such shame at his failure?

"HOW IS he?" Captain Drummond's image scowled up at Turk from the holobowl.

"Progressing, Captain."

Her image snorted. "God's sake, son. I need more than that. Can he return to duty soon? Ever?"

He stopped pacing and sank down to the floor to face her. "I don't know, ma'am. The healers have no answers yet. He… does well. But he needs quiet and dim lights still."

"And the damn blanket, I gather."

"Yes, ma'am." Turk offered a crooked smile. "And the damn blanket."

Her scowl sagged into disappointment. "We have to leave him, Turk. For now. We can't keep sitting at station dock like this."

"No, ma'am. You have runs to finish. Obligations to fulfill. I understand."

"Just make sure he understands, all right? Tell him we'll be back. We're *not* abandoning him."

"Yes, ma'am." What she implied caused a twinge of pain, though he was sure she didn't intend it. *I'm here with him. Of course you're not abandoning him.*

She signed off and Turk suffered a moment's disorientation. The *katrak*'s comm room, which hadn't changed in furnishings or equipment since he had been small, looked suddenly unfamiliar, as if he saw his home through a stranger's eyes.

*I have been away too long, seen too much, and have become a stranger.*

"Turk?" Loric stood in the door arch. "You look as if you've just stared down the maw of a hundred-year *ko'sai*."

"I'm...." Turk rose, rubbing at the side of his face. "I feel so tired sometimes, Father. I need...."

"You need a time of peace, boy. Time to heal."

He shook his head. "I would be content with a space to catch my breath."

Loric drew him into an embrace. He backed off with a choked oath. "Go bathe, boy! You can't go see your Isaac in this state. *Fah!*"

Turk shrugged, embarrassed to have neglected himself, but finding it difficult to care. "I don't get near enough even to see him properly. He certainly won't catch my scent."

Amusement crinkled the corners of Loric's eyes. "So. I should say to the healer that you have no wish to go into the *heltas* room today?"

Turk stared at him in stunned disbelief. "I can go in?"

"Eh, she said as much. But if you have no desire to...."

With a wall-echoing whoop, he swept his father off his feet and whirled him once around the room, no small feat since Loric overtopped him by several centimeters. "Thank all the spirits!"

His father laughed. "Ah, it's good to see a glow in your eyes again. I had feared you had died among the *huchtik*, after all."

With a shake of his head, Turk stepped back. "It was a close thing. On more than one occasion."

"I know. It rides behind your eyes. A warrior whose death has whispered in his ear never loses that look."

He nodded acknowledgement. His father certainly understood. Then he strode off to the bathing pool down the hall.

BRACING FOR another round of visitors, Isaac curled tight into his corner. While he had improved, he dreaded leaving the safety of his cocoon with people coming and going. Stray, unintended noises still made him flinch. Any touch on his exposed skin was still problematic.

There was Turk, appearing to take his daily post. Isaac ached to go to him, just to speak to him. The loneliness, among so many warm bodies, had worn a deep groove in his soul. There he stood, in the doorway, stoic and out of reach as always. He did an odd thing, though. He leaned against the doorway and bent to pull off his boots.

And then he moved forward, and kept moving forward. Turk actually shot him a shy smile as he strode into the room. *No one's stopping him. Holy shit, no one's stopping him!*

He sat up, suddenly wishing he'd had a shower or a shave. Turk looked so damn handsome, dashing in his Corzin clothes, dark gray trousers and bloodred vest that day. Padding barefoot through the children, cat-graceful and mindful of stray limbs, he seemed to Isaac to take up all the air in the room.

"Turk!" The hoarse whisper escaped before he could stop himself. Luckily, most of the children were far enough along in their new skin development not to flinch.

Turk patted the air with his hand, pleading for quiet. He sank down to sit in front of Isaac, carefully maneuvering his blade so it wouldn't clank on the floor. Newly shaved, immaculately groomed, he put Isaac to shame, and yet it was Turk who seemed unable to raise his eyes, fidgeting where he sat.

"It's good to see you," Isaac tried as a start.

"I...." Turk trailed off on that single syllable, settling for a nod.

"I take it back. It's freaking incredible to see you." He reached out with a blanket-wrapped hand and gripped Turk's wrist. The big man flinched, staring fixedly at the cloth. Isaac took a stab in the dark. "This wasn't your fault, you know. I'm not pissed at you or anything."

That won him a shy glance up and a half-twitch of a smile. "It eases my heart to hear you say so." The large hand turned to grip his. "But you are so pale. You've dropped weight."

"Is that a nice way of telling me I'm not so pretty anymore?"

Turk huffed a breath. "Please don't joke, Isaac."

*I wasn't.* "You saved my life, you big ox. That's not something to feel so damn guilty about."

"Hand for star," Turk murmured, rather cryptically, Isaac thought.

"I don't suppose you're going to explain that." It felt so damn good to have that huge, warm mitt envelope his, even if it was through the blanket.

"There is an old Corzin saying. When you leap to catch a star, be prepared to lose your hand."

"Charming. Is that a cautionary proverb? Think before you act kind of thing?"

"Ah, no." Turk finally met his eyes. The love shining there felt like a hammer blow between Isaac's eyes. "It is a proverb about how difficult choices come at a cost."

*Of course it is, how silly of me.* "But the courageous man does it anyway."

The little quirk of a smile grew a bit. "Yes. That is the other half of it." Then the smile faded again. "The *Hermes* has gone. The captain asks that I assure you of their return. They have—"

"Runs to finish. I know, big guy. It's okay. I didn't expect them to wait so long." *I should feel alone, isolated. But I don't.* He fought back the lump in his throat and simply gazed at that handsome face a moment, drinking him in. "Why wouldn't they let you in here before?"

"Ah. Corzin fields are disturbing to the newly shed. Too invasive. Too strong."

"Fields? Magnetic fields?"

Turk nodded, stroking a thumb over the back of Isaac's blanket-encased hand. "The little ones are far enough along that the healer said I might enter today."

"Got it."

The little ones truly had come a long way. Many of them still sat in their *heltas* blanket nests but with their heads uncovered. They spoke to each other in whispered flurries of conversation. They ate and drank as if they had hollow legs. Today, some of them even ventured naked hands out, delicately hesitant, to touch fingertips with visiting relatives.

"Can we try that?" Isaac asked, a sudden stab of longing sharp in his gut.

"If you like," Turk said, his voice no more than a breath.

He unwrapped a hand, trying first to see how it felt exposed to the air. The soft sigh of ventilation stirred over his skin. *I probably shouldn't be able to feel that.* But the sensations didn't seem too bad, nothing to make him run screaming.

*Damn. I really am a waxy color.* He flexed his fingers. Maybe it was the strange lighting in the room. Slowly, he lifted his hand, palm toward Turk, fingers splayed. A fine tremor ran through Turk's hand as he raised it in imitation.

Their fingertips touched, feather-light. High-voltage electric streamers raced from Isaac's fingers straight to his balls. He forced himself to breathe slowly and maintained contact, though every nerve screamed with the effort. Slowly, he pressed his hand closer to Turk's, mating their outstretched fingers. An earthquake ran through his arm.

"Isaac...."

He bit his lip and pressed their palms together. The dizzying rush of sensation to his groin tore a gasp from him, and he snatched his hand back, then doubled over his knees under the blanket.

"Did I hurt you?" Turk's desperate whisper reached him through the humming in his ears. "*Atenis*? Are you... please...."

"M'all right, big guy. S'okay." The blanket served as welcome camouflage since he felt himself flush scarlet. "Didn't hurt. It was just too much. I didn't want to, ah... not in front of the kids. And it was damn close." He dragged a fold of blanket over his lap, hoping its dampening effect would ease his raging hard-on. It helped, up to a point.

"Ah? Oh. I see." Turk sat still and silent until Isaac peeked out from under the blanket again. Turk spoke to the floor. "Perhaps I should be flattered."

"That you could make me come with just a touch right now? I can tell you honestly that no man's ever done that to me before."

The soft laugh that Turk forced out was too much like a sob for Isaac. He reached out with a blanket fold to stroke Turk's knee. "It'll be all right, hon. It's better than it was."

Turk's hand folded over his. Isaac found the bright warmth through the fairy-glass cloth, his voice, even at a whisper, and the heat of his gaze were enough to repair the few miles of bad road the past weeks had made of his heart.

OVER THE next few days, much to Turk's intense and everlasting relief, Isaac improved steadily. He ate more, grew stronger, and began to shuffle about the *heltas* room with the blanket wrapped close around him as his personal armor. Walking caused him unique difficulties, the soles of his feet still painfully sensitive, but he insisted he had to try.

All the younglings had gone by this time, their new skins toughened to the point where they could rejoin the larger world again as *hatra'os*, the time between child and adult. Isaac, as the room's sole occupant, said he felt embarrassed to be monopolizing the attendants' time.

"It is their charge, my heart," Turk told him. "They will soon have another group of younglings to care for."

Isaac shrugged. "Yeah, but maybe they usually take a little breather in between. Relax, get some shopping done, I don't know."

"They haven't complained. They seem rather fond of you."

"What, like a pet human?"

Turk suppressed a chuckle, pleased to hear the gentle irony in Isaac's voice again. "Perhaps. Though they have not said so." He shook out the bundle he had brought. "Here. The *katrak* sends these."

With a puzzled frown, Isaac fingered the clothes. "Thank them for me, please. But where did they get my size? I've seen lots of your folks in the past weeks, hon. They're all huge."

Now Turk did laugh. "The Corzin aren't *born* huge. These are from one of my younger brothers."

"Ha. Got it. Silly of me." He still looked puzzled, though, and held up the pouch. "I get the trousers and the slippers. But what in God's name is this?"

"For your, ah—" Turk made a motion toward his crotch and turned the pouch and thong around the right way. "Support and protection. The *irskai*-hide is soft on the inside, but the outer skin is tough. An effective shield during hand to hand."

"Oh. Practical and sexy. I like it, though I might not be able to wear it yet." Isaac tipped his head to the side under the blanket. "Why the clothes all of a sudden? Am I going somewhere?"

"The healer suggests you might try to walk the halls a bit, *atenis*. I thought you might like to be a bit less exposed to do so."

"Thanks. I appreciate that."

Isaac lifted the trousers by the top hem, gingerly between thumbs and forefingers, and began to struggle into them. Turk turned away to give him some privacy, though the gasps and whimpers became worrisome toward the end. When the little noises of distress ceased, he turned back to find Isaac sitting on the floor, trouser-encased legs stuck straight out in front of him, shivering violently.

"Are you well?" he asked softly.

"Mostly. Sort of. I think." Isaac blew out a shuddering breath. "Just this strange creepy-crawly feeling having anything but the blanket next to my skin. I can... I think I can manage. It's like plunging into cold water. Not so bad, once you dunk your head under."

Turk concentrated on smothering a dark frown as he approached to help Isaac up. His lover refused the slippers as well, declaring them too much at once, but he seemed steady when he stood.

They walked the rough-hewn hallways slowly, Isaac taking each deliberate step with a frown of concentration creasing his forehead. It was painful to watch, but Turk bit down on an offer to carry him. Isaac's pride had suffered enough.

"Turk?" Isaac began as they turned a corner. "What is this place? I mean, when you brought me in, I could have sworn I saw a city with towers and gardens. But this... this is more like a cave system."

"Ah." The return of Isaac's curiosity in full measure eased another tight band around Turk's heart. *Thank the spirits....* "This is the youngling's haven for this district. Traditionally, they are carved into the mountains, deep, protected."

"Protected from what?"

"There are predators, both on the surface and under the soil, that would eat them. Before the Drak'tar built their great cities and lived in smaller groups, children were in greater danger. Now, it is more traditional than necessary. The large predators tend to avoid the cities. And the Corzin are here in case one wanders close."

Isaac's brows drew together, an expression Turk now knew signaled his bright, flexible brain generating more questions. "So, wait. Once the kids are born, they live here? In the caves? Until they're grown?"

Turk blinked. *Those questions do hit one from strange vectors sometimes.* "Live... ah, I see. No. They spend their first life cycle here and come here for their first shed. They have their learning groups here. But otherwise they live with their nurturers."

"You mean parents?"

"Not in the biological sense I think you mean."

They passed an open archway where the new group of *hatra'os* sat, feverishly working with light styluses on astronavigation calculations. One of the youngsters turned and gave a glad cry. "Itzak!"

Learning gave way to distraction as every head turned toward the doorway, the multiplying cries of "Itzak!" causing poor Isaac to shrink back and cover his ears.

Turk leaned in the doorway, patting the air with his hand and speaking in T'tson'ae. "Gently, little ones. Not so much noise."

"But, *tach'*Corzin, he has left the room!" one protested. "Itzak is still not... whole?"

"He improves daily, but he is still sensitive. It is not his skin that needs to harden, you know."

"Yes, we know," another said, with a look of contempt for the first speaker. "Some of us simply have empty heads." The first *hatra'os* made a rude noise, which the second chose to ignore. "Please tell your *atenis*, *tach'*Corzin, that our hearts beat with his."

Turk gave them a little bow. "I will. My thanks, little ones." He turned back to Isaac and spoke in Standard. "They're concerned for you and wish you to know their thoughts are with you while you recover."

That won a smile from Isaac. "That's kind of them. I didn't know they thought of me as anything but a curiosity. Would you tell them thank you? And that it's good to see them feeling better?"

He spoke again to the learning group. "He thanks you and says he remains with you." Not precisely what Isaac had said, of course, but what Turk believed he *would* have said, had he known the forms.

From under his blanket, Isaac waved. The little ones, who had seen this before as he waved forlornly to his Corzin lover in the doorway, imitated the gesture with youthful enthusiasm, some with all four hands. He wondered what significance they had attached to it, but refrained from asking. Turk spoke to them a few moments longer since they had questions about his time as an ESTO soldier. Any adult wandering by a learning group was fair game. To not take the time to answer questions would have been shameful and the height of antisocial behavior.

When he turned back to the hall, his breath lodged tight in his chest. Isaac no longer stood beside him. He tamped down hard on the rising, unreasonable fear. Nothing could happen to Isaac here. No one would harm him. He had simply wandered off. He had mentioned that standing in one spot was as excruciating as, and more exhausting than, walking.

His ears caught a soft echo of shuffling feet. Just down the hall, then. His time with ESTO had rendered him twitchy and paranoid. *I am home. These are my people. I must stop clutching my fear to my chest.*

WATCHING TURK with the kids was fun for a few moments. He was so patient with them and they obviously saw him as some kind of heroic figure, wide eyes devouring him, hanging on his every word. Isaac grew frustrated, though, since he couldn't understand the conversation, and his aching legs told him he had to move or plunk down in the hallway.

Unwilling to worry anyone by collapsing in a heap where he stood, he opted to keep walking in the direction he and Turk had been heading. Turk would have no problem catching up to his agonizingly slow pace. A few yards down the hall, he peeked into another chamber, this one lit with a lovely, dim glow, deserted and empty except for a pool of black water in the center. Raised ledges of stone dotted the pool's circumference, benches, he assumed, perhaps for quiet reflection. The whole scene struck him as so serene and soothing, he was drawn inside.

He spread a fold of his blanket on the floor next to the pool and sank down on it, wrapping the rest tight around his body. Maybe he was rushing his healing. He felt so raw, so tired and battered. The silence here caressed him, though, easing the irritation of overstimulation. The dark water, its depths impenetrable, lay in its perfect oval like polished obsidian. Only occasional soft ripples disturbed the surface.

If he hadn't begun to doze off, he might have caught a hint of movement under the water and not been quite so shocked. When a round head broke the water's placid surface, he cried out and flung himself backward.

"Shit!" he croaked out, panting hard. "What the hell?"

Black eyes took up half the face. They regarded him steadily, one slow blink showing nictitating eyelids. The little being in the pool chirruped at him in an interrogatory way.

*Safe, you're safe, you idiot. The kids probably come to this room. Nothing harmful allowed here.*

He moved back to his seat by the pool, taking in his strange, aquatic visitor. The head was no bigger than a muskmelon, smooth, moon-pale skin interrupted only by the eyes, the tiny slit nostrils and mouth, and fingernail-sized curves on either side of the head that he reasoned were probably auditory organelles.

"Hey, there," he offered softly, unsure if his new companion was animal or sentient.

Another little chirrup and a trill answered his greeting. *Great, another being whose language I can't speak.* The round head cocked to one side. The little mouth formed an O and a single, clear note issued from it. The sound reached into Isaac, shaking him as if his bones vibrated. He scrubbed at his ears, a strange itch inside his head. The note rose half a tone. The itching localized behind his left ear. Not in his brain, then, his implant.

On some instinctive impulse, he reached behind his left ear and pressed the implant nub to activate it, knowing it wasn't a sane thing to do. He had no idea how the damn thing would react to anything after the neural changes.

The diagnostic readouts appeared in his vision, and with them, the world metamorphosed in a sudden, dizzy rush. He sensed vibrations, clear, distinct frequencies that took on color and texture. The single, clear note the pool creature still held leaped into clarity. He could *taste* the tone, feel it as he had never experienced music before, not just the note, no, but the vibrations that emanated from the creature itself, from the water, from the rocks, from deep within the planet, each note unique, each vibration its own universe of sensations.

He leaned toward the pool, one hand outstretched, wondering if the sensation would change, transform again, if he touched the creature. Was it the implant that allowed him to see this new way, or the little being in the pool?

A webbed hand broke the surface of the water. Tiny fingers reached toward his. Booted feet pounded down the hall outside.

"Isaac, no!"

Strong hands snatched him up and swung him away from the pool. Turk's chest heaved, bright blue eyes huge with fear as he clutched Isaac close. "Did you touch?"

"What?" Isaac struggled to make sense of words that sang and leaped at him. With a shaking hand, he reached up to deactivate his implant. His strange, new view of the universe abruptly ceased.

"Did you touch the hatchling?"

"The... what? That?" He pointed at the little creature, now submerged to its eyes. "I don't... no. No, we didn't touch."

Turk sank to his knees, rocking Isaac's blanket-wrapped frame in his arms. "Thank the spirits. Oh my love...."

"Why? What's got you all worked up, hon?"

"Poison." Turk heaved a shuddering breath. "The hatchlings secrete poison. You cannot touch them barehanded."

Isaac shuddered and asked in a weak whisper. "Hatchlings? You mean...."

"Yes, yes. Infant Drak'tar. They live in the pools after hatching. Poison-skinned to discourage predators." He raised his head and said something sharp and fierce to the little one in the pool. The little one gave a sad peep and vanished under the water.

*Must've been the T'tson'ae equivalent of "don't you know better than to talk to strange men?"*

"He... it didn't mean anything, hon." Isaac leaned against that broad chest, disoriented and reeling. "It was me. I don't know what happened. The implant... I turned it on. I saw... felt... it was like the world was singing to me."

Turk sat him up, searching his face, his mouth working but apparently unable to form words.

Isaac wanted to sink into the floor. "Sweetheart? Did I do something terrible? Break some rule?"

A choked sound caught in Turk's chest and he seemed to regain the ability to speak. "No. No, please don't think that." He drew a slow breath and then crushed Isaac close again. "The heart resonance. You feel it. Isaac... I have no way to know if it's the same, but I think you feel the world as we do. As the Corzin do. Or can, with your implant."

His deep voice cut off again, overcome by some emotion Isaac couldn't understand. He ignored the crawling tingles along his skin, folded the blanket over his arms, and wrapped his arms around Turk's neck to hold him tight, murmuring soothing nonsense, hoping life was going to start making sense again soon.

# CHAPTER 14: ZADRAL KATRAK

TWO WEEKS later, Isaac was able to pull on the midcalf boots Turk brought him. A short conference with the senior healer gave him clearance. Time for him to leave the nest.

"I can't take the blanket with me?" Isaac asked and cringed at the whine in his voice.

"*Atenis*." Turk smiled but he blushed to the roots of his hair. "Grown males do not walk about wrapped in *heltas* blankets. It's...."

"Undignified? Unmanly? Childish?"

"Yes."

"Fine. And here I thought I didn't have any dignity left."

Turk had brought him a new pair of crimson trousers for the occasion, and Isaac had even managed the damn pouch, though he still didn't find it comfortable. Instead of one of the knee-length vests, though, Turk had brought him a quilted jacket so he wouldn't feel so exposed both to the air and to other's eyes.

"It suits you," Turk told him with a last tug on the clasp at his throat.

"I'm not going to look like a freak? Wandering around the city all bundled up while everyone else is half naked?"

"You're very handsome, my heart. And, no, a jacket hardly makes one a 'freak.'" Turk smoothed a bit of hair back from his eyes. "The city is warm, true, but you chill so easily still."

The males Isaac had thought of as nurses—attendants was the proper term, he'd learned—said their farewells with gentle hugs. Achtik, the larger of the two, held him by the arms a moment more, speaking urgently to Turk.

"What? What's the problem?"

"Achtik worries over your eating properly." Turk's expression was quite serious, though his eyes danced in amusement. "He's making certain I have complete instructions."

"Oh." On some odd impulse, Isaac wrapped his arms around the attendant between his top and bottom arms and hugged him tight. "Thank you. You've been so kind."

A chirruping trill issued from Achtik's throat. He raised a hand to stroke Isaac's hair. The contact still sent shudders down Isaac's back, but he was able to bear it without jerking away.

"Come, *atenis*," Turk said softly. "It's time to go. They are so sad to see you leave. Don't prolong their sorrow."

With a last wave, he left the *heltas* room with Turk. This was what he had worked for, to be able to rejoin the universe, but a splinter of sorrow lodged in his heart as he walked away. Just a sentimental reaction to leaving something that had become familiar in a strange place, he told himself. It wasn't as if he couldn't come back and visit.

The corridors along their route curved gently upward until they approached what appeared to be a smooth, stone wall.

Isaac hesitated. "Did we take a wrong turn?"

Turk strode on, obviously unconcerned. The wall developed a seam as Turk neared. A section of rock pressed out and rolled up to create a door like the one Isaac had seen when he first entered the city. They stepped out onto a walkway, around a curve of stone, and the city in all its delicate, alien splendor spread before them.

"Oh. Wow." Isaac wrapped his arms tight around his ribs, feeling unaccountably small. Space stations possessed greater scale. Many of the cities on Altair Theta had taller buildings. But the sweeping grandeur of Drak'tar architecture, its graceful curves and twisting spires, its seemingly impossible feats of gravity-defying platforms and skin-thin building materials lent the structures an air of dignified mystery. Intimidating, to say the least.

"It is glorious." Turk pulled in a deep breath.

Isaac knew that misty-eyed I-didn't-know-it-was-so-beautiful-until-I-thought-I'd-lost-it look. He'd known enough veterans to recognize it. "Good to be home, huh?"

Turk patted his shoulder. "Good to be home with you."

If he had heard those words from anyone else, Isaac would have rolled his eyes and responded with sarcasm. From Turk, the words slid right through to his back brain, sending a cascade of warmth to his toes.

He barely had time to clear the lump in his throat, though. One of the odd rectangular vehicles zipping along the thoroughfares veered out of the stream of traffic and stopped beside the walkway directly in front of them. Unmanned, it settled to the roadway with a soft hiss.

"Is that for us?" Isaac asked, glancing around to see if anyone else waited for a vehicle.

"Yes."

"How did it know to stop?"

Turk pointed to the section of pavement under his feet. Branching veins of amber ran through the green stone. "Sensor pad. Should I help you in, *atenis*?"

"I'll manage," Isaac said with a frown of concentration as he tried to puzzle out how one entered the vehicle. The shallow passenger dish had beveled edges but no discernible straps or seats, and while the elegant spiral designs etching the material pointed to great care in its crafting, it struck him as a singularly unsafe way to travel.

He peered out at the layers of metallic roadway above and beneath them, expecting to see bodies plummeting from these little lunch tray vehicles at every turn and dip. When he was unable to spot any evidence of mishaps, he climbed in after Turk and sat on the floor. *They're all either crazy, suicidally brave, or they can fly and haven't told me.*

"Isn't there anything to hang on to?" Isaac forced calm into his voice.

Turk's brow furrowed but almost immediately smoothed. "Ah. You won't fall out." He reached up to tap a knuckle against a transparent surface. "Force shield. But you may hold onto me if you like."

His handsome face remained serene, though the crinkling at the corners of his eyes gave him away.

"Yeah, yeah, hilarious," Isaac grumbled. "Not nice to tease the ignorant *huchtik*."

Turk tapped out a sequence on an illuminated heads-up display and the little magic carpet vehicle proceeded along a ribbon of light, presumably to whatever destination Turk had requested. While no one could be said to drive their transports, no collisions happened, and no hesitations in route occurred as the vehicles nimbly avoided all others, large and small, on the transport ways.

*They've got one hell of a traffic control system. Autopiloted or monitored?*

Soaring, spindle-legged arches whipped past, their delicacy scorning gravity and their function not readily apparent, though Isaac saw shapes moving behind transparent sections. Cantilevered stepped buildings doubled as terraced urban gardens. No machine noises disturbed the glittering twilight of this subterranean metropolis, no scents of ozone, industrial lubricants, pollution, or waste assaulted the senses as they did in many human cities.

Isaac shrank against Turk, feeling tiny and clumsy.

"Are you well, *atenis*?" Turk's breath tickled his ear as he murmured softly to him. He stroked Isaac's shoulder. "Does the speed distress you?"

"God, no, hon." Isaac nestled back against Turk's chest with a grateful sigh. "I trained to fly fighters, remember? Don't have a problem with speed. Just a little… it's a lot to take in."

"Too much?"

"I'm fine. Really. I promise not to break." He twisted around to look at Turk. "Is it far?"

"No more than a few minutes' travel. Zadral Katrak is the oldest, charged with guarding the center of the capital and the *Sil'ke'dra*'s interests."

Isaac processed this a moment. "It was the first? And it's a family thing?" When Turk nodded, he wondered if he was activating the social equivalent of an interplanetary minefield when he asked, "So you're a direct descendant of Rolf Corzin?"

Luckily, the question didn't appear to cross any taboo barriers. Turk simply said, "Yes. Zadral is his direct line."

"You have vids of him? Was he huge like you?"

"Difficult to say from the remaining images. They say he was a big man. But the Corzin breed for size, among other things."

Distracted by a shimmering light and water sculpture in the midst of a group of buildings resembling armadillos, Isaac took a moment to catch the odd wording. "Breed for? You make it sound like you're racehorses."

"Race... horses?"

"Um, never mind."

After another turn and dip, buildings of a different style hove into view. Seven interconnected domes, one large and six smaller, surrounded an open courtyard. Half-ellipses wings stuck out from each dome like spokes on a wheel, though a broken wheel since the spokes only decorated the outward facing halves of each dome.

Turk pointed, though Isaac had already guessed. "That is home, *atenis.*"

He had been expecting something less imposing. From all he had been told about the Corzin, their mercenary bands were small, and Turk spoke of the *katrak* as if everyone were family. This wasn't a family home; this was a compound, a small village. If all the people milling around the courtyard were family, the Corzin were prodigious breeders.

*Or maybe he means "family" in a larger sense. Like clan or tribe.*

He reevaluated the "milling" part as well. No one in the broad expanse of courtyard moved aimlessly or loitered about. As they drew closer, the mass of people resolved into organized groups, rings of men encircling a pair of combatants within each circle. Men and boys, Isaac realized. Each circle seemed to represent an age group, from the smallest fighters, who might have been eight or ten, to silver-haired elders. The younger groups all had instructors who paced inside the circles, the older groups seemed to be self-refereed.

There was none of the raucous shouting and catcalls Isaac would have expected in such a setting. Certainly, all the fighting matches he had attended had been noisy affairs. Here, though, the spectators stood quietly, attentive and intense, with only the instructors calling out corrections to the younger combatants and the occasional critique issuing from an observer for the older ones.

He found it a little eerie, all that fierce testosterone under such tight control. *Odd, where are the women?* Maybe they had their own time for sparring, though he had heard that female Corzin were as ferocious as the males and the ones he had glimpsed looked like they could have held their own here. In all Turk's dealings with women, Isaac had never noticed any overt sexism. The big man seemed only to divide the universe into people who knew what they were doing and people who didn't. Did the Corzin have some strange separate but equal way of dealing with their own?

As Turk gave him a hand out of the transport, an older man broke away from one of the groups, hands held wide as he strode toward them. His blond hair held lighter streaks of silver. Time and weather had etched seams on his handsome face. There could be no mistaking the man for anyone but Turk's father.

"Isaac!" the man called in a voice that echoed off the domes.

Every head in the courtyard swiveled toward them. Isaac tried not to cringe under so many curious stares. What did they see? A scrawny, pitiful little offworld refugee?

Isaac's hands disappeared in the huge ones held out to him. The man gave him one of those tight-lipped Corzin smiles, his eyes bright and kind. "Loric. It's good to meet you."

"Welcome home, *sulden*," Loric offered softly and leaned in to kiss Isaac's forehead. "Your recovery has calmed the chill wind that blew here."

Isaac's nerves twitched at the unexpected contact, but he clamped down hard on the urge to jerk away. "Thank you."

Loric's gaze swept him up and down. "Your voice is as lovely as the rest of you. Though you are a bit thin still."

"Will he do, then, Father?" Turk asked in a dry tone.

"Very well." Loric turned to his son, his brows drawn down in a fierce frown. "Though how you deserve to keep such a rare treasure baffles me."

Turk chuckled, obviously pleased by the teasing. "I am equally stunned, Father, believe me."

"And have you written each other's names?" a new voice drawled. A figure shouldered his way out of the group of young men in their twenties. Only an inch shorter than Turk, his shoulders were equally broad, his legs long and lean in the close-fitting leggings all the men wore for sparring. Black beads glittered here and there in his auburn hair; the ones swinging from the end of his braid clacked together in counterpoint to his slow steps.

"Not yet, Nidar," Turk said, his eyes narrowed.

"Then perhaps he has not truly made his choice." When Nidar smiled, his teeth gleamed white. Isaac knew enough by now to recognize the expression as aggressive rather than friendly, though the teeth vanished when Nidar turned to him. "Beautiful Isaac, perhaps you would like to sample a few others before you make such a permanent choice? You *huchtik* do not feel as we do. How would you know it is Turk you want? You may prefer someone more... *skilled.*"

Nidar stopped in front of him, a little too close for Isaac's comfort. Oh yes, he was heartbreakingly handsome, sea-green eyes dancing with lively intelligence, but the arrogance in the challenge was all too clear. A knot formed in Isaac's stomach and he twitched back a step when Nidar reached out to stroke his hair.

"I don't need help making choices, thanks."

One moment Isaac was braving the hungry stare, the next, those sharp green eyes vanished along with the rest of Nidar in a sudden blur of motion. Isaac blinked and found him again, on the ground, pinned on his front under Turk. Isaac had missed when Turk pounced, he had moved with such blinding speed.

"You act without respect, Nidar," Turk snarled and gave a hard yank on Nidar's braid to force his head up. "Admit your error or eat sand."

Isaac expected the downed warrior to struggle or at least snarl defiance, but he laughed and coughed, since apparently he had ingested some sand already. "We've missed you, *ka'tach.* I had worried that living with the *huchtik* would slow you. Let me up. The error was mine."

Turk, still frowning, eased off and offered the redhead a hand up. Nidar accepted the help and, when he rose, clasped Turk in a bone-jarring embrace. Then he turned to Isaac and offered apologies, Corzin style, all his swagger and arrogance banished.

"*Atenis,*" Turk said with a wave toward Nidar. "This is my cousin. My father's youngest brother's son, Nidar."

"Um, nice to meet you." *I think. What just happened here?*

A dizzying series of introductions followed, to brothers (eight of them), uncles (twelve), and cousins (too many to count). Isaac greeted each politely, but after the first twenty, gave up trying to keep track. Unless "cousin" meant something other than an actual blood relation, all the men in the courtyard really were Turk's extended family. For a single child with only a handful of cousins, it proved a bit overwhelming.

"Will I meet your mother today too?" Isaac asked desperately as he bowed to perhaps the sixtieth cousin.

Turk opened his mouth, closed it, and then said slowly, "Is that... is it something you wish?"

"Is she still alive?"

"Yes, my heart."

"And you're on good terms?"

"Yes."

"Then why wouldn't I?"

"It...." Turk still looked puzzled. He glanced at his father, who shrugged. "I suppose I could make arrangements."

*All right, now I've wandered into the minefield.* An ache started behind his left eye. The sand suddenly seemed to consist of too many sharp, individual grains. Scents crowded him, male sweat, soap, strange cooking smells. Too many voices, too many susurrations of feet—he rubbed his hands over his face, hoping to banish the sudden dizziness. It only made the ground tilt under him. "Guess I'm not ready for crowds yet."

"Forgive us." Loric put a hand under his elbow to steer him toward one of the smaller domes. "You are only recently discharged by the healers. We're such louts to keep you on your feet."

"But Father," Turk protested from his other side. "I don't—"

"You do. Now that you are together, we've moved your things to a *drustel* room."

"Ah."

*A what? Where?* Isaac swallowed his irritation and followed along. He supposed if they tried to explain everything at once that his head would explode. Better for retention if he absorbed things slowly.

Turk had explained that everyone not registered as attached slept together in one big room, so it was a surprise, though not an unpleasant one, when Loric led them to a small private room with a circular bed only large enough for two.

Turk seemed unaccountably embarrassed. "We haven't.... Father, this isn't right."

"Hush." Loric waved off his objections. "Isaac needs quiet still. To put him in a room with fifty snoring youngsters and your Uncle Jerit would be cruel."

Isaac sank down on the low mattress, more futon than bed. "Thank you, Loric. Very kind of you."

With a satisfied nod, Loric left them. Isaac found Turk watching him with a guarded expression.

"Turk? What the hell?" He waved a hand in the direction of the courtyard. "What was all that?"

"I should have been training with them." Turk turned half away, one shoulder propped against the wall.

Since Turk's non sequiturs usually led somewhere eventually, Isaac waited.

"I am *tach*." He shook his head, running a hand back over his short crest. "And I should not have forgotten it."

"Great. Wonderful. So what haven't you told me now?" Isaac blew out an irritated breath.

"I... *atenis*, I have not willfully withheld things from you."

"Fine. I know. It'd be hard to know where to start if I had to take you home too. I get that. Let's start with the *tach* thing. I've heard lots of people call you that. I thought it was part of your name."

"It is." Turk stared at his feet. "Though it was not always and might not be always."

"Sometimes, hon, your nonanswers are adorable. Right now, they're driving me nuts. Does the word mean something?"

"Yes. No." Turk threw his hands up at Isaac's frustrated snort. "Translation is difficult sometimes. *Tach* could be called a rank, a job, part of what I am. For my peers, I am *tach*. The... one whose voice they follow in battle. The field commander? In *huchtik* units, the closest equivalent I saw was a sergeant, though a sergeant's autonomy is limited."

"Okay," Isaac prompted in a softer tone. "So they rely on you. They need to trust you or everyone in your battle group's at risk. And you think you, what? Betrayed your boys by leaving them?"

"No. That was something we all agreed had to be done." Turk shoved off the wall and plunked down on the edge of the bed, his hands hanging between his knees. "But since my return, my heart has been shadowed. I had no will to be with them, to spar with them, to take meals with them. I have kept myself apart. Nidar had every right to challenge me."

"Were you just depressed?" Isaac traced a finger along the veins in Turk's forearm. "Or is it...? You're having trouble readjusting?"

"I still seem to fit in my own skin." Turk turned his hands over to stare at his palms. "But I'm not certain my skin fits back in the space I had carved for it."

*Oh, I know how that feels, love. I'm so sorry.* "Maybe it'll just take time."

"Perhaps."

After a few more moments of having a staring contest with his hands, Turk shook himself, rose, and hung his weapons on pegs by the bed. He even managed a little smile for Isaac. "Do you need to rest, my heart? No one will disturb you."

"Good." Isaac pulled off his boots and hesitated, uncertain how to approach a round bed. Turk's hesitance and confusion only made the floor tilt more under his feet. They needed some grain of certainty on which to cling, some center to the strange, nebulous cloud their lives had become. *What are we now? Where are we supposed to fit?* "Lie down with me?"

Turk shrugged out of his vest and curled up on the bed, holding his arms out. He hummed at the frequency meant just for Isaac, the vibrations rumbling through the mattress and calming his nerves. With a grateful sigh, Isaac tumbled into his embrace, still fully dressed, his ear pressed to Turk's chest to hear his heartbeat and the deep resonant note.

"Babe?" he asked in a near whisper. "Have I been asking stupid questions? Did I offend anyone? Offend you?"

"No, *atenis*." Turk nuzzled at his hair. "You must ask. How do I know what is new to you if you don't?" Those strong arms tightened around him. "Though I should have guessed some of the things that would be strange for you."

"Like why there aren't any women here?"

"Yes. I should have realized that might seem odd to you, from a service where men and women serve in the same battle groups. We do work closely with them. When we go up to take our turn on station or at the outpost, when we go out on *ket'sa*, out-system, we work in tandem with groups from female *katrak'ae*. But male and female Corzin do not live together or train together."

Altairian pride bristled. Isaac had grown up on a planet where the Imperial daughters went into the service alongside their brothers. "You think the women aren't good enough?"

Turk pulled back to look at him, his brows crinkled in confusion. "Good enough for what?"

"You keep them separate—separate living quarters, separate training, separate command structures. What then, do Corzin men just go visit for a fuck when they want to have kids and otherwise the girls aren't allowed in the house?"

A scarlet flush rushed up Turk's face. He tried several times to speak, but nothing coherent emerged. Finally, he let out a mortified bark of laughter. "Ah, my heart, no Corzin woman would allow such a thing. And the male who tried it would be dead within seconds."

"So are your parents together or not?"

"Together? No, I would think not. Father is most likely in the communications room at this hour. Perhaps he is talking to my mother, since you asked after her."

"Did they ever live together? Sleep in the same bed, at least?"

Turk blinked. "No. That would have been... odd."

Isaac did his best not to scream in frustration. "So how did you happen?" He poked a finger at Turk's chest. "How did *all* those beefy, aggressive males out in the training yard happen?"

"Happen? Corzin don't simply happen, my heart. We aren't random body births."

"Oh." Isaac fumbled with this revelation a moment. "So there really is a... a breeding program?"

Turk frowned. "You make it sound so cold. Every birth is carefully considered, every child longed for. Father has had several sons and daughters with Ektra *dalk*'Corzin Krea. Genetically, their chromosomes are a perfect mix and their bloodlines far enough removed. The district birthing center helped match them, but they have known each other all their lives, respect each other. Each knows firsthand the other's skills."

"They have fought together?"

"They are from the same district. Our battle groups are often assigned to the same rotations. Yes, they have fought side by side many times."

"I thought Zadral was the *katrak* for this district?"

"Zadral is the male *katrak*, Ektra the female."

Isaac slowly pieced the bits together. He believed he was finally getting a clear picture of Corzin social structure, bizarre as it was. "Your parents were never lovers?"

Turk choked on a laugh. "Ah, no. That's an odd thought as well." His expression sobered at Isaac's raised eyebrows. "I know, my heart, I know. Other human cultures do such things. Your own parents did, I'm sure. It's simply odd to think of Loric and Krea...." He muffled another laugh. "Corzin women do not take male lovers and the reverse is true as well. I was conceived at the birthing center, egg and sperm meeting in a conception pool under the watchful eyes of attendants."

In vitro *gestation, of course.* "Does Loric have a lover?" Isaac ventured, though he had the picture now, and what a marvelous, unorthodox picture it was.

"He... did." Turk half rolled away to stare at the ceiling. "His *sol'atenis* died during the ESTO Wars."

"Oh God. I'm so sorry."

Turk swallowed hard. "He died well, they say. On his feet, fighting to the last. Father... was not well afterward. I think when he saw you, thought you dying, it took him to those dark days again, and he feared for us."

"For you."

"Yes."

He stroked a fingertip along Turk's jaw. *How bad was it for you, love? How close were you to...?* The thought sent a stab of pain through him, and he felt suddenly selfish and obtuse. During his illness and his recovery, Turk must have fought hard against despair, was still fighting with its aftereffects.

Turk's eyes slid shut under the caress. A deep moan rolled from him, sending a shiver of need through Isaac's core. "Let me touch you," the big man pleaded, his voice rough and raw, "skin to skin."

"I'll come within seconds if you hold me naked, babe."

"I know." Turk lifted a trembling hand to stroke Isaac's hair. "That's not a terrible thing."

Isaac let out a half-amused snort. "It'll just make me the worst lover, ever." Pain shone from Turk's eyes, and he hurried to continue, "I'm not saying no, hon. Just bear with me. Let me, um, kind of feel my way through this, okay?"

He ran a fingertip over the shaved side of Turk's scalp. "I'm still trying to get used to this. I guess your crest was long enough to braid once, huh?"

"Yes. Though with a lover one usually lets it fall loose."

"Oh." Now *there* was an image charged with sensuality. *First, you undress your Corzin lover, then you take down his hair, those long, fine, honey strands waterfalling through your fingers.*

He trailed down Turk's throat, over his shoulder to his chest. The contact tingled through him, raising gooseflesh, but he could control his reactions if he kept the skin to skin to a couple of fingertips. Turk's breath caught as he flicked over a nipple.

"Isaac?"

"Shh. Lie still, hon. Let me do this."

Turk laced his hands behind his head, letting Isaac explore without interference. The golden trail below Turk's navel tingled against his skin. He bent to kiss the soft hair, blood rushing to fill his cock with the contact against his oversensitive lips. The ridged muscles of Turk's abdomen tensed, standing out in hard relief, but he stayed still, his breaths coming in short sips.

"Take your pants off for me."

In three swift tugs, Turk had his trousers off and tossed across the room. Isaac sat up to drink in that long expanse of gorgeous male, clothed now only in a thong and pouch of black iridescent hide. The erection barely contained within threatened the limits of that shining pouch. Isaac ran a fingertip from balls to tip, pleased when Turk's control slipped in a twitching thrust of his hips.

He reached a hand up. "*Atenis*, please...."

"Someone's impatient today," Isaac murmured on a little grin. "Hands back behind your head for now, hon. I don't want this over too soon."

With a disgruntled sound, Turk did as he asked, giving Isaac a breathtaking view of flexing muscles as he resettled.

"Attaboy," Isaac murmured.

He leaned forward to hook two fingernails under the thong at Turk's hips and pulled the pouch down. The massive erection sprang free to slap against Turk's stomach, a moan rumbling in his chest.

Still using only his fingertips, Isaac traced the veins, amazed at how Turk arched and writhed under that spare touch, how his cock leaped to meet him, eager and needy. Granted, anticipation and abstinence probably drove his reactions, but it was almost as if he had become as oversensitive as Isaac.

With his free hand, Isaac flicked open the clasps on his jacket and shrugged out of the soft quilting. Turk's gaze devoured him, biceps twitching as he obviously fought the urge to pull Isaac close. Eyes half-closed, Isaac curled forward and ran his tongue over the tip of Turk's cock, shining with pearlescent drops of need.

He jerked back, the electric contact of tongue on heated skin sending torrents of pleasure overload straight to his balls. "Oh... damn...." Panting, rocking over his knees, he took a moment to collect himself.

"My heart?" Turk levered up on one elbow.

"S'okay, hon. Give me a sec." Isaac patted the air with one hand. "Just... that was a mistake."

"Ah." Turk's forehead remained creased as he lay back down.

*My poor love, I don't mean to put you through the gears.* "Relax, babe." He stroked the inside of one of Turk's tree-trunk thighs. "You're supposed to be enjoying this."

In answer, Turk spread his thighs with a soft sigh, giving Isaac a view that nearly derailed his desire-muddled brain entirely. He teased at Turk's heavy sac while he undid the drawstring on his trousers. He had to admit, Corzin clothes were comfortable and easy to slither out of, all except the damn pouch. For that he needed both hands back to hook his thumbs beneath the strings and yank the thing off, leaving him shivering with reaction at the overstimulation of pulling the clinging material over his aching cock.

*Sex shouldn't be this hard.* But then, sex wasn't really the problem. If he'd just wanted to come, he could've done that in the first three seconds. He returned to Turk with both hands, the fingertips on one hand caressing his engorged shaft, the knuckles of the other pressing rhythmically against the magic spot behind his balls.

"Go on, love," he whispered as Turk tossed his head and moaned. "Just go with it. I'm here with you. It's all right now."

Turk's hips rose and fell in time with his tortured breaths. His hands had slid to his sides, fingers twisting in the bedcovers. Isaac waited, every nerve on edge, his body screaming for release. The moment he felt the skin covering Turk's balls pull up tight and his panting changed to soft, desperate sounds, Isaac flung himself on top of his lover's hard body. Their shafts rubbed together in a frenzied dance. Turk's arms closed about him in a fierce embrace. The world shrank to a white-hot point of light, the pleasure on the verge of excruciating. Isaac cried out as his climax slammed through him with the force of a cesium explosion, half aware that Turk bellowed out his orgasm as well.

Directly after, with the ever-lessening earthquakes running through him in pleasurable shudders, he found he could lie in Turk's arms without feeling as if he wanted to climb out of his skin. *Probably won't last long, but I'll take it.*

"See, hon? That worked pretty well. We can do this."

A snorted laugh was all he got in answer, but Turk lay replete beneath him, finally relaxed for the first time since Isaac had been injured. *We can do this.*

# CHAPTER 15: HARMONICS

WATCHING ANY Corzin engage in hand-to-hand was breathtaking. Watching Turk was just shy of miraculous. He was, as far as Isaac could tell, the best of his generation and, in a community where one's skills determined occupation, the logical choice for a battle commander.

Martial arts had been included in Isaac's education, but even the best of the Altairian instructors would have made an embarrassing showing here. The speed and astonishing grace of these huge bodies in aggressive motion seemed to defy several laws of physics. Isaac perched atop a nearby wall to watch, safely out of the way, and while the Corzin who spoke to him did so cordially, no one, not even as a joke, suggested that he take part.

Turk had observed his battle group for the first few matches, pacing slowly around the circle, offering quiet praise and soft correction. Barefoot and bare-chested, he presented quite a distraction for Isaac, who finally appreciated how well the pouch reined in a raging erection. Now Turk sparred with Nidar, possibly the only man in the group with a chance against him, blows from feet and hands flying at frightening speed. Serious damage seemed inevitable, but they were so well matched that they blocked the majority of the blows and dodged much of the rest.

Loric wandered out from the main building and sat beside Isaac. "Good morning, *sulden*. How did you rest?"

"Better than I have in a long time," Isaac admitted, careful not to show his teeth when he smiled. "Do you mind if I ask questions?"

"I would think Turk had brought home someone dull and stupid if you did not," Loric said, his tone serious but his eyes dancing with laughter.

"Well… good." Isaac winced as Turk's fist connected with Nidar's jaw. "Ow."

Nidar backed a step, shaking his head. Turk backed off as well, bouncing on the balls of his feet. They exchanged quiet words, Turk nodded and they began to beat on each other again.

"Aren't you afraid your son and nephew are going to hurt each other?"

Loric laughed softly. "No, Isaac. This is sparring, not combat. Our youngsters are taught early to be careful of their sparring partners."

"Of course." *I'd better not ask any more idiotic questions or he will think I'm dull and stupid.* He retreated to language as a safe bet. "What does '*sulden*' mean?"

"A child of the heart. The *sol'aten'ae* of my sons are my *sulden*."

"Do you... have a bunch of them?"

"Five."

"And they all live here?"

"Four of my sons brought theirs to live here. One son went to live with his at Terous Katrak."

"Is that hard to decide? Whose family they'll live with?"

Loric shot him a puzzled glance and then shrugged. "There is no decision. They live with the elder of the pair's family."

Isaac nodded. It made sense from a genetic redistribution standpoint, and from a relationship saving one too. Clear rules meant no arguments. "So a lot of the 'cousins' I met yesterday aren't related by blood?"

"True, not originally. You met several. Edar's new *atenis*, Kerl's, Nidar's two—"

"Two?" Isaac choked on the word. "He has two partners already and wanted a third?"

"It is less usual for us than for the Drak'tar to have more than one *atenis*, but some do. Nidar's interest in you was not sexual, Isaac. It was challenge. He would not have forced the issue further with you."

"And if Turk hadn't taken him down? Or hadn't... reacted?"

"Then we would have met, the battle group and I, and Nidar would most likely be *tach* now. It would have been a signal that Turk no longer wished to be. Many of us had wondered. Even when you began to recover, he was still distant. Distracted."

"He's had a lot on his mind since the whole *Marduk* disaster."

Loric's brows drew down. "He told me there was a shchfteru attack. Beyond that, he has said little."

"Yeah, well." The image of his first sight of Turk leapt up sharp and clear. Isaac swallowed against the sudden lump in his throat. "I don't think it's something he likes to talk about." With Loric's patient, nudging questions, he related the whole of it, from the first distress call to the desperate flight from Luyten Station. Normally, he wouldn't have been able to confide in such a huge, intimidating man so quickly, but Loric's open, good-humored manner elicited immediate trust. Leading a *katrak* was obviously something one did by force of personality rather than through powerful contacts or inheritance.

Loric's fingers drummed on his forearm at the end of this recitation. "It occurs to me that we have yet to see this gravitational displacement that the ESTO people found so... menacing." He looked up from his contemplation of his boots. "Turk!"

Turk caught Nidar's fist in his hand and turned toward them. "Father?"

"Why have you not shown us your new way of singing the fields?"

"It's...." Turk let go of his cousin, hands held out before him. "It's far too dangerous to show you in the city. I have no notion of how much damage...."

"Ah. Well, then, we must go out into the wilds, I would say."

Turk paled, but he answered calmly, "Yes, Father. Everyone?"

"No. I'd think just your *hech'zai* will do."

Hech'zai... hech'zai... *right, the battle group.* Isaac cleared his throat. "And me, Loric. If it's all right."

"I would not have suggested otherwise."

Silent, tight-lipped, Turk took him by his jacket-covered arm and hustled him inside to their room. Once they were alone, Turk let go and went to rummage in his clothes chest, jaw clenched.

"What? You're mad. Okay, I get that, but if you tell me I have to stay behind, I swear I'll deck you. I don't care w—" Isaac cut off when a shirt hit him in the face. He caught it automatically, and then stared down at the heavy felt garment.

"You need warmer clothes. The surface is frozen at the worst times of year, still cold now in summer." Turk's words reached him in soft, clipped tones.

"Oh." He caught the leather pants that flew at him next and a hide jacket, thicker than his usual quilted ones. "Turk? Hon... stop a sec. Look at me."

When Turk looked up, the anguish in those bright blue eyes sliced into Isaac's heart. "They all wished to use me. The Board, the admirals, the scientists. For different reasons, but all they saw was a tool, a weapon, a thing. And now my own people will see me the same way."

Isaac put the clothes down on the bed and knelt next to Turk beside the clothes chest. "Your father needs to know his fighters' capabilities. It's not the same. This is your family. They love you."

"You can't understand, *atenis*. When they see what happens, they will fear me. Perhaps you will as well."

"Never." Isaac told him in a fierce whisper. He seized Turk's wrist in a hard grip. "You hear me, love?"

"Isaac...." Turk tried to pull away, but Isaac tightened his grip. "Isaac, you're... holding on to skin."

Pinpricks crawled over his hand, but Turk was right. He was hanging on without gritting his teeth. "See? Progress. Now it's your turn. You're scared."

Turk's eyes flashed. "I fear nothing."

"Except yourself. You're terrified."

"No!"

"You think you'll cause some horrible catastrophe. Death and destruction. You think you're a walking disaster waiting to happen!"

"*No!*"

Isaac let go and used his already tingling hand to stroke over Turk's crest. "It doesn't make you any less of a man to say you're scared."

"What if I lose control?" Turk whispered.

"Have you ever?"

"No." Turk's eyes squeezed shut. "Yes. That once. I don't remember it... may never remember. Yes, my heart, it frightens me that I do not know what I did. Does that satisfy?"

"So you lost control once in your life, under extreme duress, in a desperate effort to stay alive, battered by such enormous psychological stress that your brain blanks it out, and you think you're a monster?"

"I don't know what I am, *atenis*."

"Turk." Isaac braved the neural overload and took Turk's head between his hands. "You are a brave, honorable, honest man. Do you have any idea how rare that is? Whatever they did to you, whatever new things you can do, it doesn't change your heart. They tried their damndest to force you to do things against your nature. They failed. Do you hear me? They *failed*. You control this. You need to know what you can do."

A measured breath expanded that broad chest, let out slowly as Turk nodded against Isaac's hands.

"Guess we need to get dressed, then, huh?"

Turk rose, his paralysis broken. "Yes. Dressed and armed. Are you more comfortable with rifle or pistol, my heart?"

"Um, pistol. Why?"

"Predators."

"Great." Isaac was certain a sidearm for him would be superfluous, though. He was a competent marksman, but even Corzin kids were bound to be faster, better shots.

A soft fleece-like material lined the leather pants. The heavy shirt was double-layered as well. The boots Turk set out for him were knee high and steel-tipped, much sturdier than the soft calf boots he had been wearing. Topside was obviously much colder than the city and far less civilized. There were gloves as well of soft, supple hide. He flexed his fingers inside them. *I could touch people now, I think. Why didn't I think of gloves before?*

When they were ready, which meant Turk had armed himself with several varieties of weapon—knives, firearms, and some round items that looked suspiciously like concussion grenades—they proceeded to one of the domes at the outer edge of the compound. At Loric's touch, a four-meter wide panel separated from the side of the dome and slid upward to reveal a fleet of odd vehicles. Roofless, half-dome bottomed with benches running along either long side, they reminded Isaac of upturned tortoise shells.

*Until you spot the fore and aft gun turrets, anyway.*

Turk's battle group clambered into one of these transports. Isaac hesitated. Once, thirty big men crowding into such limited space would have enticed him to mount up damn quick. Now, the thought of so many bodies in close contact made him wince. Turk took his elbow and helped him step up into the bed, and then with spare hand signals, he rearranged his troops. His younger brother Din hurried to take the aft gun. Nidar took the front turret. Others shifted on the bench so Isaac could have the end closest to the front with only Loric beside him.

Turk kissed Isaac's gloved fingers, handed him into his seat and went forward to stand on the platform beside the front gun. A heads-up display appeared in front of him, but he didn't touch it as the vehicle rose a foot from the floor of the storage dome and proceeded out of the compound in a smooth glide. Isaac took a moment to puzzle out that the controls were at Turk's feet, the piloting done with nudges and toe-presses on floor controls, leaving his hands free for—what else?—weapons.

They traveled through the city along the rock floor, under the shining network of personal vehicle pathways, sharing the ground level, light-marked roads with larger transports. Hover barges carrying food and construction materials lumbered out of their way, much as traffic would yield the right of way to fire control back home. Outside the city proper, the ground began to rise, and this time when they headed for a sheer rock wall, Isaac knew enough not to brace for impact.

A huge door opened to the outside, the spectacular cliffs of dark malachite and scarlet scattering thought in favor of sheer wonder. Young Drak'tar males stood guard outside this portal, just as they had at the first door where Turk had carried him in. While they looked fierce and alert, Isaac suspected a hasty call would go to the *katrak'ae* if serious danger threatened. The youngsters clasped their own right fists together and raised their arms in salute as the Corzin transport whisked by.

Isaac couldn't help a smile when he spotted his flying pancakes again. He pointed to the small flock high overhead and asked Loric, "What are those called?"

"Those are *heido*."

"They're beautiful."

"Many deadly things are, *sulden*." Loric's forehead creased, his expression an older version of Turk's worried one. "Perhaps we should have taken time to brief you before we left the city."

Isaac waved a hand to indicate the brawny bodies on full alert all around them. "I don't think I've ever felt safer."

"Even so. You must be aware of your surroundings and be able to react." Loric pointed at the *heido*, dwindling in the distance. "Pretty, but their touch is poisonous. It makes the Drak'tar ill but kills humans. If one descends toward you, shoot it directly in the center to discourage it. That's the nerve center."

"Yessir."

"If you feel the ground rumble beneath your feet, for all the spirits' sakes, you *move*, boy, away from the vibration. Do you hear?"

"Yessir." Isaac swallowed hard. "Why?"

"It could simply be a smaller burrowing creature, but it could be a hunting *irskai* or worse a broody *ledit*. The *irskai* will only eat you. The *ledit* will drag you home to its many-mouthed young."

Isaac stared, hoping this was some strange bit of Corzin humor, but Loric's expression was deadly serious. "Oh. I... see. Anything else your son forgot to mention?"

Now one corner of Loric's mouth quirked up. "I'm certain there are dozens of things. He never was my most talkative child."

Without turning his head, Turk spoke in the universally aggrieved tone shared by humans suffering parental embarrassment in front of a love interest, "I armed him, Father. I did warn him the surface was dangerous."

"Of course," Loric said in a too-serene tone that drew a snort from Turk.

*They might be all business, but they're still family.* The teasing comforted Isaac, making him feel less alien and lost.

"On your thirty-six, Nidar," Turk said softly.

Nidar swung the gun a few degrees. "I have it. Not approaching us."

As the rock slowly gave way to several-meters tall, thick-stemmed grasses and bulbous, fern-like plants, Isaac made out movement among the giant plants. Nidar's gun pointed at something astonishingly huge in the near distance. From glimpses through the vegetation, Isaac's first impression was of a moving wall the size of a military shuttle. He had to increase his size estimate considerably when the beast raised a disc-shaped head on a thick, corrugated neck, a full ten meters above the Corzin transport.

"Holy shit," he whispered.

"That, my brave *sulden*, is a *ko*," Loric said.

Isaac stared, his heart feeling as if it shrank in his chest. "Will it try to eat us too?"

"No. Not intentionally. *Ko* are grazers. It may not see you while it grazes, which could be dangerous. But the most dangerous aspect of them is their curiosity. They are not... naturally graceful in their investigations."

"Great. Death by herbivore klutziness," Isaac muttered. "I think I'd rather be eaten."

Several of the nearby brothers and cousins laughed, sputtering and gasping to contain themselves as if he had said the funniest thing imaginable. *Corzin humor isn't too far from the grave. But then, that's true of most soldiers.*

"So... wait. If it gets curious about us, Nidar will have to kill it?" The *ko* was hazardous, but an amazing work of T'tson'ae biology. Its blue-green hide glittered in the sunlight and a lump lodged in Isaac's throat to think of that heroic-sized alien beauty destroyed.

Loric blinked at him, clearly startled. "Kill it? Ah... no. That would take a great deal of wasteful firepower. He would aim for the olfactory organs and discourage it. But we do not kill without need."

Plenty of nonsynthetic hides clothed them and they did eat meat. Isaac puzzled over when "need" would be. "You don't even come out here to hunt?"

"Spirits forbid." Loric's easy tone vanished, replaced by one of forbidding ice. "This territory belongs to Drak'tar hunters. Why would we do such a thing to those who take such good care of us?"

"I didn't mean to offend," Isaac said softly, offering a half bow where he sat. "My mistake. The worlds I've known were very different from this one."

Loric's dark glower immediately brightened. "No harm, *sulden*. I did say you should ask when you do not know, eh?"

*Another cultural minefield on the scanner. God, how do ambassadors do this sort of thing?*

They left the soaring cliffs behind as the rocky landscape gave way to lush terrain. The transport slid over shorter grasses and ferns, sweeping pastures in breathtaking, multi-colored hues. The chlorophyll in the native plants did not present as green, or the plants used another method of energy production entirely. The predominant colors were shades of red, yellow, and blue. In a clearing between tall stands of giant cinnamon-hued ferns, Turk slowed the vehicle and let it settle to the grass.

"Edar. Kerl. Perimeter," he ordered. The men in question leaped from the vehicle, rifles held at the ready across their bodies, and loped off into the ferns in opposite directions.

One of the smaller—by Corzin standards—young men turned in his seat to watch Edar's progress, worry and longing in every line of his body. *Edar's new* atenis.... The relationship had to be in its beginning stages for such a reaction, but he raised no protest and showed no signs of breaking ranks. The man next to him patted his knee and he turned back, face flushed pink, apparently embarrassed by his small lapse of discipline.

The scouts returned, one on the heels of the other. "*Ka'tach*, the way is clear," Edar confirmed. His resemblance to Turk was striking, though he was a few centimeters shorter and his hair was white blond to Turk's gold. He obviously shared both parents with Turk. "No hunting parties, no large forest dwellers."

With a nod, Turk turned to the rest of his command and ordered them out with hand signals, distributing them to establish a half-perimeter. Loric waited with Isaac until Turk placed all his men and stepped down from his platform to offer Isaac his hand.

"So. What do you need?" Loric asked as they stepped down into the clearing.

"A few small rocks will do," Turk murmured, his brow furrowed. "If this is merely for demonstration."

"Yes, boy," Loric said too softly for the men to hear. "Just to see. Do you distrust my motives suddenly?"

"No, Father. But what I am about to do… frightens me."

Isaac thought Loric couldn't have looked more stunned than if Turk had announced he was going to go live as a lounge singer on Triton Station. He put his gloved hand against Turk's cheek. "If you're not comfortable—"

Turk cut him off with a sharp wave. "You were right, *atenis*. I cannot hide from this. I must understand it."

From his other side, Loric put a hand on Turk's shoulder. "Lucky for us your Isaac is so wise. You're home now, my stargazing child, back with people who can help you understand."

"Trust them." Isaac bent, ran his hands through the grass, and came up with a smooth, palm-sized stone. He gripped Turk's wrist and dropped the rock into his outstretched hand. "Trust yourself."

The spare nod Turk gave him was one Isaac recognized by now as a girding of resolve. He turned to look at his men one by one. "Everyone must stay behind me as I do this. Even if the sky falls and the seas rush in through fissures in the earth, you must stay behind the shields I sing. Do you hear?"

Thirty palms struck thirty broad chests in salute. Thirty deep voices answered, "*Ka'tach!*"

Turk strode to the center of the clearing, shed his gloves and jacket despite the cold, and began to hum. The hum rose in volume until he parted his lips to sing a deep, bell-clear note. A second note joined the first, with Turk throat singing as the Drak'tar did. Standing to one side, Isaac sucked in a sharp breath when the stone in Turk's palm rose above his hand, rotating slowly.

When a third note joined the other two, Isaac shook his head, his ears tingling. *How does he do that? He shouldn't be able to….* The thought cut off as a fourth note joined the chord. Gaping, Isaac took an unintentional step closer. A hard hand closed on his arm and pulled him back. The irritation caused by an unexpected touch, even clothed, nearly had him snarling, but when he jerked around, he caught the unguarded expression of wonder and anxiety on Nidar's face.

*Right. Staying put.*

Turk's singing rose in volume and pitch, the tingling delving deep into Isaac's bones. Suddenly, Turk tensed, the stone vanished, and in that moment, his singing cut off. Half a blink later, something smacked into the largest fern bulb a hundred meters directly in front of Turk.

Pale, breathing hard, Turk ran both hands over his face. "The stone was here." He held out his palm and then pointed to the fern. "Now it is there."

Murmurings ran through the Corzin as Turk retrieved the stone. He gestured for them to cluster around and when Isaac arrived, they parted and nudged him to the front so he could see. The stone lay in Turk's palm, twisted and elongated.

The Corzin seemed impressed, but thoughtful rather than overwhelmed.

"So," Turk said, "you see the problem."

"Or solution, I suppose, depending on who you are," Loric murmured. "You begin with the magnetic fields and then rotate them?"

Turk nodded.

"The increased rotation mimics a gyroscopic gravitational drive," Edar said, and again Turk only nodded, as if his head were on a string.

"A living GEM drive," Isaac confirmed. "Which is what the ESTO people thought could be used with devastating results."

"Only some of them," Turk protested softly.

"Right. What Ranulf wanted anyway." Isaac eased closer and took the rock from Turk to examine it. "It's like the early drive experiments. Before they developed the Mondal shields. Everything would end up stretched and twisted. Living things never quite… made it."

Turk's blue eyes shot wide. "They used live subjects?"

"Um, yeah. Small rodents. Wasn't pretty." He handed the stone back to Turk. "They didn't know better until they'd tried, hon."

"Ah." Turk blinked, coming down from some memory or interior vision that had obviously disturbed him.

"Anyway, seems to me that if you want this to work like a proper GEM drive, you need to shield what you're sending."

"Yes, thank you," Turk said with uncharacteristic irritation. Some of his men took half a step back.

"Yeah, yeah, you're a smart man. You thought of that already." Isaac patted his chest. "I'm still catching up. Thinking out loud. So why didn't you? Shield it, that is."

Turk heaved a breath. "I can't. Unless I wish to be caught in a backlash. Four notes I need to shield myself and send the object on. Four notes is all I can manage." The anguish crept back into his eyes. "I have *tried*."

"It's okay, babe. You're already doing the impossible." With his gloved hand still on Turk's chest, Isaac turned to the men. "Can somebody grab another stone, please? Turk, you're going to do it again. And this time, I'll watch."

"But you've already watched," Turk said in a puzzled tone.

"Now I'm going to watch the rest of it," Isaac said with as much bravado as he could muster. He reached behind his left ear and switched on his implant. The world as he knew it vanished, replaced by the alien strangeness of synesthesia where colors exhibited taste and forms took on a symphony of notes. "Damn. I don't think I'll ever get used to that."

He must have stumbled since strong arms, several of them, closed around him. Someone spoke, he was almost certain, but he couldn't make out the words. "Guys, it's all right. I won't be able to figure out what the hell you're saying with the implant on, but I'm okay. Just need to figure out which one of you is Turk…."

That proved to be the easy part. Turk's vibrations called to him, deep, clear notes of wine red and gold that tasted of sweet fennel and basil. He shone through the explosion of other fields, steadying him, anchoring him.

"Oh, there you are," Isaac murmured as he wove his way to Turk and wrapped him in his arms. This, oh, this felt good, all the strange nerve irritations banished from his skin. Turk spoke, and then shook his head when Isaac only laughed at the rumbling nonsense words. A large hand stroked his hair. Damn, he wanted a kiss. A real, honest-to-God, tongue-tangling kiss, but this probably wasn't the best time.

"Put me where you want me, big guy. Not seeing quite… I mean, if this is how you see all the time, I don't know how you do anything but stare."

The collection of perfect sensations that was Turk said something velvet and butter cream. The arms around him tightened and then moved away. Isaac bit back an anguished cry at the sudden loss but he held fast, letting the rhythms matched so perfectly to his own move away. A different arm circled his waist, probably to make certain he stayed put, but this one, while beautiful, failed to make him feel….

Complete.

God, that was what Turk had meant. This completion wasn't something poetic or figurative; it was a real, palpable force, this meeting of perfectly matched energies. *Sol'atenis*, the completed heart… now he had seen it, *tasted* it. He dashed tears from his eyes with an impatient swipe of his mint and clarinet-tone sleeve. Now was not the time to fall apart.

When he pulled in his scattered thoughts, it became easier to see Turk, to sort through the dizzying array of added sensory input and follow what he did. This second time, he saw/heard/felt/tasted the way Turk matched resonance with the rock's magnetic field, then reversed his field to lift it, from a deep, smoky blue to a blinding cardamom yellow-orange. Isaac saw as well the moment he sang his shield note, a wall of impenetrable anise-flavored purple.

He clutched the arm encircling his waist, his fingers digging in hard as the notes rose and the stone spun to a shrieking blur. He felt as if every hair on his body stood on end, vibrating like a tuning fork in resonance to Turk's bone-rattling chord. He gasped when the stone vanished, the temporary vacuum from the gravitational jump hitting him like a sonic stun to the chest.

Shaking, he reached up to turn off his implant and hung panting and shivering on the muscular arm that supported him. Edar's *atenis*, as it turned out, was not small in any respect on close examination.

"Are you well, *lochau*?"

The deep voice rumbled against Isaac's back as he struggled to stand on his own, mortified that he would have fallen on his face without support. That the young man was polite and called him "cousin" didn't make it any less embarrassing. "I think so. That was truly bizarre." He shook his head, trying to clear the after-images. "Do you really see the world like that? The fields have color and flavor and texture and they sing to you?"

Several sets of Corzin eyes, blue, green, hazel, and gray, blinked at him in confusion. "Isaac," Nidar began softly. "The fields sing to us, if we listen. We feel the vibrations. But I don't believe I've ever tasted one or seen it clothed in color."

"Oh." Isaac drew in a slow, shaky breath. "That would be a 'no, Isaac, just you,' then. You boys all think I'm missing a few key bolts, I guess."

"The Drak'tar have given you a new gift," Loric said. "It may prove a difficult one but this does not make you mad."

Turk returned with his second twisted, distorted stone. His hand trembled as he handed it to Isaac. "Did you see what you needed, my heart?"

"I think so, hon. You okay?" *Dumb question. He's half a shade shy of gray.*

But Turk nodded. "It tires me, nothing more."

"Can you do it again?"

His brow crinkling, Turk said, "For you, I would move planets, *atenis*. But why again?"

"I want to do it with you."

"You—" Turk appeared to work that over a bit and apparently came up empty. "I don't understand."

Isaac took his hand, squeezing his fingers. "Let me stand next to you or behind you or whatever you think will work. You said you couldn't shield both yourself and the object you're sending. Maybe someone else can."

"I haven't... at least not...." Turk looked like he desperately needed to sit down. "Isaac, *can* you even sing?"

Isaac shrugged. "I can try. What's the worst that can happen? We bend another rock?"

From the looks of unhappy speculation passing over his head, the Corzin obviously imagined numerous worse things happening.

With a strangled sound, Turk crushed Isaac to his chest. "I just now have you back. I can't bear the thought... I can't."

"Of what?" Isaac mumbled from where his face lay crushed against Turk's shirt.

"What if your implant reacts badly? What if your brain hemorrhages?"

Gently, Isaac pushed back. "What if a meteor screams through the atmosphere five minutes from now and lands on the exact spot I'm standing?"

"Please, please don't joke," Turk whispered.

A surge of irritation flickered through Isaac. He shoved back, hands raised. "Now, look, I know you went through hell and I know you took the trip twice over with me being mostly dead. But I'm not some pretty little flower you picked up on the concourse. Somehow, I survived a lot of years without you, big man, so I don't need you to protect me from every damn thing. I know you have some great big brass balls. You'd better find them again, or I'll start wondering where the man I fell in love with went."

Turk's pained expression quickly slid into an angry glower. Someone snickered and the glower became a challenging glare as he stared down his men one by one. The glare landed on Isaac and with an icy tone of offense, he said, "As you wish, then."

He strode back to the center of the clearing, held out a hand, and bellowed, "Stone!"

*There you are, my fierce warrior-poet.* Isaac hid his smile and waited while half the men searched the grass for a suitable rock.

Din scurried over to place an ovoid one in Turk's outstretched palm. Without turning his head, the *tach* then bellowed, "Isaac!"

Dress him down in front of his men, yes. Disobey an obvious order in front of them, no. Isaac raced to take his place at Turk's side without another word.

"You will stay behind me," Turk growled. "It is the only reasonably safe place. You will not distract me, interrupt me, or otherwise engage me. Do you hear?"

"Yes, *ka'tach*," Isaac murmured without irony, though blood rushed to his groin at a shocking rate. His love in command mode was breathtaking. He stood behind Turk, hands on Turk's waist so there was no question that he would stay put.

Turk quirked a brow at him but only said, "Good."

He turned to face front while Isaac reached back and switched his implant on again. Better prepared and better anchored this time, he managed to keep his feet and his wits as the world exploded in synesthetic symphony. When Turk began to hum, he tried, softly at first, to see if he could match the frequencies, and found he could. He laid his cheek against Turk's back, feeling their respirations and heartbeats match as well.

*Beautiful. So disturbing, but so beautiful.*

Turk began the first note and Isaac peered around him to watch the fields form again. The shield Turk created for himself was in harmony with his own resonance, but not matching. A complementary resonance seemed necessary for shielding. Up the scale or down? Which way? Did it matter?

He concentrated on the rock, honing in on only its resonance. It was the rock, that orange-copper lamb's wool light, he had to protect. Turk began the slow climb, increasing the rock's spin. Isaac opened his mouth, his throat, his vibrating nerve endings, and let out a note. At first, it jarred Turk's careful construct, but he adjusted up and matched tones with the rock's resonance. He found he could match not only frequency, but also color and feel.

His head spun. He planted his feet, and as Turk reached that critical point in his spin, Isaac dropped his note a third, hoping to create a shield for the rock. With a sharp crack, it vanished, and he knew without looking that it hadn't worked.

He fumbled behind his ear, panting, and switched off the implant. "Once more. I went the wrong way. One more time."

"Isaac...." Turk pulled in a long, shuddering breath. A fine trembling ran through all his muscles. "Once more."

He held out his hand again. Someone must have anticipated this since a stone was slapped into his palm almost immediately. This time when Isaac pressed the nub for his implant, he kept his eyes forward, completely focused on the stone. Again, he found the note to match the spinning bit of rock. Again, he waited for that critical frequency moment. When he took his note up a third, he felt something slide into place, a new field that had not been there previously, green to complement the rock's red.

The vacuum crack slapped his sensitive ears. The rock vanished to join the flight of its brethren into the fern trunk. With a soft sigh, Turk collapsed to his hands and knees.

"Turk!" Isaac clicked off, blinking, trying to see with his normal sight again. He dropped beside Turk even as he called out to the Corzin who had gone to retrieve the rock. "Did it work? Did it hold?"

The big man was panting hard, shaking his head in fretful movements.

"Sorry, hon. Pushed you just that much too far, didn't I?"

Isaac grinned when Din handed him the stone, though. It was whole and undistorted, the same stone, save for a small chip where it had struck the trunk. He held it out where Turk could see, if he was focusing at all. "Look, sweetheart, look! It worked. It's whole. Turk, do you see?"

"I see, my heart," Turk murmured, faint and shaky. "You were right."

"Does it always take him this way?" Loric crouched by his son, his face a mask of concern.

"Actually, no. The last time he overdid it, he passed out cold and was out for hours."

"Ah." Loric gave a sage nod and held out his hand for Turk. "A bit of practice yields improvement, then."

Isaac laughed, a near-hysterical sound, but the whole day had been too far west of strange. A little hysteria was in order.

A chirrup came from Loric's pocket. He fished out a hand comm. "Yes?"

"*Ka'dalk*? The *Hermes* is approaching in-system," an older male voice crackled through the unit.

"So soon? Have they taken damage?"

"It seems probable. But they have news. Best come in."

"On our way," Loric said even as he waved the men back to their vehicle.

Nidar and Din took Turk between them, got him on his feet and moving.

A few steps later, Turk lifted his head. "Nidar. Best if you drive back, I think."

"As you will, *ka'tach*. Always so wise," Nidar agreed with a nearly stifled chuckle.

# CHAPTER 16: PRECIPITOUS RETURN

ISAAC SAT on one of the floor cushions in the *katrak*'s communications room, Turk's head in his lap. Still shaky from exhaustion, his condition had caused his men a certain amount of alarm. Some had gone to the kitchen for food, several had offered water flasks, and Nidar insisted he lie down. The fuss embarrassed Turk and he knew it made Isaac uneasy.

"I will be well, *lochau*," Turk told his cousin irritably. "An hour, no more. It simply drains me."

Nidar offered a soft snort. "Making love with your stunning *atenis* would be draining. This took you out at the knees."

In a dry tone, Turk countered, "Isaac is perfectly capable of taking me out at the knees."

"Of that, I have no doubt," Nidar said with a laugh.

"Hush, boys," Loric admonished from his place at the comm bowl. "Karil, can you replay it?"

"We've cleaned up the transmission as much as we could, but it's broken and spotty, *ka'dalk*."

*Hermes... any... receiving....* Captain Drummond's image blinked and flickered... *repeat.... ESTO battle fleet.... T'tson heading... ship's braking da—... coming in hot... any in-system ship....*

"*Dalk* Tras?" Loric turned to the steadier image at the side of the bowl, the current station commander. "Do you have them?"

"Three carriers are on intercept. They have them on scan now."

Isaac's gloved hand tightened on Turk's shoulder in a painful grip. "They will slow them, *atenis*," he murmured, patting those clenched fingers. "Don't worry so."

"Magnetic tractors?" Isaac whispered.

"Something similar, yes."

To his surprise, Isaac slid out from under him and eased closer to the bowl when Captain Drummond's message looped again to the beginning. He stared intently at the flickering image, head cocked to one side.

Loric raised a brow at this odd behavior, but didn't shoo him off, as he would have one of the youngsters. "Isaac? What do you see?"

"Sir, I know the comm system on the *Hermes* like I know my own hands. Their braking systems might be damaged, but the comm isn't."

"What does this signify, *sulden*?"

Isaac didn't appear to take notice of all the eyes on him. With calm confidence, he pointed to a flicker. "You see that, sir? That's their signal being jammed. Whatever hostile force is chasing them, it's close enough behind them to foul their transmission but not close enough to kill it completely."

"So... so...." Loric folded his arms over his chest, fingers tapping on his forearm. "System's edge?"

"Seems most likely, sir. At least at the time of this transmission." Isaac glanced up, brows drawn together. "Could they disable your outer perimeter defense?"

"With enough firepower, yes. Eventually."

Turk sat up, his weariness dropping away with the promise of battle. "Father, if we've had no perimeter alarm come in...."

"Yes." Loric nodded. "It means we have prior warning and the advantage. One we dare not lose." He rose and every *tach* in the room rose with him as if drawn by invisible wires. "*Hai'kash!* Move! Karil, full alert, every *katrak*, every *dalk* on comm now!"

Isaac had scrambled to his feet at well and now hurried to him. "Turk? What's going on?"

"*Hai'kash,*" Turk said as he strode to the wall and hit the alarm that would send everyone scrambling for the practice yard. "Full mobilization. Every Corzin planetside."

"Full...? Won't that take days?"

"Oh, no." He took Isaac's face between his hands and granted him a quick kiss. "An hour, no more." He strode for the yard where the men had already assembled, Isaac trotting at his heels. "It has been a long while since we were called to defend our home from invaders. But we are always ready."

"And the ones not planetside?"

"There will be a recall sent to those on *ket'sa*. The station and outpost have already gone on alert."

Pride filled him to see his men assembling, each one steady and capable, at the peak of their fighting skills. They gathered around in a loose semicircle, the scene repeating with every *tach*, from the youngest group barely out of adolescence with his second-youngest brother, Ard, newly chosen to lead them, to the oldest, the white-haired, wily warriors who had survived eight and nine decades.

"We go out," he told his men. "Not to fight the *huchtik* wars for them, but to fulfill the covenant. Long ago, T'tson called us home, forged us into what we are. We fight for what is ours."

"Who is it, *ka'tach*?" Edar asked.

"An ESTO battle fleet has pursued a friendly ship to the system perimeter. We believe the ship was fired upon. These are not the actions of a diplomatic mission." Turk glanced from man to man. "If this fleet is led by the man I suspect, he has shown himself treacherous and dishonorable. We go out with every expectation of battle. Do you hear?"

"*Ka'tach*!" The answer roared from thirty throats.

"*Chautae*, make me proud. Twenty minutes and we reassemble at the transports."

The men dispersed. Isaac remained at his elbow. "*Ka'tach*?"

The respectful tone made him both proud and uncomfortable. This was his Isaac, who had held him through his madness, had coaxed him back from the brink, and yet, this was also his Isaac, who fought desperately to find his footing in a strange world.

"My heart?"

"Tell me what to do."

*Stay here with Uncle Jerit when we go to the shuttles. Be safe.* But he knew that was wrong. His Isaac might be small, but he was a warrior, trained in extraplanetary tactics. He could not be left behind like a child. "Come. We have a bit of packing to do."

Packing and a visit to supplies. Isaac needed deck shoes and a proper rifle, a *lau'ec* knife and comm headset. Anxious? Yes, he was that, but his *atenis* would wish to stand beside him in battle, the way his father's had, the way his brothers' and cousins' did, shoulder to shoulder, as it should be.


TWENTY MINUTES later, Isaac found himself climbing back into the odd flipped-turtle Corzin transport, this time armed as the Corzin were, as if he were one of them. A familiar tension ran through the men; he'd seen it many times with the Marines back home. Not quite as familiar was the surfeit of tender moments, while each partnered man took advantage of the downtime during travel to speak to his love, or loves as the case might be. As one of the unattached men, Din drove on their journey to the shuttle port.

Nidar had a young man on either side, one dark with granite-gray eyes and the other white blond. Their fingers intertwined, they spoke in low earnest tones and exchanged occasional kisses with Nidar and each other. No jealousy or rivalry seemed to shadow the relationship; in fact, Nidar's *aten'ae* appeared just as concerned with each other as they did with him.

*Don't stare, don't stare, it's not anything strange for them.*

Despite his best efforts, Nidar did catch him staring and shot him a quick wink, most likely meant as reassurance. Then he had no more attention to spare, since his blond *atenis* placed his head on Nidar's shoulder and the dark-haired one turned his face for a kiss.

"Must be exhausting," Isaac murmured to Turk, who sat with his arm slung around him.

"Perhaps some nights, it is," Turk said, so deadpan that Isaac knew he hid a smile.

"How do they pick who to sleep with?"

Turk turned to him with a puzzled frown. "Pick? They sleep with each other."

"All toge—" Isaac broke off in embarrassment. He wasn't some virginal innocent, but the images his fertile imagination conjured proved a bit too vivid. "Oh."

"Ah." Turk ran a hand back over his short crest. "I see. You thought perhaps they took it in turns."

Isaac choked on the unintended double entendre. "It's not like I've never heard of a threesome. Just wondered if they're always together."

"Always? No. But at the end of the day, Nidar will bellow if his Ges and his Tash are slow coming to bed."

Nidar lifted his head from nuzzling the blond's ear. "He makes me out to be a tyrant. If I go to sleep first, without having them settled, I'm woken by a storm of knees and elbows. Best to get everyone to bed at once."

"Of course." Isaac's embarrassment ratcheted up a few clicks. He would have to remember that Nidar's hearing was extraordinary, even for a Corzin.

A tightening of Turk's arm slid Isaac closer to his large beloved. Because Turk seemed to need something with all the touching going on, he planted a quick kiss on Turk's jaw, about all he could tolerate without serious distraction, and settled his head on a broad shoulder.

"Babe? Would you ever need a third?"

"No."

"No? You sound so sure." He gestured to the trio across from them. "Apparently, it happens."

Turk hugged him tight against his side. "With you, I am complete. Our resonances mesh. There are no empty spaces. For Nidar, when he met Ges"—Turk indicated the blond—"they both knew there were still parts in their pattern to fill. When they met Tash at an exhibition, they knew they had found the missing piece."

"Must be nice, to never be wrong," Isaac muttered.

"We are sometimes wrong. Especially when we are young and unsettled," Turk said softly. "Always sad to realize such a mistake."

*And you did, didn't you? My lonely warrior-poet....* While he would never wish Turk heartache, the realization settled comfortably in Isaac's chest. Despite what appeared to be a perfect system, the Corzin weren't perfect in their pairings and did experience the pain and humiliation of failed love.

This time their trip outside the city took them along well-traveled roadways where the traffic, once again, yielded without fail to Corzin transports. They drove between high cliffs that crowded and receded from the road as they traveled. Terraces cut into some of the shining malachite and scarlet cliffs, huge fields shielded by domes as if the terraces were giant greenhouses. As they passed a field closer to the road, Isaac made out carefully spaced clusters of plants. He recognized a knobbly topped one with bright blue pods as food.

*Greenhouses, that's exactly what they are....*

Each dome exhibited a different level of opacity, some completely transparent, others a gleaming, impenetrable blue-black.

"Wonder if they're semipermeable...."

"Hmm?" Turk turned his head to follow Isaac's gaze. "Ah. To gases, yes. The plants must breathe to grow."

"And rain? How do they get water? Wait... do they need water?"

A little laugh rumbled in Turk's chest. "Yes. They do. When it rains, the *selfau*, the domes, absorb the water. The plants receive it from the domes in mist form, carefully timed and measured."

"Clever. So who owns these... what? Farms?"

"Karsk Tor," Turk said, stroking his shoulder. "They are part of the city's food supply. Food is not a—" He shifted, apparently searching for a word. "—a commodity, as it is on other planets. The Drak'tar manage supplies carefully, always enough for everyone."

Isaac's brows furrowed at that. It sounded like a hellish amount of power to give one portion of the population. "Is food ever, um, withheld? For punishment? For political maneuvering? For personal gain?"

Beside him, Turk stiffened on a sharp intake of breath and then relaxed again. "No, my heart. The *ke'dra'en* are not Altairian merchants, nor members of the ESTO Board. Any shortage causes a *ke'dra* shame, though some cannot be helped. Seismic activity. Storm devastation. But how these disasters are managed can decide whether a *ke'dra* keeps her place. Chronic shortages, mismanagement of supplies, these will quickly bring about a change in who leads."

"Got it." Isaac patted his thigh with a gloved hand. "Thanks for not getting all hissy at me. They've tried things like this system on human planets. After the colony's settled and out of survival mode, never seems to work for long. But Drak'tar aren't human." *And Corzin aren't either, not anymore.*

His hand stilled on Turk's support-beam thigh. *And maybe I'm not either.*

Soaring cliffs and *selfau* terraces flashed by as their speed increased. Isaac craned his neck, watching for a break in the surrounding rock, the opening into plateau or valley that would signal their arrival at the shuttleport. Instead, the cliffs crowded closer, bumping shoulders and blocking the sun until rock loomed ahead of them as well.

*I know how this works now.* The clear space he had anticipated would be on the other side. Isaac settled back, confident in his knowledge that a door would open before they smashed into solid rock, smug for a moment when the rock face ahead rumbled and a hangar-size doorway slid open.

The smile eroded from his face, though, when a larger rumbling above caught his attention. *Earthquake* was his first thought. The top of the trapezoidal cliff before them shook. Then it moved and split. In a deafening rumble, the entire cliff top opened, two ten-foot thick halves rolling outward. Three silver teardrop shapes leaped through this topside opening, hovered for a breath like monstrous hummingbirds, and then raced off toward the exosphere.

"That's... different." The shuttleport wasn't situated behind the mesa, the entire mesa was the shuttleport. Someday, T'tson might run out of surprises for him. Today was not that day.

"I suppose it would be," Turk said. "Imagine my horror when I saw shuttleports open to the sky, exposed to storms and wildlife."

"Well, not every planet has killer storms and wildlife that's bigger than an apartment block," Isaac grumbled.

"Believe me, this was explained to me. Perhaps one of the reasons my ESTO hosts thought me somewhat dense."

Isaac stole a quick glance at his face, but it was calm and free of any bitter edge. Planet-bound folk could be such bigots. "Wait... hadn't you ever been on other planets? Out on *ket'sa*?"

Turk shook his head. "Stations. Lifeless moons. Asteroids. A good deal of time in the dark of space. But never someone else's planet before."

"The ships that just left? Were those...."

"Corzin shuttles, yes."

A wave of bitter envy surprised Isaac. He shivered and swallowed hard. If the shuttles were so beautiful, so sleek and deadly fast, how much more astounding would the cruisers be? The carriers? The goddamned fighters? *Stop it.* Carefully, he unclenched his fist. By now, the burning need to fly should have drained out of him. He thought it had.

"Isaac?"

"Do you pilot one?" his voice grated from him, scraped raw.

"Yes," Turk confirmed slowly. "But I don't need to. We have several—"

"Are you the best pilot in this bunch of loonies?" Isaac waved a hand at the vehicle's occupants.

Everyone watched, faces curious, expectant.

"He is by far the best of us," Nidar answered for him.

"Then fly, dammit," Isaac managed in a gentler tone.

Far too cautiously, Turk started, "Perhaps once we—"

"Don't!" He flung up a hand. "This isn't the time. When your planet's not in danger, then we'll talk about what I can and can't do now. Nice, long, sensible conversation." *Until then, just fly for me, love. Don't dangle impossible hope in front of me. I'll shatter.*

"Of course." Turk laced his huge fingers with Isaac's gloved ones, not badgering, not judging, simply there and solid.

*God, I love this man.*

Then they were driving through the stone portal, into the marvel of the 'port, and Isaac had no more time for old regrets. Inside, the space opened into a huge caldera. The walls retained a jagged, untouched feel, so Isaac suspected the space was the result of a natural volcanic event rather than an excavation. Teardrop shuttles littered the caldera's floor, no order immediately apparent, but no one wandered aimlessly or seemed to have any doubt about where they should be.

Din threaded their transport through pedestrians and other vehicles alike, singing to himself as if driving through such chaotic activity was enormous fun. He pulled up alongside a shuttle near the far end. Turk's men filed out and trooped into the belly of the shuttle, presumably waiting there with its bay door open just for them.

The inside of the beautiful ship was utilitarian sparse with the middle of the bay taken up by tie downs for gear and jump seats lining either side. Turk headed up front to the cockpit with Tash, who served as his copilot and comm operator. Isaac waited, unsure where to place himself, until Nidar tapped his arm.

"Come, *durhai lochau*. I'll help you strap in," he said with a closed-lipped smile.

"*Durhai?*"

Edar leaned down on his way to his own seat. "Because you are little and fierce."

"Ah." He would have to remember to have someone show him an image of a *durhai*.

Up front, the soft patter of flight and control checks began, a comforting ritual that seemed to change little from command to command. Engine mechanics and ship design might have wild variances, but the physics of flight and the necessary precautions remained the same.

The bay door hummed, powering closed.

"Isn't Loric coming?" Isaac asked.

"He will come last," Ges said on his left as he helped with a last stubborn strap. "He directs the *hai'kash* planet-wide, and then he will remind the children of their responsibilities."

"The... children?"

Edar answered from across the bay, tight-jawed and grim, "They are the last line of defense. If we fail."

Isaac stared at him, horrified, his careful adherence to cultural openness forgotten. "You've got to be kidding. Don't the Drak'tar have any defenses of their own? Besides you?"

Next to Edar, his *atenis* lifted a shoulder in a spare shrug. "They are not warriors by nature. Scientists, artisans, musicians, nurturers. Aggression in the males is all posturing and dies out when they become attached. There are stories in the early histories of females engaging in combat over territory and males. But that is long ago, and the females are so few, one for every thirty or forty males born, too precious to risk in battle."

"Our elders along with the Drak'tar will man the cities' defenses," Nidar added with a pat to Isaac's leg. "But we are realists. The turrets and shields will not hold long against a full military assault. Our children are instructed as soon as they can walk that if the defenses fail, they fall back to the *ter'as'lok*, the tunnel systems farther underground, to protect the *ke'dra'en* and make their stand."

Ges held out his hands, palm up. "You understand, then, Isaac, why we must not fail."

Isaac looked from one to the other, all so calm and matter-of-fact about possible calamity. "You make it sound like it's inevitable. We don't even know if the fleet out there is an assault force or what their objectives might be."

"We prepare for disaster, *lochau*," Nidar said. "So that it will not happen."

*Of course.* It was an odd philosophy, but Corzin to the bone. To anticipate the enemy in all things meant there could be no surprise, and without surprise, the enemy could have no victory. *God help me, I think I'm starting to understand them.*

The shuttle rose, nearly silent on mag-lift generators. Rumbling overhead heralded the huge port doors opening. Isaac followed the men's example and settled his comm set on his head. He had made certain to ask questions before this trip out and knew how to operate the unfamiliar equipment, what channels to use and what to expect to hear on them.

Thrusters whined as they powered up. Turk's deep rumble came over the channel. "Brace for launch."

The command was all the warning they had before the shuttle shot skyward, the sudden, shocking velocity reminiscent of GEM jump acceleration. *Fast, so fast, do the shuttles pull double duty as fighters?*

The Corzin practiced strict silence during the flight up. The only voices were Turk's, as he issued brief, quiet orders, and Tash's, as he spoke to ground and station control.

Somewhere above the planet, when the claws of gravity had slipped from them, Tash announced, "We have confirmation on the

*Hermes* from station. She has been secured. Inbound now. Arrival should be minutes before ours."

Isaac made certain his mic was off before he breathed an aching sigh of relief. Nidar still heard it and gave his arm a squeeze in sympathy. *They're safe, thank you, thank you.*

Relief gave way to exhaustion and he dozed off, sleeping fitfully until the clank of docking clamps jerked him awake. Next to him, Ges snorted and twitched, and he suspected many of the Corzin had been dozing as well. Typical soldier's reaction: sleep when you can.

As they filed out, Isaac had his first glimpse of the Corzin station, not so different from any other he had seen except for the corridor's height—well over the standard of seven feet on other stations—and the colors—greens, reds, and blues that echoed the planet's natural hues rather than gunmetal gray. He didn't have much attention for sightseeing, though.

He jogged a few steps to pull even with Turk. "Do we know if Captain Drummond's aboard?"

His large beloved nodded. "She is. We're heading for her now."

"Any word on casualties?"

"None yet. The captain has not been generous with details, perhaps anticipating that transmissions could be intercepted." Turk lifted his hand and brushed a kiss over his gloved knuckles. "Try not to worry so, my heart. We'll know everything soon."

Soon turned out to be around the next bend in the corridor. They turned the corner just as Captain Drummond with her officer cadre and Corzin escort turned the corner at the opposite end. Both parties stopped in a moment of stunned recognition. Singed, bedraggled, near falling-down exhausted, still the *Hermes*'s officers were among the most beautiful sights Isaac had ever seen.

"Captain!" he cried out and raced down the corridor.

She strode to meet him, arms held out to receive his impetuous charge, though the embrace was cut short when Isaac's oversensitive nerves screamed at him.

"Well, damn, son." She clapped him hard on the shoulder as she looked him up and down. "You've gone native on us."

"Didn't have much choice in that, ma'am." He smiled for her to erase any bitter taint from that comment and fought against self-consciousness over showing his teeth. "Everyone all right? What happened out there?"

Her smile fell. "We lost Lena in engineering. The rest I'll tell everyone in conference in j—"

"Oz!" Rand slammed into him, pounding on his back.

"Don't break him, boy!" Sylvia had caught up to them to add her arms to the mess. "It's good to see you up, Oz. Damn, we thought we'd lost you."

The fire needles ran along his skin. He couldn't draw a whole breath. Heart pounding, ears ringing, Isaac shoved away and backpedaled three steps, panting hard.

"Whoa, easy, bud." Travis held an arm out to warn the others back. "Okay there?"

"Yeah... yeah." Isaac pulled in a hard, frantic breath through his nose, knowing he looked too much like a spooked horse. "I... the operation, the one that saved me... I'm a little more sensitive now."

"Far better than it was," Turk said behind him. "At first, you could not have spoken to him at all."

Travis snorted. "A little more sensitive, he says. That's why the gloves? Can't touch things directly yet?"

"Things, yes. People, no." Isaac shook off the residual nerve-overload. "I'm sorry about Lena but I'm so glad none of the rest of you were hurt."

"I lost one of my techs and my *ship* was hurt," Captain Drummond said with a black scowl. "Damned ESTO scum."

"Captain, if you'd come this way?" One of the tall Corzin women playing escort gestured down the corridor.

She was an older woman with hints of white in her golden hair and a face made more beautiful by the scar she carried proudly beside her ear. Isaac thought she looked alarmingly familiar. She turned to inspect him, her bright cerulean eyes flashing with humor.

"Ma'am," Isaac ventured softly. "Are you—"

"Hello, Mother," Turk broke in, beating him to his conclusion.

"Good to see my beautiful sons," Krea inclined her head to Turk, Edar, and Din. "You look well." She turned her attention back to Isaac. "And this must be the new one Loric mentioned."

Isaac gulped, forced to tilt his head to stare up at her when she stepped closer. *Amazon. No, I doubt Amazons were this big and fierce.* "Isaac Ozawa, ma'am." Somehow, he managed not to squeak. "Now I see where Turk gets his incredible eyes."

She laughed, a low, purring sound. "A pretty thing but bold. You'll suit *ka* Turk well." She straightened from her examination. "Send your men to assembly, *tach*, while you come with us. You have more than a stake in this, I think."

All business now, Turk nodded. "Yes, *dalk* Krea."

With the *hech'zai* dismissed, Turk, Isaac, and Nidar joined the *Hermes* officers with their escort of three as they continued on to the conference room. The room was odd by most human standards, but exactly what Isaac had come to expect by Corzin ones. Instead of a table, a comm bowl occupied the room's center. Instead of chairs, cushions lay scattered on the floor. Those gathered were older Corzin, men and women, most likely the principal *dalk'ae* from each of the planet's Tors. Loric stood casually against the wall.

*How did he beat us here?*

"Loric." Captain Drummond strode forward, hand outstretched. "Good to see you in person."

"I'm relieved to see you well and whole, Captain," Loric took her hand and pulled her in for a brief, back-pounding embrace. "You had us worried downside."

He pointed around the room in brief introductions, too many names to remember, and then gestured for them all to be seated. Isaac took a seat by the wall, out of the way and unobtrusive, though Turk and Nidar settling one on either side of him made the whole "unobtrusive" part a little absurd.

"Captain, if you will? Now would be the time for a full briefing. Your initial warning, as you most likely know by now, reached us in pieces."

Captain Drummond remained standing so she could pace while she spoke. "Right. Jammed signal. Was afraid of that."

She swept the room with her gaze and nodded, apparently coming to some conclusion. "We were on our run to Poluteles. Little Treaty planet near the center of ESTO space. Not much there, but lots of the bigwigs have homes on the rock. Custom-terraformed luxury habitats, that sort of thing, so we've made specialty item runs out there before."

"After Luyten? Wasn't that dangerous, Captain?" Turk asked. He turned an incredible shade of pink, apparently surprised at his own interruption.

"Didn't think so." She shrugged. "We hadn't broken treaty or law. We were the ones fired upon. I'd wanted to lodge a formal complaint against Ranulf while we were in Treaty space. Not that I thought it would do much good, but I wanted the real story on the official records."

"Yes, ma'am. Your pardon."

A wave and grimace was her acknowledgement as she returned to pacing. "We never got there. At the edge of Treaty space, Mr. Wilde...." She nodded to Rand. "Picked up encoded transmissions. All sorts of military traffic in ESTO space, that's nothing unusual, but our scan officer has, hmm, a curious mind. He makes a practice of hacking into coded data."

"Just to, you know, keep in practice," Rand said in a small, defensive voice.

"No one's scolding, kiddo. Sure as hell not now. You were amazing," Travis reassured him with a nudge to his shoulder.

Rand blushed crimson and sat staring at his feet, obviously trying not to grin. *How many things did you mean by that comment, Trav?*

"Yes. Good thing he does like to keep up his hobbies," Captain Drummond continued, pointedly ignoring the byplay between her officers. "This particular transmission piqued his interest since he has his programs set to red flag certain words and phrases. The words 'Turk' and 'Ozawa' came up in this one. When he had the whole thing deciphered, we weren't sure which way to jump."

"I was sure," Travis growled.

"Perfect hindsight, Humboldt. Shut it." She stopped pacing, facing her audience. "What we'd intercepted was a transmission from Admiral Ranulf to his fleet officers. He was calling in his ships for what he called a 'heroic preemptive strike to secure the safety and freedoms of Treaty space.' He painted the Corzin as terrorists and lunatics, bent on the destruction of the rest of humanity, like you boys and girls are on some weird jihad. He doesn't seem to understand that there's a nonhuman culture involved in all this. Not that it would likely change his mind."

"Why would this man believe such a thing?" Krea asked, her expression blank and placid, which Isaac was coming to interpret as how a Corzin looked when fighting confusion or anger.

"I don't think he really does. That's the rhetoric for the troops. But there are a couple of things I'm sure he does believe. One, that Turk, turned loose from ESTO control, is too dangerous to let live. And, two, now that he's come home, that he'll somehow find a way to teach the rest of you how he does this GEM-drive thing with his brain, and then you'll all be too dangerous to let live."

"So. This is not simply a raid to reclaim Turk, is it?" Loric asked.

"No. It's not. This is premeditated genocide. He wants you all wiped out. As he says, for the safety of the universe, before it's too late."

Several growls followed this pronouncement.

Captain Drummond patted the air with both hands. "Yes, I know. At first, I thought we should go to the Board. Let them know what was really happening with their renegade admiral. Some of my officers didn't agree, stating it was just as likely that the Board, or enough of the members, were in collusion with Ranulf and we'd be locked up for espionage. In the end, we didn't have a choice. One of Ranulf's scouts tagged us on scan, ID'd us, and we had to run. The only place to run was here. With the Fleet already in motion, we had to warn you."

"Bravely done, Captain," Loric said. "Though it was a close thing."

"Sure as hell was. With anyone but Humboldt in the chair, we would've been a greasy stain on one of your outer asteroids." Captain Drummond wound down, sinking onto the cushion behind her. "So what now? Have you started evacuations?"

"Oh, no, Captain. The Drak'tar will not leave their home system." One of Loric's brows twitched up. "We do what Corzin were meant to do. We stand and fight. Like lunatics."

# CHAPTER 17:
# THE MDUPEL OFFENSIVE

"TURK!" LORIC barked out, shocking the non-Corzin in the room since he had been so soft-spoken previously.

Turk shot to his feet. "*Ka'dalk!*"

"Impressions of this man, this command. You have had a good deal of contact with him."

"The *krisk* slime who nearly killed my Isaac? Yes, I have." An ominous growl rumbled deep in Turk's massive chest. Isaac reached up to take his hand, hoping to forestall an explosion.

"Objective impressions, my boy," Loric said at his driest. "We know quite well how you feel about him."

Turk fell silent, brows drawn together. Finally, he spoke slowly, "They are heavily chain-of-command dependent, these ESTO Fleets. Little independent action is encouraged. I once witnessed the trial of a sergeant whose officer had died in the field. He could not reach command and had dared to countermand orders when the situation changed after the officer's demise. While his actions most likely saved his men, he was demoted for insubordination."

Murmurs of surprise and disbelief followed this. Turk shrugged.

"They call it discipline. I found it… dangerously restrictive." He sliced the air with one hand. "No matter. It remains that this is how they operate. Rank is everything. The man in the field is expected to follow orders."

Loric flashed a hint of white, even teeth, an expression hinting at savage aggression. "Mdupel offensive."

Turk chuckled. "Father, you have learned to read minds in my absence."

"Among other things." Loric's smile reverted to one of simple amusement. "So. So. You recommend we target the flagship only?"

"Do we have specifics on their numbers and ship types?"

Isaac leaned over to Nidar to whisper, "You following this?"

"The Mdupel are a hive society." Nidar leaned in close, careful not to speak directly in his ear. "You remove the head, and the rest lose their ability to act in concert."

"Oh, we've got specs, big guy," Rand said with a bright grin.

Several of the Corzin stiffened. Hands hovered over knives. Rand's head swiveled in alarm, his eyes airlock-wide.

"*Huchtik* teeth," Loric said as if he spoke a reminder. "Nothing is meant by it."

The scan officer turned to Isaac, squeaking, "What, Oz? What'd I do?"

"Your smile...."

Rand clapped a hand over his mouth. "It's that hideous?"

With a deep breath, Isaac fought down a laugh. *I've missed you, Rand, you idiot genius. I've missed you all.* "You can't show your teeth when you smile. It's, um, like yelling 'pussy-slave' in a bar full of Altairian Marines."

"Oh." Rand shot furtive glances at the surrounding Corzin. "Sorry."

Turk crouched in front of him. "Come, Rand Wilde. I know your heart. What do you have for us?"

"Oh yeah. Hey. I forgot how huge you are up close." Flustered, Rand ducked his head and fiddled with his wrist comm. He spoke without looking up. "Can you turn on your holo soup bowl thingy? So I can talk to it?"

Turk tapped the edge of the bowl with his foot and it hummed to life. Muttering under his breath, Rand's fingers flew over the pad until he breathed out, "Ah! Got it."

A visual from one of Rand's scanners on the *Hermes* bridge hovered over the bowl, blobs of light, large and small, representing ships.

Travis threw an arm around Rand's shoulders and pulled him close to plant a tender kiss on his temple. "That's my boy."

While Isaac gaped at such a public display, Captain Drummond merely gave them an indulgent smile and Sylvia rolled her eyes.

"Okay." Rand scooted closer to the bowl to point as he spoke. "This big mama toward the back? That's the flagship. New E-class galactic carrier. Biggest freaking thing floating out there right now. These four other big guys? Older carrier models. Still monsters. You got your cruisers—five; your destroyers—seven. Buncha little scout ships but you can't get a count on them, 'cause they're in and out and the IDs are, you know, cloaked and stuff. And eight smaller frigates for the whole set. No clue about troop counts, but you soldier types probably have a better handle on that than me."

Captain Drummond's jaw tightened during Rand's excited recitation. The *dalk'ae* all wore bland expressions that Isaac translated as grim.

"That damned new carrier is a monster, but her speed is frightening," Captain Drummond broke in. "That's how they nearly caught us. We came out of GEM jump in sight of your system perimeter, and that hellish thing deceled right on our tail before she fired on us. We had your codes, at least, so we lost her once we crossed the line and your orbiting guns turned on her."

Loric looked up from the display. "Turk, would there be high-ranking officers in any of these other ships?"

"Each ship would have its captain," Turk answered. "But the command will be clustered on the flagship."

His father nodded, pulling absently on his lower lip. "Captain, if you would remain with us? Turk, if you would take the rest to the assembly room."

Inwardly, Isaac bristled at being dismissed, but he knew the *dalk'ae* didn't need all of them hovering to plan. He tugged at Rand's sleeve and jerked his head toward the door.

"Mr. Wilde?" Captain Drummond spoke as her junior officers rose to leave. "Do we have everything downloaded?"

"Yes, ma'am." Rand grabbed Travis's arm when his leg buckled. Guilt stabbed at Isaac as he realized how much it must still hurt him. "I mean, not everything. There's, like, barge loads of data in those scanners. Don't want to overload stuff. But you've got everything on those ESTO fu—I mean, creeps."

"Thank you, Mr. Wilde," the captain said at her driest.

The juniors trooped out to leave the *katrak* heads to hash out strategy with Captain Drummond.

In the hall, Nidar leaned close. He shot a glance back at Rand and murmured, "Your *chautae* speaks oddly, but he is very lovely."

Isaac blinked. He'd never thought of Rand as "lovely" but then again, he did seem to have a beatific glow about him now. "Should I tell Ges you're thinking of additions?"

Nidar snorted on a laugh. "Do you hate me so, *lochau*? It was merely an observation. I am attached, not dead."

"Speaking of…." Isaac nudged Sylvia, who walked on his other side while Turk strode before them, playing guide. "How long have Rand and Travis been… like that?"

Sylvia tried to look disgusted, but a quirk at the corner of her mouth betrayed her. "Couple nights after Turk took you downside. Trav was so down. So… I dunno. He took the whole thing hard. One night at mess, he says to me 'No more wasting time, Syl. So many years wasted.' Then he marches over to sick bay, lifts Rand up in his arms, bad shoulder and all, and carries him to one of the bigger guest cabins. Rand's had that goofy, shit-eating grin on his face ever since."

Despite the fact that he knew it was too obvious, Isaac stole a look over his shoulder at them. Yes, Travis had given Rand his arm to support his bad leg, and yes, Rand's smile as he gazed up at the pilot was unabashedly goofy, but the transformation was amazing. Separately, they had been two relatively good-looking men. Together, they were breathtakingly beautiful.

"Huh." Isaac shook his head. So unlikely, so mismatched, so… perfect. *Yeah, I understand that.* He jogged two steps to catch up to Turk. "You all right, babe?"

One blond brow lifted. "I would ask you the same."

"I feel better than I have in a long while. But you look beat."

Turk tipped a shoulder up in a shrug. "I'll rest while we wait for battle plans."

"Guess that's the best I can hope for right now, huh?"

"My heart, when this is over, I will most likely sleep far more than you wish me to."

*Just get through it with me, big guy. Me, you, my crew, your crazy family, and all the Drak kids, and I'll sit and watch you sleep for a week. Promise.*

When they reached the door to the assembly room, Isaac stopped on the threshold of the most inappropriately named meeting space in the galaxy. This wasn't a room, it was an amphitheater, a stadium, a coliseum. A huge bowl rose in a gentle gradient from a circular center platform, doors dotting the sides at several levels, Corzin of both genders and, presumably, every *katrak* lounging on the curved floor. Dark heads peppered the crowd here and there, but shades of blond and red far outnumbered them. Regardless of coloring, most of these heads turned toward them as they entered.

"Oz," Rand whispered. "They're staring at us. Is this, um, a good idea? Us being here with all these...."

"Rand, don't."

"... huge badasses?"

While the bright colors Corzin preferred gave the assembly a festive air, Isaac understood Rand's hesitation. The crowd bristled with weapons, ferocious strength on display wherever the eye turned. So many....

And yet, except for the two hundred out on *ket'sa*, this was the planet's entire Corzin population. The planet's entire defense system had gathered in this one room. Suddenly, the collected Corzin didn't seem nearly enough.

He pointed Rand toward a space halfway down the bowl. "There's our boys."

"Our boys?" Travis's brows crept up.

"Turk's boys. That's where we belong." *Yeah, our boys. That came out way too easy.*

They wended their way through groups, picking their way around long limbs. When they reached Turk's *hech'zai*, Nidar flopped down between Ges and Tash and received a kiss from each. Rand's eyes, which hadn't returned to normal size since entering the room, threatened to swallow his face. His head swiveled as he took a slow scan of the room.

"Oz," he choked out. "They're all...."

"Yes?" Isaac prompted, though he knew exactly where Rand's shock lay. "They're all huge? Gorgeous? Scary?"

Rand glared at him. "Don't be a smartass, Oz. They're all *g-a-y*."

"What are we, eight? You don't have to spell it, bud. And, yeah, I can't speak for all Corzin, but the vast majority is gay. You have a problem with that?"

"No." Rand blushed and ducked his head. "Pretty damn stellar, actually. Just didn't, you know, expect it."

Turk patted his shoulder. "Never fear. It took Isaac by surprise as well, *chautae*."

Rand blinked up at him. "What happened to the other thing you used to call me? The hatra thing?"

"You are *hatra'os* no longer," Turk said softly as they settled to the floor. "You come back to us attached, a grown male."

Face far redder than his hair, Rand retreated to fiddling with his wrist comm, obviously too embarrassed to respond. Travis rescued him with a nudge, suggesting, "Show Oz the new carrier's specs. Bet he'd appreciate that."

"Oh yeah, that's right. I'd meant to." Rand leaned forward, turning his wrist to let his personal holoimager project into the middle of their little group. A miniaturized version of the mammoth ship appeared, turning slowly. "There's the monster. See the Snowden thrusters? Five times bigger than anything tried before. Don't know how they solved the vibrational problems, but they must have or the whole damn ship would shake apart."

Isaac found himself drawn into the familiar spacer activity of analyzing other people's ships. "Gun decks?"

"Turrets all the hell over the skin. Retractable during GEM flight. Two actual gun decks, amidships, both sides. Enough firepower to take out a...." Rand stopped midsentence. His mouth snapped shut.

"A planet, one would assume," Nidar supplied in a too-calm tone.

Rand nodded, puppet-like. "Well, yeah, maybe not a whole planet. Small moon, probably. Definitely cities."

"Fighter complement?" Turk asked softly.

"Not sure. Couldn't get *all* the specs. This is still pretty classified stuff. But the hangar bays are about double what a Red Star–class carrier has."

Ges tugged at his braid. "Twelve fighter squadrons, at least, then."

"Yeah, give or take." Rand tapped, lighting up different areas of the ship as he went on, his enthusiasm somewhat dampened, his embarrassment obviously growing as every Corzin in earshot crowded around to get a look. "Engineering, crew quarters, bridge…."

"Wait, Rand, go back." Isaac tilted his head for a better look. "Back to the bridge. That's odd looking."

"What?"

Travis pointed. "Those thick bulwarks, the ones separating the bridge from the rest of the ship. Most ships have sealable sections, sure, but I've never seen this before. Seems like an inefficient use of space."

From a pilot and a veteran spacer, those were damning words indeed. Every centimeter of space on an interstellar vessel had to have some purpose, and these bulwarks….

"Rand? Are there written specs? Raw data?" Isaac prompted.

"Oh, sure. Didn't think you'd want to see the *boring* stuff, Oz," Rand grumbled as he switched to text.

"Just the bridge specs," Isaac murmured as the data rolled by. "Just the… there. Trav, do you see it?"

"Huh. I'll be damned."

"What?" Rand tugged at Travis's sleeve. "What?"

"Look here, babe." Travis outlined a bit of text between thumb and forefinger. "You see this bit? For detachable bulkheads? The whole damn bridge can separate from the rest of the ship. So if the ship's in trouble—"

"Fuckers," Rand snarled. "The brass can bail. Screw the lifepods. Screw the crew. Independent thrust engines I'll bet… yeah, there they are."

Nidar's auburn brows nearly met over his nose. "So if the ship is damaged, the ship's commander would *leave*?"

Angry mutters from the surrounding Corzin showed just how they felt about this notion.

"I suppose it's just for the worst emergencies," Isaac said, though he wasn't at all certain. "In-system flight wouldn't get them too far, after all. Wouldn't be practical for something that small to have its own GEM drive." He watched the data scroll by a few moments more. "You don't see one, do you, Trav?"

"No. Nice in-system setup, though. I've seen private envoy clippers with less power."

Murmuring farther down the bowl drew their attention, and the Corzin scattered to resume their places as the *dalk'ae* strode in. Isaac had always thought of Captain Drummond as a tall woman, but the Corzin dwarfed her until they settled around the edge of the central platform. The captain remained standing with Loric, her outward calm matching his.

Loric raised a hand and all murmuring ceased. In a voice that filled the amphitheater, he declared, "*Te'ha'dach!*"

Several thousand voices answered, the vibration so powerful Isaac's vision tunneled. "*Sil'dalk!*"

*Sil'dalk?* In that moment, Isaac realized that this normally soft-spoken, good-humored man whom he had pestered with questions was not merely the head of his own *katrak*, but the commander of every *katrak'ae*, all Corzin, everywhere. A moment of sudden disorientation swept over him, a vertiginous disconnection from his body and his surroundings.

"*Atenis?*" Turk whispered in his ear.

Isaac took his hand and twined their fingers together. One solid point in a universe that insisted on shifting and bending wherever he turned. One solid point was all he needed. *Where am I? Here, with him.*

He shivered and shifted closer to Turk as he tried to concentrate on what Loric was saying.

"...that which we had hoped never to face." Loric stood with his feet planted shoulder-width, arms crossed over his massive chest. "But that which, ultimately, we have spent our lives preparing to face.

"When we reached out to the universe again after centuries of isolation, the *ke'dra'en* hoped for civil diplomacy, exchange of ideas, perhaps even trade. What we have encountered instead is bigotry, jingoistic bureaucracy, and a man who seems to think the universe is his to order as he pleases."

He nodded to the captain standing beside him. "Captain Drummond assures me that the human universe has other people in it, other ways and solutions, other laws that would protect us. But she also assures me that any help we might request could well arrive too late. It is with the clarity of hindsight that we realize we might have been better served learning to understand the *huchtik* when we went out on *ket'sa* rather than using their wars as our training ground."

He went on to explain what they faced and played the part of Admiral Ranulf's message to his fleet where he described the deadly consequences of leaving even one Corzin unit alive. The bowl rumbled with angry indignation, several younger Corzin rising to their feet, only to be pulled back down by more cool-headed comrades.

"So... so." Loric turned off the message, for a moment looking simply like a tired, worried father.

*Nine... he has nine sons, seven of fighting age, two young enough to be left behind as the planet's last defense. How many will he lose?*

He raised his head from his contemplation of his boots. "As Sun Tzu has taught us, we must engage the enemy with what he expects. They will respond with what they have already planned, while we prepare the unexpected. The extraordinary moment."

With a courteous wave, he ceded the floor to Krea. She repeated the greeting Loric had shouted and the gathered Corzin answered in identical fashion. Sil'dalk. *Two of them. Of course.*

"Our best course of action, given what we have learned from our *Hermes* friends and *tach'*Corzin Turk, is to mount a Mdupel offensive. From what the Treaty forces know of us, they will expect and anticipate this tactic. They must believe themselves fully capable of protecting their flagship in the face of our attack. It is imperative that we appear to strike at them with all we have at our disposal. They will think us desperate and lacking subtlety."

Several heads in the crowd had cocked to the side; many expressions remained puzzled. The Corzin were waiting for the payoff. Krea paused, scanning her audience.

*And here it comes....*

"We will designate two squadrons as a *chu'tsou* strike force, their sole purpose to infiltrate the ship and take the command center. When we have Ranulf, we have the fleet."

"*Ka'dalk?*" a woman with bloodred hair called from the front, one of Krea's own since she addressed her as "*ka.*" "Who will be chosen for the strike force?"

Every Corzin in the room seemed to strain forward, waiting for who would be given pride of place.

"*Tach'*Corzin Turk!" Krea called out. When he rose, she asked him, "Do you have cause against this man Ranulf?"

A growl rumbled in Turk's chest. "*Sil'dalk,* I have cause."

"Is your cause just and honorable?"

Turk's chin rose a notch. He squared his shoulders and declared, "Before those assembled, I claim just cause. Ranulf kidnapped and tortured my *sol'atenis* for the purpose of extorting my cooperation. My Isaac nearly died and he will bear the effects of that abuse for the remainder of his life."

Krea lifted a hand, palm up, and addressed the gathering, "Does any voice speak against just cause for Zadral *tach'*Corzin Turk?"

Heads swiveled between Turk and Krea but no one spoke. She nodded, apparently satisfied. "Turk's *hech'zai* will be half the strike force. *Tach'*Corzin Liga, who has more success than any other in *chu'tsou* attacks, will lead the other half."

An older woman, her dark hair streaked with silver, rose at the back of the crowd to acknowledge. Her selection sparked no objections, either.

"So." Loric rose again. "Your *dalk'ae* will tell you your place in formation. Fight well, fight hard, *chautae*. Quarter is to be given wherever possible, aid where you deem necessary. There is no honor in slaughtering those who have no voice."

The meeting broke up as each *katrak* zeroed on their own *dalk*, the single assembly becoming several dozen. Loric came and embraced the three sons who belonged to Turk's *hech'zai* and sent them off to prepare in whatever way they felt necessary.

Out in the hall, Nidar stopped Turk and took him by the shoulders. "Find a bunk. Go rest. We are competent enough to run flight and weapons checks without you."

"But the flight path, the mineral scans—"

"Is this how the *huchtik* taught you to lead, brother?" Edar said with a snort. "That you do not trust your men and must do everything yourself?"

Turk flushed and dropped his gaze in obvious embarrassment, though he still made no move to leave them.

"What kind of attack is this?" Isaac asked, as much to distract them as to satisfy his curiosity. "This *chu'tsou?*"

"It's taken from an ancient tactic," Din answered quickly as he looked between his brothers in alarm. "And means 'from beneath.' Of course, there's no beneath in space, but the use of rocks as camouflage remains the same."

Edar's *atenis*, Hrell, touched his arm, a far better distraction. "They will look for ships. We will be nothing but space debris to them until we clamp on and board."

This explanation didn't do much more than hint at what was meant, but Isaac wasn't given a chance to probe further.

"It's only sensible, I suppose," Turk spoke as if the conversation hadn't gone on without him. "And Isaac should go to his *Hermes* shipmates, now that they are here."

"Whoa, hold on, hon." A frisson of irritation skittered over his nerves. "You think you can arm me, treat me like one of your boys, and then shove me aside as soon as it's convenient? Who do you think I *was* before you met me, anyway?"

Turk blinked at him, his eyes so tired and lost that Isaac almost felt bad for badgering him. Almost. "You were the communications officer for the *Hermes*."

"Out of necessity! I was *Fleet*, damn it!"

"But this is not your fight. You aren't Corzin...."

"Really? Hadn't figured that out myself. Thanks." Isaac wiped a hand over his face to stop his bitter sarcasm midstream. "No, I'm not. I'm kid-sized compared to you monsters. I probably can't stand up to the smallest one of you hand-to-hand. But this is ship-to-ship warfare, babe. This is what I trained for. And we're not fighting other Corzin. We're fighting people my size."

"Captain Drummond—"

"Has been doing fine without me."

Nidar folded his arms over his chest. "Can you use the weapons you carry, little *durhai*?"

"Try me."

Turk threw up his hands in evident surrender. "Well and fine. I will go find a bunk. Nidar, take Isaac to the firing range. He earns his place like any other. If he proves competent, he joins the attack."

"Sensible, as always, *ka'tach*," Nidar said with a little smile.

Isaac stood on tiptoe to plant a quick kiss on Turk's lips. "Thank you. That's all I ask. I want you to be proud of me."

A little sound caught in Turk's throat, difficult to tell if it was a laugh or a frustrated grunt. "How could I not be, my heart? You outflank me at every turn." He crushed Isaac close and then set him back abruptly to turn and wander off down the hall.

"Do I push him too far?" Isaac asked softly of Turk's brothers and cousins.

"Not yet, *lochau*," Edar answered. "But it's not difficult to tell when you've pushed Turk too far. You generally end up on the ground."

"Eating your words or eating sand," Tash added with a nudge at Nidar's ribs.

Nidar let out a sharp laugh. "Sometimes he needs to be pushed. One simply needs the courage to do so."

# CHAPTER 18: *CHU'TSOU*

"CARESS THE trigger, Isaac," Nidar instructed. "A Corzin rifle is not a weapon. It is an added limb. Treat it as you would your cock, and you might do better."

Isaac lifted his head from the rifle. "What, you don't jerk yours?"

"Nidar prefers a gentler touch," Ges offered from where he leaned against the wall.

"Some men prefer subtlety and variety over a sledge between the eyes," Nidar countered at his driest. He waved off the teasing. "You have the feel for it, Isaac. Simply a matter of becoming accustomed to different mechanics."

*Weird that everything sounds like double entendre today.*

Of course, Nidar was right about the rifle. The pistol was similar enough to Isaac's old Fleet-issue model not to cause him problems, but the plasma rifle had considerably softer, quicker action than what he'd used before. His initial shot group had been almost nonexistent.

*Have to hit the target to* have *a shot group.*

More comfortable with the weapon on the second round, he managed a respectable torso grouping on the far holotarget and connected eight out of ten times on the pop-ups.

"Will he do, love?" Tash called out from beside the door.

Nidar frowned. "Needs practice. I'd like to see a tighter grouping...."

"Nidar! Don't torment Isaac," Ges scolded. "Do you judge he can handle the weapons or not?"

His expression far too serious, Nidar gave him a short nod. "He'll do. But when this battle is over, there will be practice...."

"No more lying around eating bonbons, is that it?" Isaac laughed. "We get through this, I promise to practice till my fingers go numb."

Nidar escorted him back through the corridors to one of the huge bays lined with round bunks. While only four *hech'zai* manned the station during normal operation, the structure had obviously been built with battle-ready capacity in mind.

In a bottom bunk near the door, Turk lay curled on his side, thick blond lashes caressing his cheeks as he slept. Isaac realized they had both stopped in the doorway to watch him.

He looked up at Nidar. "You love your cousin very much, don't you?"

"We were born on the same day," Nidar offered as a nonanswer. "Closer than most brothers. When we were younger, I was sometimes jealous of him. His greater size and strength. His calm when he should have been angry or frustrated. But mostly I admire him. Do not, under any circumstances, tell him I said that." He shot Isaac a wink and then grew serious again. "There is a superstition that says cousins born together will die in the same hour. So I have a selfish interest in his health and happiness, eh?"

"I suppose you do, then."

He wandered in, wavering between a desperate desire to curl up beside Turk and a wish not to disturb him. Curling up won. He set his rifle beside Turk's in the nearby rack, pulled off his boots and slid onto the mattress. The big man shifted, settling an arm across Isaac to pull him close.

Without opening his eyes, he spoke. "You should be angry with me. And still you are here."

Isaac ran gloved fingers over his crest. "Why would I be mad at you?"

"Calling your training and your skill into question. In front of others. Had that been one of my cousins, there would have been a brawl."

"Good thing I'm not one of your cousins, then."

Turk settled his head on Isaac's shoulder just as he had when he was at his most lost and distressed. It seemed an apology and a tender affirmation all at once.

SMOOTH SKINS gleaming under the bright hangar lights, an inner life inhabited the teardrop-shaped fighters, as if they might dart out unmanned were someone foolish enough to open the bay doors, a school of bright silverfish set to devour the fabric of the universe.

"One-man craft," Turk pointed. "And two. Each squad has four of the single crew ships and one of the double crewed."

Isaac pointed in turn as well. "More speed in the one, more firepower in the other?"

"Just so, my heart." Turk ran his hand over the sleek side of the nearest two-man fighter. "This one is ours."

"So I'm your… gunner?"

"Scan, guns, yes."

"Am I displacing someone?"

Din clapped him on the shoulder. "I am pleased to be displaced. Now I will *finally* fly on my own."

"Which may be a blessing or a curse," Edar muttered as he wandered past to his own fighter.

"The light troop transport"—Turk nodded to a larger craft a few meters down the bay—"is *tach*'Liga's. Any wounded, any prisoners, we have transport for them. That, and the transport has the best equipment for boarding."

The short nap had done wonders. The prickly irritation had vanished, the weary confusion cleared from Turk's eyes. A soft note, oddly tender and poignant, rose from him as he reached out to touch the ship's canopy. Isaac blinked in shock when the ship hummed back, purring as the skin separated and slid away to expose the cockpit.

Terrible longing trembled in Isaac's stomach. *The ship talks to him, without an implant, without any artificial enhancements. I want this ship, oh, God, I want to fly… maybe with the improved implant. Maybe someday….*

A shudder ran through him as he stuffed his rampant desire into a locked mental closet. He couldn't even see straight with his enhanced implant turned on and now was not the time for experiments. He redirected his energies into absorbing all Turk's instructions as he explained the scan equipment and the gun controls. Everything had a smoother, less angular feel than Isaac was accustomed to, but the principles remained constant. In this, his size had no bearing and he could be as competent as any of his *chautae*.

"We will be running nearly silent, so we hope not to use the guns on the approach." Turk put a finger under his chin and pulled his attention away from the console. "Are you ready?"

"Yes, *ka'tach*."

A little smile tugged at the corner of Turk's mouth. "For you it should be *hei'tach*, not *ka*."

"Oh... why?"

"'Mine' rather than 'ours.'"

*Don't leave me today. Don't leave me alone like Loric's* atenis *did.* He gazed into those summer-sky eyes and managed a Corzin smile. "Mine. I like that." Arms wrapped around Turk, he burrowed against his quilted jacket as he allowed himself a moment to let Turk's scent wrap him close as well.

A few weeks ago, the lack of body armor might have surprised him, but he knew how the Corzin fought now. They created their own vibrational shields and refused to be weighed down with unnecessary layers.

Most likely, there would be lives lost on both sides, but they had surprised Isaac with their desire to avoid slaughter.

"It'll look better if there are live soldier boys and girls to hand back when you're able to contact the other governments," he had urged Loric in a private moment. "Go a long way to debunk the propaganda about Corzin as savages."

Loric had patted his shoulder. "We realize, *sulden*, never fear. I suspect most of the enemy will be little more than children."

So the Corzin dreadnoughts had orders to disable rather than destroy whenever possible and the boarding parties were to leave their weapons on stun pulse except in dire need.

They had confirmation that the ESTO fleet had punched a hole in the system's perimeter defense, the small outpost force retreating to join the main Corzin fleet at all possible speed. Across some systems, it would have taken days for the enemy to reach the planet, but T'tson lay too near the system's outer edge. A day at most to make contact, half that if they charged out to meet the incursion as they intended.

"You will need to remove a glove, my heart," Turk urged, half his attention on the ship.

*Why?* immediately leapt to Isaac's tongue but he bit back the word. *Ka'tach* or *hei'tach*, Turk was the field commander here. If he wanted to be part of this, to be an asset rather than a burden, he had to take orders without question like everyone else.

He peeled off his right glove and watched with growing curiosity as Turk pressed his naked palm against the little two-man fighter's skin. Smooth and warm, the ship hummed under his hand. *It feels alive. That can't be, can it?*

"Now she knows you," Turk explained softly. "And will respond to you."

"She does?" Isaac pulled his hand back, rubbing at his tingling fingers. "Is there a symbiont? Is it...."

"No, love. The ship isn't alive in the strictest sense. Think of her as a... highly responsive AI, able to respond to her environment independently of human control."

He blinked up at Turk, feeling absurdly dense. "So, wait. Do you really need me at all?"

"Yes. She will not fire her guns on her own. That requires a human hand."

He did his best to concentrate on the moment while Turk ran through the scan controls, oddly similar in placement and structure to the ones he'd trained on.

Isaac climbed in to take the seat Turk indicated and the big man took his place in the pilot's chair, the two crew seats back to back. The ship purred as she closed her canopy above them, a comfortable space for Isaac, a mere two inches of headroom for Turk. Moments after the ship had them safely cocooned, the klaxon sounded the vacuum warning. Several Corzin swung themselves into ships with what Isaac thought was too-casual bravado. As soon as the door sealed on the troop transport, the huge bay doors clanked, beginning their slow slide open onto the field of stars.

A dizzying feeling of *déjà vu* swept over Isaac as the ship edged toward the dark. This time he wasn't driving and this time Turk was at his side rather than dying in a grim prison cell. *Still....*

"Full circle, babe."

"Is it?"

"For me it feels like it. Last time I saw that view was when I was going out into the dark to retrieve you."

"Ah. Have I mentioned how grateful I am that you found me?"

Isaac chuckled. "You've thanked me for saving you, yes. Most beautiful thank you I ever got."

"Not merely for saving me. For finding me, for not giving up." Turk eased the ship out at the head of their fighter formation. "The universe is circular, I think."

"Could be."

"So many things are forced into circular shapes by gravitational attraction. The universe must be as well. So must all things, in the end. Infinitely circular."

"My warrior poet, you pick bizarre times to wax philosophic."

Turk reached back, squeezed his hand, and then fell silent as he turned his attention to the system readouts and his ship's demands. They headed out ahead of and in the opposite direction from the main attack fleet, which would wait until they were well on their way. Their initial goal was the asteroid ring between T'tson and its nearest outer system neighbor. Isaac understood the maneuver was about camouflage, but he didn't understand yet how they would reach the enemy fleet by going in the opposite direction.

As they approached the tumbling, spinning field of rocks, sized from gravel to small moon, Turk spoke into his headset. *"Tach 'Liga?"*

*"I hear."*

"Single formation?"

*"Group your fighters, tach. A single formation this size will ping on the scanners. We are debris, nothing more."*

"Understood." Turk issued orders, his fighters closing into tight squad formations, each quartet of single-man fighters encircling their respective two-man.

The ship's vibrations shifted abruptly, dropping in register until they rattled Isaac's bones. He twitched and panted, wishing he could leap up from his seat.

"Hold fast, *atenis*. A few minutes at this resonance, no more," Turk's deep voice barely reached him through the droning bass hum. "This sector is awash in iron-rich rock. Find me a grouping."

Arms wrapped tight around his torso as if he could keep his ribcage from splitting that way, Isaac forced his attention to the scanner displays on his left. "Thirty-six port, fifty-three below." He sent the data to Turk's display with shaking fingers. "Is it enough? For whatever you're planning?"

"More than enough, my heart. Deep breaths. There's a vacuum tube on the right side of your chair if you need it."

Isaac nodded, gulping against his nausea, understanding him perfectly. Nothing worse than puking one's guts out in zero-G and then having the results floating around one's head for the rest of the flight.

Turk's squad matched velocities with the grouping of rocks Isaac had pointed out. Most of these were smaller, no bigger than the ships, though two of the single-man fighters fired plasma bursts at the larger pieces to make them smaller still.

The ship's hum dropped even farther and Isaac ground his back teeth, doubled over his console as the sound drilled through his head. Abruptly, the droning hum ceased, and Isaac raised his head to gape at the scans. "Babe...."

"Hmm?"

"We're covered in rocks."

Turk twisted in his chair, brows drawn together. "I thought you understood what to expect."

"I, ah... well." Isaac cleared his throat. "I thought it was going to be more like using asteroids to hide our approach, not pasting them to the hull. Magnetically, I assume?"

"Yes. The rock skin will make us appear to be just that, a jumble of asteroid debris. Our opponent's sensors will dismiss us if all goes well." Turk put his hand over his heart. "The fault is mine, *atenis*. I will try to learn to explain things better to you."

"S'okay, hon," Isaac said with a wry smile. "You'd think I'd learn to ask better questions. So we head toward the flagship now?"

Turk nodded. "In no recognizable formation. We must appear as naturally occurring debris."

Isaac blinked, struck by an ancient image. *"Till Birnam Wood do come to Dunsinane...."*

"I don't understand."

"It's an old story about a man so driven by ambition that he uses everyone around him, throws all honor out the window, to get what he wants."

"And does he succeed?" Turk's gaze was back on his screens, head still cocked in an attitude of listening.

"For a short time. Then he's defeated by people he betrayed."

"Ah. It sounds like a good story for a stormy evening. You must tell me the whole of it someday."

"Promise."

Liga's voice filtered through the comm again, telling them to proceed. They orbited with the asteroid field until the field of battle came up on short-range scanners. The Corzin dreadnoughts arrowed in a deadly phalanx toward the heart of the ESTO fleet, their trajectory on a direct line to intercept the monstrous flagship. Anticipating this attempt, the ESTO battleships closed ranks, the smaller frigates moving out ahead of their line to harry the dreadnoughts, the carriers spewing fighters like milkweed seeds.

Progress halted, the Corzin ships appeared hopelessly outnumbered as their own fighters spilled from the ships in answer. Plasma fire bloomed on scan. Weapons Isaac had no name for disabled ESTO fighters, leaving them adrift and a hazard for their own forces. A Corzin fighter bloomed in a nimbus of light and vanished.

*Oh God. That was someone's* atenis *or brother or sister....* Isaac swallowed hard against an unbidden lump. The possibility that many more would die simply made it vital that they succeed as quickly as possible.

Turk's squadron broke from the asteroid field, hurtling toward the flagship as if a rock had been struck by a larger mass and flung out of its normal orbit. Most big ships had impact shielding to handle rogue debris, so the flagship's scanners wouldn't raise any alarms unless they recognized something other than rock.

"All of our ships follow?" Turk asked, intent on his flight path.

"Everyone accounted for."

While they had no visual inside their rock shield, Isaac felt the weight of the flagship pressing down on them as they drew alongside. They had agreed that cutting into the supply hold would be best, most likely short-staffed during an attack and seven decks directly below the bridge. The troop transport did the cutting, the high-powered plasma saw knifing through the hull while grapples secured the temporary airlock over their improvised entrance.

Once the troop transport was empty, the fighters broke from their squadrons one by one, nestled up to the airlock, and gave up their pilots. The ships, once abandoned, were smart enough to move out of the way for the next disembarkation. The whole operation took just under twenty minutes, with Turk and Isaac easing up to the airlock last.

Turk touched the canopy and the little ship opened just enough to let them out. Isaac unstrapped, lurching with the momentary disorientation of unsecured zero-G, and then launched himself with practiced ease through the airlock's tube. The outer lock cycled, the inner lock opened, and several strong hands caught him as he thumped out into the artificial ship gravity. Turk followed a few seconds after, nailing his dismount with considerably better grace.

Both *hech'zai* were gathered together, crouched behind storage crates, rifles held ready. It would be difficult to surprise them since the Corzin could sense the magnetic fields of living things, but that didn't mean they would have a clear shot all the way to the bridge.

"The hold is clear?" Turk crouched next to Liga, his voice a spare whisper.

"Two on duty. Tik stunned them when they came to investigate."

He nodded and rose, rifle aimed toward the door. "Nidar, go."

With Ges and Tash at his heels, Nidar raced for the next storage container cover. He checked front and held up his fist, the signal for the next group to leapfrog in front of them. In eerie near-silence, the Corzin squads glided from cover to cover, traversing the hold in efficient, disciplined fashion, never bunching up, never losing track of their surroundings. Isaac simply concentrated on staying with Turk and not tripping on his own boots.

Corridors on the lower levels in this part of the ship stood empty. Their personnel were most likely at battle stations. Either security and bridge staff had been overconfident or overly distracted by the battle raging outside, but no one challenged them or even spotted them until they had reached the deck three below the bridge.

When they did make first contact, it was with a skinny clerical type hurrying around the corner on an obviously urgent errand. Far enough down the corridor that the Corzin hadn't yet sensed him coming, he squeaked and pelted back the way he'd come. Din's shot clipped his shoulder but didn't slow down his panicked flight. When alarms sounded a heartbeat later, they gave up pursuit and raced full-out toward the access ladder to gain the next level.

The Corzin swarmed up, almost as if their feet didn't need to touch the ladder rungs. Isaac forced his body to move as quickly as possible, his heart slamming against his breastbone from exertion and anxiety. When they had gathered on the next level, their luck ran out. A squad of half-armored soldiers thundered down the corridor at them. The Corzin took what cover they could, behind support beams and doorframes, flattened against the wall, and flat on the decking, all firing. One by one the ESTO squad went down, but more soon arrived. Isaac knelt near the next ladder they needed to take up, the position better to steady his shots. A metallic ping and sizzle above his head drew his attention to the right.

"We're being outflanked!" he yelled as another squad charged at them from the cross corridor.

Those closest turned their attention to the new threat, the corridors echoing with rifle shots as everyone dove for cover and scrambled to find optimum firing positions.

Liga raised her head from her rifle and pointed up the ladder. "Turk, go! We'll hold them! Take your men and go on!"

Rather than protest, as Isaac thought he would, Turk nodded and bellowed something in T'tson'ae. The words might have been unfamiliar but the intent was clear. *Up and onward, boys!*

The Zadral men broke off the attack and swarmed up the ladder, onto the level directly beneath the access to the bridge. This time they didn't stop to gather, but continued up. When Isaac's boots hit the final level's decking, he saw what had to be the bridge entrance far down the corridor, an imposing double door with amber warning lights flashing above.

The enemy gave them no room to breathe. Shots rang out from the opposite end of the corridor the moment their last man had cleared the ladder, before anyone could draw breath to bring up his shield. They scattered for the walls.

"Move!" Nidar shouted at Ges, who still stood firing in the center of the corridor. He shoved his *atenis* behind the frame of the nearest fire suppression doorway. The chivalrous instinct cost him. Plasma fire raked his side. He crumpled, his skin smoking, rifle still clutched in both hands, eyes wide and stunned.

The *hech'zai* laid down a hail of cover fire while Tash low-crawled into the middle of the corridor to retrieve him.

"Tash?" Turk called out from his position a few meters up the corridor.

"He lives, *ka'tach!*" Tash yelled back, only the slightest crack in his voice. He bent his head, apparently to hear what Nidar whispered to him. "And he says if you take one step back this way, he will shoot you himself. He says you must keep going!"

Turk growled something under his breath that Isaac was certain must have been some inventive swearing. Isaac was about to urge him to make a decision when Turk let out an explosive breath and began bellowing orders again. Half the men stayed to hold the corridor; the others followed Turk on toward the bridge.

Unfortunately, as they spread out to make their way from cover to cover, the enemy showed a spark of genius. The fire suppression doors all slammed shut at once. Out in front, cut off from their companions, neatly trapped in a twenty-meter section of corridor, Isaac and Turk leaned against the wall, panting.

"Shit," Isaac said, the word oddly muffled in their impromptu prison.

Turk paced to the forward door, then back to the aft, tapping at the control panels. The doors remained obstinately shut. "There are always codes for these doors," he muttered. "We should have had Rand Wilde with us."

*Poor Rand would've died of a panic attack by now.* But Isaac knew that wasn't fair the moment he thought it. In a bad spot, Rand had managed more courage than his slender body should have held. "Manual override? There has to be one."

"Oh yes, but your handprint must be registered with the ship. It won't work for us. Even when I served on an ESTO ship, they would not register mine. If—" Turk broke off and turned to stare at a vent cover near the floor, his brows drawn together in a thunderous frown.

"Babe," Isaac said softly. "We can't fit you through the vent system. The spec—"

Turk patted a hand on the air to silence him. Cat-silent, the big man prowled over to the vent, his gaze never leaving the grill. Suddenly, he lunged, ripped the cover off, and thrust his arm inside the vent shaft. A strangled cry echoed inside and Turk slowly withdrew his arm, his hand fisted in a mop of curly brown hair attached to a kicking, yelling youngster in uniform.

Isaac winced as Turk slammed him up against the wall, pinning him there with a hand around his throat. "What were you doing lurking in there?"

The kid, who couldn't have been a day over nineteen, squeaked and struggled, his eyes threatening to pop out of their sockets. "My job, dammit! Lemme go, you freak!"

"Your job is to spy on people using the ventilation system?"

A sobbing breath escaped their prisoner. "Fuck you! I'm enviro engineering, not some spook!"

Turk shot Isaac a puzzled look.

"He cleans the air ducts, babe. Changes the filters. Probably *was* just doing his job."

The kid's gaze darted to him. "You're not one of them. What the hell are you?"

*I've been asking myself that a lot lately.* "I'm his." He jerked his head toward Turk. "You have a name, bud? I'm Isaac—"

Rather than being soothed by his calm words, the kid paled to gray. "You're the renegade Altairian pilot. Oh... God...."

The comment and the reaction made Isaac wonder what the propagandists on Ranulf's staff had said about him. "Well, yes, almost right."

"Please," the youngster whispered to Isaac, his eyes darting to Turk. "Please don't let him rip my arms and legs off. If he wants to eat part of me, I guess maybe a hand or something? My mom's gonna be really upset if I come home in pieces."

It took all of Isaac's will to tamp down on the laugh that wanted to fountain up from his belly. He exchanged another look with Turk, whose blond eyebrows had crept up toward his hairline. He knew Turk well enough to spot the war between amusement and offense in his eyes.

"Ah, hm, well. I do think we might have a use for your hand," Isaac managed with a straight face. "And if you're a good boy, we may even let you keep it. How's that sound?"

"Um...."

"How about a name, bud? I don't want to have to resort to calling you 'kid.' I bet you get enough of that from the older sergeants."

A glint of youthful bristle rode next to the abject fear in those dark eyes, so Isaac knew he'd hit his target. "Logan. I—I'm Logan."

"Thank you." Isaac gave him a nod and what he hoped was a reassuring smile. "Now Turk's going to keep hold of you, and you're going to give me your—Turk, is it the right or the left hand that they use?"

"Left, my heart."

"Logan, you're going to give me your left hand, and you're going to get us through these doors, all right?"

The youngster closed his eyes on a low moan. Isaac was afraid he had fainted until he said, "I'm gonna be court-martialed."

"Doubtful. You are clearly our prisoner and acting under duress. The ship's monitors will back that up." Isaac held out his hand. "I won't hurt you. Give me your hand."

As if his fingers had lead cores, Logan uncurled them from their grip around Turk's forearm. His whole arm shook as he reached out to Isaac, fingers trembling like terror-stricken birds on his palm. Isaac closed his hand around them gently while Turk shifted his grip, pulling Logan's right arm behind his back to secure him.

"Where's the override on these?"

Turk nodded to a panel on the left. "Behind there, *atenis*. You may need your knife to pop the cover."

Logan cried out, trying to pull away when Isaac drew his knife. "It's not for you. Weren't you listening?" Isaac shook his head as he eased the tip under the corner of the cover and popped it off. "What the hell are they saying about me, anyway?"

"They say… they say…." Logan swallowed hard, eyes closed as Isaac pulled his hand forward to press it against the palm lock. "That your implant went bad and you kinda, you know, tipped over the tiles."

"I went crazy?" The door hissed open and they moved down the next section of corridor to another closed door.

"Yeah. Um… yeah. And that you got the bar—the, um, Corzin all riled up. That you wanna use them to… um…."

"To what?" Isaac asked gently as he worked on the next cover. "To wreak bloody vengeance on the admiral? To destroy all of the Treaty planets in some scorched-earth campaign?"

Logan's shaking had reached the point where his palm wouldn't stay still enough for the palm lock to read. He whispered, "To conquer the universe."

The laughter Isaac had tried so hard to keep in check slipped its leash. He leaned against the door, trying to catch his breath for several moments.

"My heart, it was somewhat amusing," Turk said in a dry tone. "But could we move on?"

"Sorry, sorry." Isaac swiped at his eyes, amazed at his own odd reaction. *Hysteria, that's what it is.* "Logan, I will tell you, honestly, that I don't have any intention of conquering anything. Maybe a big bowl of stew and the bed when this is all over, but that's the limit of my lofty ambitions." He took Logan's hand again. "Listen to me. I want my friends, my family, and my love safe. I want this over. I want to go home. Isn't that what you want, too?"

The hand had steadied enough. The door hissed open. "Yeah," Logan whispered.

Before them shone their grail. The door to the bridge lay at the end of the shortened corridor.

Logan's eyes widened again. "I can't open that one for you."

"Why not?" Turk growled close to the boy's ear.

"Bridge's on lockdown. See?" He nodded up to the flashing yellow lights, a frantic edge to his voice. "I don't have access."

Turk considered that and then turned to Isaac. "Do you believe him?"

"Afraid so. It only makes sense."

With a grunt, Turk let his prisoner go. Instead of bolting, Logan sank to the decking in a heap, either too shaken or too curious to flee.

"What now, *hei'tach*?" Isaac asked. *This was all such a brave, terrible idea. We're all going to die here.* "Think we could cut through?"

"In time." Turk stood hipshot, glaring at the door as if he could slice through it with his anger alone. "Time we do not have."

Isaac chewed on his bottom lip. If only they could teleport like the shchfteru. *Then we could... wait... the chuff....* An embryonic seed of an idea began to sprout in his overtired brain.

"Logan, they can see us on the bridge, can't they?"

"Yeah, probably. I mean, all the monitor access is there."

"Can they hear us, too?"

"No, I mean, not unless they switch the comm on there by the door. And you'd hear that."

Isaac nodded, still chewing on his lip. It might work. If they could—

"What thoughts grow behind those beautiful eyes?"

He glanced up to find Turk watching him. "Babe, it's a long shot."

"Yes?"

He put a hand on Turk's arm. "The whole idea is to take the command center off the board, right? Remove the admiral and his staff officers from play."

Turk frowned, obviously following but not taking the next leap yet. "Yes. And?"

"So you and I, quite literally, remove them."

Confusion slowly bled into horror in those bright blue eyes and
Turk jerked back from him. "I will not! I'm not even certain if I could,
but if we try to rip the bridge from the ship, we leave perhaps hundreds
of lives suddenly exposed to vacuum. You ask me to—"

"Shh." Isaac stepped to him and placed a finger over his lips.
"I'm suggesting no such thing. The bridge, you recall, is detachable.
We'll need them to think we're coming in after them. If they believe it
and release the bridge capsule from the ship...."

"Then we could... yes." Turk nodded. "Without wanton damage
to the ship. Isolate it, and then we deal with it. Do you truly believe we
can? Without... distortion?"

"That last stone, hon. Just keep thinking of that. We can do this.
You and me."

Logan's gaze ticked back and forth between them as they spoke. His
expression suggested he believed the rumors that Isaac was quite mad.

Isaac crouched in front of him. "Logan, I'm going to have to tie
your hands, just so Turk doesn't have to worry about you while we
work. You just sit out of the way, and nothing will happen to you."

"Here, my heart." Turk handed down a zip tie that he'd pulled
from one of his dozen pockets.

"Thank you." Isaac took the tie and gave Logan a wink. "That's
what I love about the man. Always so prepared."

Gaping at him, Logan simply turned and complied when Isaac
asked him to cross his hands behind his back. *Poor boy, I think we're
going to scare you a lot more before we're done.*

"Okay, let's smoke out our quarry," Isaac said as he rose and then
shook his head at Turk's puzzled expression. "Never mind. How do
you want to do this?"

"Take your rifle, *atenis*. Turn the flash nozzle three clicks. Yes,
just so. Now you have a plasma torch." Turk tossed Isaac a pair of
goggles. "We can't cut through, but we can make it appear that our
intention is to *blast* through. Just make a cut large enough for one of
your concussion grenades and then stuff it in the opening. We'll
continue until we have some movement from the enemy or we run out
of grenades."

"And if Ranulf just decides to wait us out? What happens if we have to set them off?"

Turk's forehead crinkled. "That should be... interesting."

"Not exactly a confidence-inspiring phrase, love," Isaac said as he settled the goggles on his head and mimicked Turk's actions to create a little plasma flame of his own. While the high-intensity torch didn't cut through the ship alloy like butter, it did cut. *Rock-hard frozen butter, maybe. Petrified thousand-year-old frozen butter.*

Reaction from the bridge came in the first five minutes. The comm panel next to Turk squealed, followed by a voice Isaac had hoped never to hear again.

"Turk, you'll never cut through in time. Your forces are losing ground. It's just a matter of time before someone comes through that door behind you."

With a grunt, Turk pulled his pistol and shot out the control panel for the fire suppression door still closed some meters behind them. "There, Admiral, that should give us some time."

"It won't be enough, Turk. They'll cut through much faster than you can. The bridge door is two meters thick."

"It's not my intention to cut through, sir." Turk stuffed his first concussion grenade in its slot, taking his time so whoever watched on the vid feed could follow what he did. His polite calm had an eerie, artificial ring to it.

"If you surrender now, I'll issue orders to leave your boys alive. They're trapped out there. Your capitulation could gain so much for your people, your planet. So much bloodshed prevented. I didn't want any of this, Turk. You know that. What you're carrying around in your head is too dangerous for you to deal with on your own. We can still deal with each other like sensible, civilized people."

"Oh, yes? As you dealt with my Isaac?" Turk dropped the façade and snarled at the comm, teeth bared in savage ferocity. "He nearly died, Ranulf! He is now forever changed! For what you visited on him, the agony, the doubt, the self-loathing, I will make you pay in kind. I will rip your body to pieces slowly, ears, eyes, teeth, tongue, finger by finger, joint by joint, until you feel every moment of terror and pain he did! Do you hear me, Ranulf?"

Instead of an answer from Ranulf, the comm squeaked off.

"Over the top, babe," Isaac muttered as he continued his cutting. "Like you could be that uncivilized, ever."

"Perhaps not." Turk shrugged. "It matters only that he believes. And the sentiment is real. I have wished to have my hands around that man's throat many times these past few weeks."

"My ferocious love," Isaac said on a strangled chuckle as he stuffed his own grenade into the slot he'd carved for it.

The lights above the door abruptly shifted from amber to red. The blare of a klaxon ripped through the confined space. Grinding clanks echoed on the other side of the door. Servos whirred, hydraulics whined. A CG female voice somehow cut through the klaxon's braying, "Vacuum warning. Do not attempt to open. Imminent vacuum hazard in thirty seconds. Vacuum warning. Do not attempt to open...."

Logan's eyes threatened to swallow his face. "Holy shit! The admiral's bailing?"

"I believe his intention is merely to move beyond my reach, youngling." Turk laced his fingers and cracked his knuckles as he spoke. "I hope to oblige him and move him considerably farther. Isaac?"

"Just a sec, babe. Logan, move down past that first fire doorway. Attaboy. Just stay there and you won't get hurt." Isaac watched until their captive had scooted down the corridor to the requested vantage point and then slung his rifle across his back. He waited while Turk put his palms flat on the door, humming, intense concentration creasing his brow. "Have they moved off? Can you tell?"

"They are detached," Turk confirmed. "I have the shape of it."

He put his hand on Turk's shoulder. "I'm switching the implant on now, so talking to me won't get you too far."

Turk patted his hand and actually gave him a wink. "I'm relieved that's not always the case, *atenis*."

*Teasing? Now?* He rose up on his toes to give Turk a soft kiss. Then he wrapped an arm around the expanse of Turk's chest and reached behind his left ear to press the implant switch. The corridor shattered into the now-familiar cacophony of sensation. He wrapped both arms hard around Turk, his anchor, his rock, and waited, letting Turk feel his way through his part of the field building.

The build took longer than it had with the stone, which was not surprising since they dealt with a far larger and more complex object. The indistinct humming he began with felt to Isaac like searching, gauging. Then Turk shifted, most likely setting his hands more comfortably on the door, and the hum gathered color and force. The cardamom-cardinal-tree-bark note enveloped him, vibrating deep into his bones. The vibration wasn't the unpleasant one he'd received from the fighter craft, though. This one had him pressing up tight against Turk's back, wanting more. He hoped he wasn't going to end up humping Turk's leg before they were through.

The second note joined the first in bright cerulean-lemon-rind and the third in a wave of deepest violet-ginger and silk. Isaac reached out for the triad, finding his place in it, then reached out farther along the notes, out to the bridge capsule Turk now held in his web of resonance. He felt the shape of it, the flavor of it, outlined by the harmonic fields Turk created. The moment Turk added his fourth note, the one that would create the GEM effect, Isaac reached past and planted his note between the bridge and the deadly, spinning field. He sang his shield for all he was worth, lungs burning, head pounding, but he forced himself to keep going. He had to succeed.

It would be disastrous to Turk's slowly relayering confidence if he killed with his gift now. It would be disastrous for T'tson if Admiral Ranulf died under mysterious circumstances, unable to answer for his crimes, or to even be accused of them.

Turk shifted in his arms, muscles straining. The notes reached their full pitch and strength. For a moment, it seemed the bridge capsule resisted, that it was too much mass to shift. Isaac tightened his grip on Turk as he felt him waver. His imagination might have been working on overdrive, but through their resonances, he felt as if Turk drew strength from him, enough for one last Herculean effort. His notes pushed at the mass, shoving it through the spinning field.

With a palpable snap, the bridge capsule vanished with that right feeling, that feeling of all the correct harmonies still in place that let Isaac know it had gone through with the shield intact. Of course, only recovery of the capsule would prove him right. He hoped they hadn't sent it too far.

Isaac reached back to switch off his implant. With the loss of support, Turk collapsed and Isaac went down with him, unable to hold his weight with one arm but too stubborn to let go.

"Turk? Sweetheart?" Isaac panted out. Waves of dizzy nausea swept over him; the corridor kept graying in and out. Logan was saying something. He couldn't piece the sounds together into words.

He let Turk slide down, his head landing in Isaac's lap. Squinting, he managed to make out the sparks and heated line of a torch cutting through the closed fire door at the other end of their foreshortened corridor. *Time's up. Here they come.*

"Mr. Ozawa?" Logan was walking toward them on his knees. "Is he all right?"

Isaac blinked at him, surprised at the quaver in the boy's voice. *Right, he's only been scared half to death.* "Is he breathing? I can't quite... see."

"Yeah" came the soft answer. "Mostly."

Isaac pulled in a hitching breath. "That works for now. You'd better get behind us, bud. I don't want you hurt if your friends come through shooting."

"No... I'll...." There was a stubborn note in Logan's voice. "I'll talk to them. Just keep your hands off your weapons, Mr. Ozawa, and it'll be okay. They'll take him to sick bay. It'll be all right. You'll see."

Isaac nodded, his blurred vision glued to the shallow, uneven rise and fall of Turk's chest. A drop of moisture hit his hand. He swiped impatiently at his eyes. *Not now, Ozawa. Don't you fall apart now.*

The section of sliced door fell inward with a hollow clang. Logan squeaked in alarm. Instead of ESTO black and gray, the corridor filled with the bright hues of Corzin warriors.

"Stay by me, Logan. Stay still. They won't hurt you," Isaac murmured.

"There they are!" Liga shouted and Isaac raised a shaking hand in acknowledgment.

Corzin of both genders pelted down the hall to them, relief and worry evident in equal measures.

"*Tach* 'Liga." Isaac put his fist to his chest in a pale approximation of a Corzin salute. "It is done. The piece has been removed from the field. At least I believe so. This young man is tech, a noncombatant."

Liga murmured into her headset and then gave him a spare nod. "It is done, Zadral Isaac. Our carrier outside confirms the bridge capsule cannot be found on scan."

She crouched down behind Logan to free his hands. Edar and Din arrived then to gather Turk up and Hrell lifted Isaac in his arms.

"I can walk," he protested, though somehow his head had come to rest on Hrell's broad shoulder.

"Perhaps so, *durhai lochau*," Hrell said. "But perhaps you've done enough for one day."

He gathered bits and disjointed pieces as the Corzin raced back the way they had come. Another *hech'zai* of fighter ships had broken through the lines and reached the flagship. With reinforcements, the Corzin had been able to regroup and secure their wounded. The fighting in the ship's corridors had suddenly become disorganized and strange, with squads more apt to flee from the Corzin invaders than to engage them.

They were, in Din's words, "a shamefully dispirited herd of *lechta*."

The troop transport they piled into was attached to one of the conventional airlocks, which made it easier to load the wounded. Nidar already lay secured on a stretcher, the ugly burns along his right side covered in a clear film. Ges sat at his head, face buried in his hands, Tash at his feet, stoic and stone-faced.

Edar strapped Turk into the stretcher directly opposite and Hrell put Isaac down on the jump seat by Turk's head. He found he couldn't sit up any longer and curled over to rest his head on Turk's shoulder. Everything hurt, pounding, aching pain all through his joints and muscles, careening around his head, making it impossible to think two thoughts in succession.

They let him stay there, though Din settled on his other side with a hand on his back. The transport moved off from the ship, leaving behind hell only knew what scenes of panic and chaos. But Isaac didn't care. He didn't have the energy to do anything but watch Turk's chest shudder and rise, hitch and fall.

Sometime during the flight back to the station, the unthinkable happened. Turk's chest fell and stopped. Isaac watched, waiting for a gasp, a twitch, a hint of breath resumed. A wedge of ice slammed into his heart, threatening to split it in two.

"Turk?" he whispered, reaching out to stroke that beloved, handsome face. Nothing. "Babe?"

He slid from his seat, heedless of flight rules, and took Turk by the shoulders, shaking hard. "Turk! Damn it, don't do this! Breathe!"

"No...." The anguished word came from across the aisle as Ges slid to his knees beside Nidar. "Not now, beloved. Please... not now."

"You can't die!" Isaac yelled in Turk's face. "Then Nidar will die too! You can't do that! I won't let you!" He yanked Turk's head back and forced his mouth open, covering mouth and nose with his own, forcing the air from his aching lungs into Turk's recalcitrant ones. "Breathe, damn you!"

He felt himself lifted and he screamed and flailed with his fists, trying to connect with something, anything. "Let me go! Let me go! He'll die!"

"Hush, hush, Isaac," Hrell murmured to him, jerking his head to the side to dodge another blow. "We need to get the respirator on."

"Respirator?" he repeated, feeling stunned and stupid. He put his hands to work wiping the tears of rage and grief from his face.

"Yes." Edar took his chin in a hard grip, his voice fierce and stern. "You must stop this now. It's unseemly, this wailing while he might yet live. When it is time to grieve for him, then grieve, but not before."

His insides turned to slow, glacial ice inside him as he watched them fasten the respirator mask over Turk's face. Din tore his jacket and shirt open to attach squares of shining material, most likely cardiac regulators. *This is what you do for wounded men in full arrest. You hook them up and wait for the doctors to tell you they're really dead.*

"I can't...." He clutched Hrell's arm as his legs turned to tissue paper.

"I have you, Isaac. Let's sit you down by him again. The healers have come up on station. They will see to him as soon as we dock."

Isaac shook his head, though he allowed himself to be led back to his seat. "Hrell, I can't… if he dies… there's nothing left."

Hrell crouched in front of him, his cloud-gray eyes patient and kind. "It is a decision every man must make at some point, Isaac. To go on or follow the one we love into the dark. If it comes to that, the spirits forbid, but if it does, remember you have family. We will be your shelter, your bulwark if you need us. If you let us."

"But, I'm not—"

"Family, *lochau*. You are family."

Edar put a hand on his lover's shoulder. Stern, laconic and even a bit distant, Isaac had thought of Turk's next youngest brother as all of these, but a glint of moisture marred his glower now. "Rest, Isaac. There is nothing else to do at the moment."

With a nod, Isaac curled up with his head back on Turk's shoulder. Across the bay, Tash had finished hooking Nidar up to life support as well. He held Ges close, stroking his blond hair, murmuring in his ear. Isaac had the unkind thought that if Nidar died, at least they would have each other, but he knew that was wrong. Nidar's death would rip a hole in two hearts rather than just one.

"You can't die, big guy," Isaac whispered, his ragged voice lost in the whisper and sigh of the respirator. "We haven't even written our names together yet. I still have to tell you about *Macbeth*. You need to… there's so many damn things you need to. Don't go, babe. Just don't."

He clung to hope and consciousness with equal ferocity and refused to look at the yawning dark threatening to swallow him whole.

JUNIOR OFFICERS came and went in the corridor, peering at the forbidding bridge door, yelling into wrist comms and at each other. When the patrol finally came for him, Logan still sat stunned and unmoving on the decking where the fierce, beautiful barbarians had left him. So bright, so alive. He'd never seen people so full up to the top line with *life* before, not only the Corzin, but Ozawa too. The way he had looked at that huge, gorgeous blond, Logan thought the heat in those eyes would scorch the hull. *Love like that, you only find it in stories, right?*

"You hurt, kid? Those savages rough you up?"

He looked up at the sergeant's gruff voice, one that held as much scorn as concern, and shook his head. "No. I'm... I'm all right."

"Come on, kid. Let's get you down to sick bay. You look a little shocky." A hard hand dragged him to his feet, propelled him along whether he wanted to go or not.

He fingered the zip tie in his pocket, the one thing the Corzin had left behind. *I wish you had taken me with you....*

# CHAPTER 19: CIRCLES

*A QUIET place.* Walls painted in gradations of deep blue, lighting dim enough to soothe his aching head, Isaac reasoned he had landed in another medical ward of some kind.

A soft snore came from his right and Isaac turned, hoping against hope. But, no, the owner of the snore turned out to be Loric, who slept sitting up, chin on his chest, arms wrapped tight around him. The singed ends of his braid rested on his forearm. Heavy lines of exhaustion furrowed around his eyes and mouth.

Isaac hated to wake him from most likely the first peaceful moment he had snatched, but his anxiety grew every second he was conscious. Turk had been taken from him, whisked away by Drak'tar healers. With that last sight of Turk, the last of Isaac's strength drained from him, and he passed out in the attendant's multiple arms.

"*Ka'dalk?*" he ventured, his voice raw and hoarse.

Loric's eyes snapped open. He stretched, a huge, aging predator. "*Sulden*, how do you feel?"

"Better than before. I'm more worried about Turk, though."

With a sigh, Loric leaned forward, arms on his knees. "He sleeps. The healers tell me there were issues with his heart. They make repairs as we speak."

"I nearly killed him." Isaac buried his face against his forearm, throat closing over on that stark epiphany. "I asked him to do the impossible and he did it. And it nearly killed him."

A huge hand stroked his hair, as if he were a toddler again woken from nightmare. "Isaac, for you he would move entire star systems, it's true. But in this, I believe you overestimate your influence. Turk is a hero born. If it took his death to secure the safety of his people and his planet, he would have died a dozen times without hesitation. Sometimes a father wishes for more sense, but there it is."

Isaac managed a strangled, wordless affirmation. He fought for a whole breath and then another before his brain restarted. "But he'll be all right, won't he?"

"My most stubborn child? Death wouldn't dare try to take him unwilling."

With a hiccupped breath that couldn't quite be classified as a laugh, the hard bands around Isaac's heart eased. "The Fleet? The capsule? Casualties?" He struggled to sit up but found he could barely raise his head.

"So. Yes." Loric leaned back against the wall again. "The Fleet is in the process of surrender. I say this since surrender has been ship by ship, each individual captain forced to make the choice without orders from above. A few pockets of shipboard fighting remain, a last, few bits of desperation. Nothing serious. Your friend Rand is tracking the bridge capsule. He believes he has found its trace just outside the system."

"Life signs?"

"We have no word on that yet. Casualties… some on either side, but not as many as could have been. With the beast decapitated, there was little fight left in it."

"Nidar?" Isaac asked in a croak.

"Struggles to remain with us. If sheer will guaranteed survival…." Loric drew in a slow breath. "One hopes. One surely does."

Din poked his head around the doorway, whispering, "Father, is he awake?"

"You may ask Isaac yourself, my boy," Loric said with a little smile.

"Ah, good." Din strode in, overcrowding the room with his youthful energy. "The healers say it would be best if they are together. I'll carry him, Father. You look so tired still and—"

"Din." The single, growled word stopped him short. "You must learn to begin at beginnings. And to do it politely."

"But the healers…."

Loric waved a hand. "Isaac lies right there in front of you, fully conscious, in full command of his faculties. Start again, please."

Even in the dim light, Din's flush was visible as he placed both hands over his heart and bowed in apology. "I have erred, please—"

"It's okay, bud," Isaac cut him off, his patience too short for courtesies. "Say what you came to say."

"The healers are finished with Turk. They say it will be best for him to have you beside him, so they sent me to fetch you. With the *tessil* still on your back, they thought it best if you were carried."

"The... what?" Isaac twisted. What he had thought was a pillow against his back was instead a strange little contraption attached *to* his back. It moved with him, a soft, pliable passenger stuck to his skin like a leech. The comparison made him shudder.

"It helps you heal, fiercest of my *sulden'ae*," Loric said gently. "Gives you moisture and extra air to breathe."

*IV and oxygen in one package....* "Oh. Guess I needed it, huh?" He snagged the corner of his blanket and pulled it around his body, *tessil* and all. While he hadn't had much reaction to Loric touching his hair, he had been stripped to his pouch and didn't want to twitch when Din picked him up. "Okay, hon. I'm set. Cart away."

Brows raised in a good imitation of his older brother's best quizzical look, Din obviously understood enough to slide hard arms underneath and lift Isaac against his chest. Smaller than Turk and Edar, more compact and sleek, still Din was more than up to the job of carrying one slender comm officer.

An air of serious medical intervention suffused Turk's room. Instead of a carpet to rest on, a raised platform dominated the center. Raised sides of shining black material reflected the light and hid the patient. Soft machine susurrations whispered mysterious interrogatives. The sight was so unexpected, Isaac took a moment to register the figure standing by the platform.

"Hey, sweetie!" Dr. Varga turned to give him a beaming smile and then quickly closed her mouth to hide her teeth. "You look alert and focused, at least. How do you feel?"

"Tired. Not so bad. Turk?"

She nodded to the odd platform. "Looks like a giant bento box, doesn't it?"

"Yeah. Don't think I want to think of Turk as sushi, though, if you don't mind."

"Sorry, Oz." She flipped her braid over her shoulder with a chuckle. "You, I wasn't too worried about. Yes, your body had all the earmarks of a man who's run a double marathon without water, severe dehydration, depressed vitals, but with that lovely little *tessil* thing, you turned around fast. The big guy, though"—she nodded to the black-sided platform—"had a major cardiac incident."

"Incident?"

"Ruptured coronary arteries in several spots."

"Did you... fix it?"

Dr. Varga laughed. "Oh goodness, no! I wouldn't have dreamed of interfering. But the Draktar healers let me observe. Absolutely fascinating. No artificial implants, no synth replacements, all Turk's own biomatter, reformed and reengineered. Amazing. And zero chance of rejection."

Her lack of anxiety heartened Isaac considerably. "So he'll be okay? He'll... recover?"

"Things look good right now. But if he never quite regains his precoronary stamina and strength, I don't want you shocked. You need to be prepared for the long haul, Oz."

"I get it, Doc, don't worry. All I'm asking is for him to live, for me to hear his voice. I'll never push him again."

Loric let out a soft snort. "For that, he would never forgive you."

*Right, of course. Just not pushing too hard, too soon.* Isaac glanced up at his transport and pointed to the patient unit. "Din, could you?"

The maneuver proved awkward with Din reaching up and over the side to place Isaac in beside Turk, but he managed, only a short grunt hinting at the strain.

"There you are," Isaac whispered, finally able to confirm the rise and fall of Turk's chest, the small movements of his features as he dreamed. Complexion too pale, body too inert, still Isaac had never seen a more beautiful sight.

Warm, humidified air misted from the sides of the patient bed, the surface some firm yet yielding material that supported the body without stress. Isaac had expected a patchwork of tubes and wires, but Turk lay in his natural state, a blanket covering him to his waist, one solitary tube snaking out by his hip. Apparently, even the Drak'tar had not been able to find a way around the necessity of a catheter.

Fingernail-size scars decorated Turk's skin along his sternum, as if from an overly enthusiastic lover. These seemed to be the only visible evidence of the repairs to his heart. *Neat work, there.* He took Turk's hand and kissed his knuckles, wondering why his oversensitized nerves didn't kick up a ruckus. Not that he would complain if his body had decided to settle down a few notches.

"Gentlemen," Dr. Vargas said in her best "I'm the expert here" voice. "I think it's time we left our boys alone."

Din started to protest, "But what if—"

She cut him off, albeit gently. "Isaac, there's a call pad by your head. You press that if you need anything, even if you're just worried and you want someone in here. All right?"

"Yes, ma'am."

Then it was just him and Turk again, as it had been in that first sick-bay meeting, though now the handsome face was achingly, heart-wrenchingly familiar rather than merely intriguing. Isaac had memorized every plane and line, every angle and shadow.

A fierce storm had chased them from their first meeting all the way to this moment. It had finally caught them in its teeth, tossed them ass over elbow, and then roared past them. In its wake, a strange, anticipatory silence reigned, leaving Isaac disoriented and rudderless. *Now what?*

Turk shifted, his brows knitted together, perhaps struggling against some distressing dream.

"I'm here, babe," Isaac murmured as he scooted closer.

He wanted to crawl on top of his massive lover, drape himself over that hard body, and hold him tight, but he was afraid of putting any pressure on Turk's chest. He settled for sliding a hand under the blanket to rest on Turk's stomach. A low murmur rumbled in Turk's chest.

"Shh, just rest. Need to get strong again, you and me." Isaac chewed on his lower lip a moment and then, though he felt self-conscious and a little silly, he began a lullaby his mother had sung to him after his worst night terrors. "*How many stars does night sew into*

*her blanket? Can you count them? Can you count them? One to sweep*
*day's dust away, one to call the moons to play....*"

His hoarse, ragged voice smoothed out as he sang, gaining
strength, finding pitch. Turk's forehead smoothed. A corner of his
mouth tugged up. For now, that was enough and Isaac nestled beside
him, content.


"ITZAK."

The voice gave him a gentle, insistent shake.

"Itzak."

Startled out of a sound sleep, Isaac rolled onto his back. The *tessil*
had vanished while he slept. He blinked at the nonhuman face above
him, unable to place who she was for a blank, brain-stuck moment,
perhaps since he had never seen her in one of the long, quilted coats
before. Soon, though, the red bangles on her wrists and the spectacular
emerald and turquoise crest registered.

"*Sil'ke'dra*? You came up to the station?"

"There seemed need." She leaned over the high walls of the bed
to stroke Turk's hair when he shifted. "*Ka'Turk, hidach.*"

Isaac sat up, rubbing the side of his head against lingering sleep.
"You said that to him when we first came, ma'am. What does it mean?"

The odd trill of a Drak'tar chuckle washed over them. "I suppose
you would say that it means all will be well. Okay. Is this not the
expression I hear from your *huchtik* friends?"

"Yes." He watched the odd sight of Turk calming under her huge
hand. "But you didn't come all the way up here to visit us, I don't think."

"No. I have need for advice. For human things and human words.
From people not born to T'tson. You."

"Me?"

She tilted her head to the side. "You doubt, Itzak. You have
doubted for many years, I think. But I have watched. More lives in you
than you...." She hesitated over a word.

"Admit?"

"Yes." She held her arms out to him. "Come and meet. We have much to talk over."

He pulled the blanket close, sliding an anxious glance between her and Turk. "I don't want to leave him alone."

"The attendants will stay with him, reassure him, soothe him if he wakes."

Isaac heaved a slow breath, unsure of what help he could possibly be in his exhausted, confused state. She simply stared at him, patient and unmoving, until he let her help him to the floor, where his knees promptly gave way. One long Drak'tar arm snaked around him, and he managed a slow hobble down the hall leaning against her warmth.

They reached the conference room without Isaac collapsing, only to find an argument in progress.

"... not a good idea! The whole damn Board's gotta be crooked!" Rand shouted in agitation. "All those old Treaty codgers are bent all to hell!"

"Mr. Wilde," Captain Drummond raised her voice to drown him out. "I would suggest we not allow our opinion of an entire governmental body to be colored by someone's single bad experience in their judiciary system."

His face crimson, Rand subsided, hunched in his chair, muttering.

"Didn't catch that last part?" Dr. Varga prompted.

Travis put a hand on Rand's arm, his jaw tight, his words ground out. "He *said* we should contact Admiral Uchechi directly. I agree. We have to deliver these boys and girls to someone and he's the one man in ESTO's command structure we *know* isn't crooked."

"We can't tight-band a transmission from this far out," Sylvia said, looking to Isaac for confirmation. He shook his head as he took a place by the wall. "Too many hands to go through. If Rand can intercept, so can any other techie brat out there."

Isaac shut his eyes. He wasn't up to dealing with tired, prickly personalities, and Loric's scowl was growing darker with each sentence.

"Not *any* other."

"Shut it, Wilde, you had your say. It has to be the whole Board or—"

"No," Isaac said on a weary sigh. The room's silence prompted him to open his eyes. Everyone sat staring at him.

"No, Mr. Ozawa?" Captain Drummond sat forward, hands clasped on the table. "No to what specifically?"

The *Sil'ke'dra* settled beside him, her tail curled around him, her presence giving weight to his words he didn't want, her confidence giving him the courage, nonetheless.

"It's not enough. Only contacting the Treaty planets allows this mess to fall into the black hole of their politicking. They may find it more expedient and less embarrassing to sweep all this under the carpet. They may do all sorts of insane, stupid things on too little information and someone wanting to appear the heroic statesman." He looked up, addressing the governmental leader beside him. "I suggest a general broad scope transmission. Every public channel, every planetary news outlet. Altairian Empire, ESTO, Adanai Collective, Galactic Hansa, everyone. From you, *Sil'ke'dra*. The transmission should come from you."

"Should it?" She blinked her golden, saurian eyes slowly. "Why do you think this, *ka* 'Itzak?"

He returned her blink at her use of the possessive for him. *Our Isaac?* "Forgive me if I'm speaking out of turn, ma'am. But I think at this point, your best defense is no longer isolation. Continue to shut yourself off and the rumors grow. Humans, at least the humans out there"—he waved a hand toward the universe at large—"are frightened by what they don't know. Maybe, *Sil'ke'dra*, it's time to join the galactic community. On your terms, before the community forces their terms on you because they think you're a threat."

"What is it that we threaten?" Her melodious voice sounded puzzled, perhaps even hurt.

"Apparently, with your Corzin army, you and I are set on conquering the galaxy."

Her trilled laugh ended on a snort, Drak'tar disbelief or disgust, Isaac wasn't certain. "Territorial disputes? As in ancient days? Are they still such... what is the word, Itzak?"

"Barbarians?"

"Yes. Barbarians." She said it slowly, careful with the *b*'s. "And this is what you bid us join?"

"The treaties and the intersystem courts curb the barbarism, ma'am. No government wants any other to seize too much power. No one wants the old wars of conquest to start up again, or the wars of defensive aggression that followed. Opening diplomatic relations would give you a voice in this system, would grant you protection against incursion without a single life threatened. Ambassadors rather than fleets of warships."

"We do not leave the system, Itzak. Neither do I wish for a sudden herd of strange humans descending upon us."

"But you have citizens who do leave the system. Sensible, adaptable, open-minded...."

She nodded. "Yes. It is truth." A few more slow blinks. "Come. You will help me with this message to the galaxy, Itzak."

"Me?"

"Ma'am, I've rarely met a man better with words," Travis broke in.

"And he's pretty damn smart about all that history and political stuff," Rand added helpfully. "Academy educated and all that."

"Inquisitive to a fault," Loric added. "But as sharp as a *lau'ec* knife."

Captain Drummond rose, fists planted on the table. "I didn't hire you on as comm officer for your pretty face, Mr. Ozawa, though it didn't hurt."

"Um, thanks a lot everyone," Isaac grumbled. "Doc, aren't I supposed to be resting?"

"Sure, sweetie, but you can do this from bed. I don't see why not."

Isaac hunched under his blankets. "I think I've just been thrown under the proverbial autoloader. What happened to 'I've got your back'?"

"Best man for the job, Oz," Sylvia said with an amused gleam in her eyes. "*Semper fidelis.*"

Isaac stabbed a finger at her even as Loric helped him stand. "Do *not* throw that Fleet crap at me, Casalvez! Don't even try it!"

Sylvia just snickered and to Isaac's amazement, Rand punched her in the arm and joined her. She whispered something to him and he all but collapsed in a fit of hysterical giggles. Clearly, the *Hermes* officers had been under too much stress lately.

A LOW thrum of sound brought Turk to awareness. *Was I or was I not just dying again?* A deep, throbbing ache centered in his chest, so perhaps that was still the case, though otherwise he felt warm and comfortable, the desperate feeling of clinging to life having deserted him.

His lips curled in a smile when he caught Isaac's scent and then the familiar, soothing hum of his field. If he had to die, at least his *atenis* was beside him. Though, as he listened, his forehead creased. He wouldn't have thought Isaac would sound quite so animated and confident while he lay dying.

When he cracked an eye open, the black wall of a *sart* bed greeted him. He had been in one before, after the *irskai* had bitten him when he was ten and he had nearly bled out. Whatever his current condition, it wasn't good.

A gentle hand smoothed over his crest. Isaac leaned over him to kiss his jaw. "Hey, there."

"Isaac." His voice was a spare whisper. He stared at the beautiful, golden face above him. This felt so familiar.... "You are here... aren't you?"

"I'm here, babe. I'm real. Good to see those blue eyes again."

Something seemed off, though. Turk coughed and gathered breath to speak. "You're touching me. Without your gloves."

"And you're complaining?" Isaac's bright smile warmed his heart, even though those dark eyes looked so tired. "Seems our last bit of trauma settled something in my brain. I still don't *like* being touched by other people, but I can stand it. Touching you is different, though. Doesn't make me twitch at all."

A large, crested head loomed above them. "You are awake."

"*Sil'ke'dra!*" He struggled to sit up, but only managed to get an elbow under him before he collapsed back, panting. "What has happened? Isaac... why...?"

Isaac pressed on his shoulder, keeping him down. "It's okay, hon. We're alive, we're on the station. You did what you had to do and kept everyone safe. The *Sil'ke'dra* is on station to, hmm, facilitate the surrender and start the next part of the process."

Turk pressed Isaac's hand to his cheek, his head spinning. "Small words. Short sentences, little man."

"Bridge capsule. Shunted out-system. You did that. It's drifting. Lost engines. Being retrieved. Massive heart attack—you; half-dead from exhaustion—me. Both fixed. You need rest."

"And?" Turk nodded to the *Sil'ke'dra*, still patiently looming above them.

"Diplomacy. She wants to send a message. To the human galaxy. No more keeping the planet secret. No more hiding."

"Ah?" He thought on that for a moment and believed he understood the wisdom of it.

"You would like to hear this message Isaac has helped create, yes?" Drak'tar nostrils closed and flared.

There was only one possible answer. "Yes."

She leaned two arms on the black wall and began, "To the several governments of the human galaxy, we send this urgent plea. I am *Sil'ke'dra* Lenta, the matri-arch—" Drak'tar lips stumbled over the unfamiliar word and she glanced at Isaac for confirmation, only continuing when he nodded. "—of a planet in the KS901 quarantined zone. Recently, our system suffered an invasion from a hostile force, our planet, our very existence as a race threatened...."

Turk listened attentively as the *Sil'ke'dra* described the attack and her desire to reach out to the human governments, to prevent such misunderstandings in the future, to open lines of communication and exchange. Even as he listened, though, part of him wondered at how her eyes devoured Isaac and what her plans were for him. He loved her dearly and trusted her without question, but such rapt attention from her came with consequences. It had always been so.

THE ATTENDANTS had to bring a box for Isaac to stand on to see over the side of the *sart* bed.

Tash glanced up, and then buried his face against Nidar's shoulder again. In a few hours, it would be Ges beside him again. With only room for two, they were all universally miserable.

"Little *durhai*," Nidar whispered. His side, after several grafts and repairs to several organs, looked more red-raw than black now, though the healers said he might be slower on that side now. "Good to see you greeted the next day."

"And you." Isaac leaned on the bed wall. "We thought we'd lost you there. You and Turk."

"What did I tell you, little one?" Nidar granted him a spare smile. "He could not die without me. And since he is too spirits-forsaken stubborn to die, I had to stay."

"I would hope so. You wouldn't be a very good cousin, abandoning him now."

Nidar cocked an auburn brow at him. "Now? What have you not said, *lochau*? You will become as bad as him at this rate, closed-mouthed and uncommunicative."

Isaac laughed. "I don't think there's any danger of that. But the *Sil'ke'dra* has decided to send Turk and me on a new sort of *ket'sa*."

"Oh, yes? Where is the battle?"

"Diplomacy, not battle. She's created a new job for us. *Ket'haras*."

"The outward voice?"

"Ambassadors, most of the galaxy calls them, but, yes. Turk, for his part, thinks it's fine to go on our own. Me, I'd rather have people at my back I can trust. Advice I can rely on. People handy in a bad spot if it comes to that."

"He thinks to go out there again without me?" Nidar struggled to sit up, much to Tash's distress. "I *will* have words with him if he thinks any such thing! After the last disaster on his own? I'll snap his foolish, stubborn neck myself."

Isaac helped Tash press him back to the bed, though he smiled at Nidar's reaction, the one for which he had hoped. His fire, his humor and his sense would prove invaluable over the next few months, Isaac was certain. "When you're both better, you can brawl all you want. Don't worry. I won't let him leave without you."

"Nothing will ever be the same, will it?" Tash asked on a hard swallow.

"No, *lochau*," Isaac said gently. "Everything has changed. But I know the Corzin have the courage to face change. To embrace it."

"Even if Isaac must drag us by the hair to do so," Nidar grumbled, though his eyes glinted with amusement. "Lead the charge, little *durhai*. We will follow."

Isaac left them with a little smile. *One piece secured. Next, Captain Drummond.* He found her in the docking bay where the *Hermes* repairs were nearing completion.

"Morning, Isaac." She put down the microwelder she had been using on one of the smaller servos for the braking mechanism. "You almost look yourself today, son."

"Almost feel myself, Captain." He settled on the packing crate next to her. "I guess I should really give you a formal resignation, shouldn't I?"

"Probably best to enter it into the log." She turned the tool over in her hands. "Hate to lose you, but I can't expect you to sit comm now that you're slated for ambassador status, now can I?"

"About that, Captain." He had wanted to simply barrel through his request, but sitting with her in the huge, echoing bay, he hesitated, anxious and awkward. She had been an autonomous captain for so long, how could he ask her to go back, to serve another government?

"Spit it out, boy. You have something to say to me, say it. Too far down this road now."

The statement led him to believe she had some suspicions, so he forged ahead. "We've been receiving messages back over the last couple of days, from the Collective, from the Hansa, from Altair, all reaching out with careful diplomatic feelers, but all wanting to establish contact. The Empire makes all the right relieved noises about my wellbeing, too. Funny how they didn't care so much when I was just a despairing private citizen, isn't it?"

"No, son, not funny at all. But you're high profile now. You know how these things work."

He heaved a breath, not quite a sigh. "I know, Captain. I'm not so bitter about it anymore. Guess it's just force of habit. Anyway, the return messages we've sent have been with the *Sil'ke'dra*, Turk, and I together. She wants it clear that out there, we are her Voice; we speak for the planet. We heard from the Treaty Board today and from Admiral Uchechi. The admiral is coming to take charge of what the Board is calling the 'renegade fleet bent on criminal action.' If they had any hand in the invasion, they're being careful to distance themselves."

"They'd sure as hell be stupid not to," Captain Drummond growled.

"Yes, ma'am. The upshot of it all is that Turk and I are being sent to Terranova for talks with the Board and to stand witness in the several trials they have planned for Admiral Ranulf and his top brass. We'll be taking a few of the Corzin with us, but not a whole *hech'zai*. Don't want this to look like a military operation."

"Right. The more civilian you boys look, the better, I'd say."

"With that in mind, the *Sil'ke'dra* thought it best if we didn't arrive at our diplomatic missions on a troop transport or in a Corzin dreadnought."

"Here it comes," she muttered.

"She'd like to offer you, the *Hermes*, and her crew a new line of work. That of diplomatic transport as the T'tson consulate ship."

Captain Drummond frowned at the microwelder, her eyes boring through it as if everything from the past few months was its fault. "Son, I appreciate her confidence, but why the hell me?"

"Because you are nonmilitary and independent. You know the flight lanes and the docks. Because *I* trust you and Turk does. *Chautae.* We need someone at our backs we can count on, but someone who doesn't appear to the rest of the universe as a threat. I go into port with a Corzin pilot and Corzin warriors as crew, and dock masters everywhere are going to panic. No one's ever seen Corzin before except in the middle of a battle."

"Dammit, son, these folks don't exactly have a traditional economy. How would I pay my crew? Or docking fees for that matter? How would I pay for supplies or repairs or upgrades?"

Isaac cleared his throat. "Well, you know diplomatic ships don't pay docking fees." He patted the air with both hands at her impatient snort. "I know, I do understand. That's not the half of it. I did have a long talk with Herself about finances, trying to figure out how the

Drak'tar would fund anything in the larger galaxy. Convinced they'd have to start dealing in some of their amazing bioengineering, I was asking her about their ships. Construction, materials, that sort of thing. But then I happened to ask where they obtained the lumanium for their intersystem drive shields. She waved an airy hand and told me it's *common* here. Just lying around the planet and its moons."

Captain Drummond's head shot up. "The hell you say."

"That's what I thought too. So I had Rand and Sylvia help me with mineral scans. The whole system is lousy with lumanium. They have enough here to flood the market at will, to control the market, in fact."

"Good lord, son. Have you talked to Elaine in finance? Gotten some good banking contacts for them?"

"Yes, ma'am, we're working on all that." Isaac laced his fingers together and stared at his boots. "I know it's asking a lot. Giving up your status as an independent contractor, for one. I don't know what we'll run up against in the future, so I'm not offering a safe life. But it would be steady employment. No worrying about where the next contract will come from."

She rose to pace, tapping the microwelder against the palm of her left hand. "And what would we be to the Drak'tar?"

"As far as Drak'tar law goes, we would be our own *katrak*, a new one. Turk and I, the *Hermes*, and the few Corzin we have with us."

She paced and stopped, paced and stopped for four more turns around the packing crate. "I have to run this by my officers, Mr. Ozawa. The ship's stakeholders all have to be in agreement on such a major shift in employment."

He held up his hands in acquiescence. "That's all I ask, ma'am. Plenty of time to think. We can't go anywhere until Turk's cleared medically."

"A few years ago, I would've told you I'm too old for something new." She shook her head, the overhead lights catching in her steel gray hair. "Now I'm not so sure. Change. You're bringing it, and I'm not sure I want to be left behind."

"Talk to them, Captain." He gripped her arm. "All I ask."

Later, toward the evening of the station's day cycle, he meandered back to Turk's new room, tired but satisfied with progress on all fronts. Turk had been moved from the *sart* bed to a regular round floor bed, a sure sign that he was well on his way to recovery.

A nice quiet dinner with Turk, a chance to curl up with the big man in his arms, just the two of them….

The crowded room dashed those hopes to tiny slivers. Loric sat by Turk, Din, Edar, and Hrell nearby. Travis and Sylvia stood propped against the wall, with Rand sitting at Travis's feet. A holoimage of an unfamiliar Drak'tar floated above a portable comm bowl in front of Turk.

*This looks bad.*

"Everything all right?" Isaac asked through the blood pounding in his ears.

"One hopes it will be," Loric answered, his expression chiseled from granite. "My son tells me he never took you to register before we came up to the station."

Turk sat with his back against the wall, face parchment pale, gaze fixed on his lap.

Loric went on, "For this, he feels deservedly ashamed. You must forgive me as well, Isaac. With all that went on, I had no idea he had been so neglectful."

"So this is a rifle-barrel registration? You're forcing him to make an honest man out of me?"

"We"—Loric waved a hand at those assembled—"your family and friends, have decided to insist. We have the registrar online and only await your consent."

Not at all pleased by the ambush, Isaac crossed his arms over his chest. "What if I say 'no'?"

Turk's head shot up, his expression full of shocked anguish. "Isaac!"

"It's not as if you actually *asked*, now is it?"

With shaking hands, Turk fumbled his blankets aside, shifting with every evident intention of crawling off the mattress onto the floor. With a sharp cry, Isaac intercepted him. "What the hell do you think you're doing?"

"Preparing to ask, *atenis*," Turk said in a hoarse whisper, his breaths coming in whistling gasps. "To get on my knees and beg, if necessary."

"Stay there. Don't move." Isaac knelt instead, his arms wrapped around Turk. "I didn't mean it. I'm sorry. Just kinda shocked by all this. Please don't hurt yourself, babe. Please."

"Still, the question remains unasked." Turk leaned against him, regaining a bit of control after a few gulps of air. "Isaac Daichi Ozawa, would you write your name with mine? To be joined under the law and in sight of witnesses? Mine as I am yours, for as long as we draw breath?"

Isaac wanted to shout "yes!" but with so many eyes on them, the feeling of occasion seemed to demand more. "Zadral *tach'Corzin* Turk, I will. Mine as I am yours. Now and always."

Turk took the light stylus Edar held out for him. Isaac had to help steady his hand as Turk wrote his name where the registrar officer indicated on the image.

When it came his turn, Isaac hesitated. "I can't write in T'tson'ae characters."

"No matter, *sulden*," Loric reassured him. "It is your signature, in your hand, that matters. Write your name as you always have."

He wrote his signature twice, once in Standard script and once in kanji characters, since they looked more at home beside T'tson'ae. "There." Isaac planted a kiss on Turk's lips. "Happy?"

"Nearly fainting from it," Turk breathed out against his skin.

"I think that's something else, babe. Lie back down."

"So now you're an old married couple?" Rand's smartass comment was ruined by a little sniff.

Isaac turned to his Corzin family. "*Ka'dalk*, is that it? We're attached?"

"You are attached." Loric kissed his forehead and then bent to kiss Turk's. "And now, my friends, my sons, thank you for standing witness, but I think it best we leave Turk to his rest."

They filed out with hugs and congratulations, and finally Isaac had the quiet he needed. "Babe? You okay there?"

"Better now. When I thought you might refuse me...."

"Sweetheart, after all we've been through? Besides, you've completely ruined me for any other man. How could I ever accept another lover after having a Corzin?"

Turk quirked a brow at him, and then his face settled into a too-serious expression. "True."

Isaac snorted and buried his face against Turk's shoulder, laughing until tears rolled down his cheeks.

"THAT'S A *durhai*?"

Ges had found him an image while they waited for the *Hermes* airlock to synch with their assigned lock on Terranova's orbiting station. The creature looked like a dust ball with teeth. Lots of teeth.

"Yes."

Isaac waved a hand at the image, while he shot a look at Nidar. "*This* is what you've been calling me? Not exactly flattering."

"I never said you looked like one," Nidar countered. "But the *durhai* are fierce."

"Normally, they are solitary and stay far from the cities," Turk added with a little shudder. "But in the worst drought years, they swarm and run rampant, eating everything in their path. Everything."

"Keeping them from the *selfau* domes is not a pleasant task," Tash said.

Isaac felt certain that was one of the worst understatements of the century. "But I'm not some crazed, devouring beast. Not like I rolled over a bunch of Corzin and flattened them."

"You think so, *ket'haras*?" Nidar said with a wry smile. "I have felt quite flattened more than once since meeting you."

He managed a little chuckle at the teasing, though he wasn't comfortable at all with the image. "All right, gentlemen, remember we are a diplomatic party. We are not here to pick fights. Smiles with teeth are?"

"Simply an attempt to appear friendly," Ges answered.

"Right. I know it's built into your wiring, but please don't forget it. And an extended hand?"

Tash sighed and rolled his eyes. "Is not a threat. Isaac, we have it."

"Uh-huh." Isaac pointed to Ges, spinning his *lau'ec* knife around its handle. "And what have I said about weapons?"

Ges slammed the knife back in its sheath as he flushed bright red. "No weapon drawn unless we're attacked."

"Right. You're our security, so it's fine to look serious and intimidating, but *not* fine to look like we're here to cause trouble."

"*Ket'haras*," three deep voices answered, somewhat subdued.

The lock cycled. Beside him, Turk drew in a slow, measured breath.

"All right, babe?"

Turk kissed the top of his head. "Well enough, my heart. Perhaps I am a bit anxious about facing the Board again."

"They have no power over you anymore." Isaac leaned against him. "You're coming before them as a person now rather than an object for them to dispose of as they wished." He looked up into bright blue eyes clouded with worry. "I bet it's stranger for them than it is for you."

"Perhaps." Turk nodded, his stance relaxing a hair.

They stepped through into the station, signs pointing them to customs. Normally, Isaac would have been worried sick about bringing weapons through, but he had found that, as a diplomat, he was entitled to carry, and his security was expected to be armed. He had managed to secure permits for two weapons apiece, pistol and *lau'ec* knife for each of them.

The customs gate at the end of their docking tube was better manned than most Isaac had passed through. Four serious, sharp-uniformed young men and women, their expressions, he thought, more than a little anxious. He gave them a cheerful good morning and stepped through the scan tube first, his weapons immediately lighting up the boards, which flicked to green again when the system located his permits.

A square-jawed young man at the other end of the tube held a hand scanner. "Ambassador, if I could have your retinal, please, to confirm your permits?"

Isaac stood still to have his left eye scanned, pointedly relaxed and cheerful so his companions would remain relaxed as well. Turk stepped into the tube next. Alarms shrieked.

The young man developed a worried frown. "Ambassador Zadral, are you carrying… grenades?"

Stopped in the middle of the scan tube, Turk put a hand to his jacket. "Ah. My apologies. Matter of habit. I forgot they were there."

"Sir, if you could step back through the tube and leave any items you don't have carrying permits for in the secure bin? Please?"

"Of course." Turk turned back around without hesitation and emptied his pockets of concussion grenades, placing them in the secure hazardous items bin. Isaac supposed he should have been grateful that Turk had limited himself to four.

When he had cleared the scan on his second pass, Isaac poked his head around the tube to speak to the rest of their party. "Gentlemen, if any of you have unauthorized weapons, now would be the time to rid yourself of them. We'll get a receipt and retrieve everything when we come back to the ship."

After a bit of embarrassed shuffling, Ges and Nidar both began emptying their pockets of their private arsenals. Grenades, EM field disrupters, a wicked-looking neurotox pistol—Ges's—and a forearm-length butterfly knife—Nidar's—went into the bin. Tash hadn't moved, his jaw tight, his expression mulish.

"Tash?" Isaac called softly. *Please, please don't make a scene. We just got here.*

"I don't see how we are to protect our *ket'haras'ae* without being properly armed. It simply isn't sensible," Tash muttered. "Especially after the last time *ka* Isaac guested with these people."

Nidar stood hipshot, arms crossed over his broad chest, head cocked as he regarded his recalcitrant *atenis*. "My love, my own, we most certainly *cannot* protect them if we are detained for carrying unlawful weapons." He nudged Tash with his elbow. "And the day we need more than knife and pistol to take on a *huchtik* assailant…."

Tash threw his hands up in surrender, an astounding array of items making their way from pockets to bin, including throwing stars and a folding-stock rifle. The ESTO soldiers watched with an interesting mix of astonishment and admiration in their expressions.

"Thank you for being so patient with us," Isaac said to the soldiers when his companions had all been cleared. "So nice not to be barked at coming through the tube."

One of the young women, a smile twitching at her lips, said, "Our pleasure, sir. Believe me."

Heads followed them as they strolled through the station, all the way to their commercial shuttle. While Turk would have preferred taking one of the shuttles from the *Hermes* down instead, the mountain of permits involved for a private shuttle, even a diplomatic one, gave Isaac a monstrous headache. *Maybe when I'm better at all this, more experienced with all the right channels.*

They passed a group of women with the parcels and bags of people returning home from vacation. A low whistle came from the group, the women whispering to each other and giggling like teenagers as they ogled. Nidar gave them a cheery wave and a wink, setting off a veritable storm of whispering and covert pointing.

Certainly, some stares were suspicious or openly hostile, but most people they passed eyed them with curiosity, with interest, or with outright lust. It put a little spring in Isaac's step that so many of their fellow travelers viewed the Corzin as a bunch of extraordinarily handsome men rather than a menacing war band.

"Explorers, love." He tucked his hand into the crook of Turk's arm. "That's what we are."

"This is hardly an undiscovered place," Turk said with a pat to his hand.

"The place, no. The people? Lots to discover."

"Perhaps so."

FOUR DAYS later, Turk sat beside Isaac in the enormous chairs reserved for important visitors in the Board's assembly room. They sat on the same dais, in the same semicircle as the Board members. It was far different from when he had sat facing the Board, at the table a few meters below, where he had felt small and lost.

He still felt a bit lost amidst the long-winded, convoluted speech of politicians, but with Isaac beside him, he would never again feel insignificant.

Admiral Ranulf's trial was ongoing, he had watched footage on the news vids with Isaac the previous evening, but they wouldn't be called to testify for a week at least, so for now, their days were comprised of hour after hour of political wrangling. There had been endless rounds of questions and drafts of long agreements regarding territorial lines and the beginnings of trade, nonaggression agreements, and statements of apology.

He glanced up to where Nidar stood with his *aten'ae* by the wall with the other security. His cousin rolled his eyes in sympathy at the long-winded representative's endless speech.

Then Isaac was speaking, pulling his attention back to the proceedings. "Mr. Caulfield, I must object to the phrase 'Corzin army' in regard to the human population of T'tson. The Corzin are not a standing army."

The representative at the podium frowned, white brows knitting together. "I was led to believe that this is precisely what the Corzin are, Ambassador Ozawa. I see no reference to any other occupation for them. The Draktar use them as a military force."

Turk put a hand on Isaac's arm and leaned forward to answer. He had learned the power of his deep voice in the first day of talks. It carried well in this room and when he spoke, seldom and sparingly, the sound of it caused people to sit up attentively.

"This is, perhaps, an understandable misconception, Mr. Caulfield," he said. "But the Drak'tar have never used us as an army."

"But the Corzin battle squads—"

"Your pardon, sir, but does your planet have no mercenaries?"

Mr. Caulfield ignored the question, instead asking in a pointed tone, "So in what capacity are the Corzin engaged on your homeworld, Ambassador?"

This was a question he had discussed with Isaac at some length, since his little *atenis* had the foresight to anticipate it. "We are, first and foremost, civil defense, sir. Search and rescue, fire suppression, disaster recovery. We man the system's stations, provide tech support for scientific ventures, act as test pilots, vermin control, and, on the rare occasion when it's necessary, law enforcement. We have our own art and music. We do not live in barracks, but in family homes where we raise our children and care for our elderly."

Isaac's soft voice followed his. "I would suggest, esteemed members of the Board, that references to the Corzin be amended to indicate an ethnicity and a cultural group rather than a military organization."

"Objections?" The Board supervisor glared around the assembly hall for a reasonable time allowing anyone to dare object. Then he waved a blue-veined hand. "Have all references to the Corzin as an army stricken from the documents. Amendments to be made in Section twenty J, Section thirty-four C, Section...."

The supervisor droned on and Turk began to suspect that all the endless bureaucracy had aged the Board members prematurely. His mind wandered again even while Isaac diligently made notes in his document reader. Turk felt a bit guilty about drifting off while Isaac remained so focused, but no one could argue that his lover was far better at this than he was.

The hour finally arrived when even the bureaucrats began shifting restlessly in their chairs. No matter how convoluted the arguments or how complex the issue, the assembly would adjourn at sixteen hundred without fail. At ten minutes to the hour, they reached a new agenda item, the proposed "cultural exchange program."

Even Isaac seemed to have run out of patience. "Ladies, gentlemen, I would very much like to discuss this topic in depth. But before we adjourn for the day, we would like to make it understood that there will be very clear, specific profiles the *Sil'ke'dra* will consider for candidates."

"As you say, Ambassador, we are nearly at the hour," an elderly woman near the end of the Board table said. "But could you supply, perhaps, a sampling of these criteria?"

"While candidates must be of legal age, we will not consider any candidate beyond the age of twenty-three. Psychological profiles must show Bruegger adaptability and tolerance scores over three hundred. Candidates must score in the ninety-fifth percentile in language aptitude and show a demonstrable talent for scientific or technical work. Active military, of any branch, will not be accepted."

The supervisor arched his bushy eyebrows at Isaac. "Is it the Silkedra's intention, then, to ensure that the criteria cannot possibly be met?"

"Not at all, sir. But these must be extraordinary young people, able to adapt successfully in often lonely and difficult conditions. This is not a summer vacation on Adanai Caba. The Drak'tar are an ancient, nonhuman culture and I cannot stress that enough. They are in no way human. We wish to avoid any possible... incidents."

Murmurs of agreement ran through the assembly. Apparently, Isaac had picked just the right word for his audience.

"Very good, Mr. Ozawa. We will take this up as the first agenda item in the morning. Ladies and gentlemen, we are adjourned for the evening. Good night."

As the assembly rustled to their feet, Turk tucked Isaac under his arm and steered him straight for the door. Nidar, Ges, and Tash fell in step right behind to further discourage anyone desiring Isaac's attention. While Isaac would have been gracious and stayed to talk to whoever felt the need, the days were long and Turk knew all the close contact with unfamiliar people wore on the little man's nerves. The previous evening, Isaac had been shaking when they finally reached their hotel room. He had vowed to guard his love's health more closely after that.

Outside, the daylight had softened to early evening, purple shadows stretching across the green that bisected the government buildings. Isaac rested his head against him and heaved a long sigh.

"Tired, *atenis*?"

"Tired. Hungry." Isaac glanced up at him. "I want to eat out tonight. We should walk downtown and hunt up a good restaurant."

Turk indulged himself for a moment, simply gazing into those glorious dark eyes. "Hmm. There is an Altairian restaurant not far from here, if you wish."

"Yeah, well, it's probably not authentic."

"I can't speak to that, but the food is good."

"And how do you know this?"

Turk planted a soft kiss on those upturned lips. "I was stationed here for some months, you know. They didn't keep me in a cage."

"Oh, right. I didn't realize you were actually *here*." Isaac turned to walk backward. "You boys up for some Altairian home cooking? If it's a good place, we'll be sitting on floor cushions instead of chairs, just like home."

"Whatever pleases you, Isaac," Nidar said with a smile. "So long as—"

He broke off as running footsteps neared. Turk joined his cousins as they closed around Isaac in a defensive circle.

"Mr. Ozawa? Sir? I know you probably don't remember me...." A young man ran up to them, hesitating when he saw the wall of bodies. He seemed familiar.

"Logan?" Isaac peered around him. "Of course I remember you."

"You do? Oh, that's... thank you. I mean... I've been watching on the news feeds, so I knew you'd be here. I heard about... about the exchange and all." Logan pulled himself up straight. "I'm going to apply, sir."

Turk pinned him with a gaze, though he kept his voice soft. "Why?"

"Why, sir?" The young man fidgeted from foot to foot, his eager anxiety filtering out into the air around him.

"Yes, why? The last time we saw you, did you not believe I was going to dismember you alive and devour you?"

Logan ducked his head. "Yessir. Sorry. But I only had what I'd heard to go on. I knew it wasn't true after the first five minutes."

"Ah."

"We're not taking any military personnel, Logan," Isaac said gently. "You did hear that part, right?"

The head of tousled brown hair picked back up. "I'm civ now, sir. My two years were up and I chose not to renew. The sergeants gave me hell, but I just couldn't. Not after...." He shrugged, either running out of words or too shy to say what he meant.

"After?" Nidar prompted. "After seeing Corzin for the first time?"

Logan's eyes threatened to devour his face as he looked at Nidar and nodded.

"This is not the venue to go looking for a boyfriend," Isaac said.

"No, sir. I... I know." The crimson climbing the boy's face told the world he had at least harbored fantasies, though. "It's not that."

"Then let's go back to Turk's first question, Logan. Good God, I don't even know if that's your first or last name."

"Logan Cordoba, sir."

"All right, then, Cordoba. Why? What makes you want to spend time with a bunch of weapons-crazed lunatics?"

The boy met Isaac's gaze head on, a fierce light burning in his eyes. "Life, sir. I've never met anyone else so *alive*."

Isaac stared at him so long the boy squirmed. Then he nodded and held out his hand for Logan to shake. "Good... good. The program probably won't be online for a few days yet, but when it is, you apply and send me your scores. If they're good enough, I'll put in a personal recommendation for you."

"You will? Oh, *thank* you, sir!" The boy flung his arms around Isaac's neck and then immediately bounced back, flustered and as red as the sunset. "Thank you, sir. You won't regret it."

Isaac looked a bit bemused as they watched the boy run off again, but a slow smile spread over his face. "You know, babe, I think I lied to Logan Cordoba."

"Did you?"

"Yes. You remember when I told him I had no intention of conquering the galaxy?"

"Yes."

"I think maybe I do want to. One heart at a time."

Turk allowed himself a little chuckle and tucked Isaac's hand back into the crook of his elbow. "Of that we had no doubt, my love."

As he strode across the green, his brilliant, beautiful beloved on his arm, his *chautae* at his back, the expanse of grass before him became more than a lovely park. The whole of the universe suddenly stretched out before him.

ANGEL MARTINEZ, the unlikely black sheep of an ivory tower intellectual family, has managed to make her way through life reasonably unscathed. Despite a wildly misspent youth, she snagged a degree in English Lit, married once and did it right the first time, (same husband for over twenty-five years) and gave birth to one amazing son (now in college.) While Angel has worked, in no particular order, as a state park employee, retail worker, medic, LPN, call center zombie, banker, and corporate drone, none of those occupations quite fit.

She now writes full time because she finally can and has been happily astonished to have her work place consistently in the annual Rainbow Awards. Angel currently lives in Delaware in a drinking town with a college problem and writes Science Fiction and Fantasy centered around gay heroes.

Website: http://angelmartinezauthor.weebly.com/
Facebook: https://www.facebook.com/amartinez2
Facebook Author Group:
https://www.facebook.com/groups/495188947277007/
Twitter: @AngelMartinezrr
E-mail: ravenesperanza@yahoo.com

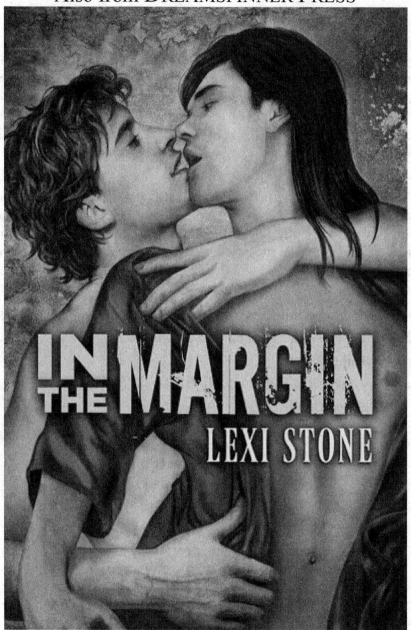

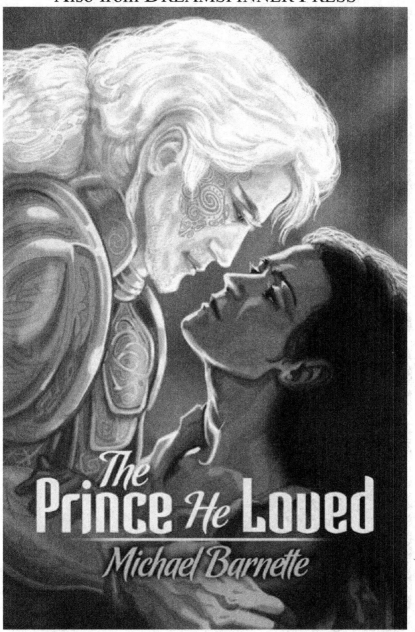

CPSIA information can be obtained
at www.ICGtesting.com
Printed in the USA
FSOW04n2212160917
38597FS

9 781627 989008